I0613547

Forging Forgiveness

by

C. B. Clark

This is a work of fiction. Names, characters, places, and incidents are either the product of the author's imagination or are used fictitiously, and any resemblance to actual persons living or dead, business establishments, events, or locales, is entirely coincidental.

Forging Forgiveness

COPYRIGHT © 2022 by C. B. Clark

All rights reserved. No part of this book may be used or reproduced in any manner whatsoever without written permission of the author or The Wild Rose Press, Inc. except in the case of brief quotations embodied in critical articles or reviews.
Contact Information: info@thewildrosepress.com

Cover Art by *The Wild Rose Press, Inc.*

The Wild Rose Press, Inc.
PO Box 708
Adams Basin, NY 14410-0708
Visit us at www.thewildrosepress.com

Publishing History
First Edition, 2022
Trade Paperback ISBN 978-1-5092-4293-1
Digital ISBN 978-1-5092-4294-8

Published in the United States of America

Candace Cooper's breath fogged out in plumes in the frosty, late afternoon air as she pumped her arms and loped along the narrow trail. Yesterday's rain had turned to sleet, and overnight, two inches of fresh snow blanketed the trail. Something caught her eye, and she slowed to a stop, turned around, and walked back three yards.

What the heck?

Indentations—a heel, the pad of a big toe, and the four, smaller indents of the other toes—were clearly formed in the smooth dusting of snow. The set of small, narrow footprints tracked along the snowy trail, veering into the deeper shadows of the forest. Someone had walked in his or her bare feet down the cold, snow-covered path.

The wind gusted against her damp face, and she shivered. Late November was too cold for anyone in their right mind to be out in the mountainous backcountry of northeast Colorado walking around without proper footgear. She squatted for a closer look. A smear of dark red, stark against the white snow, marked the heel depression of each left footprint. She touched the red splotch with the tip of her gloved finger. A rust-colored smudge stained the light blue cotton. Her heart rate kicked up.

Blood!

Praise for C. B. Clark

FORGING FORGIVENESS is award-winning author C.B. Clark's eighth romantic suspense published by The Wild Rose Press. MY BROTHER'S SINS placed first in the Melody of Love Romance Writing Competition. BROKEN TRUST placed second in the 2017 Best Romance Novel Critters/Preditors & Editors Reader's Poll. TWISTED LIES placed first in its category in the 2021 PRG Reviewer's Choice Awards.

BITTER LEGACY, BROKEN TRUST, and SECRET BETRAYAL are out in Audible.

"TWISTED LIES definitely gets five stars! I can't wait for another great read from this author who knows how to put the right amount of chemistry to make the perfect stories!"

~ *Trully*

"Wonderful story with lots of emotion."

~ *Katherine H*

"Loved HEALING HEARTS and the characters! I could not put it down."

~ *Jane C*

Dedication

As always, For Douglas, my favorite fan.

Chapter 1

Candace Cooper's breath fogged out in plumes in the frosty, late afternoon air as she pumped her arms and loped along the narrow trail.

Yesterday's rain had turned to sleet, and overnight, two inches of fresh snow blanketed the path and weighed down the limbs of the tall pine trees.

Hey, what was that?

She slowed to a stop, turned around, and walked back three yards.

What the heck?

Indentations—a heel, the pad of a big toe, and the four, smaller indents of the other toes—were clearly formed in the smooth dusting of snow. The set of small, narrow footprints tracked along the snowy trail, veering into the deeper shadows of the forest. Someone had walked in his or her bare feet down the cold, snow-covered path.

The wind gusted against her damp face, and she shivered. Late November was too cold for anyone in their right mind to be out in the mountainous backcountry of northeast Colorado walking around without proper footgear, let alone barefoot. She squatted for a closer look.

A smear of dark red, stark against the white snow, marked the heel depression of each left footprint.

She touched the red splotch with the tip of her

gloved finger. A rust-colored smudge stained the light blue cotton. Her heart rate kicked up.

Blood!

Sinking back on her heels, she peered into the forest's deepening shadows and shuddered.

Only four o'clock in the afternoon, and the sun was already disappearing behind the mountains. Nothing stirred. Even the squirrels were quiet, as if the silent forest watched and waited.

She knew this area of the park, ran the trails in the summer and snowshoed over the flatlands in the winter.

Nothing manmade existed out there—no houses, no cottages, nothing but trees and wild animals.

Most visitors to Creighton Springs State Park stayed on the well-groomed gravel walkways and didn't venture far from the parking lot.

She never saw anyone on the hilly trail, not in winter.

Yet, as recently as this morning, or early afternoon, someone had gone this way—and in bare feet. They'd left a blood trail. If that person was injured, maybe they needed help.

She slipped off her gloves and traced her finger along the impression. Too small to be an adult male or female's footprint. Her gut clenched.

A child?

God, no! Please don't let it be a child.

The unspeakable horror of the past reared over her like an attacking beast, and she sagged onto her knees, her heart pounding as if threatening to burst from her chest. A piteous moan escaped her lips. Not again. Dear Lord, please, not again.

Hot tears burned her eyes.

A loud crack reverberated throughout the silent forest.

She bit back a scream and surged to her feet. Gunshot?

An instant later, another sharp boom filled the air.

The piercing sounds of distant rifle fire were unmistakable. But no way would anyone be shooting. It was illegal to hunt in the park. Besides, it was too dark for a hunter to see his target.

Her heart thundered, her breath frozen in her chest.

Seconds passed, turning into minutes.

Her back tingled with the certainty she was being watched, but she couldn't move, could only stand there and listen, waiting for the next shot.

The forest remained hushed.

The sun dipped behind the mountains, and the valley filled with dark shadows as night settled in.

A snap of a branch breaking shook her out of her paralysis. The breath she'd been holding whooshed out, and she fumbled in her backpack and drew out her headlamp. Slipping the elastic strap over her forehead, she switched on the light.

Following the thin beam of light cast by her headlamp, she jogged down the trail. Her legs wobbled, and she stumbled over slippery roots and rocks, staggering, almost falling, but she dug deep and kept running.

The parking lot where she'd left her car was an hour's walk, but if she ran, she could make it in half that time. Heart thumping, her lungs burning, she raced around a bend in the trail but lurched to a stop at a flicker of movement in the trees on her right.

A large shadow separated from the trunk of a fir

tree and formed into the shape of a man.

She shone her headlamp into the forest.

The beam of light revealed a tall man with broad shoulders wearing a camouflage-patterned coat and baggy, green cargo pants. A gray woolen toque hung low over his forehead, and a thick black beard covered the lower half of his face. A rifle was strapped over one shoulder.

"He…hello?" Her voice was thin and reedy. He wasn't a park ranger. Not in that getup, but he had to be the person shooting, considering the enormous rifle slung over his shoulder.

Not one part of his body moved. He didn't even blink.

Hands shaking, she peeled off her gloves, letting them fall to the ground, and yanked out the can of pepper spray she carried in a canvas holster strapped around her waist. Sliding off the safety guard, she held the can up, the nozzle pointed at the unsettling stranger. "Who are you? What do you want?"

The man remained still and unspeaking.

Her heart thundered in her ears. "Hey, I asked you a question. What do you want?"

Behind the beard, he smiled, his lips stretching wide, his teeth gleaming in the headlamp's beam. In the encroaching darkness, his muscular frame appeared larger, his demeanor even more threatening.

Fear clawed her throat, and her primal instincts kicked in. *Run!* The urgent command roared through her, but her knees locked and refused to obey. Her breath puffed in and out in frantic huffs. "Don't come any closer." Gripping the can of pepper spray so tight her hand ached, she shifted her finger on the trigger.

The frightening smirk remained fixed on his brutish face.

An eternity passed. The cold settled in, and her fingers holding the can grew numb. The can slipped, but she grabbed the cold metal before it fell and tightened her hold, bringing up the nozzle and pointing the sprayer into the trees.

What the heck? She blinked and blinked again.

He was gone.

She turned her head, sweeping the area with the headlamp light, but the feeble light only penetrated a few yards, making it impossible to tell if he was hiding in the shadows waiting for her to drop her guard. A shudder rippled along her spine.

An owl hooted, and the haunting call broke through her paralyzing fear. Stuffing the pepper spray into the holster, she spun around and sprinted down the trail. She slipped on the snowy ground and tripped over a hidden root, slamming her knees on the hard, snow-covered dirt, yelping at the sharp pain. She peered over her shoulder, but it was too dark to see if the man had followed her. Clambering to her feet, she raced on.

Chest heaving, lungs burning, she burst through the trees into the parking lot and stumbled toward her red, economy-sized car. She dug in her pocket for her keys. They slipped through her cold fingers and fell.

No, no, no!

She dropped to her knees, ignoring the pain, and sifted through the snow. Her lungs wheezed as she hyperventilated, her heart jackhammering. Brushing snow and wet pine needles aside, she grabbed the key ring, stood, and punched the car's Unlock button. She ran to the driver's side and jumped into the front seat, slammed the door shut, and hit the Lock switch.

Her hands shook so much she dropped the key fob twice more before jamming the key into the ignition.

The engine rumbled to life, and twin headlight beams strobed the darkness, revealing the deserted parking lot and the surrounding tall, ghostly trees.

She stomped her foot on the gas, and the vehicle shot forward, fishtailing out of the gravel lot. The headlights swept over the forest as she turned onto the access road.

The bearded man emerged from the line of trees and stood with his legs braced wide on the shoulder of the road.

She swallowed back a scream and gripped the steering wheel, keeping her foot crushed against the gas pedal, skidding on the narrow, single-lane road. The car headed for the ditch, but she wrenched the wheel to the left, and somehow the vehicle stayed on the road. She shot a glance in the rearview mirror, and her blood chilled.

He still stood on the side of the road, watching her barrel out of the park, the long rifle cradled in his arms.

Gripping the steering wheel so tight her knuckles turned white, she sped down the road as the first snowflakes floated to the ground.

Chapter 2

Her hand jerked, and the hot coffee in her cup sloshed, threatening to spill onto the tiled floor. She slammed the mug on the kitchen table. More coffee slopped out and puddled on the oak table. She smoothed the palms of her damp hands on her pants as anger burned through her veins.

"You're certain you saw a bearded man packing a rifle out there in the woods?" Detective Breacher studied her, a bored expression on his fleshy face. "It wasn't a deer or a moose or a tree's shadow?"

She bit hard on her bottom lip to stop the sharp retort threatening on the tip of her tongue. Past experience with the prickly man had taught her he didn't react well to criticism. "I know what I saw. I heard two gunshots, and minutes later, the man appeared, holding a rifle. I called out to him, but he didn't say anything; he just stood there watching me, smiling." She shuddered and rubbed the goose bumps prickling her arms. "There was a storm approaching, and it was getting dark, but I saw him as clearly as I see you."

He cast a surreptitious glance at his watch and frowned, making it clear she was wasting his time. "And yet, my men and I didn't find any tracks, any sign of this man, nothing to indicate what you allege happened." He reached into his coat pocket and dug out a pair of light-blue gloves and tossed them onto the table. "We did find these buried under the snow. Yours, by any chance?"

She nodded. "I took off my gloves right where I saw the man." She shot the detective a frustrated look. "You didn't find any tracks. How could you when it snowed all night? Any footprints the man left would've long been covered." After she tore out of the park's parking lot, she'd called the cops the second she had cell reception. The officer she spoke to requested she come to the police station and provide a statement.

She'd spent hours in the stuffy, overheated building, being shuffled from one police officer to another until she'd ended up at Breacher's desk. He'd run through the same questions all the other cops had asked, and then he'd assured her the police would look into the incident as soon as possible. He told her to go home and wait for his call.

As soon as possible turned out to be hours later when the sun rose, hours during which six inches of fresh snow blanketed the town and surrounding countryside.

Breacher had shown up at her townhouse that afternoon to tell her what he and his men *hadn't* found. And now he was acting like she'd made up the entire incident. She wasn't surprised. She'd faced the same stubborn resistance from him and other police personnel countless times in the past. Why had she thought this time would be different?

"Nope. No sign of him at all."

She bit her lip and stared out the kitchen window at the falling snow. A headache throbbed. She hadn't slept the previous night. Aside from it being the anniversary of *The Incident*, every time she closed her eyes, the terrifying image of the bearded man rose before her. Even worse, was the sickening feeling she'd seen him somewhere before. She couldn't put her finger on why he was so familiar, but whatever the connection, his very presence filled her with fear.

She lifted her cup, pleased her hands weren't shaking, and gulped the steaming liquid, relishing the tendrils of warmth spreading throughout her body. She hadn't felt warm since she'd roared out of the dark parking lot in a panic. "Look, Officer Breacher—"

"*Detective* Breacher." His hooded gaze fixed on her.

She'd forgotten he'd been promoted years ago, though how he'd advanced in the police department was beyond her. "That man was up to no good. Just before I saw him, I heard two rifle shots." She heaved a sigh. "Surely you and your men found something…footprints, shell casings, blood?"

He shook his head. "We located the trail you were on, and we found your gloves and a few impressions of your running-shoe prints in the snow under the trees where the snow hadn't covered them, but there weren't any other signs. No indication anyone else was out there, that's for sure." He scratched his beard-shadowed chin. "If this man was in the park yesterday, there's no sign of him."

She set down her cup and rubbed her throbbing temples. "What about the bare footprints in the snow? And the blood?"

The corners of his mouth quirked. "Right. The footprints. You say you saw footprints in the snow…bare, bloody footprints."

His patent disbelief stoked her fury, but she reined in her anger. Telling him off would feel good—okay, it would feel great—but it wouldn't convince him she was telling the truth, and it wouldn't help find whoever had left the footprints. "Look, I know what I saw—four, or maybe five, human footprints were impressed in the fresh snow, indicating someone followed the path along the ridge and headed into the forest. A smear of what I'm sure was blood stained the snow where the left heel impressions were.

"It's pretty clear someone's out there, hurt and needing help. I mean, why else would anyone be in the park at this time of year walking in the cold snow in their bare feet?" She sat back and crossed her arms over her chest. "That's why I called the police. Someone needs help. The footprints were small, so probably a child. The man I saw is involved. I know it."

Once again, he glanced at his watch, and made a poor job of suppressing a yawn. "My men and I spent all morning traipsing through that forest. We didn't find anything out of the ordinary, nothing unusual, and especially no bare footprints." He smirked. "And no blood or injured child either."

He might as well have added that they hadn't found green aliens lurking in the forest for all the weight he put on her description of the frightening events of the previous evening. Her fight drained, deflating like the air fizzling out of a balloon. "You think I made this up." She spread her arms. "Why would I do that? Why would I waste your time?"

"You tell me." His bushy, gray eyebrows quirked. "It was a full moon last night. That always brings out the crazies or the delusional." His thick lips curled, making clear what category into which he lumped her. Setting down his coffee cup, he stood, his knee joints popping with the effort. He stuffed his notepad into his coat pocket. "Don't get me wrong. I believe you saw something, but it wasn't what you thought. The temperature was pretty cold yesterday, and by your own admission you were near the end of a long, arduous run."

Buttoning up his trench coat, he faced her. "Overexertion happens all the time. A person gets tired, dehydrated, and the mind plays tricks. You *thought* you saw footprints in the snow, and you *thought* you heard rifle shots, and you also *thought* a man was lurking in the trees watching you." He shrugged. "Who knows? Maybe you heard a branch snap under the weight of the snow. Or maybe you saw an elk and mistook it for a person. You wouldn't be the first." He wrapped a black-and-white striped woolen scarf around his thick neck. "Lots of elk out in those woods."

"What about the blood? Did I imagine that too?"

"All I can tell you is we didn't find any signs of blood to corroborate your story."

She jumped to her feet. "So that's it? You're done? You're not going to investigate further?"

"What's to investigate?" He blew out an aggrieved breath. "Look, I'll keep my ears open. If I hear anything, if any other visitors to the park report seeing this guy or—" He didn't bother to hide his smirk. "—bloody, bare footprints in the snow, I'll let you know."

Yeah. Sure, he would. The second he walked out her townhouse door, her complaint would be buried under a stack of nuisance complaints.

"Thanks for the coffee, Ms. Cooper. I'll see myself

11

out." He strode down the short hallway to the front door.

"Detective Breacher, wait."

He grasped the door handle but turned back to her. The furrows in his brow deepened. "What is it?"

"What about missing persons reports? Has anyone disappeared from the area recently? A child or a woman?" She blinked. *Missing persons*? She was reaching for straws. But she wasn't imagining things, and she wasn't crazy. *Someone* had made those tracks in the park. *Someone* had walked on his or her bare feet through the cold snow and left bloody footprints in their wake. She couldn't shake the certainty that same someone was in serious trouble. And somehow, the bearded man was involved.

"Is anyone missing?" He chuckled. "It's a big state. Our county alone encompasses almost seven thousand square miles. There're about a half-dozen or so individuals reported missing every year. Most show up, but—" He shrugged. "—one or two are never heard from again."

"Didn't a young girl go missing upstate a few weeks ago? The story was on the news." She should have thought of the missing teen when she saw the footprints, but with the anniversary of her sister's kidnapping and all the angst and guilt that came with that fateful date, and seeing that man in the forest, she wasn't thinking straight. "The footprints were small, probably those of a young woman or older child. Could they belong to the missing girl?" Her heart chilled. "Is it possible the man with the beard is involved?"

He opened the door. For a brief second, compassion shone in his faded blue eyes. "Look. I know what the date is, and I know what you went through with your sister. I was there. Remember?" He huffed out a breath. "But this isn't the same thing, not by any stretch. The girl who's missing?" His lip curled. "She's a runaway. No one's out in the woods abducting young girls and holding them hostage. You can take that to the bank." The fleeting warmth faded, and he stepped through the doorway and onto the front porch. "Have a nice afternoon." He strode down the sidewalk to his tan-colored, police-issue sedan.

Her headache ramped up to a four-alarm blaze, and she closed the door, secured the dead bolt, slid the security chain into place, and latched the heavy-duty metal lock. She plodded down the hall to the bathroom and fumbled in the cabinet over the sink for her antianxiety pills.

Cursing, she fought with the child-protection cap. When the lid finally popped off, she dropped the plastic bottle, and tiny blue pills scattered across the bathroom tiles.

She fell to her knees as sobs shook her, and then she collapsed onto the cold tiles.

Chapter 3

"All right. That's it for today." Candace stared out at the sea of young, bored faces. "Don't forget your final term papers are due next week."

A collective groan filled the room as the students stood and gathered their books, laptops, and coats.

"If you need assistance, you know my office hours." Raising her voice over the noise as they stampeded toward the exit, she smiled at their eagerness to escape the stuffy, over-bright room.

It was Friday afternoon—dates, keg parties, movies, video games—all awaited. Any thoughts of studying or working on a term paper were put on hold until Sunday afternoon when the panic of the looming deadline struck home.

She gathered up her lecture notes and slid her laptop into its leather case. Who could blame them? They were young. Life was meant to be enjoyed to the fullest. They didn't have any worries or fears. They thought they were invincible and nothing bad would ever happen—not to them.

She couldn't remember a time she'd been so free. Burdened by a lifetime of guilt, she lived with the sure knowledge that if she let down her guard, the nightmare of what happened to her sister would destroy her.

Instead of heading out for a night on the town with friends, she'd do what she always did—go for a run and then spend the evening at home on her couch, watching a movie. Maybe she'd splurge and order in Chinese food to have with her glass of white wine. Exciting times.

The door slammed after the last of the students, and the large lecture theater was empty.

The lights in the hall blazed and drilled into her eyeballs. More than three months had passed since that day when she'd run in Creighton Springs State Park and found the footprints in the snow, but she couldn't get them out of her mind.

Was she overreacting? The police thought she was. The bearded man was probably an innocent visitor to the park. But if so, where had he parked his vehicle? And why was he packing a rifle? Protection from wildlife? Nah. Most bears had hibernated by late November.

Something fishy was going on or he would have responded when she called out to him. Were her gut instincts right and his intentions nefarious? She shuddered. Had he hurt someone? The questions, one after the other, tumbled on constant rewind through her brain.

Daytime was usually okay. She kept busy preparing lessons, marking papers, and teaching her anthropology classes at Briggston Junior College, and she pushed the ever-present concern to the back of her mind.

The nights were a different story. Alone, and with nothing to distract her, the unsettling images flooded her...the bloody, small, human footprints in the snow, the bearded man, her numbing terror, her worries she hadn't done enough, that someone was in trouble, that history was repeating itself, that—

"Dr. Cooper?"

She startled at the deep male voice and dropped the papers. They scattered like leaves in a wind across the scuffed oak floor.

A tall, lean man, clean-shaven, with wavy dark hair that brushed the collar of his white shirt, stood at the top of the tier of seats. He was too old to be a student, but too young to be a parent of one of her undergraduates. There was an air of authority about him, something that screamed cop.

She backed up until the lectern pressed against her back.

He smiled, revealing a blinding flash of white teeth. "Sorry to startle you, Dr. Cooper. Dr. Hong, the college dean, told me you'd be here." He moved down the steps, reached inside his coat pocket, and pulled out a slim, black leather wallet. Stepping closer, he flipped the wallet open and held it before her.

She squinted, but the words were a blur, and she tugged her glasses from her leather bag on the desk and slipped them on. The images cleared. A shiny metal police badge was on one side of the wallet, his photo ID on the other. "How can I help you, Detective Farrell?" She crouched and started picking up the papers scattered across the floor.

"Here." He knelt beside her. "Let me help."

They reached for the same paper, and their hands grazed.

An instant zing of awareness shot from her hand direct to her stomach. Their gazes connected, and for a heartbeat, she stared into his eyes—hazel irises, shot with specks of gold. She snatched back her hand and jumped to her feet, her heart pounding.

He finished gathering the papers and set them on the lectern. "Here you go."

He smiled again, and tiny crinkles appeared at the corners of his all-too-captivating eyes. No man should have such long, sweeping dark eyelashes.

He was tall, really tall. She was five ten, and he towered over her. She gulped and backed up a step, bumping against the lectern.

It wobbled and would have fallen over if he hadn't reached past her and grabbed the stand and held it steady. "Easy there." He righted the lectern but stayed where he was, so close his suede jacket brushed her blouse.

His aftershave—a subtle woodsy scent—washed over her, and butterflies fluttered in her stomach. "Thanks." She winced as the word squeaked out.

"No problem." He unleashed his devastating grin again like it was a secret weapon. "I'm sorry I startled you."

Drawn into his intense gaze, she couldn't look away. Searing heat flushed up her neck and onto her cheeks. She inhaled a steadying breath and drew herself together, forcing an all-business smile to her lips. Stepping back a step, she removed her glasses and slid them into the case. "How can I help you, Detective?"

He slipped the wallet back into the pocket of his brown-suede coat, but before he could respond, the door at the top of the lecture theatre banged open, and a young man strode in.

"Sorry, Dr. Cooper. I forgot my notebook." He bounded down the stairs and along a row of seats and retrieved a black binder. Retracing his steps, he paused and eyed the tall detective. "Everything okay in here, Professor?"

She nodded. "Fine, thanks. Have a good weekend, Zack."

"Thanks, Dr. Cooper. You too." He opened the door and charged through. The door banged closed behind him.

"Do you have an office?" The detective gestured at the vast auditorium. "Somewhere more private we can talk?"

Her stomach lurched. Did his visit have something to do with her sister? After all these years, had the police finally found Charlene? As soon as the faint tendril of hope entered her brain, she rejected it. His visit wasn't about her sister. He wouldn't come all the way out to the university to update her. No, the handsome detective was there for another reason.

This wasn't the first time the police had come to the college. A few months back, a student had been attacked and raped on campus. The police had talked to the victim's instructors and fellow students to see if they'd noticed anyone following her.

As far as Candace knew, the rapist was still free. The poor girl hadn't returned to class, and the last Candace heard was she'd taken off the rest of the semester. She shoved back the disturbing thought of young women at risk on campus and focused on the detective.

He was watching her, his dark eyebrows raised, waiting for her to answer his question.

Her cheeks heated. "My office is just down the hall. Will that work?"

"Perfect." He smiled that devastating smile.

Her legs turned to jelly, and she grabbed onto the wooden lectern to hold steady. It had been a long time since she was so attracted to a man. A very long time.

"Shall we go?"

She blinked. "Go where?"

His grin widened, and a twinkle sparkled in his hazel eyes, as if he were all too aware of his lethal effect on a woman's hormones. "To your office. You were taking me there so we could talk in private."

Right. Her office.

A fresh wave of heat engulfed her face, and she hid her burning cheeks behind a fall of hair. "Yes, of course. Follow me." She released her death grip on the lectern and crossed the room to the door, praying her legs would support her, and she wouldn't make any more of a fool of herself than she already had.

He followed her out of the lecture theatre and down the busy corridor, dodging clumps of lingering students who talked and joked with one another, or texted on their cell phones, oblivious to those around them.

She halted before a frosted glass door with her name inscribed in black letters across the front, fished in her skirt pocket for the key, and unlocked the door. Holding the door open, she gestured for him to precede her into the tiny office.

His larger-than-life presence seemed to fill the small space and suck out all the air. She set her stack of papers and briefcase on her desk and hurried to the window and slid it open, breathing in gulps of fresh air.

He closed the door but remained standing, as his sharp-eyed gaze took in the miniscule room.

She had the unsettling feeling he noticed every detail and was making judgments. Did he know about her past? Of course he did. The kidnappings had been all over the news, and he was a policeman. He'd have access to the old case files. He would've checked her out before coming to the college. She shook her head, refusing to allow her thoughts to feather into the past.

"Nice office." His voice was noncommittal. "You have some interesting things."

She'd always liked her tiny office, found it cozy and comfortable. But now, viewing it through his eyes, she noticed the stacks of books piled on every surface, the dusty plaster model of a Neanderthal skull set atop the overflowing bookshelf, the limp, yellowing fern she'd forgotten to water again, and the piles of student papers she'd yet to grade.

She shoved aside a coffee mug with an inch of greasy-looking liquid coating the bottom, brushed crumbs from the sandwich she'd eaten at lunch off the desktop, and settled on her creaky leather desk chair. "Would you like to sit down?" She pointed at the visitor chair.

"Thanks." He hefted the stack of books from the seat and set them on the floor. Lowering his bulk onto the orange plastic chair, he stretched out his long legs, and crossed his booted feet, looking relaxed. Too relaxed.

The silence dragged on. The steady ticktock of the institutional metal clock on the wall behind him marked the seconds as if in slow motion.

She cleared her throat. "How can I help you, Detective?" she asked for the third time.

He picked up a carved wooden mask from the corner of her messy desk and ran his long fingers over the incised designs. "This is interesting." He fixed her with a piercing gaze. "What is it?"

"A Kwakuitl burial mask."

"Neat."

Neat? Who said neat anymore? "It's more than four hundred years old, so please be careful." She looked at the clock again and sighed. The frustration of dealing with the police after her sister's kidnapping, made her nervous, but this too-handsome detective really set her on edge. Besides, she wanted to get her run in before the sun set. Ever since she'd encountered the bearded man in the state park, she'd been careful to run only in daylight and never in the park.

He set the mask back in the velvet-lined wooden box. "Really? That old, huh? How come it's not in a museum?"

"I didn't steal it, if that's what you're thinking." She smiled, but her lips were stiff, her attempt at humor a failure. "I uncovered the mask during an excavation on Theodore Island in the Salish Sea last season. After I've finished my research, it will be repatriated to the local indigenous group. It's really quite unique…" She stopped her rambling and rubbed the tightness in the back of her neck. "I assume you're here for a reason, Detective Farrell. If you don't mind, I'd like you to get to the point." She glanced meaningfully at the stack of unmarked papers.

"Of course." He withdrew a small, spiral-bound notebook from his coat pocket. "Forgive me. It's late and the end of the workweek. I'm sure you're anxious to get on with your weekend plans."

"I don't have any plans." She bit hard on her lip to stop any more too-personal confessions escaping.

"Really?" He studied her, his narrowed hazel-eyed

gaze probing. The corners of his mouth twitched as if he were holding back a grin. "Huh." He flipped open his notebook and consulted his notes, though she had the distinct feeling he knew every word written in the notebook. "I'm new to the Briggston Police Department, and I've been assigned to a missing person's case."

Every cell in her body zinged to full alert, and a spark of hope flared. "Is—" She struggled to form the words she'd waited so long to ask. "—is this about my sister? Did you find Charlene? Is she alive?"

A furrow formed between his dark brows. "Your sister? No. Is that what you thought?" His face softened. "I'm sorry."

The spark died, replaced by anger. She hated the compassion, the pity, the kindness, especially from strangers. Their sympathy brought back all the old feelings of helplessness, loss, and guilt. "So then why are you here?" Her voice was sharper than she intended.

He consulted his notes. "Last November 16th, you reported to the police that you discovered some unusual footprints in the snow while you were running in Creighton Springs State Park. Is that correct?"

Her breath caught in her throat. Had the cops found the bearded man who starred in her nightmares? Had they located the person who'd walked on bare feet in the cold snow? Had they—

"Dr. Cooper? Do you remember reporting unusual footprints in Creighton Springs State Park last November?"

She blinked and met his gaze. "Yes, of course I do."

He leaned forward on his chair and rested his

elbows on the desk. "In your statement to Detective Breacher, you indicated you were running in the state park and came across some bare footprints in the snow. You then heard two rifle shots and encountered a bearded man who frightened you."

Her stomach tightened, and she nodded.

"Care to tell me more?"

"Why? Detective Breacher wasn't interested. He thought I mistook the footprints for animal tracks, and the rifle shots I heard were branches breaking or an animal crashing through the trees."

"But you thought different."

"The prints were human. I'm sure of that." She pointed at the model of the ancient Neanderthal skull. "I'm a physical anthropologist, and I study early humans. I know a human footprint when I see one, whether it's encased in million-year-old stone or fresh snow." She huffed out a breath. "The prints had the high arch that's distinctive to homo sapiens. No question, they were made by a person."

"So, you found these footprints?" He motioned for her to continue.

She spread her hands, palms down, on the scarred desktop. "Unfortunately, by the time the police ran their investigation, it was late the next morning, and it had snowed six inches overnight. The footprints were buried."

"How many footprints did you see?"

She shrugged. "I'm not sure. It was getting dark, and even though I had my headlamp on, the light was poor under the trees. I followed the prints for a few yards along the ridge trail until they veered into the forest." She brushed a curl of hair behind her ear.

"There were drops of blood on some of the heel imprints."

His eyebrows rose. "You saw blood?"

"Yes, blood stained the snow where the person's left heel would have been."

The ticking in his jaw accelerated. "Did you tell Detective Breacher about the blood?"

"Of course. I was worried someone was injured. That's why I called the police."

He sat back and crossed his arms over his chest. His coat gaped open, revealing a snug-fitting white T-shirt and the firm muscles in his chest and abdomen. He stared out the window for a long minute, and then he met her gaze. "You'd better start at the beginning and tell me everything."

She inhaled a steadying breath. "It was a Wednesday, and my 1:30 class was cancelled, so I decided to go for a run to clear my head. It was a beautiful day, and that late in the season, I'd have the park to myself." She wiped her clammy hands on her skirt.

Running was her life—her escape from the confines of four walls. Nothing was better than the fresh air brushing her face, the burn in her muscles, the steady, soothing rhythm of her feet pounding the ground. She ran most days of the week and always alone, pushing her body to move faster, run one more mile, climb one last hill, seeking escape from the noises in her head and her onerous burden of guilt.

Her running routes varied from the busy sidewalks of town, along country roads past cultivated green fields, and on a treadmill in the gym when winter snows covered the ground. But her favorite place to run was on the rugged trails of Creighton Springs State Park. The beauty of the evergreen forest, the rushing river, glimmering lakes, and the surrounding mountains with their snow-covered peaks soothed her soul.

"Er…Dr. Cooper?"

She picked up a pen and tapped the nib on the desk in a rapid staccato. "Sorry. It's been a long week." The drumming was loud in the small office. Too loud. Inhaling a deep breath, she tossed the pen aside and clasped her hands on her lap. "I followed the loop trail around Mercer Lake. That route only takes a couple of hours, and I planned to be back at my car long before dark. I didn't count on having to climb over a couple of deadfalls blocking the trail. I guess the big wind storm the previous week blew down some trees."

She unclenched her hands and straightened a stack of papers on her desk. "I-I was running out of light, and that's when I found the footprints." Squirming in her chair, she crossed and uncrossed her legs. "Right after that, I heard the rifle shots."

"And the only person you saw was the man with the rifle?"

"The parking lot was empty." She smoothed a lock of hair behind her ear. "I thought I was alone."

"Let's focus on the footprints for a minute." He tugged out the stub of a yellow pencil from his coat pocket and held it poised over his notebook. "Do you remember where the footprints joined the trail?"

"I'm not sure. I was running, and the trail was covered in snow." She inhaled a shaky breath. "At first, I thought the prints were animal tracks. I mean, no one would be walking in their bare feet. Not in that temperature, and…" Her voice faded. Did he really want to hear all this? She shouldn't let his good looks fool her. He might seem interested in her thoughts, but he was a cop, and past experience had taught her cops had their own agendas.

His expression remained inscrutable. "What about the blood? Tell me more about that."

She studied his face. It was impossible to read what he was thinking by looking into his hooded hazel eyes. Did he believe her? Or was he like Detective Breacher and just going through the motions, crossing t's and dotting i's so he could dismiss her claims with the clear conscience of having done his due diligence?

Her stomach tightened as once again the questions that had haunted her for the past three months reared in her mind. What if the footprints belonged to someone who was in trouble? A child. An injured child. If she'd followed the tracks into the trees, would she have found the person? She should've pushed Detective Breacher harder and made him take her seriously. She should've—

"Dr. Cooper?"

The detective's deep voice pierced her self-castigation. She met his penetrating gaze, and a rush of heat flooded her face. "Sorry. You were asking about the blood, right?" She sucked in a breath. "Like I said, the blood smears were where the heel of the person's left foot would have landed, as if whoever made the tracks had cut her foot on something."

His eyes narrowed. "*Her*?"

She shook her head, not understanding.

"You said that whoever cut *her* foot." If possible, his eyes narrowed further, and his gaze zeroed in on her like twin laser beams. "Why do you think a woman made the tracks?"

She squeezed her hands together. "I don't know. They could've been left by an older child, possibly a teen." She struggled to visualize what she'd seen that day…small, narrow human footprints, with a high arch. "They seemed too small to be from an adult, but I can't be certain. The light was fading, and the tracks were in the shadows."

He scribbled in his book. "How fresh do you think the blood was?"

"I-I touched the blood, and it was sticky. It stained my glove." She licked her dry lips and voiced her worst fear. "You don't think a child was out there that day, do you? One who was hurt and needed help?"

He leaned forward. "Do you still have those gloves?"

"No. I threw them out. I couldn't bear the thought of having someone's blood on them, and Detective Breacher made it pretty clear that he didn't believe me." She bit down on her bottom lip. Why had she thrown out the gloves? She should've known better. The bloodstain could've been sampled for DNA evidence.

His jaw hardened, and his mouth firmed into a thin line. He turned and stared out the window.

She followed his gaze.

The afternoon sun shone on a rolling expanse of lush green grass, shaded by the tall, stately firs of the college common. Daffodils, their vibrant yellow heads bobbing in the breeze, bloomed in the manicured flowerbeds.

Clusters of students lazed on the lawn. Two young men, dressed in T-shirts emblazoned with the college's football team's logo and long, baggy shorts, tossed a football back and forth.

Laughter, the sounds of conversation, birds tweeting in the bushes outside her office window, and the faint rush of traffic from the ring road around the campus, travelled through the open window.

"I'd like you to take me there."

She swung back to him. "Out there? To the college common?"

The corners of his mouth twitched. "No. To Creighton Springs State Park. I want you to show me where you saw the tracks."

"But months have passed. It's spring now. There won't be anything to see."

He arched his dark brows.

The heat in her cheeks flared to a four-alarm blaze. Stupid comment. Of course, he knew the footprints would be long gone. "What—" She swallowed. "—what do you think you'll find after all this time?"

He shrugged. "We won't know until we look." He stood with an easy grace for such a tall man and stuffed his notebook and pencil into his coat pocket. "So, I'll see you tomorrow?"

"Tomorrow? But tomorrow's Saturday."

The crinkles at the corners of his eyes deepened. "Yes. I'm aware of that."

He wanted her to go with him *tomorrow*? An image of the bearded man rose before her, and she shuddered. He'd exuded menace, and his very presence had terrified her. Afraid of encountering him again, she hadn't been back to the park. And now this detective wanted her to go there with him the next day. She pushed her fears away. "I guess that would work."

"Great. I have your home address. How about I

pick you up at nine?" He strode to the door without waiting for her agreement, twisted the handle, and opened the door.

"Detective Farrell?"

He looked back at her. "Yes?"

"Why now? Why are you interested in those footprints after all these months? Detective Breacher made it more than clear he thought I was wasting his time."

His eyes turned the icy green of an alpine lake. "Just over three months ago, fifteen-year-old Amanda Jacobs vanished in the middle of the night from her bedroom in her parents' house in Cardion. There's been no sign of her since."

Her stomach plummeted. All too well she knew the devastation the missing girl's family would be feeling as they reeled from their daughter's disappearance. "Cardion is miles from the state park. You can't think the footprints I saw are connected to this missing girl."

"I'm investigating every possible lead." His mouth tightened. "We need to find her." He stepped into the hall and closed the door behind him with a solid thunk.

She sagged back in her chair. A young girl was missing. Was her disappearance connected to the bare footprints Candace saw in the state park three months ago? If so, she'd let the poor girl down when she'd desperately needed help. She rubbed the increasing tightness in the back of her neck.

Tomorrow. One way or another, she'd know tomorrow. And then she could deal with her guilt. She leaned forward and rested her head in her arms on the desk.

Tomorrow.

Chapter 4

Candace shrugged off her daypack, tugged out a plastic water bottle, and held it out to the detective. "Want a drink, Detective Farrell?"

"Please, call me Aiden." He smiled, flashing a row of even, white teeth.

"Okay. Aiden it is." His name rolled off her tongue like velvet. "Would you like some water, Aiden?"

He shook his head. "I'm fine, thanks." He studied the river below. "It sure is pretty out here."

The clear waters of the Eggleston River frothed white as they roared over massive basalt boulders and snaked through a narrow canyon eighty feet below. The winding dirt path followed the river along the edge of the ridge through a mature Douglas fir forest and past the clear, aquamarine waters of Mercer Lake. Yellow and purple wildflowers dotted the emerald-green mossy ground.

She breathed in the sweet scent of rising sap carried on the fresh spring breeze.

The incessant drone of insects, and the rumble of the distant rushing water filled the air.

She brushed a smear of dirt off the knee of her hiking pants. "I'm surprised we haven't seen other hikers. This trail is pretty popular on Saturdays."

"Have you been back here since that time you were running and saw the footprints?"

She shivered and wrapped her arms across her chest. "No. I-I—"

"I understand. You were afraid you'd run into that man, but you can rest easy. He wouldn't hang around, especially if he were up to no good."

"I know my fears are groundless, but I…" She bit down on her bottom lip. Once spring arrived, and the snow and ice melted, she'd wanted to return to the park, wanted to run along its winding trails, but she couldn't get over her nervousness. Even now, with a handsome, armed detective at her side, she couldn't help peering into the thick stand of trees searching for someone lurking, watching them. She swiped her sweat-dampened hair off her forehead. "How is our being here helping?"

"I want you to pinpoint where you saw the footprints."

"Why? I don't see how showing you where I saw the tracks three months ago will help. We don't even know who left the footprints. Detective Breacher suggested they were made by a naturist connecting with Mother Earth by walking barefoot through the forest."

He chuckled. "Maybe." His easy grin faded. "But maybe not."

After he'd left her office yesterday afternoon, she'd spent the evening on her computer searching news sites for information about missing persons in Colorado. The news stories were easy to find—dozens and dozens of articles about missing teens and young women—all very disturbing. She was shocked at how many people were missing. Most were women, the majority of them young.

Fifteen-year-old Amanda Jacobs was the most-recent person who'd disappeared, and the circumstances were all too familiar. She'd vanished from her bedroom in the middle of the night in Cardion. The last anyone saw of her was when she said good night to her parents and headed to bed.

Her mother had gone to Amanda's room to wake her for school the next morning, but she wasn't there. Her bed had been slept in, but Amanda was gone. The bedroom window was open, and no one was certain if she'd run away, or if she'd been taken against her will. She hadn't been seen or heard from since.

That was three months ago.

Candace had spotted the footprints in the snow around that time. Was there a connection? Or was she placing too much weight on her uneasy gut feelings? The face of the bearded man filled her vision, and she shuddered and rubbed her chilled skin.

"Damn." Swatting at a cloud of hungry mosquitoes buzzing his face and arms, Aiden swore again. "Are the bugs always this bad?"

She fished in her pack for a small bottle of insect repellent. "Sometimes they're worse." She handed him the bug spray. "Try this. It'll help."

"Thanks." He moved a few feet away and sprayed a cloud of the repellent over his arms and legs. Squirting some of the insecticide into the palms of his hands, he smeared the oil over his face and the back of his neck.

She couldn't help smiling. "You don't get out in the woods much, do you?"

"Is it that obvious?"

She looked pointedly at his once-pristine tennis shoes. The white canvas sides were coated in mud. Tiny green burrs furred the long white laces.

His face reddened. "I guess I should have worn hiking boots." His warm laughter rumbled from deep within his broad chest.

Her insides melted, and she couldn't help but chuckle in return. His laugh was infectious. "You think?"

"Give me a break. I'm new to the area. I moved here a month ago from Seattle, and I've been working so hard I haven't had a chance to get proper hiking clothes."

"Briggston must be quite a change from the big city." She'd lived in the small, rural town of twenty thousand, nestled in the heart of the Rockies, her entire life. The surrounding county had everything she liked… rivers, towering snow-capped mountains, a myriad of spring-fed, azure-blue lakes, and hundreds of acres of protected forest. Creighton Springs State Park, with its miles of trails, was one of her favorite places to run, cycle, and snowshoe. Or at least it had been until she'd encountered the creepy bearded man.

Aiden swatted at a fly buzzing his head. "This is pretty country, but you could sure do something about these damn bugs. I miss the ocean, and the beaches, and my favorite coffee shop." He slapped a mosquito that landed on his arm. "People in Briggston are friendly though. Small town, I guess. Everyone knows everyone."

She winced. That was the one thing she didn't like about Briggston—people had long memories—too long. She couldn't walk down the street without someone stopping her and expressing sympathy for her loss. The pity in their eyes brought back the pain and made the guilt fresh again. She'd thought of moving to a town where no one knew her sad story, but the possibility that Charlene would return one day kept her in Briggston.

She checked her wristwatch. "We'd better get moving if you want to look at the area where I saw the footprints and make it back to town by afternoon." She hefted her pack, slung it over her shoulders, and continued along the narrow trail.

Still slapping bugs, he followed.

Fifteen minutes later, she stopped and studied the moss-covered ground. The area looked different in the spring with all the new growth, but she recognized a large rock threaded with distinctive gray-and-white quartzite streaks. "There." She pointed. "That's where I noticed the first footprint."

He squatted and studied the ground, brushing aside dirt and leaf litter. "Are you sure?"

She pointed at the striped boulder. "I remember that rock."

He studied the surrounding forest for a long time, as if he hoped the trees would reveal the answers he sought.

"Do you think the footprints belonged to that missing girl? Is that why we're here?" The question had haunted her since she'd learned about the missing teen, and it kept her awake the previous night. The thought of a young girl in the forest in the dark and cold, in bare feet, injured, and fleeing her abductor, sickened her.

She should have done more that day, listened to her inner voices warning her something was terribly wrong and insisted Detective Breacher search the area sooner. If she had, maybe Amanda Jacobs would be home with her family and not another sad statistic, a face on a missing person's poster. She crossed her arms over her chest. "Do you think she was here? Is that even a possibility?"

Aiden scrubbed his whiskered chin. "You said the prints were small, like those of a woman or a teenager."

"That's what I thought, but snow can distort the size of tracks. For all I know they could have been made by a small man's foot."

"Maybe."

She shivered, though the day was warm. "Why would a kidnapper bring her to the park? Cardion's a long way from here, and there aren't any houses close by. The park outhouses and open-sided shelters in the picnic areas are the only buildings. Where would he keep her?"

His face was grim as he studied the dense forest. "I promised her parents I'd find her." He huffed out a breath. "Show me where the footprints headed into the trees."

She led the way along the winding, narrow trail and around a bend and stopped. "I think this is where the tracks veered into the bush."

"You're certain?"

"I think so." She shrugged. "Everything looked different. A winter storm was coming, and it was getting dark."

He shoved leafy branches and prickles aside and fought through a thick tangle of wild rose bushes and red willows. Rubbing a long red scratch on his arm, he frowned. "The undergrowth's pretty thick, and even in the fall, these brambles would've blocked the way."

"That's what surprised me. Why would anyone

head into the bush? You'd think they'd stay on the trail where the walking's easier, especially if they were injured." *Unless they were running from someone; someone who wanted to hurt them.* Again, she shuddered.

He reached into the back pocket of his jeans and pulled out a roll of fluorescent pink flagging tape. Using his teeth, he ripped off a strip of tape and tied it to a branch.

"What're you doing?"

"Marking this spot so the K9 team knows where to start their search radius."

"You're planning to bring in search dogs?" Finally, someone was taking her concerns seriously. Warmth flooded through her, and hope flared, but then she recalled how long ago it was that she'd seen the tracks in the snow, and her hope fizzled. "Will the dogs be able to pick up on anything after all these months?"

He scratched his arm. "I don't know, but there's a young girl missing, and I sure as hell intend to do my damnedest to find her." His mouth firmed, and a tiny pulse throbbed in his jaw. He ripped off another strip of flagging tape and tied it to a branch overhanging a stump.

She pointed out two more places where she thought she'd seen the footprints before she lost them in the maze of trees and thick undergrowth.

He tied a pink ribbon by each spot she indicated.

When she was finished, he stuffed the roll of flagging tape back in his pocket. "You did great. This'll help a lot."

A menacing-looking cloud covered the sun, dark shadows deepened under the trees, and the wind picked up. She shivered in the sudden chill. "Looks like a storm's on the way."

"I think I have enough for now. Let's head back. I'd like to get the paperwork started." He shoved through the bushes to the path and set a fast pace as his long legs ate up the trail.

She had to jog to keep up, and by the time they descended the hill to the parking lot, she was out of breath.

They crossed the gravel lot to his black SUV, and he tugged out an electronic key ring and unlocked the doors. Holding the front passenger door open, he gestured for her to climb inside.

She settled onto the supple leather seat and strapped on her seatbelt.

He strode around to the driver's door, slid behind the steering wheel, started the vehicle, and pulled out of the parking lot onto the narrow access road.

"Can I ask you a question?" She shifted on the seat, so she faced him.

He shot her a look. "Sure."

"How come you left Seattle? I mean, Briggston is a small town. We don't have fancy coffee shops or high-end restaurants." She bit the inside of her cheek. His personal life was none of her business; yet, for some reason, she wanted to know everything about him. "This place must be pretty boring for a big-city detective like you."

His hands tightened on the steering wheel, and his knuckles turned white.

He was silent for so long she didn't think he was going to answer. "Look, I'm sorry. It's none of my business—"

"Briggston isn't boring." He plastered an obviously forced grin on his face. "I met you, didn't I?" He scratched a red welt on his neck. "And there're all these lovely bugs. What more could a man want?"

His attempt at flirting fell flat, but she returned his smile. The man had secrets. That was obvious. He'd avoided answering her question.

Interesting.

Chapter 5

Aiden stuffed his hands into his pants pockets and shivered in the cold wind. If only he'd worn a heavier coat. The weather in these damn mountains changed every ten minutes. When he left the house, the sun was shining, and the temperature hovered in the mid-70s. It promised to be a beautiful spring day, but by the time he reached the park, the clouds had moved in, and the air had cooled ten degrees.

Go figure.

Organized chaos surrounded him.

The dog handlers unloaded the scent dogs and freed them from their carriers.

The excited animals yipped and whined, eager to begin the search. Their long tails whipped back and forth, and their pink tongues lolled as they tugged on their leashes.

The high-pitched baying, the harsh commands of their handlers, the incessant squawk of handheld radios, and the rumble of voices filled the air in a discordant jumble.

Aiden rubbed the back of his neck, scratching at one of the many bug bites he'd acquired from his trek into the wilderness with Candace Cooper. The bites weren't the only souvenir of the day. Not by a long shot. Candace was a beautiful woman. She'd caught his attention all right. He'd been so distracted by her long, silky looking dark hair braided into a single braid that reached her narrow waist, and eyes the color of sapphires, he'd barely been able to form coherent sentences.

Loud barking broke into his fantasies, and he gritted his teeth. *Get your mind off the woman and focus.* This was his operation, and his reputation was on the line.

Was Breacher right? Was this search a fool's quest, and Aiden was wasting taxpayers' money? Would his ass be in the shitter if the media heard about this adventure? He scratched a red welt on his arm. What choice did he have? A child was missing, and he'd walk through the fiery gates of Hell and face the very Devil himself if doing so led him to find her.

He wasn't a fool. He knew the stats. After all these months, the odds of finding Amanda Jacobs alive were slim to none. But he wouldn't rest until he'd followed every lead and tracked down every clue, no matter how flimsy or farfetched.

He swallowed a lump in his throat as he recalled the pale, stricken faces of the missing girl's parents. The agony of losing their daughter had staggered them. Their expressions were haunted, their eyes sunken, and it was all they could do to stand without collapsing.

Even though he knew better, he'd promised them he'd find Amanda. And damn it all, he would. He just prayed she'd be alive when he found her. He swatted a mosquito that had braved the cold to buzz his face, searching for fresh blood.

"You don't really think this'll work. You're not that desperate to redeem yourself. Are you?"

Aiden grimaced at his partner's rough, smoker's

voice. "I know, Joe. The odds are a zillion to one those footprints were made by our missing girl, but it's all we have."

Ever since he'd broached the idea of using scent dogs to attempt to follow the blood trail Candace Cooper was certain she'd seen last November, Joe Breacher had been riding his ass. He wasn't the only one. Pretty well every cop at the station thought the venture was a waste of time and money. When Aiden presented the idea to the captain, she'd been skeptical, but willing to let Aiden go ahead.

A fresh blast of wind straight out of the north sliced through his coat, and he shivered again. When Lexington Rhodes called that morning and said he had three hours to devote to the search, Aiden had jumped into his car and raced to the park.

He'd been trying to set this search up for a week, but the unseasonably early spring and warm temperatures had brought out scads of outdoor enthusiasts, and missing hikers were keeping Rhodes and his team of search-and-rescue dogs busy. This was the only opening they had for months.

It was now or never.

Joe snorted, tugged out a cigarette from the battered pack he carried in his shirt pocket, and stuffed the cigarette in his mouth. "If you ask me, this search is a waste of bloody time and money. Those dogs aren't gonna find a damn thing." He fished a lighter from his coat pocket and flicked it with his thumb. A tiny flame flickered, and he cupped his hand around the flame and lit the end of his cigarette.

Lexington Rhodes strode over, his gray eyes flashing fire, his auburn handlebar mustache bristling.

"Don't smoke that, Detective."

"Why the hell not?" Joe growled.

"I don't allow people to smoke around my dogs. It affects their scenting abilities."

Joe puffed out an aggrieved breath, stubbed out the burning end of his cigarette, and stuffed both lighter and cigarette back into his pocket, muttering under his breath. He was a lifelong smoker, evidenced by his nicotine-stained fingers, yellow teeth, and heavily lined face, not to mention his annoying smoker's cough.

"All set, Lex?" Aiden asked.

"Max sure is." Lexington petted a large male golden retriever prancing at his feet.

The dog's furry tail thumped the ground, raising a small cloud of dust.

"He loves this work."

Betty-Ann Covington, Lex's helper, approached holding a German shepherd-cross, the mixed-breed dog straining at the lead. The animal's muscular body vibrated with excitement. "We're all set. Where do we start?"

Aiden pointed along the ridge trail. "I marked the spots where our witness says she saw the blood smears. You'll find the strips of pink flagging tape about five hundred yards down the trail beyond the river. You can't miss them."

"Okay." Lexington hefted a bulky nylon pack onto his back. "With any luck, we'll see you soon."

"Are you sure I can't go with you?" Aiden asked. The thought of cooling his heels by the vehicles while Lexington and his helper and the search dogs did their work was unbearable. He had a good feeling about this venture. The information Candace provided about the strange, bloody footprints she'd found in the snow three months prior had set off a tingling deep in his gut.

And he listened to his gut.

Well, most of the time. There was that situation in Seattle when he— He shut off the thought. Not now. Definitely not now,

"Sorry, Aiden." Lexington shook his head. "The dogs work better if there aren't strangers around. Too many distractions." He settled a red cap over his gleaming baldhead. "You'll know if they find anything. They'll start barking like banshees."

Aiden scratched an insect bite on the back of his neck. "Good luck."

Lexington patted the retriever's golden head. "My boys don't need luck. They're the best in the state. If there's any blood trace out there, they'll find it."

The two handlers, their dogs barking and straining at their leashes, headed down the trail at a trot.

The second they were out of sight, Joe pulled out his cigarette and lit it with the plastic lighter. He inhaled deeply and blew out a plume of fragrant smoke. "You ask me, this is a waste of our friggin' time. We should be at the station working on that stack of paperwork weighing our desks down instead of standing in the middle of the godforsaken wilderness freezing our asses off." Another cloud of smoke filled the air. "You can't really believe our missing girl is out here."

Aiden bit back a sharp retort. They'd been through this a dozen times. Joe hadn't made any secret of the fact he thought the search a waste of time and resources, but after the captain agreed to Aiden's plan, Joe had grudgingly come along. "Where *should* we be looking for her, Joe? Because if you have a better idea, I'm all ears. Last I heard, we were out of leads."

Joe's forehead furrowed, and he puffed on his cigarette. "What about that kid who said he saw her at a bus stop near Riemer Road two weeks ago?"

"The patrol cops followed up on that lead. The city bus driver is positive he didn't pick up a girl with Amanda Jacob's description at that stop on the day in question. The security cameras on the bus confirmed that."

A gust of wind blew cigarette smoke into his face, and Aiden coughed and waved his hand, shooing away the smoke. "If you ask me, I think the kid made up the sighting. He was looking for attention and called the tip line. We get hundreds of calls like that every week." He scratched another bug bite. "The reward the family offered has brought out all the nutcases."

"This is bullshit, and you know it." Joe tossed his burning butt on the ground and crushed it beneath his shoe. "I can't believe we're standing here like a couple of doofuses, while two mangy mutts try and sniff out a blood trail that's more than three months old." He hawked up phlegm and spat on the ground.

Aiden reined in his irritation and disgust. From the moment Joe Breacher had been assigned as his partner, the man had been a thorn in Aiden's side. They didn't get along.

Not. At. All.

Thirty years of working as a detective had jaded Joe, and he didn't hide the fact he was counting the days until he retired. Until then, he was just putting in time. His idea of effective police work was swilling coffee and eating pie and ice cream at Donna's Diner and reading the crime report in the newspaper.

Any suggestion Aiden made in a case was met with his partner's resistance and outright scorn. He'd been tempted to go to the captain about his concerns, but he was under no illusions about his standing in the Briggston Detective Division.

After the fiasco in Seattle that came damn close to ruining his career, he was desperate for a job. When the captain of the small, rural Briggston Police Force offered him a position to assist with the recent bump in the number of missing women and girls in the county, Aiden had jumped at the opportunity like a drowning victim grabbing a life ring. His work was his life. If he wasn't Detective Aiden Farrell, then who the hell was he?

Joe cursed and swatted at a bug. He dug out another cigarette, his irritation evident on his world-weary face.

Aiden didn't care what his partner thought. He was over it. The man was a waste of a badge. It rankled that Joe had brushed off Candace Cooper's report of the bloody footprints and had only conducted a cursory examination of the park. Sure, it was a stretch, but what if those were Amanda Jacobs's footprints? What if the man Candace saw in the woods was Amanda's kidnapper? He rubbed at the tightness in his chest. This case could've been solved months ago.

Joe blew a cloud of noxious smoke in Aiden's face. "Even if the dogs find anything—and I don't for a sweet goddamn minute think they will—what will it prove?" He tapped his cigarette, and gray ash floated to the ground.

Aiden strove for calm. "Why didn't you include the

blood smears in the report you filed?"

"Because that Cooper woman made the whole friggin' thing up." Joe huffed out a breath. "She's deranged. Not that I blame her. You know her background, right? Her sister was one of the Forgotten Five. The girl we never found. Ever since, Cooper's been a pain in the butt, demanding we continue the search, even though the poor girl's gotta be long dead.

"This is just more of the same. Candace Cooper will do anything to draw attention to her sister's case." Joe's eyes slitted against the billowing cloud of smoke. "That's why I didn't take her report seriously, and it's why I'm damn sure we're wasting our time." He spat on the ground. "She thinks the creep who abducted her sister and the other girls is out there, still kidnapping young women."

He sneered. "I wouldn't put it past her to have made up the whole damn story." His lip curled. "Bare footprints in the snow in the middle of the goddamned wilderness in November? Please."

The urge to defend Candace roared through Aiden. "I read the old reports on the Forgotten Five case. The guy who kidnapped those girls got away. The cops never caught him. He could still be around the area and back at it. Maybe he took Amanda Jacobs."

Another gob of phlegm hit the ground. "The only reason you're so het up on following through on Candace Cooper's nonsense is she's a hell of a fine-looking woman." Joe snickered. "Oh, don't think I didn't notice the way you looked at her. It's time you started thinking with your brain, Farrell, and not your dick."

Aiden's hands fisted in his pockets. Joe was hard to

take on the best of days. Today wasn't one of those days. "If you're so against this, why did you come along? You could've stayed at the office and worked the tip line or finished that stack of reports you're so concerned about."

Joe released a perfect smoke ring into the crisp air. "You young cops are all the same, full of fire and righteousness, figuring you're gonna save the world." He guffawed, the sound thick with phlegm, and spit again. "One of these days, you're gonna wake up and realize half the people we deal with are losers, and the other half are outright liars."

Aiden opened his mouth to vent his outrage, but the distant sound of frenzied barking halted the words. "They found something!" His heart raced.

They found something!

Chapter 6

The piercing ring of the doorbell broke through the soft-rock song playing on the music station on the television. Candace dropped her red marking pen on the coffee table and glanced at the clock on the mantel. Her stomach knotted. It was late—too late for a casual visitor.

She tossed the stack of papers onto the couch and crept to the living room window. Edging aside the heavy curtain, she peered outside. The front porch light illuminated a tall, dark-haired man standing outside her front door.

Aiden!

Her unease vanished, replaced by a different kind of nervousness. She ran her hand over her hair, tucking stray strands of hair behind her ears. Smoothing the wrinkles from her T-shirt, she walked down the hall to the front door. She twisted the deadbolt, slid back the security chain, unsnapped the spring lock, and opened the door. "Detective Farrell." She leaned her head back. She'd forgotten how tall he was. She'd also forgotten he was drop-dead gorgeous.

No. She hadn't forgotten. Not for one nanosecond. He'd featured prominently in her fantasies this past week. And now he was standing at her front door, looking impossibly handsome.

His cheeks were flushed from the cold night air,

and his hair was rumpled, as if he'd run his fingers through the glossy, dark strands. "Mind if I come in?"

A wave of heat flooded her at the certainty he'd caught her drooling. God, she hoped not. "Of course." She stood aside and gestured for him to enter the small two-bedroom townhouse.

He strolled past her, and she caught an enticing whiff of something spicy and definitely masculine.

By the time she gathered her senses and closed and locked the door, he stood in the middle of the living room.

"Nice place."

Don't just stand there gawking. Say something. Anything. He isn't that good-looking. She snuck another glance at him and gulped. Who was she kidding? He was a curl-your-toes and knock-you-breathless hunk. "Um…ah…er…would you like to take off your coat? Can I get you some coffee? A glass of water?" Her voice was a thin squeak.

He grinned, and she stumbled back a step.

His smile widened as if he were all too aware of the power of that devasting grin. "No thanks. This won't take long."

She tottered on wobbly legs to the couch and plopped onto the cushions.

He pointed at the papers on the couch. "Looks like you were working."

"It's the end of term." She laid a hand on the pile and straightened the papers. "I have to get these graded by Friday."

"I apologize for disturbing you at this hour."

"It's okay. I'm almost finished." Their gazes met, connected, and locked. Another thing she'd forgotten—

the unusual color of his piercing eyes—almost green and sparked with gold. She swallowed.

"Is it all right if I sit?" He pointed at a chair beside the fireplace.

"Of course." *Come on, Candace. Get a grip.* "Please sit down."

He settled on the flower-patterned, upholstered chair and stretched out his long legs and crossed his booted feet at the ankles.

The music, the warm spill of light from the table lamps, and the flickering flames in the gas fireplace lent the room a cozy, intimate ambience…almost romantic. *Easy, girl. He's not here for a social visit.* She perched on the edge of the cushion and clasped her hands on her lap. "How can I help you, Detective?"

"For starters, please call me Aiden." He smiled. "I thought we were friends."

Friends. Oh my. She covered her mouth with her hand, hiding what was surely a goofy grin.

"The K9 team searched Creighton Springs State Park today. They found something."

All thoughts of his muscled biceps vanished. "They did?"

"Right where you said you saw the footprints." He smoothed the palms of his hands over his faded jeans. "I'm not an expert, but the dog handlers were pretty confident the canines scented human blood."

"Really?" Vindication flooded her, and she clasped her hands together to stop from fist pumping the air. She'd been right all along. She hadn't imagined the bare footprints or the blood spots. "How can they be sure? I mean, it's been months."

"The handler told me scent dogs are able to detect

even the smallest traces of blood for up to twenty-four months."

She tucked an unruly lock of hair behind her ear. "Are they certain it's human blood and not blood from an injured animal? Can the dogs differentiate between species?"

"Lexington Rhodes's dogs are highly trained. They're one of the few K9 units in the country capable of conducting this type of search. He's positive they detected human blood."

A chill rippled along her spine, and she shivered even though the gas fireplace was on, and the room was warm. "Did they find anything else?" *The missing girl? A body?*

"That's the hitch. The dogs followed the trail into the woods for another fifty yards or so, but then they lost the scent."

"How can that be? Whoever made those tracks didn't just vanish into thin air."

He threaded his fingers through his hair. "The K9 team ran a complete search radius and scouted the area, but the dogs didn't pick up any other hits."

She blew out a breath. "So, where does that leave us?"

"Us?" The corners of his mouth twitched.

Her face heated. "I-I mean, you, the police, the investigation." She stumbled over her words like a teenage girl crushing on the captain of the football team.

He flashed a grin, but before the full force of his smile struck, his face settled into somber lines. "Are you certain there wasn't another vehicle in the parking lot that evening?"

She shook her head. "My car was the only one in the parking lot when I arrived and the only one there when I left."

"And you didn't encounter a vehicle on the access road?"

"Not until I turned onto the highway." Unable to sit still, she crossed one leg over the other and swung her foot. "I didn't see any people either, at least, not until I encountered the man with the beard."

He leaned forward and rested his elbows on his thighs. His gaze zeroed in on her. "And this guy was standing in the trees near where you saw the footprints?"

She nodded. "His clothes were camouflage-patterned, and he was standing still, so I'm not sure I would've seen him if I hadn't been on alert because of the two gunshots."

His eyes narrowed. "Did you speak to him?"

"That's what was so weird. When I first spotted him, I waved and called out hello—" She swallowed, but her mouth was too dry. "—you know, like you do in the backcountry when you see someone? But he didn't respond. He just stood there. His silence unnerved me, and he had a rifle." The lump in her throat was the size of a boulder. "And then—" She snapped her fingers. "—just like that, he vanished." She blew out a breath. "It freaked me out, and I got the heck out of there. I ran all the way to my car."

"And that's when you saw him again."

She shivered. "It was almost full dark by the time I reached the parking lot. I started my car and pulled out of the lot. I wanted to find cell service so I could call the police. Something about that man frightened me. I knew he was up to no good, and I was worried that someone was out there in the cold, injured and bleeding."

She uncrossed her legs and bounced her toes up and down, tapping a frantic beat on the hardwood floor. "When I turned out of the parking lot onto the access road, my headlights shone into the trees, and there he was." The image of the bearded man and his sinister grin flashed before her, and she rubbed her arms for warmth. "He'd followed me. I jammed my foot on the gas and sped out of there. I don't know how I stayed on the road." She stopped drumming her feet.

A weighty silence descended, sucking all the oxygen from the room, making it hard to breathe.

The antique clock on the mantel ticked the seconds, each sonorous tick sounding like a deafening boom.

A vehicle passed on the street, the whirr of its tires on the wet pavement filtering through the living room window.

Somewhere, out in the neighborhood, a dog barked.

He cleared his throat. "Could you identify this man if you saw him again?"

"I think so." Who was she kidding? Of course, she could. It'd been dusk, and the bearded man was in shadows, but when her headlights swept over him, he'd been in full view as if under a spotlight.

His tall, burly form was clad in a camouflage-patterned parka and baggy cargo pants, and he wore knee-high, heavy rubber boots. A gray wool toque had been pulled low over his forehead, but she was able to make out his large, crooked nose and unkempt, bushy black beard. The shadows under the trees were too deep to see his eyes, but she'd felt his feral gaze and sensed the danger. She jumped to her feet and crossed to the fireplace and switched the flames to high.

"I'd like you to meet with a police artist and see if the two of you can come up with a sketch of this man." His eyes narrowed. "Would you be okay with that?"

"I guess." She swallowed. "Do you think the man I saw, and those footprints, are connected to the missing girl?"

He tapped his long fingers on his thighs. "I don't know. The dogs proved that at some time in the past several months, human blood was spilled in that forest." His gaze zeroed in on her. "You saw footprints and blood spots in the snow around the same time Amanda Jacobs went missing. That's quite a coincidence, don't you think?" He stood and stuffed his hands into the front pockets of his jeans. "I'm following up on every lead, no matter how tenuous—anything I can do to find her and bring her home to her parents."

He seemed sincere in his desire to find the missing teen. She shouldn't lump him in with all the other investigators she'd butted heads with over the years. "Of course I'll meet with your sketch artist. Anything I can do to help."

He nodded. "Good. I'll see if I can set something up for tomorrow, if that works for you."

"I'll make it work."

Her cell phone rang, the piercing tone loud and strident. She stared at the phone vibrating on the coffee table and slid a glance at the mantel clock. A chill rippled through her. *Damn.* She'd forgotten to mute the ringer.

Every night for the past two months, like

clockwork, the phone rang at ten o'clock. She'd answered the first call expecting it to be from a friend or a student needing help on an assignment. The caller hadn't said a word, but she'd heard heavy, labored breathing.

She'd hung up.

The next night, she received another phone call. She'd answered that one as well and again, was met with unsettling silence. The third night, she didn't answer, but the phone rang again and again, until she finally picked up and clicked Answer, only to be met with more silence and heavy breathing.

After that, she ignored the calls. No matter how many times the phone rang at night, she didn't answer. She'd considered going to the police and reporting the disturbing calls, but her experience with Detective Breacher and other cops like him had taught her she couldn't count on the authorities. They wouldn't take her seriously. And so, she'd gotten into the habit of turning off her phone's ringer in the evening. Somehow, she'd forgotten tonight.

The strident ringing persisted.

"Aren't you going to answer that?" Aiden's piercing gaze studied her.

Her hand shook as she reached for her cell phone on the table beside the couch and checked the call display.

Unknown caller.

As she'd expected. She shut off the ringer, silencing the insistent noise, and schooled her expression to mask her unease. "Telemarketers." The lie slid off her lips.

"It's late for them to be calling. Those companies

have no shame." He headed for the door. "I'll leave you to your marking."

She followed him.

He eyed the elaborate locking system on her front door. "Are you afraid of something?"

"Afraid?" The word choked in her throat. "What are you talking about?"

He nodded at the sturdy metal latch, chain-link door guard, and the jimmy-proof dead bolt she'd paid a fortune to have installed three months ago after her encounter with the bearded man in the forest. "This is quite the setup."

She forced a laugh. "Just being safe. You know…a woman living alone."

"Smart. You never know what weirdos are out there." He undid the locks, one after the other, opened the door, and stepped onto the well-lit porch. "I'll be in touch." Tightening the collar of his brown suede jacket, he bounded down the steps and strode along the sidewalk to the gleaming black SUV parked under a streetlight. He climbed into his car and slammed the door closed.

She released the breath she'd been holding, closed and locked the door, twisted the deadbolt into place, slipped the chain into the security guard, and slid the metal safety latch to the closed position. Following her nightly ritual, she prowled around the house, moving from room to room, examining each window and ensuring the latches were secure. When she returned to the front door, she activated the high-end alarm system.

Only then could she breathe.

Chapter 7

Aiden gripped the steering wheel and stared at Candace's town house and blew out a shaky breath. He swiped his damp forehead with the back of his hand, as hot and bothered as a kid at his first dance. He'd gone to her house to tell her the results of the K9 search. Just doing his job, right?

Not.

He could've phoned and told her what the dogs had found and asked if she were willing to meet with a police sketch artist. Or he could have asked her to come down to the station and discuss the findings. Instead, he'd gone to her house…at night…alone.

At the end of shift, when Aiden told his partner he was going to Candace's house to inform her what the K9 team had uncovered, Joe curled his lip and told him to go shoot his wad. He wanted nothing to do with Aiden's foolish endeavor, and with that scathing comment, and a smirk on his fleshy face, he'd strode out of the station.

Joe didn't have any interest in pursuing this lead…or any lead for that matter. He was convinced the bloody footprints were a figment of Candace's imagination, no matter what the K9 dogs had found. He'd made his feelings clear on the subject to the point where Aiden was ready to punch the smirk off the man's bloated face if he brought up his disbelief again.

Besides, at this time of night, Joe was settled on a barstool at his favorite drinking establishment, swilling back another round of whiskey and boring those around him with his heroic exploits as a renowned Briggston Police detective.

Aiden had spent hours at home, struggling with his decision. A phone call was too impersonal. He wanted to see her face when he told her what the K9 unit had found, wanted her to know that her unease was justified. So, he'd ignored the warning bells ringing in his head and, in spite of it being well past a decent hour for an official police-business call, he drove to Candace's house and knocked on her door.

A mistake.

A big one.

When she opened the door, she'd taken his breath away. Her dark hair was mussed, the silken strands free of the single long, heavy braid she favored. Her pale-pink, loose T-shirt and baggy pajama bottoms with multi-colored stars dancing across the flannel did little to conceal her curves.

And then there was her scent—floral with a hint of cinnamon. One whiff and his heart started pounding, and his blood sizzled and headed south. It had required all his police training to keep his expression impassive and his hands off her. But like an idiot determined to ruin what was left of his career and reputation, he'd wiped the drool from his face and sailed through her front door.

The entire time he was in her house, all he could think about was how soft her skin looked and how damn pretty her blue eyes were with their sweep of long dark eyelashes.

Jesus H. Christ!

He should've learned from the shitstorm that went down in Seattle. If he had any sense left in his brain cells, he'd do the right thing and keep his distance from the all-too-lovely Dr. Cooper. Once she met with the police sketch artist, and he had a picture of the guy she'd seen in the state park, he wouldn't need her anymore. If anything came up, he could always send Joe to talk to her.

He grimaced. Nah. He wouldn't do that. No one deserved Joe, not even the most hardened of criminals. And Candace was anything but a hardened criminal. A vision of her long dark hair gleaming like a raven's wing, her creamy skin and full mouth—

Jesus!

He clipped himself on the back of his head. Only a fool would sit in the dark outside her house mooning like a lovestruck puppy. If he didn't get moving, her neighbors would call the cops. He grimaced. And wouldn't that be something? Joe would have a hell of a good chuckle.

Something was going on with her. That phone call was weird. He didn't believe for one second the caller was a telemarketer. When the phone rang, she'd jumped a foot, and her face lost its color. She'd tried to hide it, but she was afraid. But why would she lie? Why not tell him if she was getting harassing calls? Add in the overkill lock set up on her front door, and it was pretty obvious she was frightened.

He shook his head. Whatever it was, the smart move would be to leave it alone. Her problems were none of his business. Jamming the key into the ignition, he shoved his foot on the gas, and the SUV roared to life.

He stilled.

The shrubs separating Candace's townhouse from the one next door were shaking, the leaves trembling as if from a sudden strong gust of wind. He checked the leaves on a tree overhanging the driveway. The leaves were still. Prickles of alarm tightened the hairs on the back of his neck.

A flicker of movement, more branches waving, leaves fluttering, and a large, dark shape shifted deeper into the shadows.

Too big for a raccoon or a neighbor's dog. He squinted into the dark. A person. Had to be. Every cell in his body zinged to full alert. Someone was lurking outside Candace's house. He shifted the car into Park and reached under his coat and unsnapped his holster cover.

A car headed down the street toward him. Its headlights swept the lawn and the decorative bushes lining Candace's driveway.

A black cat yowled, streaked out of the shrubs, and raced across the grass and vanished behind the neighbor's house.

Aiden released his breath and eased his grip on his gun and slumped back on the seat. *Jesus*. What the hell was wrong with him? He was seeing bad guys behind every damn tree.

When he joined the Briggston Police Force, he'd read the state's unsolved missing persons' files and discovered Amanda Jacobs had been abducted from her home two months prior and was still missing. Missing kids were his weak spot, and since then he'd worked nonstop to find her, putting in long hours after his shift at the precinct was done, working from home on weekends, chasing down leads, no matter how tenuous. He'd driven to Cardion and re-interviewed the girl's family and friends and followed up on the hundreds of tips called in to the station's crime stopper's tip line.

The case was tragic. Fifteen-year-old Amanda had vanished from her bedroom sometime during the night, leaving no trace of where she'd gone. Nothing her parents, or any of her friends or teachers, said, indicated Amanda would've left home willingly. She wasn't the party type, she did well in school, she didn't have a boyfriend, and as far as anyone knew, she didn't use alcohol or illegal drugs.

In the months since her disappearance, the police and dozens of volunteers had searched the forest surrounding Cardion and the nearby mountains and back roads for the missing girl. They'd even dragged the Crozier River that ran through town, and nearby Kluscus Lake.

The citizens of Cardion were on high alert, but no one had seen Amanda, and no sign of her had been found. With no leads to follow, the task force had dwindled, and the case stagnated, as other crimes occurred and moved to the forefront.

But he hadn't given up. He was determined to find Amanda. Candace Cooper's sighting of bloody footprints in the snow was the first viable clue he'd had in months. No matter what his partner thought, Candace was a credible witness. Aiden believed her. It wasn't just his attraction for her that was talking. At least, he hoped it wasn't.

He yawned and rubbed his eyes. He'd better go home and get some sleep. Tomorrow was going to be another long day. With a final glance at the dark shrubbery, he shifted the car into Drive and pulled onto the street.

Chapter 8

Candace yanked open the heavy, glass-fronted door to the Briggston Police Station and stepped inside.

Uniformed cops and civilians milled about the cavernous lobby, their voices echoing off the vaulted ceiling.

She joined a snaking line of people waiting to pass through security. Once through the metal detector, she approached the front counter.

A bald, heavyset, uniformed officer looked up from a file he was reading and peered at her through thick smudged lenses. "Yes?"

"I have an appointment with Officer Mulhoney."

He tapped computer keys and consulted the screen before him. "Your name?"

"Candace Cooper."

He stiffened and his eyes narrowed, probably in recognition of her infamous name, but he pointed across the lobby. "Down the hall. Third door on your left." He kept his gaze on her as she turned and crossed the lobby.

She followed his directions, but she halted in the wide hallway before a large bulletin board filled with posters of wanted felons and missing persons stapled to its pitted surface. Amanda Jacobs's name jumped out from a tattered poster, and her heart skipped a beat.

Amanda's slim, heart-shaped face was framed by

long, wavy, dark hair that hung past her shoulders and was held back on one side by a red, plastic hair clip. She had trusting blue eyes and the open, friendly smile girls her age possessed, confident nothing bad would ever happen to them.

Where was she? Were those her footprints Candace had seen in the snow at Creighton Springs State Park? Had Amanda run away from home and hidden in the forest? No way. No teenager would seek refuge in the middle of the wilderness, especially in the cold, wet days and freezing nights of November in the mountains. A young girl on the run would head to a friend's house or vanish into the bright lights and crowds of a big city like Denver.

But what if someone abducted her and took her against her will to the isolated state park, and somehow, she'd managed to escape?

Candace's stomach flipped over. If she'd followed the footprints into the forest that day, she might have found Amanda. Instead, she'd let her fear of the bearded stranger rule her, and she'd run to the safety of her car and left that poor girl out there. Guilt flooded her along with the sting of tears, and she fished in her purse for a tissue.

Twenty-two years ago, when Charlene disappeared, Candace had prayed for someone to find her. If a concerned citizen had come forward with a clue, some small piece of evidence, her sister could have been found, and Charlene wouldn't have had to endure years of atrocities. If help had come even one day sooner, maybe Charlene would be here today, married to a wonderful man, a mother with children of her own, and Candace wouldn't be so emotionally scarred, or...

She cut off the speeding train of toxic thoughts. She'd been over this scenario a million times. There were hundreds of maybes, a thousand what-ifs, but none of those wishes would change the stark reality of what happened, none would bring her sister home, and none would heal Candace's emotional wounds. She swiped her hand over her damp eyes.

The nightmare days and weeks after Charlene vanished were seared into Candace's brain. After a few months, the police had stopped looking, the search parties had disbanded, and the media moved on to other tragedies, but she and her parents never gave up hope. They never stopped looking. The certainty Charlene was alive kept them going day after unendurable day.

Charlene's abduction changed Candace forever, and the tragedy transformed the whole family. Their lives were divided into two distinct worlds—the golden times before Charlene was taken, and the dark nightmare after. After wasn't a good place. Not for anyone, especially an impressionable twelve-year-old girl, grieving the loss of the older sister she adored, and weighed down by a truckload of guilt.

The situation worsened when the other missing girls were rescued and returned to their families. At first, there was joy in their release and hope Charlene was finally coming home. The investigators found evidence that proved Charlene had been in the old farm shed where the other missing girls had been held, but she was gone when the police raided the farm.

Just hours before the police arrived, the kidnapper had freed Charlene of her bindings and dragged her, kicking and screaming, out of the shed. When no sign of either Charlene or her abductor was found, despite extensive searching, the police were convinced the man had killed her and buried her body deep in the woods where she'd never be found. After a few more months, they stopped looking. The suspension of the federal task force, with all its manpower and resources, was the worst—the total annihilation of hope.

Charlene wasn't coming back.

Ever.

The family fractured.

Candace isolated in her room, withdrawing, not talking, not feeling, not thinking, just existing.

Her mother died five years later of invasive breast cancer.

Two years after that, her father succumbed to a massive stroke.

But Candace knew better.

The medical diagnoses were wrong. Devastated by the loss of their oldest daughter, John and Marilyn Cooper had died of broken hearts.

Her own scars ran so deep in her psyche, she wasn't the same Candace, and would never be the same person again, no matter how many therapy sessions or prescribed medications.

The grief and guilt had nearly killed her, but her anger at the authorities, the media, the townspeople, everyone who'd given up on Charlene, dragged Candace out of her misery and propelled her to action. She became a crusader, determined to do whatever it took to keep her sister's name in the news, to force the police to keep looking, to convince everyone to not give up on Charlene.

Candace wiped her hand over her damp face and

forced her thoughts from the past. Reliving the nightmare that had shaped her life wouldn't bring Charlene back.

She studied the youthful face on the missing person poster. Had the same fate befallen Amanda Jacobs? Had she been abducted, and was she being held in some remote cabin? She shuddered. After all these months, was there a chance Amanda was still alive?

Candace bit down on her bottom lip, determined to do her best to describe the bearded man to the police artist and hope his picture would help the police track him down. He could be innocent and not connected to Amanda's disappearance. Maybe he had been out for a walk in the forest, but every cell in her being screamed otherwise.

She turned from the bulletin board and smacked into a wall of solid muscle. A familiar male scent washed over her, and she stumbled back a step. Her breath whooshed out. "Aiden!" Mere inches separated her from the handsome detective.

His hazel eyes sparked with golden lights. "Hey, Candace." He smiled and intriguing tiny lines creased beside his eyes. "You're here to see the police sketch artist?"

She nodded.

He looked over her shoulder, and his smile faded. "You were looking at Amanda Jacobs's poster."

She nodded again though he hadn't asked a question. "I hope you find her."

His brow furrowed, and he studied the poster and then stared at her. He edged around her and tapped the poster. "You two could be sisters, you know that? You both have long, dark-brown hair and vivid blue eyes."

She rocked back on her heels. He was right. The physical similarities were there. Amanda could be her younger sister. Her mouth dried. Why hadn't she noticed the resemblance? "I'm sure that's just a coincidence. There are hundreds of dark-haired, blue-eyed women in this state."

"Yeah, probably." His narrowed gaze kept switching from the photograph on the poster to Candace and back again.

She sucked in a steadying breath and made a show of examining her watch. "Look at that, I'm late for my appointment." She backed up and smacked into the wall. Heat flushed her face. "I'd better go."

"Don't let me detain you." He smiled, his eyes sparkling with tiny diamonds. "Thank you for doing this. It might help."

Her legs turned rubbery under the full-wattage power of his smile. It was either stay and kiss the man or flee. Like a coward, she chose flight and sidled past him and fled down the hall, all too aware of his gaze pinned on her back. The desk sergeant had said the office she wanted was the third door on the right. She tapped on the battered metal door.

The door swung open, and a tall lean man with thinning red hair stood in the doorway. "You must be Candace Cooper." He held out a large, bony hand. "I'm Officer Mulhoney." After they shook hands, he gestured her into his tiny office. "I've been waiting for you."

"Sorry, I—"

"Don't worry about it. You're here now." He removed a teetering stack of papers and books from a metal chair by the lone window in the small, messy office. "Have a seat."

Once she was seated, he picked up a large sketchbook and a mechanical pencil from the overflowing metal desktop and sat on a facing chair. "Okay. Let's get started."

Recalling the frightening man in the forest and trying to visualize every detail drained her, but an hour later, the drawing was complete.

Officer Mulhoney held up the sketch. "What do you think? Does this look like the man you saw?"

She sucked in a breath and gripped the sides of the metal chair, holding steady as the room swirled. "That's him! How did you do that?"

He grinned, his eyes twinkling. "You're a good witness. You recalled an amazing amount of detail." He stood. "Now—"

The door opened and Aiden stepped into the room. "All done?"

Officer Mulhoney nodded. "We just finished." He held up the sketch.

Aiden studied the picture and then looked at her. "That's the man you saw?"

"I think so."

"Okay. We'll have copies made and sent out to every patrol car and beat cop in the state." He turned to Officer Mulhoney. "See if we can't get this on the evening news. The more people who see this sketch, the better chance we have of tracking this guy down."

"But what if he wasn't doing anything wrong? What if he was just out for a walk in the forest?" Even though she was certain the bearded man was up to no good, she didn't want to cause him trouble if he was just a fellow hiker.

"You said you heard two gunshots."

"I'm pretty sure I did."

"And he was packing a rifle. Shooting off firearms is illegal in the park, so if he's the one who fired the shots, he broke the law." Aiden scratched his whiskered chin. "I'd say it's worth the risk of embarrassing him, wouldn't you? A young girl's life is at stake." His eyes narrowed. "Besides, he spooked you. Over the years, I've learned to trust my instincts. If someone feels sketchy, they're probably up to no good. At the very least, he's a person of interest."

She swallowed, her mouth arid dry. The bearded man *had* frightened her. Something about him—his wide-legged, aggressive stance, the way he smiled— something dark and forbidding, rocked her to her core.

Aiden nodded at Officer Mulhoney. "Email me that sketch, will you? I'll get started." He wheeled around and left the room.

Officer Mulhoney's red eyebrows arched. "He's a man on a mission. Let's hope his hunch pays out, and— " He tapped the sketch. "—this guy's our perp. We need to find that poor girl before..." He stopped, his cheeks flaming.

She shuddered at what he'd been about to say. *Before it was too late. Before Amanda Jacobs was killed.* Heart lodged in her throat, she rose and picked up her purse. "I guess we're finished."

"Thank you for coming in today. I know this wasn't easy."

She paused in the doorway. "I hope that sketch helps."

He patted the paper. "This is more than we had an hour ago. With any luck, this picture will help us locate this guy, and we'll figure out what he was up to in the park that day. If we're lucky, he's the kidnapper. We all want Amanda home safe and sound."

Her legs wobbled as she retraced her steps out of the building, down the front stairs, and across the street to the shopping center parking lot where she'd left her car. She was exhausted. All she wanted was to get home and slip into a hot bath.

Her small, red, hybrid car was in the third row, squashed between a massive gray SUV and a dust-covered, blue minivan. She tugged out her keys from her coat pocket and hit the unlock button. The car chirped, and the doors unlocked. She walked around to the driver's door but paused, her hand on the door handle. The back of her neck tingled with the unsettling sensation she was being watched.

The large parking lot was almost full. Vehicles of every description filled the slots. Shoppers, pushing overflowing shopping carts or carrying bulging plastic bags, exited the mall entrance in search of their cars. Others crossed the parking lot heading toward the main entrance.

She scanned the busy lot. Everything appeared normal, but the uncomfortable tingling continued. Was someone watching her? Or was she overreacting like she had so many times during the past months—thinking she saw the man from the forest behind every bush and in every car that passed her house?

A man and a woman held the hands of two small children who chattered in excited, high-pitched voices, as they weaved through parked cars toward the mall entrance.

A small white car wheeled off the street into the

parking lot. The driver steered the car into a spot two stalls over. The car door opened, and an elderly woman climbed out. She shuffled around to the back of the vehicle and retrieved an armful of reusable shopping bags from her trunk and headed toward the stores.

Normal people going about their day.

Candace squinted against the glare of the midday sun and stilled.

One row over. A person sat behind the wheel of a battered gray pickup. The light reflected off the truck's cracked windshield but revealed the driver's dark bushy beard.

Despite the sunglasses covering his eyes, she sensed the penetrating power of his gaze. Her heart caught in her throat. The man from the forest! She rubbed the back of her neck. *Don't be silly.* Recalling the facial features of the stranger she'd seen in Creighton Springs State Park for the police sketch artist had put her on edge. Lots of men had beards these days. Facial hair was in style.

Heart hammering, she yanked open her car door, leaped inside, and slapped her hand on the door's lock button. She dropped the key fob twice before sliding the key into the ignition.

The car roared to life.

Mashing her foot on the gas, she backed out of the parking spot, sped through the parking lot, and shot onto the busy street, cutting off a black sedan.

The driver blew his horn and shot her the finger.

She careened down the street and sped through a yellow traffic light. Six blocks later, she checked the rearview mirror. Not a gray truck in sight. Easing her foot off the gas, she slowed to the speed limit.

Loosening her death grip on the steering wheel, she switched on her turn signal and eased to the side of the road. Wiping the dampness from her brow, she laid her head against the headrest and closed her eyes. What the hell was wrong with her? In her panic to escape the parking lot, she could've killed someone. And for what? Because she thought the bearded man from the forest was in the mall parking lot watching her?

She inhaled a shaky breath. People sat in their vehicles all the time while they checked their cell phones. Or he could've been waiting for his wife who was shopping in one of the many mall stores.

Maybe.

Or just maybe the pinging in her gut was right, and he was the man from Creighton Springs State Park. A chill rippled along her spine, and she sucked in a sharp breath. He'd followed her. The past several months she'd had the unsettling sensation she was being watched. She knew it was crazy, but she couldn't shake her unease. That was why she'd had the extra locks installed on her doors and the expensive alarm system set up.

The previous night, she'd awakened in the early hours of the morning, and on her way to the bathroom, she'd slid the curtain aside and peered out her bedroom window.

A truck was parked on the street outside. The glow from the streetlight down the block shone on the vehicle's light-colored hood, revealing a flicker of movement inside the vehicle as if someone were sitting behind the steering wheel.

Her heart slammed against her ribs. She glanced at the bedside clock. At this time of night, the houses were dark, the street still. Her neighborhood was a quiet one, the houses filled with young, working families and retirees who were in bed by eleven.

She didn't recognize the vehicle. The truck didn't belong to one of her neighbors. A guest maybe?

The truck's engine roared to life, and the twin beams of its headlights strobed the dark street. The vehicle pulled away from the curb and slowly moved down the street.

She blew out a ragged breath and nearly sagged to the floor in a wave of relief. The person in the truck was a late-night visitor leaving her neighbor's house. That's all. Nothing to worry about.

She continued to the bathroom, relieved herself, drank a glass of water, and headed back to bed. Stopping by the window, she slid the curtain aside and studied the deserted street.

Nothing out of the ordinary. No gray truck. No bearded man.

Closing the curtain, she crawled into bed.

Hours later, she was still awake, still wondering, unable to shake the anxiety percolating through her.

She'd seen the truck again. At least she thought the gray truck in the mall parking lot was the same vehicle. The truck the prior night had been light-colored, but under the glow of the streetlight, it was impossible to tell if the truck was gray, or light blue, or tan.

She rubbed her temples with the pads of her fingers, hoping to ease the dull throbbing. *Call Aiden.* She grimaced. And tell him what? That she suspected the man she'd seen in the forest so many months ago was following her? He'd think she was nuts.

Her mouth twisted in a rueful smile. And just

maybe he'd be right. She'd come so far, worked impossibly hard to conquer her crippling anxiety. The irrational fear that one day the man who'd taken her sister would return for Candace filled her every moment. She imagined monsters around every corner.

Her fears were ridiculous, but she couldn't shake them. She threaded her fingers through her hair. Instead of freaking out and driving like a kamikaze through the downtown streets, she should be arranging a session with her therapist.

Or focusing on her afternoon class. She'd finished marking the students' term papers. Some of the essays were poorly researched and filled with sloppy writing, and a few contained complete paragraphs plagiarized from well-known sources. Those students would not be pleased with their low marks. But a few of the essays were well-researched and well-written. Those students deserved their A grade.

She restarted the car and pulled back onto the road. Taking the next right, she drove with studied care, but she couldn't stop checking the rearview mirror to ensure the gray truck wasn't following.

Chapter 9

Candace flicked off her office light and closed the door and locked it behind her. It was late Sunday night, and most students and staff were in their dorms cramming for final exams or at home with their families. The usually bustling corridor was empty, and her footsteps echoed hollowly as she strode past dark faculty offices and an empty lecture theater to the stairs.

The utter emptiness of the deserted building was unnerving, and she hurried her steps.

The custodial staff had finished their cleaning rounds an hour ago, and the building had been silent ever since.

A prickle of unease tightened her stomach. She never stayed at work this late. She liked to be safely tucked in her townhouse when the sun went down, but with everything going on, she'd fallen behind in her work, and end-of-term deadlines loomed.

The building creaked around her, and she was almost running by the time she reached the end of the hallway and shoved open the fire exit door. She stepped onto the dimly lit landing and leaped down the stairs. Her chest was heaving when she slammed open the door and entered the main foyer.

A campus security guard sat behind a large wooden desk in front of the main entrance. A hockey game was playing on a small television set on top of the desk.

When he saw her, he turned the volume down on the game and smiled. "Burning the midnight oil, Dr. Cooper, I see."

"You know what end of term is like, George." She nodded at the television. "Good game?"

George Baker was a fixture at Briggston College. He'd worked as a college security guard for as long as Candace could remember. Always cheerful and friendly, he was a fervid fan of the local hockey team. He had front-row-center season tickets when the Bobcats played in town, and he watched their televised games when they played out of town games.

He took off his wire-framed glasses and polished the lenses with his shirttail. His forehead creased. "I tell you, if the Bobcats don't do any better this next round, I'm burning my season tickets."

She laughed. "I'll believe that when I see it. You're their biggest supporter. I don't know what they'd do if you weren't sitting in the stands cheering them on."

He chuckled and settled his glasses on his face. "You know me too well. I guess I'm a sucker for punishment." Shoving back his chair, he pushed to his feet. "I'll walk you to your car. It's dark out there." Since a young coed had been assaulted on campus six weeks prior, George and the other campus security guards had agitated for more guards and brighter sidewalk and parking lot lighting.

The college was under tight budget constraints, and so far, nothing had changed.

"Thanks, but I'll be fine." She smoothed her palms on her jeans. The thought of leaving the safety of the faculty building and walking to her car alone in the dark filled her with fear. But she hated to tear him away from his game. Her therapist told her she needed to conquer her unreasonable fear of dark, lonely places. Besides—she patted the bulge in her purse—she had her can of mace and her cell phone.

"Okay. If you're sure." He focused on the television screen and cheered. "Yes!" He pumped his fist in the air. "The Bobcats scored! They're ahead by one. I knew they could do it. Go Cats!"

"Goodnight, George. See you tomorrow." She headed toward the glass exit doors.

He waved a hand, her presence already forgotten.

She thrust open the door and stepped into the night. A blast of cold wind struck her, and she tightened the collar of her coat.

It had rained sometime during the evening. Puddles pooled on the sidewalk, and the air was damp. Patches of fog hung in the air.

Faint streaks of light from the widely spaced streetlights filtered through the leafy branches of the tall trees lining the sidewalk, casting the walkway in dark, shifting shadows.

She shivered and huddled into her coat, already regretting not asking George to escort her.

A footfall sounded behind her, and she cast a glance over her shoulder.

Nothing.

She clutched her purse to her chest. She'd done this walk to the faculty parking lot countless times, though never so late at night. She was always vigilant. A woman couldn't be too careful, but tonight she jumped at every noise and peered into the shadows.

Another footfall, the scrape of a heavy boot sole against pavement.

Tensing, she fumbled with the catch on her purse and fished out the can of mace. She shot a look behind, but the sidewalk was empty.

Headlights lit up the narrow road, and a car drove slowly by. Water splashed as the car's tires drove through mud puddles. The faint glow of light cast by a streetlight lit the car's interior, revealing a blonde-haired woman behind the wheel. The car continued along the road until it was out of sight, and the campus was once again deserted.

Candace released a shaky breath. A cold wind gusted loose strands of hair across her face. She couldn't shake the sensation she was being followed, but no matter how often she looked behind, she didn't see anyone. She should return to the faculty building and take George up on his offer to walk her to her car. *Don't be a ninny*. No one was following her. She'd done this walk dozens of times, and she'd never had a problem.

In spite of her reassurances, the certainty something dark and menacing was closing in had her hurrying her steps. The sense of being watched from the darkness remained acute. She was almost running by the time she reached the parking lot.

Her car, parked under a tall elm tree, was the only vehicle in the lot. Raindrops beaded on the car's shiny red surface. She sucked in a shaky breath. Why hadn't she parked near one of the parking lot lights? But it was daylight when she'd arrived, and she hadn't planned to stay so long at work. Working through the stack of student papers, she'd lost track of time. One minute the sun was shining, and the next time she looked out the window, the dark of night had settled in.

She fumbled in her purse for her keys.

A hand jerked her arm with such force she was knocked off her feet. She screamed. Thick fingers dug through the thin fabric of her coat into her skin and muscle, stopping her fall.

Her purse, her car keys, and the can of mace fell from her hands. Lipstick, loose change, her cell phone, and her wallet spilled onto the wet pavement. She opened her mouth to scream again, but a large, callused palm slapped over her mouth silencing her. She was yanked back against a hard, masculine body. A nauseating wave of garlic, fried onions, and stale cigarette smoke washed over her. She gagged, as terror iced her gut.

The rapist!

He was going to rape her. Just like he'd assaulted that coed. Adrenaline fired through her, and she jerked and twisted, kicking and punching her attacker, fighting to escape. One of her blows struck home, and he grunted in pain.

Yes!

She fought harder, determined to break free.

He tightened his grip, and his arm jammed across her neck.

Her lungs burned, and her chest heaved as she struggled to draw in breath. She clawed at his arm, her nails digging deep, drawing blood, desperate for air.

A rough voice snarled in her ear, "Stop fighting or I'll slit your throat."

The prick of a sharp blade sliced the tender skin on her neck just below her ear. A trickle of warm blood trailed down her neck. Terror rocketed into the stratosphere. Her mind raced, skittering from one frantic plan to another.

The mace!

Out of the corner of her eye she saw it. The small, red cannister lay inches from her feet. If she could grab the can she could—

"How ya doin', Candy Girl?"

Warm spittle spattered her face. She froze. *Candy Girl*? Only one person had ever called her Candy Girl, and that person had vanished twenty-two years ago. Her heart clenched, and her worse nightmare, the one that kept her up at night, rushed at her like a freight train.

It's him! The monster who took Charlene and the other four girls had returned for her. Just like in her nightmares.

Spots clouded her vision, and her ears rang. She needed air. Now! Panic roared, and she bit his palm, sinking her teeth through the thin glove and into flesh, tasting blood.

He cursed, and for a heartbeat, the pressure on her neck eased.

She sucked in a breath and screamed like a banshee. He grabbed her, but she fought harder, kicking, twisting, and bucking. Her booted foot connected with his shin.

He grunted.

Victory soared through her, fueling her fury, and she struck again.

Arm raised, he lunged and stabbed.

A sharp prick on her neck, like a bee sting.

He cackled and held up a syringe. "You can't get away from me, Candy Girl. I've got plans for you. Big plans."

Loud ringing in her ears dulled his words, and a

warm lassitude washed over her. Salty tears flowed unchecked down her cheeks. Sheer nothingness grasped her soul, threatening to engulf her. Her muscles grew heavy and leaden, each leg weighing a ton.

Keep fighting!

Her body refused to obey. An icy coldness settled deep in her belly, and fingers of ice invaded her blood. The glow from the distant streetlights faded in and out in nauseating waves. Her legs wobbled. She sagged.

"Hey! What are you doing over there?"

"Let her go!"

Distant voices, shouting, feet pounding on the pavement.

The painful grip on her arms loosened. Her knees buckled, and she collapsed in a boneless heap onto the unforgiving ground. Her head snapped back and smashed the pavement. A jolt of pain, and bright splotches of light filled the night. The world dimmed, but she fought to stay conscious, to be aware, to fight, to live. But her legs and arms wouldn't move, her muscles leaden.

"Ma'am? Are you okay? Did he hurt you?" A man's blurry face loomed above her.

She opened her mouth to speak, but her throat closed tight as if a boulder were lodged inside, and no sounds emerged.

"Call an ambulance!" Another male voice, distant and muted as if the speaker were under water.

The world darkened and transformed into a fathomless black abyss, and she fell, spiraling into the dark.

Chapter 10

Aiden paced back and forth across the narrow corridor outside Candace's hospital room, trying not to inhale the strong medicinal stench that saturated the air. He jammed his hands into the front pockets of his jeans to stop from punching the wall. Ever since he received the call about the attack on Candace at the college, a fury raged through him.

He scowled at the closed door. He'd been in her room, but he only managed a glimpse of her pale face before an arrogant witch of a nurse, who would have put Nurse Ratched to shame, ordered him out. A team of nurses and doctors remained, tending to the unconscious patient.

The attending doctor had told Aiden the preliminary lab tests revealed Candace had been injected with a high dose of ketamine. When the ambulance arrived at the crime scene, she was out cold, and as far as he knew she still was.

He'd been on his way home from his daily workout at the gym after putting in ten long hours in what was fast becoming a fruitless search for Amanda Jacobs, the missing girl, when his police radio alerted him to the attack on Candace. He'd pulled a three sixty in the middle of the road, ignoring the blaring horns of the drivers he cut off, and raced to the college.

Even with breaking land-speed records, by the time

he got to the scene, the paramedics had her strapped on a stretcher and were loading her into the back of an ambulance.

Police emergency lights and the ambulance's red-and-blue flashing lights strobed the dark parking lot, creating an eerie, otherworldly scene.

A uniformed cop was taking the statements of three fraternity brothers.

Farther back, a small crowd of onlookers watched the unfolding drama.

Two other cops roped off the crime scene with long strands of yellow police tape.

Aiden's heart skipped a beat at the small, dark pool of blood on the wet pavement. A black leather purse he recognized as Candace's lay on the ground. Cosmetics and other paraphernalia spilled from the open bag. A set of car keys glistened in the rain, and a can of mace lay on the ground by her car's back tire.

Joe, chewing on a thick wad of gum, approached. "'Bout time you got your sorry ass here, partner. I thought you were gonna take a pass."

Aiden bit back a sharp retort. "What the hell happened?"

Joe blew a bubble and popped his gum with a loud snap. "Looks like another assault." He shook his head. "When will these women learn? I mean, how can they be so stupid? A coed was attacked on this campus a few weeks ago, and what does—" He jerked his thumb at the ambulance as it sped out of the parking lot, lights flashing, sirens blaring. "—our good professor do?" He curled his upper lip. "She walks alone, at night, through the campus to her car." He pointed at the small red two-door coupe. "If that weren't bad enough, she parked under that tree and as far from the parking lot lights as possible." He blew another bubble. "I ask you, what the hell was she thinking?"

Aiden brushed off his partner's comments. No woman deserved to be attacked, no matter where she walked or where she parked her car. The campus should be a safe place. For everyone. He glanced at the puddle of blood, and his gut tightened. "What happened?"

"I told you." Another loud pop from Joe's gum. "Our vic worked late and left her office and walked out of the building to her car alone."

It took all Aiden's self-control not to yank the gum out of Joe's mouth. "And?"

"The security guard in the foyer of her office building confirmed the time she left. He warned her to be careful and offered to walk her to her car, but she refused." Another pop. "Like I said, stupid."

Aiden had had enough. "What are you doing here, Joe? It's after hours."

"I heard the call on the radio." Joe shrugged. "I was curious to see what trouble the Cooper woman was up to now." His eyes narrowed. "I could ask you the same question, partner. Why are you here?" He waggled his bushy eyebrows. "Booty call?"

Instead of punching the smirk off Joe's face, Aiden swung away and crossed to a uniformed officer who was taking photos of the red car. "Hey, Murray."

The gray-haired cop hung his camera by a strap from his shoulder. "Hey, Aiden." He shook his head. "Our victim was damn lucky." He pointed at the trio of young men. "If those kids hadn't come by when they did, the perp would have raped her for sure. The witnesses said the guy had a knife to her throat."

A chill settled over Aiden. "Did he cut her?" He stared at the blood, unable to look away.

"She had a nick on her throat, but it looks like the blood occurred when she fell and hit her head on the pavement. The paramedics think she has a mild concussion." He frowned. "She was injected with some sort of drug. We found a used syringe." He held up a small plastic baggie. A needle was visible through the clear plastic.

Aiden's gut knotted. "Thanks, Murray. When the techs arrive, make sure they examine every inch of the crime scene. The perp must've left some sort of trace. I want to pin this jerk's ass."

Murray nodded and raised the camera and snapped another photo.

Aiden ground down on his back molars so hard he feared they'd crack. This sort of assault was all too common. These scumbags thought they had the right to attack a woman and take what they wanted by force. Candace was one of the lucky ones. She'd live another day. Many victims weren't so fortunate. He forced back his fury and approached the three witnesses. He nodded at the cop. "I'll take it from here, officer."

The cop backed away, and Aiden focused his attention on the three young men. He wrinkled his nose at the alcohol fumes filling the night air.

Their eyes were bloodshot, their gazes glazed, and they were unsteady on their feet.

"I'll need a statement from each of you." He beckoned to a tall, lanky, red-haired man. "You first. The rest of you wait here." He led the way to his car and ushered him inside.

Aiden walked around to the driver's side and slid behind the wheel and fixed the witness with a steely look. "What's your name?"

"Caleb. Caleb Hartford."

"Okay, Caleb. Tell me what happened."

The young man fidgeted on the seat, clasping and unclasping his hands. His face was pale, and the freckles sprinkled across his nose and cheeks stood out like fly spatter.

"Me and the guys were walking back to our dorm from the campus pub." He grimaced. "We had a few beers." He waved his hands. "You know, to celebrate the end of term and all."

No kidding. Judging by the kid's slurred speech, he'd had more than a few drinks. Aiden nodded. "Go on."

"We were crossing the common heading back to our dorm when a woman screamed. We'd heard about the girl who was attacked a few weeks back, so we ran over and saw this guy wrestling with a woman." His face flushed. "Right away we could tell he was holding her against her will. It was dark, but we could see he held a knife to her throat. She was kicking and fighting him, and..." His Adam's apple bobbed in his thin throat. "Trevor, that's my roommate, he hollered at the guy to let her go, and the guy dropped her like a rock and took off.

"We were shocked when we saw it was Dr. Cooper." He wiped his gleaming brow with the back of his hand. "She's one of the good instructors. She really cares about her students. Everyone likes her." He sniffled, and his eyes shone with unshed tears. "Is she gonna be all right? I mean, when we got to her, she was

out cold, and she was bleeding. I know we should've chased after the guy, but we were too worried about Dr. Cooper and calling 911."

"You did the right thing. You probably saved her life."

Caleb sat up straighter and wiped his streaming nose. "Do you think so?"

Aiden knew so. He shuddered to think what would've happened if Caleb and his friends hadn't come by. The fact the perp had a knife, and he came prepared with a syringe filled with some sort of date-rape drug no doubt, indicated he meant business. No way would Candace have stood a chance. The slimeball would've hauled her off somewhere dark and private and raped her. That's what happened to the poor coed a few weeks ago. He shook off his dark thoughts and refocused on the witness. "Did you see where the guy went? Did he have a vehicle?"

"He ran across the parking lot and into the trees along the common. I didn't see a car."

"Did you get a look at him?" Aiden's heart thudded in his chest. This was the tricky part. Few witnesses to a violent attack recalled many details of the attacker. Aside from the fact Caleb had been drinking, the shock of witnessing a violent assault often blinded people.

Caleb grimaced. "I'm sorry. It was dark, and they were in the shadows, but he was a big guy. He towered over Dr. Cooper, and she's a tall woman."

Aiden nodded, fighting back smoldering rage. "Anything else? Any little detail you can remember may help us catch this guy."

Caleb shook his head. "No, I don't think so." He

looked at Aiden, his red-rimmed eyes pleading. "I'm sorry."

"It's okay. You've been a big help." Aiden's lie filled the car's interior. The boy's description of the attacker fit thousands of men and wouldn't help the cops find the bastard, but Caleb and his friends' intervention had stopped the perp, and for that, Aiden was grateful. "An officer will take you to the precinct and get your official statement. Thanks for your cooperation. Your actions saved Dr. Cooper's life."

He climbed out of the car and motioned for Caleb to do the same.

The student started to walk away and then stopped. "Detective?"

Aiden looked up from his notes. "What is it?"

"I think the guy had a beard, but I can't be certain."

A beard! Aiden's gut pinged. The man Candace saw in the state park had a beard. Had he followed her to the college and attacked her? He shook his head. Nah. He was reaching for straws. The attack on Candace was a random event, a serial rapist intent on finding a vulnerable victim. But still...a bearded man... "Send one of your friends over, will you?"

The next witness, Cory Sinclair, a third year Education major, described the same scenario as Caleb. He didn't have any new details to add.

The third witness, Trevor Lorenco, was the most inebriated, and his statement didn't differ from the first two men, other than he thought he heard a vehicle off in the distance after the attacker ran. Of course, he hadn't seen the car, but he was pretty certain the motor was a diesel, so maybe a truck. A complete description would *have been asking too much. Cases were never that easy.*

Caleb was the only witness who noticed the man's beard. None of the other two men mentioned a beard. Maybe they were too fixated on the knife in the attacker's hand, or the guy didn't have a beard. That was possible too. So, what did that leave? A tall man, possibly with a beard, maybe driving a truck.

Zip.

His only hope was that Candace got a look at her attacker.

Aiden paced the hospital corridor and rubbed his throbbing head, trying to make sense of the attack. The knife and syringe indicated premeditation. The attacker was looking for a victim, and he'd come prepared.

The question was—had he come looking for Candace? Was she the intended victim? Or was it just her bad luck to be in the wrong place at the wrong time? His gut twisted. Was the perp the same bearded man Candace encountered in Creighton Springs State Park?

What were the odds?

Zero to nil.

A few weeks ago, a young coed had been attacked on the university campus. The assault had occurred just after Aiden moved to Briggston. He and Joe weren't assigned to the case, but having made a point to read every open case file, Aiden was familiar with the details. Aside from not having a life, he wanted to prove himself, to show his new coworkers that he had skills, damn good skills.

The victim, Lori-Anne Carson, was returning to her dorm from a late-night frat party, and someone grabbed her from behind, dragged her into the bushes, and sexually assaulted her. The guy left her bruised and battered, but alive. The police investigated, but there weren't any witnesses, and they still hadn't caught the perp.

The same guy could've attacked Candace, but the pinging in Aiden's gut told him there was more to tonight's vicious attack. These sickos tended to stick to a pattern, one that worked in the past. The guy who'd raped the coed hadn't used a weapon during the assault, and the victim hadn't been stuck with a needle and shot full of ketamine. Could be, the perp was progressing, learning from each attack, or the attacker could be someone else entirely. There were a lot of slimeballs out there.

The door to the hospital room opened, and a doctor strode out. "She's awake, Detective. You can see her, but only for a few minutes. She's pretty disoriented."

"Thanks." Aiden inhaled a breath and pushed open the door and stepped into the room.

Chapter 11

The overhead fluorescent lights blazed, illuminating every corner of the sterile room. Candace lay on a narrow hospital bed. Tubes snaked from hanging bags of clear fluid into her arm. A machine beside the bed beeped, recording the hills and valleys of her heartbeat and blood pressure.

Her face was unnaturally pale, her eyes closed, dark circles like bruises beneath her long dark lashes. A gauze bandage was wrapped around her head. More padded gauze dressing covered the cut on her neck, and another small patch showed where she'd been stuck with the needle.

His heart lodged in his throat as the burn of anger built like a bonfire, and he vowed to catch the bastard who'd done this. His hand shook when he touched her arm and trailed the pads of his fingers across her cool, smooth skin. He turned to the nurse hovering over the patient. "The doctor told me she'd regained consciousness. Why isn't she awake?"

"The drug's still in her system. She'll come in and out of consciousness for a few more hours." The woman adjusted a dial on the bedside monitor. "Most people injected with ketamine recover in thirty minutes to an hour. She's been under almost two hours, so we know she got a pretty hefty dose."

"How's she doing?" He swallowed past the catch

in his throat, unable to tear his gaze from the pale, unconscious woman on the bed.

The nurse stripped off her nitrile gloves and tossed them into a yellow plastic toxic-waste disposal bin. "Her blood pressure is still high, and her pulse is tachycardic, meaning it's faster than normal."

His gut twisted. He'd dealt with victims of ketamine before, and it was never a pretty sight.

The drug, originally designed for veterinary use to subdue large mammals, was sold illegally in clubs and often used as a date-rape drug. When injected into the bloodstream, the fast-acting anesthetic knocked a person out in as little as one minute. The drug induced vivid dreams and hallucinations. The disconcerting feelings of mind-body separation and numbness could last for hours and cause confusion and disorientation in the victim. They often didn't remember the attack.

The nurse crossed the small room, switched off the bank of bright overhead lights, and closed the blinds. "When she wakes up, the light's going to bother her, so let's keep it dim in here." She shot Aiden a look. "I'll give you five minutes, but then you're going to have to leave." The stern-faced nurse left no room for disagreement. She strode to the door, flung it open, and swept into the busy corridor.

Aiden wiped the moisture off his upper lip and studied Candace's pale face. Behind her closed eyelids, her eyes shifted from side to side, and the muscles in her body jerked and twitched as if she were still fighting her attacker.

What the hell happened? Who assaulted her? And why? The witnesses' statements weren't much help. All he could do was hope she remembered what happened and could describe her attacker. One thing was certain—when he tracked down this maniac—and he would—he'd slam the man's sorry ass in jail.

His cell phone buzzed in his coat pocket. He tugged the small phone free and studied the caller ID, frowned, and punched the answer button. "Joe. What's up?"

Joe's gravelly voice roared in his ear. "Where the hell are you?"

"At the hospital. Why?"

"Typical. I'm out here in the pissing rain working my ass off, and you're holding the Cooper woman's hand." Sarcasm dripped from each word.

Aiden bit back a stinging retort. Past experience had taught him his partner enjoyed goading him, and it was smarter to ignore his snide comments. "What've you got? Did the crime scene techs find anything?"

The loud crack and pop of bubblegum blasted over the line. "All three witnesses are at the station giving official statements, and I have uniforms checking with students in the dorms to see if they noticed anyone suspicious lurking around campus."

Aiden waited, but Joe remained stubbornly silent. He heaved a breath and asked, "And?"

Another snap as Joe popped a gum bubble. "Nada. No one saw a damn thing. Turns out, it's the end of term, and everyone was in their dorm room studying for finals." Another crack of gum. "Everyone, except our witnesses. Those boys may flunk out of college, but they're heroes. That's for damn sure. If it weren't for them confronting the assailant, Dr. Cooper could be raped or dead."

The thought of what could have happened chilled

Aiden to the bone. Candace had been lucky. Damn lucky.

Joe continued his report. "We bagged and tagged the syringe we found by her car. Looks like the perp dropped it after he injected her and didn't have time to retrieve it when the frat boys showed up. Let's hope he left his fingerprints or DNA behind."

"We don't have much to go on." Aiden gripped the phone tighter. "The doctors here say her blood work indicates she was injected with ketamine. She's still out of it."

"How long you gonna babysit that woman?"

"As long as it takes."

"Whatever, Loverboy." Joe's snarky words drilled deep. "It's late, and I'm freezing my balls off. I'm booking out. See you in the morning." The connection ended.

Aiden stuffed his phone in his pocket, Joe's use of the derogatory label reverberating through his brain.

Loverboy.

The Seattle media ghouls had dubbed him Loverboy. The name left a foul taste in his mouth, and his hand shook as he grabbed a plastic water glass sitting on the bedside tray and drained the water.

He'd made one mistake, and that lack of judgment had ended a child's life and almost destroyed his career. Briggston was his chance at a new start. He'd learned his lesson. He wouldn't commit the same transgression again.

No damn way.

Candace called out, her cry laced with panic and fear. Her legs jerked, and her hands tightened into fists as if she were fighting for her life.

He laid his hand on her shoulder and squeezed, offering her unspoken comfort, hoping that in her drugged stupor she knew she was safe, sensed he was there.

Her body recoiled as if he'd struck her, and her mouth opened in a silent scream.

He snatched his hand back.

Her eyelids fluttered, opened. Her gaze was unfocused, her pupils dilated to the size of quarters. She moaned. Tears leaked from the corners of her eyes and dampened her tangled dark hair. After a heartbeat, she closed her eyes and her body stilled as she relaxed back into unconsciousness.

Chapter 12

She was floating in a dark abyss, circling in dizzying rotations. Stars blazed, piercing the darkness, and she reached for their fiery beauty, but grasped only emptiness. The pinpoints of light vanished, but still she spun, revolving in the endless void.

"Candace? Can you hear me? Wake up."

She struggled to open her eyes, but her lids were weighted with stones. An incessant high-pitched beeping drilled like knives into her brain. A strong chemical smell stung her nostrils.

"Candace, come on, it's time to wake up."

Wake up? She wasn't sleeping. She was…the thought faded, and once again she was floating, weightless, rising into the air, drifting through space.

And then she wasn't.

Her eyelids popped open. She blinked under the burn of piercing light. The room spun, her stomach roiled, and she tasted bile.

"Candace, can you hear me?" A man leaned over her, his warm breath caressing her face.

"Wha…?" The word stuck in her throat, her tongue thick and furred.

"You're in the hospital, but you're going to be fine. You're safe."

Hospital? What was she doing in a hospital? Had she been in an accident? Was she injured? She couldn't

C. B. Clark

think past the fierce pounding in her head. A kaleidoscopic blur of terrifying images filled her vision—disabling terror, cruel, hurting hands, fighting for her life, a sharp sting on her neck, the metallic smell of blood, a pinprick of pain, loud voices, and then falling, more pain, darkness—

"Candace, stay with me. You're safe. Do you hear me? You're safe."

A familiar voice broke through her panic, and she blinked away the gossamer threads of fear.

Aiden hovered over her. His handsome face was pale, his green eyes filled with concern.

She swallowed, her mouth desert dry, her tongue thick.

"That's it. Breathe, slow and easy. The drug is still in your system, and it's affecting you. That's why you feel a bit strange."

Drug? She fought the beckoning darkness and blinked to clear her blurred vision. The only drugs she used were her prescription antianxiety pills and the occasional over-the-counter analgesic. "I was drugged?" The words slipped from between her cracked lips, her voice a rough croak.

"Here." He held a plastic glass with a bendable straw near her mouth. "Drink this."

Lifting her head an inch or two from the pillow, she sipped, drawing cool water into her parched mouth. The moisture soothed her raw throat. "What—" She licked her lips. "—why are you here?"

His forehead furrowed. "You don't remember what happened?"

"I worked late. It's always busy at the end of term, but this year, I'm way behind." The pounding in her head amped up on the Richter scale. She couldn't think, couldn't focus. The blinding lights, the incessant, piercing beeping, brain fog. Her chest heaved as she struggled to draw in breath. Her body ached, and a bone-deep exhaustion dragged at her, pulling her down into the depths. "What…happened…to…me?"

"You were attacked." Anger sparked in his light eyes.

Her breath caught in her throat. "Attacked?" Why couldn't she remember? "Who—" She swallowed. "—who attacked me?"

"We don't know. The perp ran away, but we'll find the bastard." He bristled, his face tight, his eyes fierce. "You can count on that."

An image of cruel hands grabbing her, fingers digging deep into her flesh flashed before her. She touched her neck and winced. The raised edges of a bandage, a sharp ache beneath. "Am I hurt?"

A thundercloud darkened his face. "You were injected with a strong dose of ketamine. The doctor says you'll be fine once the drug clears your system. You also have a slight concussion and a cut on your neck."

Her mind whirled, but she latched onto one word. "Ketamine?"

He nodded. "It's a club drug. Sometimes called Special K or Vitamin K."

"I've heard of it. Last year…one of my students was given some, and then…she was raped." Her heart slammed in her chest. "Wait! Was I—" She licked her lips as she struggled to force out the terrifying words. "—was I raped?"

"No. You weren't." He sat on the edge of her

narrow bed, his warm thigh brushing her leg. "Three frat boys scared off the attacker. You were lucky."

She squeezed her eyes shut and smoothed her fingers over the dressing on her neck, trying to remember. Nothing, just a haunting black emptiness and the certainty there was something she was forgetting, something important. "A female student was attacked on campus a few weeks ago...one of my students. It was terrible.

"The university's supposed to be beefing up security, but they haven't received the funding yet." The room wavered, the walls looming closer and then receding. Her head pounded with an unbearable ferocity.

The door burst open, and a tall, blonde woman in a multi-colored, floral top and matching scrub pants strode in followed by an older, dark-haired woman wearing a white lab coat.

The woman in the white coat spoke, "Glad to see you're awake, Candace. I'm Dr. Young. You had us pretty worried."

The crushing weight of exhaustion cascaded over her, and Candace closed her eyes. Refusing to give in to the drug, she dug deep, and using superhuman strength, she forced her eyelids open to narrow slits, unable to form words, her lips numb.

The doctor patted Candace's arm. "It's okay. Don't try and talk. I know you're tired." She placed her warm fingers on Candace's wrist and checked her pulse. "Your heart rate is better. That's good." She looked at the beeping machine. "Your blood pressure is down too." She turned to Aiden. "Has she said anything?"

"She's a bit confused. She doesn't remember the

attack."

Candace fought the pull of blackness, struggling to keep awake, but her body sank deeper into the mattress, her arms leaden weights, her legs boneless. The darkness beckoned, and she fell into the void.

****

The second the doctor gave the okay, Candace dressed in her wrinkled-and-bloodstained clothes, called a ride share, and headed home. She hated hospitals—the chemical smells, the constant noise, the hard, uncomfortable bed, the bland food, the too-cheerful nurses—everything. They reminded her of the nightmare in the years after Charlene went missing and her parents' health failed. She couldn't count the number of hours she'd spent in the Intensive Care Unit, watching first her mother succumb to the cancer that was eating away at her, and then her father dying of a broken heart. Leaving Candace an orphan at nineteen.

Besides, she didn't have time to lie around in a hospital bed being poked and prodded by a seemingly endless stream of nurses and doctors. She had exams to grade. Second-term marks were due at the end of the week. She'd never been late turning in her marks, and this wasn't going to be the first time. If she allowed the trauma of the violent assault to change her routine, the attacker won. She wasn't about to let that happen. He'd already taken so much from her.

Maybe it was because she was still reeling from the vicious attack, or the ketamine was lingering in her system, or maybe the fact every inch of her body ached, or she hadn't slept in who knew how long, but every time she closed her eyes, a confusing blur of images of the terrifying assault flashed before her. Add in the onslaught of the decades-old guilt that washed over her, and she was a mess.

It should have been me.

The familiar refrain stabbed deep into her soul. Charlene was the good daughter, the responsible one. She made her bed every day, she never left wet towels heaped on the bathroom floor after her shower, never talked back to their parents, and was top of her class in academics, and a star athlete. Not like Candace, who left a mess wherever she'd been, argued with their parents over the house rules, and struggled with math.

Yes, it should have been me.

The condemning, yet all-too-familiar, words blazed through her brain as if lit by a neon light. She should've been the Cooper sister who was kidnapped. She should be missing and presumed dead.

Not Charlene.

Her.

A sob hitched in her throat, and she collapsed onto the couch and pressed her damp face into the soft cushions, giving in to the bottomless sea of swamping guilt.

The cushion was wet and her throat raw when she sat up and swiped tangled damp strands of hair off her face. Beating up on herself wouldn't bring back Charlene. Crying wouldn't change what happened. Nothing would. Her therapist had told her countless times she had to leave the past in the past and move on with her life. Like she hadn't been trying to do that for the past twenty-two years.

She sniffled and grabbed a tissue from the box on the coffee table and blew her nose. Was that why the man attacked her last night? A chill rippled through her.

Was he somehow connected to Charlene's abduction? A low moan escaped her mouth, and she collapsed once more on the cushions.

No!

The denial blazed through her. That wasn't possible. No way. The man who attacked her and injected her with ketamine was the same person who'd assaulted Lori Ann Carson last month. He was lurking around the campus, looking for another victim. Candace had given him an easy target…walking alone late at night to her car parked in a secluded and poorly lighted parking lot. That's why he'd chosen her. That was the only reason. To think otherwise was a possibility more frightening than the assault itself.

The doorbell pealed.

She jumped, and some of the papers she'd been planning to grade slipped off the couch onto the floor.

Aiden.

She'd forgotten he'd called and told her he was coming over. The thought of the handsome detective, with his tall, muscular body and comforting presence soothed her distress. She grabbed a handful of tissues and wiped her face. Balling up the damp mass, she shoved it under a couch cushion out of sight. Standing on shaky legs, she slipped her bare feet into her fuzzy slippers and shuffled to the door.

Catching a glimpse of herself in the hall mirror, she frowned. When he'd phoned two hours ago and said he wanted to stop by and ask her a few questions, she'd agreed. She hadn't wanted to be alone in her empty house, startling at every sound, terrified the man who'd attacked her had found out where she lived and would strike again.

103

She had it all planned. She'd work on correcting the term finals for an hour and then jump into the shower and dress in her nicest jeans and that pretty blue sweater she'd bought last week. She grimaced. So much for her plan. Now, instead of looking her best, she was wearing baggy pajama pants and an old, ratty T-shirt with stains of an undetermined origin spotting the front. Her hair was a mess. She hadn't combed it in who knew how long, and the dark tangled strands fell about her blotchy, tearstained face. Add in a swollen bottom lip and the bandage wrapped around her neck, and she was a real piece of work.

Way to make an impression.

The doorbell pealed again.

Smoothing her hair as best she could, she straightened her top, and undid the security locks. She opened the door to a blast of cold air, gasped, and stumbled back a step.

Chapter 13

"Afternoon, ma'am." Detective Breacher smiled an oily grin.

"Detective Breacher. I wasn't expecting you." She wilted under his steely stare. What was he doing there? More importantly, where was Aiden?

Breacher's smile widened as if he took pleasure in her confusion and discomfort. "You thought my partner, Detective Farrell, was coming to call. Am I right?"

She licked her dry lips, wincing at the sting of the small cut on her bottom lip. "He called a while ago and told me he wanted to update my statement from last night's attack."

A small bubble of pink gum appeared at the corner of his mouth. He flexed his thick lips and popped the bubble with a loud crack. "Loverboy's busy right now, so you got me." His eyes narrowed. "That's all right, isn't it?"

Loverboy? Who was he talking about? Her head throbbed, and she pushed the confusing name aside. "Yes, of course, it's fine." Her lie fell flat at his feet. The last thing she wanted was to talk to the cynical detective, especially when she felt so vulnerable. She chewed on her wounded bottom lip, ignoring the pain. The thought of rehashing the previous night's attack made her tremble, but to relate the terrifying events to this unfeeling man almost drove her to her knees.

But she wanted the person who'd attacked her caught before he hurt someone else. If that meant giving her statement to the arrogant detective, she'd do it. Besides, he couldn't discount her story this time. There were witnesses, and the hospital tests of her blood showed evidence of the drug her attacker had injected into her. She expelled a shaky breath and stepped aside. "Come in, Detective."

He brushed past her, and without bothering to wipe his mud-spattered shoes on the doormat, strode into her living room as if he owned the place.

She closed the door and followed, girding her loins for the coming ordeal.

He shrugged out of his trench coat and dropped it onto the couch, scattering the remaining stack of exams. "Let's get this done. I have a load of paperwork waiting for me back at the station." He plopped onto a chair, wincing as if his knees hurt. Tugging out a small tape recorder, he set it on the coffee table in front of him. "Okay if I record this conversation?"

"I guess." Her legs wobbled as she sank onto the couch. She stuffed her hands between her knees to hide their shaking.

A weighty silence descended. Out on the street, a dog barked, followed by the happy squeals of children playing. Her furnace kicked in with a quiet whump. The digital clock on the DVR machine clicked another minute, and then another, and another.

He drew out a small notebook and a stub of a pencil. Licking the tip of the pencil, he wrote in the notebook. Finally, he looked at her. A deep furrow grooved between his thick, gray eyebrows. His bulbous nose was pitted with tiny red dots, and his cheeks were ruddy as if he were a heavy drinker. A small square of blood-crusted tissue was stuck to his jaw where he'd cut himself shaving. He smiled, but the smile didn't reach his cold eyes. "Okay. Let's get started."

He asked her stilted questions as if he were reading from a script in the police manual, showing no emotion on his fleshy face as she relayed what she recalled of the terrifying attack.

She answered as best she could, but her memory was spotty. Her stomach knotted, and her head ached as she struggled to recall the frightening events of the vicious attack. Other than vague impressions of her overriding fear and pain, she recollected very little. There was that niggling certainty she was forgetting something, but no matter how hard she tried to remember, the thought was as ephemeral as a wisp of smoke.

His voice remained flat and unemotional. His every gesture, every facial expression, made clear he thought the interview was a waste of his time, and he was just going through the motions because he had to.

Twenty long minutes later, he closed the notebook with a snap and stuffed it into his shirt pocket along with the pencil. Leaning over, he punched a button on the recorder to stop the recording and slipped the compact machine into his coat pocket. He rose to his feet, his knees cracking. "Well, I guess that's that. Thanks for your time."

"Wait, Detective." She stood. "What's going to happen? What are you doing to find the man who attacked me?"

He heaved a breath. "Look, Miss Cooper—"

She'd had enough of his blatant contempt. "It's *Doctor* Cooper." She instilled the stern, no-nonsense teacher voice she used on difficult students into the words, the one guaranteed to make him sit up and take notice.

Their eyes met, and she wanted to punch the air when he shifted his gaze away first.

He cleared his throat. "Dr. Cooper."

He spoke her name like he was enunciating the name of a career felon, but she let his condescension go. One victory against this pompous ass was enough; besides, she was exhausted, and every inch of her body ached. She wanted him to leave so she could have a nap.

"You haven't given us much to go on." He shrugged. "You don't know what the guy looked like, and you can't remember if he said anything. If it weren't for those frat boys, this whole story could be another one of your concoctions. Those boys were drunk. Who knows what they really saw?"

Her breath whooshed out. "What? Are you—" Her fury was so visceral she stumbled over the words. "—are you implying I made up the attack?"

"Of course not." The corners of his mouth tightened. "All I'm saying is that no one saw the perp. Just you and three drunk kids—students of yours, I understand."

Heat seared through her. She tightened her hands into fists to stop from clawing the smug expression off his florid face. "How do you explain the ketamine in my system? And the cut on my neck? To say nothing of the concussion I suffered. Do you actually think I orchestrated the attack? For what? Attention?" She blew out a breath. "Ask your partner. Detective Farrell was at the hospital last night. He talked to the doctors. He knows what happened."

"Ah, yes, my partner." He smirked and grabbed his coat from the back of the couch. "I'll just bet he believes you."

She blinked. Where was his attitude coming from? She understood that he didn't care for her. They had a history, but his snarky tone made clear he didn't respect Aiden.

"If I were you, *Doctor*, I'd be careful around Farrell. He has a soft spot for the ladies, especially pretty ones like you." He buttoned up his coat and stepped closer and waggled his unruly eyebrows. "Why do you think a hotshot detective like him ended up in Briggston?"

She stumbled back from the blast of his sour coffee breath. "What are talking about?"

"You're a smart woman. Check it out. The story was all over the Internet." He turned and strode to the door. "I'll let you know if we find the guy who attacked you, but don't hold your breath." He opened the door, stepped onto the porch, and closed the door with a decisive thud.

****

Aiden pulled into the driveway and frowned.

An unmarked police cruiser was parked at the curb.

The front door of the townhouse opened, and Joe stepped out.

Aiden yanked out the keys, unsnapped his seatbelt, thrust open the door, and jumped out. "What are you doing here, Joe?"

Joe grinned a shit-eating grin. "My job. Why?

What are *you* doing here?"

"I thought we agreed we'd interview Dr. Cooper together." Aiden shoved back the sleeve of his coat and studied his watch. "You said you'd meet me here at three. It's three o'clock." His eyes narrowed. "What the hell are you doing, Joe? What game are you playing?"

"I got here early and decided not to wait for you. It doesn't take two of us to question a victim." Joe dug in his pocket and held up a tape recorder. "Don't worry. I interviewed the good professor, but she doesn't remember anything useful. I got buttkiss." His lip curled in a sneer. "No surprise there."

"You took her statement?"

He tapped the recorder. "Got it all right here. What's wrong? You don't look happy." His wide-eyed, fake-innocent gaze met Aiden's. "I don't get you, *partner.* I thought I'd save you time. I knew you were busy at the crime lab checking out the results on that syringe found at the crime scene. You should be happy I'm carrying your share of the load."

Aiden's gut curdled. Joe looked like the proverbial cat that ate the canary. Something was fishy, that was for damn sure. In the two months he'd worked with him, Aiden had learned that Joe would go to any length to avoid work. The guy made no secret of the fact he was putting in time, counting the hours and minutes until he retired next month. No way in hell would he go out of his way to interview a victim. Aiden stormed over, stopping inches from Joe. "What are you up to?"

Joe spread his hands wide. "Saving your ass, man."

"What the hell are you talking about?" His fury was so hot he spit each word out between his clenched teeth.

Joe jerked his thumb at the small white townhouse behind him and arched his bushy eyebrows. "Think about it...a hot, young woman...and you...in her house...together...alone." He snorted. "I mean, come on, *Loverboy*. Use the brain in your head and not the one in your pants for once." He smirked. "Like I said, I saved your sorry ass, though I'm starting to doubt if it's worth saving."

Aiden ached to punch the smarmy bastard in his smug face. He jammed his clenched fists into the front pockets of his jeans and counted to ten. No way would he give the jerk the satisfaction of watching as Aiden got sacked by the captain for assaulting a fellow detective. He pasted a patently false smile on his face. "Why, thank you so much, Joe. I appreciate you looking out for little old me." He stomped closer until his chest bumped against Joe's. "I'll remember this, partner. Believe me, I won't forget."

Joe's face paled. He swallowed, his Adam's apple riding up and down in his thick throat and made a show of checking his watch. "Well, will you look at that? I gotta run." He scuttled to his cruiser and jumped inside. Before he closed the door, he looked back at Aiden. "Aren't you coming?"

Aiden shook his head. "I have a few questions to ask Dr. Cooper."

"I'll just bet you do." Joe slammed the car door, revved the motor, and with a screech of tires, pulled out into the street and roared down the road.

Aiden rubbed the back of his neck. Every muscle in his body was strung as tight as a guitar string. A white-hot rage blazed through his cells. Damn Joe. Damn the man to hell. Ever since Aiden had been assigned to the older detective, Joe had done his damnedest to show Aiden just how little he thought of his new partner and his detective skills.

The debacle in Seattle followed him like a bad smell he couldn't shake. The best he could do was suck it up, put his nose to the grindstone, and hope his hard work would show Joe and the others like him in the department that he was good at his job. Damn good. And he deserved a second chance.

Joe's patent disrespect, though annoying, didn't surprise Aiden. The ignominious, and very public, dismissal from the Seattle Police Department and the sordid reasons behind the edict weren't a secret. Any fool with a computer and access to the Internet could find all the lurid details posted online. If that didn't work, there was the very effective cop-gossip train.

Aiden wasn't proud of what he'd done. Hell, he'd crossed the line, then made a fatal mistake, one that resulted in the death of a child. He deserved his punishment.

And more.

He didn't blame his commanding officer for firing him, or his fellow Seattle detectives for turning their backs on him. He'd taken his whacks, but he hadn't expected that getting back on his feet and redeeming himself would be so damn difficult.

He understood Joe's initial contempt, but he'd figured that after a few weeks, once Joe saw how hard Aiden worked and his dedication to the job, Joe's antagonism would ease. He slapped his hand on his thigh. No such luck. Joe seemed to take it as his personal mission to undermine anything Aiden did.

Today was no different.

Aiden had called Candace and arranged the interview, and he and Joe had been all set to leave the precinct and go to her house to take her official statement when the call from the crime lab came in.

The crime-scene techs had discovered something interesting in the syringe found at the scene of the attack.

Aiden arranged to meet his partner at Candace's house at three o'clock, and then he went to the crime lab.

His lip curled. He should've known. The second Aiden walked out of the police station, Joe had jumped in his car and raced to Candace's house. The question that burned a trail of fire through his gut was…why? What did Joe hope to gain by jumping the gun? Was it solely a matter of wanting to get ahead of Aiden? Was he protecting Aiden like he said? Or was there more behind his actions?

He studied the townhouse with its neat garden beds, trimmed shrubs, and swept sidewalk. A gust of wind whipped down the street, raising tiny cyclones of dust in the air and scattering dried leaves left over from the previous fall. A fat raindrop plopped onto the sidewalk. Another landed on his coat sleeve. In the next heartbeat, the heavens opened up, and rain poured down in sheets.

He tightened the collar of his coat and raced for the front door.

Chapter 14

The doorbell pealed, and Candace jumped, startled at the loud ring. She rubbed her burning eyes and sat up, smoothing her tangled hair off her face. Had she locked the door? She couldn't remember. She'd been so exhausted when Detective Breacher left, she'd stumbled to the couch and lay in a daze as disjointed memories of the attack pelted her.

Another ring was accompanied by loud rapping on the door. "Candace? Please open the door. It's me, Aiden."

She stilled. What was he doing there? She'd already given her statement to his partner.

The doorbell pealed again.

She pushed to her feet and stumbled down the hall. The security chain dangled, and her heart caught in her throat. She hadn't locked the door! Anyone could've entered her house without her knowing. Anyone. She shuddered.

He knocked again, startling her out of her frightening thoughts. Inhaling a deep breath, she clasped the door handle and opened the door.

He stood on the small concrete porch. His hair was mussed as if he'd threaded his fingers through the glossy strands, and a lock of dark hair hung over his forehead. Drops of rain spattered his brown suede jacket. His golden gaze bore into hers, and he smiled.

"Hi."

Under the power of his thousand-watt grin, her tiredness vanished. "I didn't expect to see you. Your partner just left."

He grimaced. "Yeah. Sorry about that. Joe can be a bit rough around the edges."

"A *bit* rough?"

The corners of his eyes crinkled, and he laughed.

She chuckled but winced at a sharp jab of pain in her neck where her attacker had crushed her throat.

His laughter stopped, and he frowned. "You're hurting. I'm sorry."

Their gazes met and held, as a thousand unsaid words exchanged between them, words neither could speak aloud.

He leaned closer, and she read the need in his heated gaze.

The sudden desire to kiss him overwhelmed her, and she moistened her lips. A car horn tooted, and she jerked her head up.

A vehicle passed her house and turned into her neighbor's driveway.

Aiden cleared his throat, stepping back two paces, looking like a boy caught stealing candy from the corner store. He opened his mouth to say something, but no words emerged.

She exhaled the breath she'd been holding. "You'd better come in." She gestured toward the open door.

Looking uncomfortable and guilty, he stepped into the house.

What the heck just happened? Had they really been about to kiss? No way. They hardly knew each other. She was vulnerable. That's what was going on. After last night's attack, she wasn't thinking clearly. Who could blame her? She'd been assaulted and shot full of ketamine. For all she knew, the man who'd grabbed her could still be after her.

She shuddered and checked the neighborhood. Aiden's black SUV was in her driveway, and other than her neighbor, who was unpacking bags of groceries from his car, no unfamiliar vehicles were parked on the street, and no strangers lurked in the shrubbery. At least no one she could see. A frisson of ice slid along her spine, and she hurried inside, closing and locking the door. She gestured for Aiden to follow her to the living room.

He slipped off his high-top white sneakers, left them on the mat by the door, and followed her. Shrugging out of his jacket, he folded it, draped it over the back of a chair, and settled on the couch. "I know my partner took your statement, but I have a few questions I'd like to ask you if you're up to it."

She remained standing by the window. "I don't think your partner believes my account of the attack last night."

"Did he say that?" His eyes widened, and a splash of red flushed his cheeks.

"Not in so many words, but his attitude made his thoughts pretty clear."

"I know this must be difficult, but do you mind telling me what you remember from last night? Will you go over the details again?" Sincerity shone in his hazel eyes, making it clear he was on her side.

She sighed and sank onto a chair. "I don't remember much."

He nodded. "Just tell me what you do remember.

Any detail, no matter how small, might help us catch this guy before he strikes again."

"Do you think he will?"

"I do." His gaze bore into hers. "If he's the same perp who attacked that student a few weeks ago, and now you, he'll do it again." A muscle twitched in his jaw. "Unless we stop him."

She inhaled a deep breath, and for the second time in less than an hour, recounted the previous night's terrifying events, starting with leaving her office late, talking to the security guard, and walking to her car in the faculty parking lot. By the time she finished, her throat was raw, and she was drained. She stood on shaky legs and headed to the kitchen. "I need something to drink. Do you want some water?"

"Sure." Jumping up, he followed her to the kitchen. He leaned his hips against the counter and threaded his fingers through his hair. A dark curl fell across his forehead.

For a brief second—the merest heartbeat—she forgot the previous night's nightmare, forgot why he was there, and focused on that one glossy curl. She itched to touch the wayward lock, to feel its silkiness slip between her fingers. She stepped closer and raised her hand but froze at the sight of a vivid red bruise on her wrist, a stark reminder of why he was there.

Jerking away, she bustled about the tiny kitchen, getting glasses from the cupboard and filling both glasses with water from the tap. Retrieving ice cubes from the freezer, she plopped two cubes into each glass and handed him one, pleased her hand didn't shake.

"Thanks." He took a sip. "I'm not surprised you remember so little about the attack. Ketamine has that effect." He drank more water, and then set the glass on the counter. "Is there anything you do remember? Even just an impression you got from the guy…anything at all?"

A foul taste filled her mouth. She drained her glass, but it wasn't enough. Turning on the tap, she refilled her glass and drank again. "I think…maybe…" A chill rippled through her. "Just before I blacked out, he said something. At least, I think he did."

Aiden's gaze drilled into hers. "Okay. That's good. Take your time."

She rubbed her throbbing head, feeling the tender lump at the back of her skull where she'd hit her head on the unforgiving pavement when the man shoved her to the ground. "I was so frightened. His arm was pressing against my throat, and I couldn't breathe. He held something sharp, a knife, I think, to my neck." She touched the bandage on her neck, and then the small, bruised injection site. "I felt a sharp prick like a bee's sting, and the next thing I knew, everything blurred, and I was so tired, I couldn't keep my eyes open, couldn't stand…" She swallowed back a sob. "Just before I passed out, he whispered something into my ear."

As if she were watching a horror movie, the terrifying images flashed before her. The man's sweaty stench, his hot, rancid breath, the suffocating pressure of his arm cutting into her throat… Tears sprang to her eyes and flowed down her cheeks. The sob she'd been fighting to hold back escaped. She remembered. "Oh my God!"

Hello, Candy Girl.

In the next breath, she was in Aiden's arms, pressed close to his solid, reassuring warmth. Her tears dampened his shirt.

"It's okay. No one's going to hurt you. Not anymore. You're safe now." His soothing voice rumbled deep in his chest. He rubbed her back, holding her close. "We'll find him."

She closed her eyes and breathed him in…coffee, fresh spring air, male. For the first time in years, a feeling of safety and contentment filled her, and she burrowed into his strength as the tears flowed.

But instead of holding her, his body stiffened, and he loosened his embrace and backed away, putting three feet of space between them. A frown furrowed his brow, and his gaze focused somewhere over her shoulder. "I apologize. That was out of line."

She shivered at the loss of the warmth of his muscular body. "I remember what the man said." Grabbing a handful of tissues from the box on the counter, she wiped her tears.

He turned from the window and faced her. "Go on."

"He knew my name." Her breath hiccupped in her throat, and fresh tears stung her eyes. "He called me…*Candy Girl*." Her knees gave out, and she collapsed on a kitchen chair and covered her face with her hands. "Only one person ever called me that name. Only one."

"Who was that?"

She swiped at her tears with the back of her hand and tried to speak over the lump clogging her throat. "My sister. Charlene called me Candy Girl." The room swirled, and she grabbed the table and held on, fighting the rush of painful memories. "You must know about her. The story was all over the news. She was kidnapped twenty-two years ago and held captive in a shed on a farm in the forest with four other girls. When the cops raided the farm, Charlene wasn't there. The man who kidnapped her took her with him when he escaped." She hiccupped a sob. "He..." She couldn't finish, couldn't speak aloud the terrible words. "No one has heard from her since."

His eyes narrowed. "Are you sure you heard right? That's what he said? He called you Candy Girl?"

"I think so." She shuddered as she recalled the cruel voice whispering in her ear, the stench of stale cigarette smoke, the heat of his body... She met his gaze. "How could he know my sister's secret pet name for me, unless—?"

Aiden held up his hand. "Hold on. Let's not get ahead of ourselves."

"But he called me Candy Girl. How could he know that name if Charlene didn't tell him?" She swiped the back of her hand over her damp face. "He's back, isn't he? Isaiah's back." Her stomach roiled. The name was enough to strike terror into her heart and turn her into a quivering mess. For twenty-two years, Isaiah had been the monster of her nightmares, the reason she awoke in the middle of the night with her pillow damp, tears streaking her face, and her heart thudding.

The media dubbed the missing girls the Forgotten Five because it was months before the authorities realized a serial kidnapper was operating in the state. Investigators assumed the girls had run away. It wasn't until Charlene vanished, leaving indisputable evidence that she'd been forcibly abducted, that the police connected the dots and realized the other four girls had been kidnapped as well. Some of the victims had been missing almost two years.

When the girls were finally rescued, they told the authorities that a man called Isaiah had kidnapped them and held them against their wills in that cold, dark farm shed, chained to metal stakes cemented into the ground. He'd repeatedly and viciously abused them until they'd given up hope of ever seeing their loved ones again.

The media was all over the story and featured the horrifying details of the Forgotten Five's incarceration on every newscast. Four girls had been rescued from the monster. The country celebrated. Medals were awarded to those in command of the task force.

Four girls freed.

Not five.

One girl never made it home—her sister.

Candace lay awake at night wondering if Charlene was still alive, still being kept hostage, waiting for rescue. The cops believed she was long dead, her body buried somewhere in the wilderness, murdered by the man who took her. Candace refused to accept that. She and her sister had been close. She'd know if Charlene was deceased. Her gut told her she was still alive. And so, Candace hoped, prayed, and begged any god that might be listening to bring her older sister home.

Now she had proof. Finally. Charlene was alive!

The only way the man who attacked Candace and injected her with ketamine could know the secret name Charlene had called her was if Charlene told him. And the only way he knew Charlene, was if he was the one who took her.

Aiden cleared his throat. "I was a kid at the time, but the story of your sister and the other girls' disappearances and subsequent rescue was all over the news. Reporters vied with each other to get the salient details. Maybe some reporter found out the pet name your sister called you and ran it on a newscast, and your attacker heard it."

"But we didn't tell anyone. Not—" She blinked back tears. "—not even my parents knew. It was our secret."

A furrow formed between his dark brows. "Maybe Charlene told one of the other hostages, and when that girl was rescued, she told someone, and they told someone else. Briggston is a small town. People gossip. The whole Forgotten Five situation must've rocked this state to its core."

He set his glass on the counter. "Think about it. Candy is a common diminutive of Candace. You're a popular instructor. Everyone on campus knows your name. The fact that the creep who attacked you knew the name could mean he lives in the area and overheard people talking at Ed's Diner or Marv's Barber shop or the campus cafeteria."

Her mind whirled. What he said made sense. She rubbed her aching temples, exhausted. Her eyes burned and her body was spent. All she wanted to do was crawl into her bed and forget last night's attack, but she had to ask, had to speak the terrifying words aloud. "Do—" She swallowed. "—do you think there's a possibility Isaiah has returned?"

His expression softened, and sympathy filled his hazel eyes. The truth was written in the soft expression on his handsome face.

"It's okay. I get it. You don't believe me. You're like all the other cops. You think I'm so desperate to find my sister that I'm imagining things that don't exist.

You're just like your partner." Unable to fight a second longer, she laid her head on her arms on the table and closed her eyes, hoping he'd leave.

"You're exhausted and upset." He rested his hand on her shoulder. "No wonder, after the ordeal you've been through."

The warmth of his large hand seeped through her shirt, heating her skin. She opened her eyes and lifted her head and met his golden gaze.

"I'll look into this. I promise I won't rest until we find this guy. You don't have to be afraid." He removed his hand. "Okay?"

She nodded because that was what he wanted, but a dark cold closed in, and an icy chill settled deep in her bones. No matter what he said, she knew the truth. The man who took her sister was still out there, watching, waiting… She shuddered and rubbed the goose bumps on her arms.

"Look, I know you're tired, but I just have a few more questions." His eyes softened. "Are you okay with that?"

Again, she nodded. The sooner he finished his questioning, the sooner she could collapse in bed.

"Great. Thank you." He squeezed her shoulder. "There weren't any fingerprints on the syringe, so we're guessing the perp wore gloves. The lab techs found something interesting in the mixture of the drug he used." He tugged out a notebook from his coat pocket.

She clasped her hands on her lap. "It was ketamine, wasn't it? That's what the doctor told me."

His jaw tightened. "This wasn't your typical club drug. The Special K sold on the streets has a different chemical signature. The drug you were injected with is the type of ketamine only sold to veterinarians. It's a tightly controlled drug, and not easy to access without proper paperwork."

"Are you saying I was injected with a drug meant for animals?" The throbbing in her head amped up to an all-out tsunami of pain.

"The ketamine he used on you was ketamine hydrochloride, the pure pharmaceutical grade. Most ketamine sold on the streets in the US and Canada comes from Mexico. The dealers cut the ketamine with other chemicals to make the high greater and the drug more addictive. The ketamine that monster injected into you was pure."

She rubbed her aching temples. Her brain felt as if it were stuffed with cotton, and his voice was muffled, as if it came from deep inside a tunnel. "What difference does the type of ketamine make? The doctor said the effects would wear off in a day or two, and I'll be fine. Right?"

"We think your attacker could be a veterinarian, or someone with access to a vet clinic."

"He's a vet?" She jolted upright.

"It's a definite possibility." His gaze lasered in on her. "Is that significant? Do you know any veterinarians?"

She lurched to her feet. "I need to lie down."

Taking her not-so-subtle hint, he nodded and retrieved his coat from the couch and headed to the front door.

She followed him, fighting through the fierce pounding in her head, struggling not to collapse on the floor. *Her attacker was a veterinarian.* The terrifying words pelted her brain like a hail of bullets.

"If we learn anything new, I'll be in touch."

"Okay."

He grasped the doorknob and opened the door. "If you remember anything else, please call me." Tugging out a small card from his back pocket, he pressed it into her hand. "I mean it, Candace, call me any time. Okay? I'm going to get this guy. Believe me. I will."

She nodded, but she wanted to grab him and haul him back inside. She didn't want him to go, to leave her alone with her fears. Instead, she said goodbye. The second he stepped over the threshold, she closed the door and set all the locks and hit the alarm button. She stumbled down the hall to her bedroom and crawled into bed, tugging the covers up to her chin.

Candy Girl.

Shudders wracked her body, and she whimpered into her pillow, as the long-ago past reared over her like a coiled, venomous serpent.

No question now. Isaiah *was* back.

Chapter 15

Candace threw off the covers and kicked her legs free of the tangled sheets. She'd lain awake for hours, tossing and turning, unable to sleep. Every time she closed her eyes the taunting voice of the man who'd attacked her filled her head.

Candy Girl.

She shuddered and jammed her hands over her ears, but it didn't stop. The frightening name repeated, again and again, as if imprinted on an endless audio reel.

She had to do something, anything to block out his voice. She'd tried reading, watching her favorite old movies, playing video games, marking test papers. Nothing worked. Sitting on the edge of the bed, she rubbed her tired eyes. Her body craved the restorative release of sleep, but her mind wouldn't shut down.

There were some sleeping pills in the bathroom cabinet, but she didn't like taking pills at the best of times, and this definitely wasn't the best of times. A large dose of ketamine had been injected into her. Adding another sedative to the mix wouldn't be a good idea.

But she had to do something. She couldn't sit there all night, staring at the walls, listening to that insidious voice inside her head. Grabbing her robe from the hook on the back of her bedroom door, she slipped it on and tied the belt around her waist. Shuffling down the dark hall, she flicked on the light to her home office and sat on the chair in front of her desktop computer. She needed a distraction, and what she was about to do was just the ticket.

Detective Breacher had called Aiden Loverboy and hinted Aiden was involved in something shady when he worked for the police force in Seattle. At the time, she'd ignored the insinuations, but now she couldn't stop thinking about them.

She studied her homepage on the flickering screen. Aiden had been kind to her. He'd treated her with respect, and now she was going to delve into his past, a past he would've told her about if he wanted her to know. Over the last few days, she'd begun to think of him as more than just another cop.

Much more.

Not only was he one handsome hunk of a man, but there was something about him, something honest and real that called to her soul. Of all the cops she'd dealt with over the years in her quest to keep her sister's case front and center in the police's active case files, he was one of the good ones. He cared about the victims and saw their cases as more than a means to a high solve rate.

Yet, there she was—about to violate his privacy. She shoved back her chair and stood. No, she wouldn't do this. If he wanted her to know about his past, he'd tell her. Until then, his previous life was none of her business.

She headed to the kitchen and heated a cup of water in the microwave. When the timer beeped, she removed the cup, tossed in a tea bag, and dragged it through the hot water. Ever since Charlene had gone missing, she hadn't trusted any man. How could she when he could be the person who'd abducted her sister? Ridiculous, she knew, but to her, the fear was all too real.

All these years, she'd lived with the knowledge she'd been sound asleep in a bed in the same room beside where her sister slept, when Charlene was dragged from her bed and carried away by a monster. Candace hadn't wakened, hadn't screamed for help, or done anything to save her sister. The guilt kept her awake at night. Her therapist told her she needed to stop blaming herself and move on with her life.

Easier said than done.

She'd undergone years of intensive therapy before she felt comfortable enough to go to the store on her own; years wasted as she hid behind locked doors, startling at every sound, terrified the man who took Charlene had come back. She'd stopped going to her classes at school and started correspondence courses, missing out on prom, meeting new friends, and attending parties and dances like other young people.

After her parents passed, she'd finally gathered her courage and ventured out into the world beyond her front door, but she was always looking behind her, searching the shadows, certain she saw someone waiting, watching. She'd lost track of the number of times she'd called the police and reported seeing the infamous Isaiah, the man who took her sister.

At first, they'd arrived, sirens blaring, lights flashing, guns ready, only to discover she'd identified the wrong man. When the same scenario played out again and again, the cops took longer to arrive, and their cruisers were silent. Eventually, they stopped coming.

She'd tried, done her damnedest to put the terrifying events behind her. She finished high school and went on to the university and earned her Bachelor of Arts degree. After that, she'd continued her studies and received a doctorate in Anthropology, and now she was on tenure at the college.

In spite of her academic and career successes, she continued her crusade to find Charlene. She showed up at the police station at least once every few months and demanded updates on the search for her sister. Her persistence didn't make her popular with the local police, but she didn't care. All that mattered was they didn't forget Charlene, and they continued their investigation.

She wasn't a complete fool. She knew the odds of finding Charlene alive were slim. The police were probably right, and Charlene was long dead, but Candace wouldn't rest until she knew the truth about what happened. Tears burned her eyes, and she blinked them back. Maybe snooping into someone else's previous life would take her mind off her own sordid past.

She picked up her cup of tea and headed back to her home office and settled before the computer. Steam rose in the air, bringing with it the soothing scent of chamomile as she set down the cup and started typing.

Her tea was cold by the time she pushed back her chair and shuffled to the window and shoved aside the curtain.

The streetlights shone on the quiet street. In the cold green light, her lawn looked surreal. The carefully pruned bushes along the edge of her property cast deep shadows.

Nothing stirred, but she couldn't dispel the sensation someone was out there, watching, waiting. She shivered and dropped the curtain back into place.

Grabbing her cup, she wandered into the kitchen and poured the cold tea into the sink. She refilled the cup from the tap and set it in the microwave and pushed the Start button. As the water heated, she fought back a yawn and rubbed her burning eyes. She didn't think she'd ever been so exhausted. It must be the residual effects of the ketamine and the trauma of the vicious attack.

The microwave beeped, and she opened the door and removed her cup. Swishing a new tea bag through the steaming water, she carried the cup to the living room and sank onto the couch. She blew on the hot tea and sipped. The tea filled her with a comforting warmth, dispelling the chill that had settled like a block of ice in her chest.

The Seattle news headlines from last year were all similar...*Detective's Illicit Romance Results In Toddler's Homicide...Seattle Detective's Actions Lead To Child's Death...Loverboy Detective Sent Packing...*

She lifted her cup and inhaled the soothing scents of flowers and sunshine. Aiden had made a mistake, a big one, one that almost destroyed his career. According to the articles, he was the detective in charge of the case of the abduction of four-year-old Suzi Grantley.

Marissa Grantley, a single mother, reported her daughter missing when she disappeared from the backyard. The mother had left the toddler alone for a few minutes while she ran inside for a treat. When she came back outside, the child was gone.

A Seattle detective team, led by Aiden, investigated. Witnesses recalled seeing a suspicious white van in the area the day the girl vanished, and an extensive search for the van began. When the owner of the white van was tracked down, he turned out to be a delivery driver for a package distribution company. He was taken in for questioning, but the police couldn't prove he was involved in the case, and so, after only a few hours, the delivery driver was released.

Two weeks later, Suzi Grantley's bloodied and beaten body was found by an early morning dog walker in a nearby park. Her body had been hidden under a log and covered with leaves.

The tragedy rocked the city, and the cops pulled out all the stops, determined to find the murderer. For months there weren't any suspects, and the investigators were stymied, even as pressure mounted to find the child's killer.

As lead detective, Aiden worked closely with the victim's mother, Marissa Grantley, interviewing her countless times and offering emotional support to the distraught woman. According to the media, over the many weeks of the investigation, his relationship with Marissa crossed the line from professional to personal, and they became lovers.

None of that would have mattered, or even come to light, if the case hadn't taken an unexpected turn. Investigators discovered Marissa Grantley had a history of anger-control issues. She'd been fired from several jobs for threatening fellow employees. A neighbor came forward to say she'd often heard Marissa yelling at Suzi, and once witnessed her slapping her daughter across the face.

As evidence against the mother mounted, Aiden's professional lapse rose to the forefront. Charged with murdering her daughter, and facing a lengthy prison term, Marissa Grantley's lawyer revealed her relationship with Aiden to the media. Probably in the hopes of having her potential life sentence reduced and redirecting the public's outrage onto the Seattle Police Department.

All hell broke loose. The press dubbed Aiden Loverboy, and the public's anger against him exploded.

But the story didn't end there. After Marissa Grantley's conviction for first degree murder, her lawyer sued the police department and Aiden for unprofessional conduct. The police department denied Aiden had an inappropriate relationship with the suspect, but the media wasn't buying it. A few more days of lurid headlines, and Aiden was dismissed from the force.

Candace sat back and curled her legs under her and sipped tea. The story was shocking. If what she read was true, Aiden had made a terrible mistake. One that ruined his career. But there were holes in the allegations against him. He'd never issued a statement to the press, never publicly defended his actions. The man she knew, the one who believed her when others didn't, who offered her much-needed comfort and support, wasn't someone who'd cross the line. His job was too important. He wouldn't risk the life of a child for sexual gratification. If he thought for a moment Marissa Grantley was guilty, he'd have turned her in.

His steely resolve to find Amanda Jacobs was

proof of his dedication to his job and his desire to help people in need. She hadn't known Aiden long, but she knew deep in her gut that he'd never do something that would compromise a case.

She set her empty cup on the coffee table. He must have gone through hell all those months the media hounded him, labeling him Loverboy in order to sell more advertising space. He lost his job and left his home in Seattle under a cloud of distrust and infamy. What a step down for him to move from the bustling city of Seattle, where he worked hundreds of cases a year, to the sleepy town of Briggston. Other than the Forgotten Five kidnappings twenty-two years ago, the most exciting crime was when a group of teenagers broke into the high school and egged a teacher's classroom.

But things had changed. In the past six months, the Briggston crime rate had skyrocketed. A young coed had been sexually assaulted, Amanda Jacobs disappeared from her bedroom in the nearby city of Cardion, and Candace was attacked and drugged. She shivered in the house's early morning chill and walked down the hall to the thermostat and turned up the furnace.

She was glad Aiden was in town. Not just because he was working hard at solving her case. He was also doing everything he could to find Amanda Jacobs. If anyone could find the missing teen, he could. He was a good cop. She'd stake her life on his integrity.

She yawned and rubbed her aching eyes.

A cold, gray light filtered through the edges of the curtains covering the living room window. The long, sleepless night was over.

Finally.

It was Monday, and she didn't have any classes scheduled until Tuesday morning. The thought of filling the empty hours, keeping her mind busy so she wouldn't dwell on the events of the past few days, exhausted her. Maybe she should crawl back into bed and try and sleep.

She shook her head. No way. She refused to cower in her house like a frightened child, jumping at every noise, waiting for the man who'd attacked her to strike again. Pushing away from the counter, she strode out of the kitchen. It was time she stopped being a victim and took action.

Chapter 16

Aiden pushed back from his desk, stood, pressed his hands on his aching lower back, and stretched. Unable to get the image of Candace's pale, stricken face out of his mind, he hadn't been able to sleep. He'd arrived at work well before dawn and had been hard at it for the past four hours.

After he'd left her place, he was jacked, certain Candace knew her attacker. Her reaction to the revelation that the perp was possibly connected to a veterinary clinic proved that. She may not realize it yet, but she knew the scum, all right. He'd stake his badge on that. Add in the fact the attacker called her by name, and it was a fricken' certainty.

Candy Girl.

That was the name she said the perp had used; the name only her sister, who'd been abducted twenty-two years ago, had called her. That fact alone changed the dynamics of the case.

The assault on Candace in the faculty parking lot was a deliberate, premeditated act. The perp had followed her and attacked her when she was alone and vulnerable. Was it the same man who'd taken her sister and the other four girls so many years ago, the man they knew only as Isaiah? Was that even possible? Despite a nation-wide manhunt, Isaiah had eluded the police, and to this day, he was free. After all these years, why would he return? And why target Candace?

He rubbed the knot in the back of his neck. So many questions, and not an answer in sight. No wonder he hadn't been able to sleep. On his first day on the job at the Briggston Police Department, he'd used his department-issue computer and downloaded the summary file of the Forgotten Five case. The rest of the files, the records of the hundreds of interviews, the countless crime tip call ins, and the results of the thousands of man hours of police work put on the case hadn't been uploaded to the server and were stored in a basement somewhere upstate.

The Forgotten Five case was the biggest crime event the state had dealt with in the past fifty years. All levels of police were involved—federal, state, and local. Even the Briggston campus police helped with the search. All that policing created tons of paper. He'd been plowing through the investigation reports for hours, and he'd barely made a dent.

Four girls, all in their teens, went missing over a period of twenty-six months. The girls were from towns spread throughout the state, but the events surrounding their disappearances were eerily similar. They vanished from their bedrooms in the middle of the night, leaving no indications they were planning on running away or where they might have gone. At the time, the police assumed the girls were runaways, as in each case, there weren't any witnesses or accounts of suspicious characters in the area, and no obvious signs of break-ins.

It wasn't until Charlene Cooper, the fifth girl, disappeared under similar circumstances that the authorities began to suspect they were dealing with a serial abductor. The press had a heyday with the sensational story and dubbed the girls the Forgotten Five.

Charlene was fifteen when she vanished in the middle of the night from the bedroom she shared with her younger sister. Twelve-year-old Candace was asleep in a bed four feet from Charlene's, but she hadn't heard a thing. The parents didn't know their daughter was missing until they went to waken their daughters for school, and Charlene was gone.

Candace slept through the entire abduction. No wonder she'd fought so hard to convince the cops to keep searching for her sister. The certainty that, but for the fact Charlene's bed was closer to the bedroom door, Candace, and not her older sister, would have been the missing daughter must eat at her. Experts called it survivor's guilt, and Candace had it in spades.

Investigators determined the perp gained access through the house's unlocked front door. He'd ascended the stairs, crept into the girls' bedroom, and stolen away with Charlene. The only signs of a struggle were the bedsheets tangled in a twisted heap on the floor.

The police had nothing to go on...no witnesses to the abduction, no DNA evidence left by the perp, no sightings of strange cars in the neighborhood...nothing, and the attending officer had written Charlene off as a probable runaway. The Amber Alert didn't go out until the following day when the mother noticed blood spatter on her missing daughter's pillow.

Valuable hours had been lost, but the alarm had been raised, and a manhunt began. Dozens of searchers spent hundreds of hours combing the nearby woods and fields, but there was no sign of the missing girl.

Three weeks later, acting on an anonymous tip phoned into the case hotline, the cops raided an isolated farm on the outskirts of Mitchell River, a town south of Briggston, and found four of the missing girls. They were locked inside a dilapidated shed behind the farmhouse, and each girl was chained by her ankle to a metal post cemented into the ground. They were filthy and emaciated, their bodies covered in multiple contusions.

Four girls were rescued that day. Charlene Cooper wasn't one of them.

According to the rescued girls' statements, Charlene had been held captive, chained to a post in the shed with them, but two hours before the police raid, Isaiah had taken her from the shed. They never saw him or Charlene again. None of the girls knew why he'd taken Charlene or where he'd gone.

Aiden slumped in his chair and rubbed the back of his neck. The case was disturbing. The sordid details of the brutalities Charlene and the other victims suffered at the hands of the beast who'd abducted them curdled his stomach.

While he read through the investigation notes, an idea niggled at the back of his mind, finally coalescing into a startling revelation. The similarities between the long-ago abductions of the five teenage girls to the Amanda Jacobs's case were too many to ignore. The girls were of a similar age and build, all between fifteen and seventeen years of age. They had long black hair and light-blue eyes, and they'd vanished from their bedrooms in the middle of the night.

He dug the pads of his fingers into the knot of muscle in the back of his neck. He was reaching for the impossible. The abductions, separated by so many years, weren't connected to Amanda Jacobs's disappearance. There was no way on Earth that the man they called Isaiah had returned and restarted his kidnapping spree.

He thought back to his interview with Candace the previous day. She'd been shaken and traumatized when she recalled her attacker's words. *Candy Girl*. The same pet name her sister, and only her sister, had called her.

She was even more upset when he mentioned his theory that her attacker could be a veterinarian. Hell, a strong breeze could have blown her over. He'd wanted to press her further, to drill down and find out why that fact was significant, but one look at her pale face, trembling body, and the raw fear in her eyes, and he didn't have the heart to push. She'd been through a horrendous experience, and it was obvious she was still reeling from the effects of the drug.

Going against his better cop judgment, he'd left and given her the space and time she so obviously needed, but the second he was in his car, he regretted his decision. He needed to find the man who'd attacked her before he hurt someone else. Candace could know a clue that would help solve the case. He punched the steering wheel. Once again, he'd let his personal feelings for a subject get in the way of good, solid police work.

But he'd be back, and the next time he wouldn't go so easy on her. The dirtbag who'd assaulted and drugged her would attack again. No question. The next victim might not be so lucky. The next victim could end up dead.

Aiden's job was to find the perp and lock him up

before he struck again. Candace was the key. He knew that with a visceral certainty. Grabbing his mug, he slugged back the cold dregs of bitter coffee.

His partner believed the footprints Candace saw in Creighton Springs State Park were left by an elk or some other wild animal.

Joe wasn't alone. There was even a theory going around the precinct that the footprints were part of a college prank created by kids with too much time on their hands. Other cops were so overwhelmed by the sheer number of cases they were working they just didn't give a damn. Bottom line—no one believed the tracks in the snow had any connection to Amanda Jacobs's disappearance.

No one, but Aiden.

Deep in his gut festered the certainty that the snowy footprints and Amanda's abduction were connected. Amanda Jacobs's disappearance and Candace's violent attack the other night somehow revolved around Creighton Springs State Park and a mysterious bearded man. Whether any of those events were connected to the Forgotten Five case was another scenario entirely—one he wasn't about to put out there yet. Not until he had something more substantial than his gut to back up his theory.

He wove through the maze of dented metal desks, nodding good morning to the detectives who were straggling into the bullpen for the start of shift, as he headed to the break room. Focused on the coffee machine and his desperate desire for another hit of caffeine, he didn't notice he wasn't alone.

"How goes the battle?"

Aiden jumped at Joe's gravelly voice, and hot

coffee slopped out of his mug and spilled on his hand. Cursing, he set down the pot and his cup and turned on the tap and ran the back of his scalded hand under the cold water.

"What the hell, man? You're as skittish as a nun in a whorehouse." Joe chuckled and munched on a chocolate-covered doughnut.

Aiden turned off the water and dried his hands with a wad of paper towels. "You're here early." Joe usually shuffled into work a half hour, or more, late for the start of his shift. He had a dozen excuses—his car wouldn't start, he had a flat tire, he ran into heavy traffic, he'd booked an early doctor's appointment—but he was never early.

Never.

Aiden eyed his partner. Something was up. Something was definitely up. He grabbed his cup and slurped. The strong black coffee was bitter and thick as mud, just the way he liked it. He drank again.

"I could say the same about you. You look like hell. Been here all night?" Joe spoke through a mouthful of doughnut, spraying crumbs on his white shirt and the floor.

Aiden frowned and backed up a step. Although Joe's interest seemed genuine, Aiden was too tired to care about whatever was going on with his taciturn partner. He drained his cup, poured more coffee, and slurped. The zing of caffeine zipped through his bloodstream, pushing aside the heavy weight of exhaustion. "It's this damn case. I've spent the better part of the night researching cases of missing girls from across the country, trying to find any similarities to Amanda Jacobs." He slugged back more coffee. "You wouldn't believe how many young women are missing. The numbers are staggering."

Joe shrugged. "Most of those girls are runaways. They're probably living on the streets of Denver selling themselves for drugs. Sad, but there's not much we can do to help them." Joe swallowed the last bite of his doughnut and wiped his chin with the back of his hand. A smear of chocolate icing lingered at the corner of his mouth. "They don't want to be found."

Joe's cynicism was almost too much to bear, though his partner was right. Lots of the missing cases involved young girls who'd left home of their own volition and vanished into the bowels of a big city, caught in the clutches of some pimp, and selling their bodies to support a drug habit.

But not all of them. Not Amanda Jacobs. He grabbed a paper napkin from the metal container on the counter and handed the napkin to Joe. "You got something…" He pointed at his own mouth.

Joe took the paper napkin and dabbed at his mouth. "Thanks."

"About the Candace Cooper assault." Aiden leaned his hips against the counter. "Did you get anywhere checking with local veterinarians? Any of them missing ketamine?"

Joe grimaced. "Do you have any idea how long that's gonna take? There are a lot of vets in this town, let alone the entire state." He picked a doughnut crumb from a crease in his white, collared shirt and popped the morsel in his mouth. "Besides, tracking down the ketamine's a waste of time, if you ask me. No way the guy who attacked the Cooper woman is a veterinarian. This perp is smart. He knew we'd trace the drug to the veterinary market. It's gotta be a false lead." He smacked his lips.

Aiden bit back his irritation. "Not all criminals are geniuses. That's why prisons are full. This case is important. A young girl is missing, and time is running out. We need to track down every lead." Working with Joe was like going several rounds in the boxing ring. His crusty partner fought him every step of the way, resisting any suggestion that involved hard police work. "We need to stop this guy before he attacks someone else."

Joe crumpled the greasy doughnut wrapper into a ball and tossed it into a dented metal garbage can. "I'm still not sure I believe Candace Cooper. I mean, you know her history, right? After what happened to her sister, she's been a bug up our asses, always after us to keep looking for Charlene, even though everyone knows her sister's probably long dead and buried somewhere in the mountains. We'll never find her." He shrugged. "Unless some hunter stumbles upon her bones."

Aiden bit his lip to stop from snapping. "Really? So, because of what happened to her sister, you think Candace made up the attack?" He blew out a breath. "Did you *read* the medical report? She has a minor concussion, a slice on her neck from a sharp object, a puncture wound from a needle, and a body pumped full of high-test ketamine. You really think she did that to herself? Just so the cops will keep looking for her sister?"

Joe shrugged again. "Stranger things have happened."

Before Aiden could blast his partner for his

blockheadedness, the captain stuck her head in the door. "My office. Both of you. Now."

Aiden set down his cup and met Joe's raised eyebrows. He shrugged and strode out of the break room and through the maze of desks to the captain's office.

Joe slouched behind.

Chapter 17

Captain Judy Cerroli was a middle-aged, no-nonsense career cop with a hard edge. She'd risen through the ranks, broken through the glass ceiling, and beaten down the old boys' club with her impressive solve-and-conviction rate. Most of the cops who worked at the Briggston Police Station respected her.

In Aiden's case, it was more than respect. He owed her. Big time. She'd gone out on a limb and hired him when no one else would, showing a faith in his detecting abilities he so desperately needed. She'd given him a chance to redeem himself, and in the process earned his undying loyalty.

He tapped on the doorframe. The captain hadn't looked happy when she ordered him and Joe to her office. Something was up, and whatever it was, he was pretty certain he wasn't going to like it.

"Enter." Seated behind her desk, a frown on her weathered face, she pointed at the two plastic visitor chairs. "Sit."

Aiden's gut tightened at her gruff command. Ever since Amanda Jacobs had gone missing, the captain had been on a tear to find the young teen. Pressure from above, and the clamoring of the press made her cranky. But at that moment, she looked more than upset. She looked downright pissed.

Her gray eyes were hardened steel, her mouth

drawn in a tight line. A few strands of her silver-streaked hair had escaped her usually neat bun and floated about her face, adding an unexpected softness, so at odds with the angry set of her mouth. She slapped a piece of paper on her desk. "We have a body."

Aiden's head jerked up. "A body?" His heart sank. "They found Amanda Jacobs?"

"No, it's not her." The captain shook her head. "Two days ago, hikers in Lynn Canyon found human remains. The ME examined the body and determined the victim was a young female, with signs of blunt force trauma to her skull, a broken jaw, and cracked ribs. She'd been bludgeoned to death." She opened a file folder and tapped her finger on a paper and read from the medical examiner's report. "The approximate age of the victim was sixteen."

"Do they have an ID?" Aiden ground down on his back molars.

The captain shook her head. "Not yet."

"What's this girl's death got to do with us?" Joe asked. "Lynn Canyon isn't in our jurisdiction."

She shoved a folder toward Aiden and another to Joe. "Take a look."

Aiden flipped open the file and studied the color photograph of the victim. His stomach sank to his toes. The girl in the picture had long, dark brown hair, big blue eyes, and a grimace of permanent terror and the blank stare of death on what used to be a pretty face. The floor fell out from under him, and he scrubbed his face. "She looks like our missing teen, Amanda Jacobs." *And Candace Cooper*. But he didn't say Candace's name aloud. Not yet. Not until he knew the lay of the land.

Cerolli nodded. "That's what I thought."

Joe tapped his fingers on the photograph. "Come on, you two. You're reaching. Lots of girls have long dark hair. Big deal. Long hair's the style these days."

Aiden ignored him and focused on the captain. "So, there's a possibility the two cases are related? Do you think—" He stopped. He didn't have any hard evidence. It was just a gut feeling, and he knew all too well what Joe thought of gut feelings.

The captain's gray-eyed gaze zeroed in on Aiden. "Spit it out, Farrell. What are you holding back?"

"The Lynn Canyon victim and Amanda Jacobs have similar appearances." Aiden sat forward, swallowed, and took the leap. "Candace Cooper does as well. I know she's a lot older, but—"

Joe blew a loud raspberry. "Come on, Farrell. Just because you have a hard-on for the pretty professor, doesn't mean the cases are connected. The perp who attacked her was probably a junkie looking for easy cash for his next fix."

Aiden's face flamed, and he fisted his hands, but before he could tell Joe just what he thought, the captain's hard-edged voice cut in.

"That's enough, Breacher." She pinned the older detective with a glare guaranteed to shut up even the most-hardened felon.

Joe slumped in his chair and crossed his arms over his chest, a mutinous look on his florid face. But he shut up.

Captain Cerolli smoothed her hand over the file folder. "The medical examiner who worked the homicide victim's case in Lynn Canyon said her blood showed a high concentration of ketamine. And here's

147

the kicker. It's the same chemical signature as the ketamine found in Candace Cooper's blood." She drew in a deep breath. "So, it's looking more and more like the cases are related."

"What?" Aiden's heart thumped. "Are you saying we might have a serial killer on the loose?" If not for the intervention of the drunken frat boys, Candace could have been killed. Had the attacker planned to kidnap and murder her? Was that why he'd injected her with enough ketamine to knock out an elephant? His heart thumped so loudly he was surprised the others in the room couldn't hear its furious pounding. Candace was at risk. The man who'd attempted to kidnap her would try again. He'd seen it before. The sick perverts refused to accept failure. They didn't stop pursuing their chosen victims until they were caught and tossed in jail.

The captain and Joe were watching.

He schooled his expression and forced himself to breathe and think like a cop, not some guy who really liked a woman and feared for her safety. Besides, this wasn't just about Candace. Time was running out for Amanda Jacobs. She'd been missing more than three months. No one spoke the words out loud, but everyone knew the statistics. The longer a victim remained missing, the less chance she'd be found alive. Every minute counted.

"Detective Farrell? Are you all right?"

He blinked as the captain's stern voice drew him out of his troubling thoughts. The concern on her face made it obvious his attempt at calm hadn't fooled her. "Yeah. I'm fine."

She studied him for a long minute, and then tapped

the file folder on her desk. "As I was saying, we can't be certain, but it looks like the three cases could be connected. Whoever murdered the girl in Lynn Canyon may have also kidnapped Amanda Jacobs. He could be the same perp who attacked Dr. Cooper the other night."

"Come on, Captain. You're not buying into this cockamamie theory, are you? Candace Cooper's way too old. She's like in her thirties, right?" Joe snorted. "You know what these wackos are like. They pick a type and stick to it like a religion. No way would a guy like that change the age range of his victims." Joe cracked his knuckles, the popping sounds loud in the tension-filled office. "The perp who killed the girl in Lynn Canyon isn't the same guy who attacked Candace Cooper. I just don't see it."

"We need to view this situation with an open mind." She raised a finger. "First, we have a sixteen-year-old homicide victim, a missing fifteen-year-old girl, and an adult female who was attacked."

She raised a second finger. "Two of the victims were injected with animal-grade ketamine." Another finger joined the first two. "All three woman have similar appearances—tall with slim builds, long, dark-brown hair, and blue eyes." She held up a fourth finger. "And finally, all either vanished or were attacked within the past three months." Her eyes narrowed, and her mouth thinned. "I think there's a good chance we're looking at a serial offender."

"What about Lori Ann Carson?" interjected Breacher. "She was attacked and raped at the college, but she's a blonde." He sat back with a smug look on his face. "How do you factor that attack into your little scenario?" Joe cracked his knuckles again.

Aiden winced at the annoying popping sound. "The perp who assaulted Lori Ann was someone different entirely. She wasn't injected with ketamine. But, like I said, these are just theories." He inhaled a steadying breath and caught the captain's eye. "There's something you should know—something I just learned."

She leaned forward. "What's that?"

"When I interviewed Candace...er...Dr. Cooper, she remembered another detail about the attack." His heart rate kicked up, and he rubbed his icy hands together. He was really going out on a limb now. "She recalled something her attacker said."

She arched her brows and nodded for him to continue.

"He called her Candy Girl."

The crease between her brows deepened. "The guy knew her name?"

Aiden nodded. "According to Candace, the only person who has ever called her that was her older sister, Charlene Cooper. It was their secret pet name." The mention of Charlene's name was like a bomb detonating in the small room.

"Charlene Cooper?" The captain's eyes widened. "She was one of the Forgotten Five, wasn't she? The girl they never found?"

He nodded. "She's Candace Cooper's older sister."

The furrow between her brows deepened. "Dr. Cooper is certain that's what her attacker said?"

He nodded.

"Interesting." She tapped her fingers on her desk. "How would the perp who attacked Candace Cooper know the secret name her sister called her?"

Aiden shrugged. "No idea."

"Wait a minute." Joe blew out a breath, spraying droplets of spit across the room. "This is ridiculous. There's no way these cases are connected. You're not buying his ridiculous theory, are you, Captain? That's—"

She held up her hand, stopping his outburst. "Until we learn something different, we're treating these recent cases as if they're connected. As for linking them to the Forgotten Five case—" She grimaced. "Let's hold off on that until we get more evidence. If the media caught wind, they'd go ballistic."

She rested her elbows on the desktop and fixed Aiden with a thoughtful look. "Detective Farrell, I want you to talk to Candace Cooper again. From what I've read, people injected with ketamine can have memory recall hours or even days later. I want to know every detail of what she remembers from that night. If we're right, and these cases are connected, she's our only witness. We also can't lose sight of the fact a child is missing. Finding Amanda Jacobs has to be our priority."

A frisson of unease slid down Aiden's spine. "How are we going to protect Candace Cooper?"

Captain Cerroli's forehead furrowed. "Let's not get ahead of ourselves." She nodded at Breacher. "Joe could be right. Maybe we're reaching for straws. There's no way I'll get funding to assign a protection detail for Dr. Cooper on what little evidence we have."

Aiden bit back his frustration. Candace's life was at stake, but it always came down to money. City budgets were tight, and a small police department like Briggston had few discretionary funds. Besides, the captain had a point. There was no definitive evidence the three cases were connected. It was all speculation.

Joe stood, and his knees popped. "Okay, Captain. Nice talk. My partner and I'll arrange another interview with Candace Cooper." His tone made clear how unappealing he found that idea.

"Not so fast, Breacher. Both of you don't need to talk to the witness. I want you to work another angle."

Joe paused, his hand on the door handle. He arched his shaggy brows.

"I want you to continue to check out veterinary clinics in the area. Find that source of ketamine."

Joe frowned. "But tomorrow's Saturday, and I've been working extra hours all week. I was planning on—"

She cut him off. "We have one dead girl, a missing teen, and a college instructor who was assaulted. The pressure's on. The top brass wants this case solved yesterday. If we can find where this lowlife's getting his drug of choice, maybe we can nail him." She blew out a breath. "I don't care about your personal plans. I want you both hard at work all weekend long, if that's what it takes. The chief okayed overtime hours on this case."

Joe opened his mouth to protest, but the captain held up her hand. "I don't want to hear any excuses. Until Amanda Jacobs is found, this office doesn't rest." She leveled her gaze at first Aiden and then Joe. "You hear me?"

Joe's expression turned sour, but he nodded. "I'll get right on it."

Aiden shot his partner a look. Joe never worked weekends. Not ever. He belonged to a competitive bowling league that met every Saturday morning. Missing a match because the older detective had to work a case would definitely rankle, but he wouldn't go against a direct order, not when he was so close to retirement.

"I'll set up a follow-up interview with Dr. Cooper as soon as possible." Candace was in danger. He knew that with a visceral certainty that had his heart thumping. Someone, whether it was Isaiah, or some other perverted snake, was after her. The nightly phone calls, the attack on campus…all were connected. Given the chance, the perp would strike again. It was up to Aiden to stop him before that happened.

The phone on Captain Cerroli's desk rang. She grimaced. "That's probably the chief wanting an update." The phone pealed again, and she waved them out of the room.

Aiden hurried to his desk, gathered his stack of case files, and stuffed them in his leather case, one thought raging—protect Candace. No matter what he had to do, he'd make damn sure she was safe. She'd suffered enough in her life. He turned to head out, but Joe blocked his way.

"Lucky you. You're spending the weekend with the all-too-pretty Dr. Cooper, while I'm running my ass off tracking down veterinarians." His lip curled in a sneer. "You're the one with a dog. You should be checking the vet clinics."

Aiden threaded his hands through his hair. He didn't have time to stand around sparring with his cantankerous partner. "Look, Joe. I know you have a beef with me, but it's time you got over it. This case is too important to allow petty differences to get in the way." He hefted his bag and hung the strap over one shoulder. "You heard the captain. She assigned us each a task. I don't know about you, but I'm going to do my damnedest to find Amanda Jacobs and catch the jerk who abducted her."

He shoved past Joe's stocky frame and stormed out of the detective bullpen. He should have offered to switch assignments with his partner. The last thing he should do was spend more time alone with Candace. She was attractive, honest, and incredibly courageous. Her wounded vulnerability struck a chord. No matter how hard he resisted, she'd managed to knock down the walls he'd erected, and all he could think of was her.

He'd made a mistake before and messed up big time. No way in hell would he go down that road again. He clomped down the stairs to the lobby, pushed through the exhausted duty cops heading home after their twelve-hour night shifts, shoved open the reinforced glass door, and stepped onto the empty sidewalk.

It was still early. Rush hour, or the morning six-car lineup at the town's only downtown traffic light, hadn't started yet, and the street was quiet. He fought back a yawn. It had been a hell of a long day, and it wasn't even eight o'clock. He'd been hard at the job since well before dawn, and all he had to show for his labor was a dead teenager and a shitload of questions and wild theories.

He strode down the sidewalk to the police parking lot. His SUV was parked between a green van and a tiny white, two-door hybrid. He unlocked the driver's door and settled behind the wheel.

Every cell in his body demanded he talk to

Candace. She knew something about the case she wasn't telling him, and he had every intention of finding out what that was. He couldn't shake the certainty the clock was ticking. Every second counted if they hoped to find Amanda Jacobs alive. Candace was smack in the middle of the case. What her role was in this nightmare, he had no idea, but the case was finally building momentum after being stagnant for months.

But before he could question Candace, he had to take Tracker for a quick walk. The poor dog had been locked in his crate since Aiden had left in the middle of the night, and Tracker's bladder would be bursting.

He strapped on his seatbelt and started the car. With a quick glance in his mirrors, he pulled out of his parking spot and onto the street.

Chapter 18

Candace stuffed a plastic-wrapped ham-and-cheese sandwich and two granola bars into her backpack. She filled a reusable water bottle from the tap and jammed it in the outside pocket and conducted a quick inventory of the items she'd already packed—first aid kit, waterproof matches, raincoat, hat, sunscreen, bug spray, a topographic map.

All packed. Set to go.

Soft, golden morning light streamed through the kitchen window. The sky was the clear, fragile blue of springtime in the Rockies. In the distance, the mountains gleamed with a dusting of fresh snow, but down in the valley, the leaves on the trees glowed with new life; the daffodils and crocuses in her garden bloomed, their yellow and purple heads opening to greet the new day. A robin hopped across the dewy lawn searching for breakfast.

It was a beautiful morning, but her heart didn't sing like it normally did at the prospect of a day filled with warm sunshine and fresh spring breezes. Instead, her heart was heavy, weighted down with what she'd remembered the man who'd attacked her had whispered.

Candy Girl.

Even though the kitchen was warm, she shivered. The attack on her wasn't a random act. She'd been targeted. Her attacker knew her name. That alone raised alarm bells. Had Isaiah, the man who kidnapped her sister, returned after all these years? Was he the one who'd assaulted her? Had he taken Amanda Jacobs and restarted his kidnapping spree? Her knees wobbled, and she grabbed onto the counter.

After the police raided the old farmhouse in the mountainous backcountry and discovered the four missing girls, the hunt for the man who'd abducted them and absconded with her sister intensified. All levels of police were involved—county sheriff's departments, Highway Patrol, the state police, and even the FBI.

As the traumatized girls revealed details about their months of incarceration, the full horror of what they'd endured shocked even the most-hardened police officers. Isaiah had promised he'd return for the girls and punish them if they talked, and they were provided police protection, but when months went by with no sign of Isaiah, the bodyguards were recalled, and the girls allowed to go on with their lives, such as they could, considering the trauma they'd suffered.

But now, twenty-two years later, another young girl was missing, abducted from her bedroom in the middle of the night just like the earlier kidnapping victims. Candace had been attacked by someone who knew the secret pet name only Charlene knew. No question—as far as she was concerned, Isaiah was back. Unless someone was copying his crimes. A shudder rippled through her at the frightening possibility.

She had two choices—hide out in her townhouse and wait for the police to find her assailant—or take action and do something that might help find Amanda

Jacobs. Candace hadn't been able to help her sister, and she lived with that guilt every day. But if there was the slightest chance Isaiah had returned and taken Amanda, Candace couldn't live with herself if she didn't do everything in her power to find her. Even if that meant heading out into Creighton Springs State Park…alone.

The thought of encountering the bearded man in the forest almost brought her to her knees, and she stumbled across the kitchen and collapsed onto a chair. A sob hitched in her throat, and she buried her face in her hands as another flood of memories engulfed her.

The night Isaiah came for her sister, and left Candace sound asleep a few feet away, changed her life forever. Every detail of that night and the following morning was tattooed on her brain—the book she was reading about a boy with a lightning strike scar on his forehead and magical powers, the golden glow cast by the string of fairy lights hung on the purple walls, the tattered posters of teen idols, the familiar fuzzy softness of her purple-and-pink striped comforter, her innocence, her naïve belief that life was fair.

Charlene stomped into the room, slammed the door and ripped off Candace's quilt and tossed it on the floor. "You little brat!" She held up a blue plastic bottle. "You used all my shampoo." She tossed the empty bottle onto Candace's bed. "I told you not to touch it. You know it's my favorite."

"I'm sorry. I didn't mean to use all of it." Candace sat up and grabbed the bottle and tossed it into the garbage bin. "I promise I won't do it again."

Charlene plopped onto her own bed and slipped under the covers. "Well, you'd better convince Mom to buy some more shampoo." She was still frowning, but the anger had left her voice.

"Please don't be mad at me." Tears burned in Candace's eyes. "I told you I was sorry."

Charlene heaved a heavy sigh. "I'm not mad at you, Candy Girl. I just wish I had my own room." She picked up her CD player and set it on her lap and slipped in a CD. "I'm too old to be sharing a room with my baby sister." Switching the machine on, she popped on a set of headphones, sat up against her pillow, and turned up the music. "Now go to sleep before Dad comes up and tells us to be quiet." The tinny beats of rap music filled the small room.

Candace retrieved her quilt from the floor, turned out her bedside light, and curled on her side on her bed. Charlene had been agitating for her own room for months. Their parents were talking about renovating the attic and moving Charlene in there. Candace didn't want her sister to move out. She liked sharing a room with her, liked knowing she wasn't alone at night.

Charlene turned up the volume, singing along with the lyrics.

Candace groaned and stuffed a pillow over her head. Maybe Charlene was right, and it was time they had their own rooms. Maybe having her own space wouldn't be such a bad thing after all.

The nightmare began the next morning. She woke to her mother's loud, frantic cries. Charlene's bed was empty. The blankets were tangled and tossed on the floor. Candace and her parents searched, but Charlene wasn't in the bathroom down the hall, the kitchen, or anywhere else in the house. Her father looked in the garage and the yard, while her mother contacted Charlene's closest friends.

The police were called, but the young rookie officer who attended, Officer Joe Breacher, assured the family that since there were no signs of forced entry, no witnesses, and no proof Charlene had been kidnapped, she'd probably left of her own accord. He suggested they post missing-person posters at the bus depot and in cafes along the highway, and he assured the family Charlene would probably return home soon. Most runaways did.

The next day, Candace's mother noticed tiny spots of blood on Charlene's pillow. She called the police again.

Another officer came to the house and took away the pillowcase. When tests showed the blood wasn't Charlene's, or anyone else's in the Cooper family, an investigation into Charlene's disappearance began.

Aside from the tangled sheets and blood spots, the investigators found a scattering of pet hairs on the bed.

The Coopers didn't own a pet.

Further investigation revealed the hairs were from multiple domestic animals.

The lightbulb finally went on, and the police realized they were dealing with a serial kidnapper. Four other girls in the state, who'd been missing for months and labeled runaways, were now determined to be victims of abduction. In each case, pet hairs were found on their bedsheets.

When the police speculated that whoever abducted Charlene gained entrance to the house through the unlocked front door, Candace was distraught. The Coopers always locked their doors at night, but the night Charlene was kidnapped, after the family was asleep, Candace snuck outside.

Her teacher had talked to the class about something called a blood moon, and Candace wanted to see if the moon really looked red. Late that night, after everyone in the house was asleep, she stood on the front lawn, shivering in her pajamas, and peered up at the night sky. Heavy clouds covered the stars, and the moon was invisible. Disappointed, she went back inside the house, tiptoed up the stairs to her bedroom, and climbed into bed.

The guilt Candace endured at the knowledge that she'd left the front door unlocked kept her awake at night. Her pain and remorse were as sharp today as twenty-two years ago. Scrubbing her hands over her tearstained face, she inhaled a deep breath.

After the other Forgotten Five girls were rescued, the media hounded Candace's family like jackals. They camped their news vans on the street in front of the house and followed the family whenever they left home, shouting questions they couldn't answer. The phone rang day and night with requests for interviews and offers of book and movie deals. Everyone wanted a piece of their tragedy.

The spotlight was intense, and for months, Candace and her family hid inside their small house, the blinds closed, doors locked, living in gloom and guilt, their grief poisoning the air.

The police said there was nothing they could do, as long as the reporters stayed on the street and didn't trespass on private property. They promised the furor would die down, but it was months before the street in front of the house cleared of strange vehicles and the phone stopped ringing, months before the family could attempt to heal their wounds.

C. B. Clark

Years of counseling, and a steady dose of antianxiety medication and sleeping pills, weren't able to ease Candace's burden of guilt, but on the advice of her therapist, she stopped being a victim and took action. She read every word the media wrote about The Forgotten Five and fought for, and won, access to the police files on the case. She was determined to do what the police, with all their resources, hadn't been able to accomplish. *She* would find Charlene.

Her fixation on finding her sister affected her life, and instead of dating, attending football and basketball games and parties like other young people, she spent her free time researching the Forgotten Five case and following up on leads, no matter how tenuous. She contacted the Briggston Police Department so often she became *persona non grata*. Whenever she showed up at the station house with what she was certain was a new lead to the case, she was met with closed doors, or worse—looks of pity.

Her efforts were for naught. Twenty-two years later, her sister was still missing, and Isaiah remained at large. She grabbed a handful of tissues from the box on the table and blew her nose.

The first years in college were rocky, but by her third year, she'd chosen a major and begun to enjoy the new normal of life after Charlene's disappearance. She settled on the field of physical anthropology. The study of early humans fascinated her. She didn't need a therapist to tell her that escaping into the prehistoric past was her way of avoiding the nightmare reality of the present.

She went to graduate school and earned her doctorate. All her hard work paid off when she secured her teaching position at Briggston College. Life settled into a routine of teaching classes, researching, and field studies. She hadn't called the police demanding an update on the Forgotten Five case for months. What was the point? No one believed that Charlene was still alive. No one cared. Not really. There were too many other tragedies occurring on an almost daily basis, and the police had only so much manpower.

She thought she'd moved on, and she was finally dealing with the defining tragedy of her life. A bitter laugh burst out of her mouth. *Yeah. She was over it, all right.* She'd been living in a false bubble. The disturbing events of the past months brought back the angst of the old tragedy.

She couldn't get Amanda Jacobs out of her mind. What if the footprints and the drops of blood she'd seen in the park that day so many months ago were Amanda's? The poor girl could have been fleeing her captor. The tall, bearded man Candace saw watching from the dense trees could be Amanda's kidnapper. Was she being held in some dark, cold place, waiting for rescue?

The disturbing thoughts kept Candace tossing and turning all night. Throw in a pounding headache and frightening, but vague, memories of the vicious attack in the faculty parking lot, and it was a wonder she wasn't hanging from the ceiling screaming like a gibbering monkey. Somehow, she was holding it together, but just barely.

But today, she was going to change all that. She was going to make a difference and direct the energy she wasted on guilt, into action. Today, she was going to Creighton Springs State Park to retrace her steps of that cold November day along the Eggelston River.

Instead of stopping like she had when she went to the park with Aiden, where the footprints veered off the trail and headed into the forest, she'd follow the many narrow, twisting deer trails through the thick bush. Maybe somewhere deep in the woods she'd find a remnant of cloth, a deserted cabin, or evidence of a camp, some indication that would prove Amanda had been in the park.

The K9 dogs had searched the area. The chances of finding any clues after all this time were slim to none, but she couldn't live with herself if she didn't at least try.

The phone rang.

She checked the caller ID and hit the Cancel button, just like she had the previous six times Aiden had called. If he knew her plans, he'd try and talk her out of the trip to the park.

Opening the cabinet under the sink, she hefted the large canister of bear spray she'd bought at the hardware store after she was attacked on campus. Mace was all well and good, but bear spray was intended to stop a charging bear. She could only imagine what the powerful pepper spray would do to an attacking human.

She slipped the can into its canvas holster and strapped the belt around her waist. Zipping up her backpack, she gulped a final swig of coffee from her ceramic mug. Hefting the backpack over her shoulder, she scooped her cell phone and sunglasses from the counter and grabbed her car keys from the bowl by the front door.

The doorbell pealed.

She jumped and pressed her hand to her chest to

slow her racing heart.

Isaiah! He'd come for her.

Calm down. Isaiah wouldn't ring the doorbell and announce his presence. He'd want the element of surprise on his side. Shaking, she peered through the door's peephole. Her breath whooshed out.

Aiden stood on the stoop.

Another bout of shaky nerves flooded her body—this time, not caused by fear of personal harm, but the concern she was beginning to like him far, far too much.

Chapter 19

She fumbled with the security chain, unlocked the deadbolt, twisted the lock and cracked open the door. "Why are you here? Has something happened?" A hundred scenarios flashed through her, each one more frightening than the one before.

"Good morning, Candace." His gaze shifted to the backpack slung over her shoulder. "Going somewhere?"

"I was heading out for a walk. I thought some fresh air would distract me." Her hand fluttered to the healing wounds on her neck.

"Looks like it's going to be a nice day, that's for sure. I plan on taking advantage of the sunshine too." He jerked his thumb at his black SUV parked in the driveway. A large hairy dog perched on the front seat, his mouth open in a goofy grin, his long red tongue hanging out. "I promised Tracker a good long walk, but first, I have a few more questions I'd like to ask if you can spare a minute." He phrased it as a request, but the determined look in his eyes made clear he wouldn't be put off. "I tried to call, but…" He arched a dark brow.

Heat flamed across her cheeks. "Did you? I didn't hear my phone ring."

"Huh." His tone made clear he didn't believe her. He glanced at his car and the panting dog. "On second thought…" He shuffled his feet and grinned, looking like a young boy skipping school. "Why don't Tracker and I tag along? I can ask my questions while we walk." He shrugged. "It's a great day. Be a shame to waste it."

She bit her bottom lip. She couldn't tell him her plans. He'd think she was nuts.

The light in his eyes faded. "Unless you don't like dogs."

She studied the dog.

His big hairy head hung out the open window, and he watched her with dark, soulful eyes.

"I like dogs." She blew out a resigned breath. She'd never been a good liar. "You might as well know I'm going to Creighton Springs State Park." She set the house alarm, hefted the backpack, stepped onto the porch, and closed and locked the door.

He rocked back on his heels. "What? Why?"

"I want to check the area where I saw those footprints again." She couldn't look at him, certain she'd see derision on his handsome face. "I need to do something to help find that missing girl. I can't stop thinking that if I'd confronted that man, pushed the police harder…" She stopped. She didn't owe him an explanation. She could walk wherever she wanted.

A weighty silence settled over them, broken only by the twittering of birds in the tall, leafy elms at the end of her driveway, and the swish of tires as a car passed on the street.

"Okay."

She blinked. "Okay?"

He nodded. "Sure. Let's do this." He paused. "As long as you're fine with Tracker and me tagging along."

For the first time that morning, she smiled. "Let's

167

go." How could she refuse? She was a sucker for dogs, and having an armed Aiden and his big dog beside her on her search was a bonus. *In more ways than one.*

"Great." He grinned. "Let's take my car."

Anticipation bubbled through her as she followed him down the walk to his SUV. She was spending the day with him, and she didn't want to question why that made her heart sing.

Aiden shooed the big, hairy dog off the front seat and into the back of the SUV, and then he gestured for her to climb into the newly vacated front seat.

A cloud of dog hairs wafted in the air as she settled on the seat and strapped on her seat belt. The belt brushed the wound on her neck, and she winced. The painful reminder of the attack erased her happiness. Even though her memories of the assault were vague and disjointed, she'd never forget her terror when the man whispered her nickname into her ear.

Aiden started the car and backed out of the driveway and onto the street. "Here we go. Off on our adventure."

Tracker woofed in agreement.

Aiden chuckled, the rich, warm sound filling the car.

His teasing, lighthearted tone didn't fool her. Tension radiated off him in waves. Something had changed since the last time she'd seen him. He was on edge, and he checked the rearview mirror far too often. What was he looking for? Did he think someone was following them?

She breathed in slow, deep breaths, inhaling through her nose and exhaling out her mouth, fighting to quell her rising anxiety. She eyed the bulge of

Aiden's service revolver in his shoulder holster under his jacket. A gun beat a can of bear spray any day.

He drove with skill and confidence, one hand on the steering wheel, the other on his thigh, tapping to the fast-paced beat of the country-and-western song playing over the car radio.

At this early hour, the streets were free of traffic, and they made quick time through the downtown core and onto the main road leading out of town toward Creighton Springs State Park, thirty miles distant.

The radiant hues of orange, crimson, and pink bled into the cloudless sky like fire as the sun rose over the mountains in the east. With each mile, her heart beat faster, and she gripped the leather armrests. This *adventure*, as Aiden called their trip, was a long shot. Maybe they wouldn't find anything. Maybe? Certainly. But at least she'd tried, and at long last, she was taking action.

****

"Looks pretty busy." Aiden pulled the car into the nearly full parking lot and turned into a parking space. "Guess we aren't the only ones who wanted to get out of town early today."

Candace undid her seat belt and opened the door. "It's the first nice weekend this spring, and it's a professional development day for teachers, so there's no school. I'm not surprised people are here. Once we get away from the parking lot, we won't see anyone. Most folks don't venture far from their vehicles."

Tracker whined and panted in the back seat, trembling in excitement. He shook his big body, raising a cloud of gray-and-brown hairs that floated in the air and settled on every surface.

Aiden retrieved Candace's daypack from the trunk, loosened the nylon straps, and shrugged the pack over his shoulders, surprised at the weight of the small bag. What the heck did she have in there? He opened the door to the back seat and latched the leash onto Tracker's collar. "Okay, boy. Out you get."

The dog bounded out of the vehicle, barking and prancing in circles, his big paws raising a cloud of dust.

He grinned at Tracker's antics. "Someone's pretty happy to be going for a walk." Then he slid a glance at Candace. "All set?"

She nodded, though her face was pale, and shadows clouded the depths of her vivid blue eyes. "I think so."

He frowned. When she hadn't answered his phone calls, his inner alarm bells clanged. Maybe she was in bed recovering from her ordeal and was too tired to answer the phone, or maybe—and this possibility chilled him to the bone—maybe her attacker had returned.

So, he'd gone against protocol and shown up unannounced on her doorstep. One thing led to another, and the next thing he knew, he was suggesting he and Tracker join her on her hike.

This search was a waste of time and energy. The chances of finding some indication Amanda Jacobs had been in the state park in November were slim to none. But Candace was determined to do this, and so he'd offered to join her. That way he could keep an eye on her and question her about her attacker like the captain had asked him to.

Joe would make Aiden's life miserable if he knew Aiden was strolling in the forest with Candace, but he didn't give a damn what his partner thought. She was in danger. Every cell in his body twigged to that. He wasn't about to let her head into the wilderness on her own. Not after the foiled attack the other night. The perp could be watching her, waiting to strike again.

A black minivan pulled into the lot and parked. The door slid open, and two teenagers tumbled out, their excited chatter carrying like magpies across the large lot.

An older, gray-haired man climbed out of the van, slammed the driver's door, and strode around to the rear of the vehicle. He lifted the hatch and wrestled out three mountain bikes. In minutes, the three park visitors had strapped on helmets, mounted their bikes, and pedaled out of the parking lot and down a trail.

Tracker whined, tugging at the leash.

Aiden petted the dog's shaggy head. "Okay, boy. Let's go."

Tracker took off like a shot, almost jerking Aiden off his feet.

Aiden stumbled over the uneven ground, hanging onto the leash, running to keep up with the excited beast. Served him right for leaving the high-energy dog cooped up in his crate for the past few days while Aiden put in long hours on the case. He'd managed to take Tracker on a few quick rips around the block, but the dog needed a good run.

"Hey, you guys, wait up."

He glanced over his shoulder.

Candace was jogging behind.

He tugged the leash, slowing the rambunctious dog to a trot. "Sorry. He hasn't had a run in a few days."

She laughed, and it was if the angels came out to

sing. Her cheeks flushed, and her arresting blue eyes sparkled. A dimple grooved in her left cheek.

He gaped and stumbled over a root, barely managing to right himself. He'd never seen her laugh, not an outright chuckle. And why hadn't he noticed that cute dimple? It was all he could do not to touch the intriguing indent.

Stop! Focus on the case, not the pretty girl. The warning blazed through his frontal cortex, but it didn't quell the excited flutter deep in his gut.

They cleared the parking lot and started along a well-maintained, graveled path.

Tracker strained at the leash, threatening to dislocate Aiden's arm as they jogged past a man and a woman pushing a stroller with a sleeping toddler bundled in the seat.

A minute later, they passed a middle-aged couple with a white miniature poodle in tow.

The little dog lunged at Tracker, snarling and snapping.

Tracker raced by, too intent on the intriguing smells on the trail to pay the aggressive poodle any attention.

When they turned onto the narrow, winding trail that led along the ridgeline, Candace stopped. Her chest heaved, and she was puffing. "You can let him off the leash now. We shouldn't meet anyone on this trail, and he looks like he needs a good run." She grinned. "Besides, I think your arm's a good two inches longer than when we started."

She chuckled, the sound like the sweetest musical notes rising on the clear morning air. The shadows lurking in her vivid blue eyes had vanished, and the lines of strain on her face softened.

For a moment, he forgot to breathe, forgot where he was, forgot everything but the beautiful woman.

A squirrel chittered from atop a pine tree, and Tracker lunged, jerking the leash, almost toppling Aiden, snapping him out of his fantasies. Aiden unclipped the leash and released the slobbering dog.

Tracker shot after the squirrel like a canine bullet, his long tail wagging, his mouth open in a wide grin.

Aiden rubbed his aching arm and hurried after Candace as she set a brisk pace along the same narrow trail they'd taken a week ago when she showed him the area where she'd seen the footprints.

Tracker raced ahead, zigzagging into the forest, chasing one intriguing scent after another, his joy at being out in the woods evident in his rapidly swishing tail.

The sun had risen over the distant mountains and beat warmly on Aiden's head.

The sky was a clear robin's-egg blue. Spring burst from every corner of the forest. The breeze carried the sweet scents of burgeoning leaves, morning dew, and rising pine sap. The piping trills of birds resonated from the bank of trees. Morning dew on a spider's web strung between two branches, glistened likc tiny diamonds.

After thirty minutes of hiking along the path, they passed the striped rock Candace had pointed out the last time they were there, but instead of stopping, they branched off onto a narrow game trail and headed deeper into the trees.

Tracker charged out of the forest, hot on the heels of a fluttering butterfly, his long, red tongue lolling.

"He's having fun." Candace grinned. "How long have you had him?"

As if he knew they were talking about him, Tracker ran to Aiden and sat panting at his feet.

"A couple of years. I wasn't planning on getting a dog, but..." He fumbled in his pocket for a dog treat and offered one to Tracker.

The treat disappeared in a nanosecond, and Tracker whined and looked piteous, begging for more.

Aiden laughed and handed the dog another dog biscuit. "Believe it or not, this big galoot is a trained cadaver dog. He hurt his back and hips during a training exercise and couldn't do his job anymore. I knew a guy who knew a guy who knew a guy." He shrugged. "Anyway, I mentioned I was thinking of getting a small dog in a few years, and the next thing I knew this big beast was riding shotgun in my car." He rubbed Tracker's floppy ears. "We've been a team ever since."

What he didn't say, was just how important Tracker was. Without the dog, he doubted he would have survived the challenging past year. Knowing his dog thought the sun rose and set on Aiden and didn't think less of him for the mistakes he'd made, kept Aiden going day after day when it seemed as if everyone else had given up on him.

Tracker galloped into the bush and returned with a stick in his mouth. He perched at Aiden's feet, cocked his ears, and dropped the stick.

Grinning, Aiden picked up the slobber-covered chunk of wood and tossed it into the forest.

Tracker barked joyously and gave chase.

Aiden chuckled. "Now instead of searching out cadavers, he uses all that expensive training to sniff out squirrels. He's always finding some sort of animal bone on our walks. He has quite the collection in the back yard. Once, he brought back a full set of moose antlers." He chuckled again. "They were bigger than him."

"Are you thirsty?" She pointed at a water bottle strapped to the pack on his back.

He nodded. "I didn't bring any water."

"Good thing I came prepared, then." She smiled. "I don't mind sharing."

He shrugged out of the backpack and tugged out the water bottle and handed it to her.

Unscrewing the cap, she raised the bottle to her mouth. The long, pale column of her throat…the pursing of her soft-looking pink lips as she drank…

The breath whooshed out of his chest as if he'd been punched. *Wow! Just wow!* He tore his gaze away. She was a beautiful woman, inside and out, and God help him, he was attracted to her. Not just attracted— smitten, enamored, besotted, whatever the hell he wanted to call it. But the feelings were wrong, and acting on the attraction spelled trouble. He *wouldn't* make the same mistake again.

No. Damn. Way.

"Aiden? Want some water?"

He blinked. "Wha-what?"

She held up the water bottle. "I asked if you wanted a drink."

He forced a chuckle. "Yeah. Thanks." As he grasped the water bottle, his hand brushed hers. He sucked in a steadying breath at the jolt of electricity from the brief contact. Gulping water, he fought to hide his reaction. He turned away and stuffed the water bottle back into the pack.

He was a cop. She was a victim of a violent assault. His job was to question her and find out what she was keeping from him so he could catch the perpetrator and prevent more attacks. That's why he was there. That was the only reason—to solve the case. He was just doing his job. *Yeah, right.* He tried to ignore the small, heckling voice in the back of his brain, but the snide words continued. *You keep telling yourself that, buddy.*

He shot her a glance, and his heart stuttered. Man, he was in trouble.

Big trouble.

Chapter 20

"I think this is where I lost the footprints."

"You're right." He pointed at a strip of pink flagging tape tied to a branch. A fly buzzed his ear, and he swatted the annoying bug. Once again, he hadn't brought bug spray, and once again, he was a prime target for the hordes of buzzing insects that called the park home. A cloud of hungry mosquitos surrounded him, while not one bug bothered Candace. "Did you bring any bug spray?" He cursed and swatted a mosquito that landed on his neck looking for breakfast.

She unzipped a pouch in the back of the pack and tugged out a small canister. "I never hike without it."

He took the can, careful not to brush his fingers against hers. "Thanks." Stepping a few feet away, he sprayed a cloud of repellent over his body. His eyes watered, and he coughed and gagged at the acrid stench, but the bugs disappeared. Hallelujah!

"If you plan on doing more hiking in the woods, you'd better come prepared." She smiled. "This is only the start of the season. The bugs will be a lot worse in a few weeks."

"They sure seem to like my city-slicker blood."

She laughed. "It's probably all the lattes, mochas, and espressos you city folks drink."

Her musical laughter was contagious and impossible to resist, and he chuckled.

"Why did you move to Briggston?"

He was so distracted by that adorable dimple flashing in her cheek, it was a minute before he realized what she'd asked. His smile fizzled. "What are you talking about?" But he knew. Oh, yes, he knew. The only surprise was, she'd waited so long.

Her forehead crinkled into a frown. "I'm sorry if I'm prying, but your partner mentioned you moved here from Seattle." Her attempt at a smile failed miserably. "Most people do the opposite. You know, move out of the small town to the bright lights of the city."

He cursed under his breath. Damn Joe. Trust him to gossip. For a heartbeat he thought about lying, making up some story about how he'd always wanted to live in a small town, but he saw the truth in her blue eyes. She knew the sordid details of his ignominious escape from Seattle, but she was too nice to come out and accuse him of anything. Instead, she was giving him a chance to explain. He sank onto a moss-covered log and patted the space beside him. "You might as well sit down. It's a long and ugly story."

She sat beside him and picked up a twig and twirled it with her fingers. "You don't have to tell me. Your past is none of my business. I'm sorry I asked."

He clenched his hands so tight his fingers hurt. "It's not like it's a secret. The details are all over the Internet."

Her face flushed a bright red.

"You looked me up, didn't you?"

She didn't meet his gaze. "The Internet articles said you were fired from your detective position with the Seattle Police Department."

He nodded. "The Department didn't have a choice.

They had to let me go."

For the first time since they'd started the uncomfortable conversation, she met his gaze. "The news stories implied you'd made some poor decisions. The situation must have been horrible."

He chewed on the inside of his cheek and tasted blood. "I made a bad mistake. A big one. If it weren't for my actions, we'd have figured out the mother was the perp a lot sooner. Maybe we could've saved the child."

"Will you tell me what happened?" Her voice broke. "But only if you want to."

He met her gaze, read compassion, and not the avid curiosity and distrust he'd feared, in the blue depths, and he inhaled a deep, steadying breath. "I was the detective in charge. It was my first big case, and I was pretty cocky. I thought I could save the world." He grimaced. "As it turned out, I couldn't even save one little girl."

"The media accused you and the mother of having an affair. They dubbed you Loverboy."

He unclenched his hands and spread them on his thighs and studied the thick cords of blue veins on the tanned skin on the backs of his hands. Revealing the details of that terrible time was hard, harder than anything he'd ever done. Made all the more difficult because he cared about her, cared what she thought of him, both as a man and a cop. But she had to know the ugly truth. Maybe once she realized how flawed he was, the attraction that flared between them would fade, and she'd stay well away.

He heaved a breath. "The reporters believe I was having an inappropriate relationship with the mother, and because of that, I didn't suspect her until it was too late." He picked up a pebble and tossed it over the bank. "They were wrong. I felt sorry for Marissa. Who wouldn't? Her child had been kidnapped, and she was distraught, but I didn't cross the line. We didn't have an affair, no matter what she, her lawyer, or the media say."

A crow landed on a fir bough in a nearby tree, its weight bending the branch. The big, black bird's chestnut-colored eyes met his, and it cawed as if mocking him.

A sudden lassitude descended, and all he wanted to do was lie down, close his eyes, and sink into oblivion. He gritted his teeth until his jaw ached. He wouldn't take the coward's way out. He'd started this sordid tell-all; he was damn well going to finish. Candace deserved the complete and unvarnished truth.

"I didn't sleep with her, if that's what you're wondering." He heaved a shaky breath. "But what I did was a thousand times worse." He slipped off his cap and threaded his fingers through his hair. "I was so certain I knew who the culprit was, I ignored the evidence that was right in front of me. I believed everything that woman said, every damn lie." A long silence ensued. Tears burned his eyes, but he blinked them back. "I blame myself for that little girl's death."

"So that's why you didn't defend yourself." Her voice was soft, as if her throat was coated with liquid honey. "You think you deserved to be punished. You believe Marissa killed her daughter because you didn't stop her in time."

"I should've seen through her lies. That's my job— to find the bad guys before they hurt anyone." He met her gaze even though he knew his eyes must be streaked with red and tear-filled. "All the signs pointed at Marissa, but I thought I knew better. A child paid the price for my arrogance."

She shifted closer and rested her hand on his thigh. "You can't blame yourself for what happened. Marissa was a liar and a manipulator. She would've murdered her daughter no matter what you did. You were the scapegoat."

He stared into her eyes, desperate to believe her, but the burden of guilt was too entrenched and refused to ease. "We're wasting time sitting here rehashing the past. Nothing's going to change what happened. I screwed up. Nothing will bring that little girl back." He lurched to his feet. "Let's get going."

She stood and faced him, her hands on her slim hips. "Are you finished with your little pity party?"

He blinked.

"It's time you stopped blaming yourself and cut yourself some slack. You did the best you could with the information you had." Two bright spots of red stained her cheeks. Her blue eyes flashed fire. "You're a good cop. You really care about the people you help. If you'd had the slightest indication the mother was the kidnapper, you'd have arrested her. I know that, and you do too."

He wiped his hand over his damp eyes. Could she be right, and he wasn't at fault? Was that even a possibility? For the first time in over a year, he didn't hate himself.

She moved a step closer. "Look. You know my story. I've lived with survivor's guilt most of my life. I wake up at night blaming myself for Charlene's disappearance."

"You were just a kid. It wasn't your fault. If you'd woken up when the perp was in your room, he could've killed you, or taken you too."

"You don't understand. It *was* my fault." Her eyes glistened with tears. "I left the front door unlocked."

"What?"

She nodded. "Yep. It was me. There was a special type of full moon that night, and I wanted to see it. After everyone was in bed, I snuck outside. When I came back inside, I forgot to lock the front door." She shuddered. "If it weren't for my stupid mistake, the man who took Charlene wouldn't have been able to get into the house. He would have gone somewhere else."

Silence settled over them. Birds tweeted in the bushes, the crow cawed again, insects buzzed, but he stood there, frozen, locked into her tortured gaze. The same painful shadows that he saw reflected in his eyes every morning when he looked in the mirror dulled her blue eyes.

In the next breath, he was holding her in his arms. What started as an offer of comfort and compassion, transformed into something else, something beyond his control. He kissed her sweet lips, and one kiss led to another and another. He couldn't get enough.

She pressed her body closer, her soft curves melding with his muscular hardness.

He loosened her braid and tangled his fingers through her silky hair. His chest heaved, and his blood heated and headed south.

Her moan was the sweetest music he'd ever heard, and he deepened the kiss, exploring her warm, moist mouth. He smoothed his hands over the swell of her hips.

Tracker barked, the sharp sound acting like a splash of cold water.

Sanity returned, and he dropped his arms and stumbled back a step. "I'm sorry. I shouldn't have done that." *Shouldn't have done that*? Hell, that was an understatement. He was on the job. Kissing her was all shades of wrong. He was supposed to be grilling her, not making out. Lives were at stake, hers especially.

Her face was unreadable, her eyes dark, the pupils dilated. Her mouth was red and swollen from their kisses, her cheeks flushed.

She smoothed the tendrils of hair he'd freed with his passion and inhaled a breath. "We're quite a pair, aren't we? Both so filled with guilt, that's all we see."

A rush of warmth flooded him. She understood. She got him. Just like he got her.

Oh man. He was done for.

He liked this woman. God help him. He really liked her.

Chapter 21

Hefting the pack over his shoulders, he whistled for Tracker, and motioned for Candace to take the lead. "Show me the way."

She pointed along the narrow deer trail to a twisted tangle of willows and prickle bushes. A pink ribbon flapped in the breeze. "The footprints headed into the forest there." She moved off the trail and into the bush.

He followed, wincing as brambles grabbed at his clothes, and he stumbled over unseen roots and rocks.

Tendrils of sun filtered through the leafy branches high above and dappled the forest floor where a thick layer of pine needles covered the ground and muffled their footsteps. Green moss coated the north-facing sides of the thick, scarred tree trunks.

"What are you hoping to find?" He brushed past a cobweb where a huge black spider lurked on a shiny silken thread. The high-pitched whine of a mosquito filled his ear, and he slapped the back of his neck. "The K9 squad searched this area, and they didn't locate any signs other than the scent of human blood—" He jerked his thumb behind him. "—and that was back there."

"I know this is probably a waste of time, but I have to do something. I can't sit at home waiting for…" She shrugged. "I just want to do whatever I can to find Amanda Jacobs."

He brushed a pine needle from her cheek. "You're

pretty sure those footprints you saw were hers, aren't you?"

Her cheeks flushed pink. "I don't know, but someone was out there that day. And they were injured."

His fingers lingered on her soft skin. The alarm bells in his brain rose to a deafening clamor. He jerked his hand back. "Okay, let's see what we can find." Her gaze met his, and once again there was that instant connection, the one that both warmed his soul and terrified the shit out of him.

"Great." She picked up a stick and tossed it for Tracker.

The dog bolted, returning in seconds, the stick clenched in his mouth. He dropped it at her feet and sat, tail wagging, hope glistening in his beseeching gaze.

Aiden prayed his own face didn't carry the same look of desperate longing as his dog's.

"I can't help feeling there's something here, something everyone's missed." She turned an imploring gaze on him. "What if the footprints I saw belonged to Amanda? What if she escaped her captor and was running for help, and I let her down?" She swiped her glistening eyes. "What if I could have saved her?"

Against his better judgment, he touched her arm. The jolt of electricity staggered him, but he didn't remove his hand. Not this time. A man was only so strong. "You did everything you could. You called the police. They searched the area, and we had the scent dogs here a week ago. There's nothing more could've done."

She wiped her damp eyes with the back of her hand. "I want to find her. I don't want her to end up like my sister." Her voice choked, breaking on a sob. "I don't want her family to suffer."

He gathered her in his arms again and held her close. The embrace felt even better this time. "Hey. It's okay." Her perfume, something floral and infinitely feminine, washed over him, and he smoothed tendrils of silken hair off her damp face. "We'll find her. I promise you. If not today—tomorrow, or the next day—but we *will* find her."

He regretted the words the second they were out of his mouth. How could he make that promise? Amanda Jacobs had been missing more than three months. The odds of finding her alive after all this time were a billion to one.

But he was going to try to find her. He'd promised her parents, and now Candace, so he was going to give the search for the missing girl his damnedest.

****

Candace burrowed deeper into Aiden's embrace, seeking comfort and reassurance, and easing of her guilt. A stick landed on her foot with a heavy thunk, and she looked down and smiled in spite of her tears.

Tracker perched in front of her, his liquid brown eyes gazing at her, pawing her foot. He whined and jumped back, his rear end raised, his bushy tail waving like a flag. The stick, the bark wet with slobber, lay on the ground at her feet.

Aiden released her and stepped back.

Embarrassed at her meltdown, she fumbled in her pocket for a tissue and mopped her wet eyes and blew her nose.

Tracker barked and pawed her foot again.

"Okay. Okay." She picked up the slobber-covered

stick and tossed it far into the thick bush. "Good luck finding that."

Tracker blasted after the stick.

"Are you okay?"

Aiden's quiet voice reached her over Tracker's excited barking. She nodded, still not meeting his gaze. "I'm not usually so emotional." Well, that was an outright lie. Ever since the attack the other night, she'd been a basket case. She'd lost track of the number of times she'd broken down.

"A missing child is a terrible thing." His deep voice filled the space between them. "You, more than most people, know that. We all want to help. We all want to find Amanda."

A heavy silence descended, broken only by Tracker's distant barking, the wind rustling in the trees, and a crow croaking atop a nearby tree.

Aiden cleared his throat. "Do you want to head back?"

The air was rich with the fragrance of new leaves, rich, dark loam, and growing plants. The sky was a clear azure blue, and the sun, filtering through the branches, was a warm caress on her shoulders. Giant pine trees towered above her, their twisted roots creating humps like serpents in the soft ground. A bee buzzed, flitting from one brilliantly colored wildflower to another.

She inhaled a deep, restoring breath. "I'd like to keep going, if you have the time." If they stumbled across some sort of indication Amanda had been in the woods, so much the better. If they didn't, at least she'd escaped the stuffy confines of her house, and a respite from her constant fear that someone was watching.

His forehead furrowed. "Are you sure?"

She spread her arms wide. "This day's too beautiful to waste."

His frown didn't ease.

"Unless you have to be back at work?"

"I do have a lot of work to do, but I still have a few questions about the attack the other night that I need to ask you." He rubbed his whiskered cheeks. "Let's find a lunch spot, and we can talk. Is that okay?"

A few questions.

Her heart skipped a beat. For a moment, she'd forgotten he was a cop, forgotten why he showed up at her door that morning. Tagging along with her on this walk was his way of getting her to open up. He was there for work. Only work. She'd best not forget that. "Sure." Her voice was flat.

"Great." He whistled.

Tracker bounded into the small clearing, a stick clenched between his teeth.

"Come on, boy."

They headed into dense undergrowth, following the slight indentation of a narrow game trail.

He led the way, holding branches for her as he thrust through the tangle of willows and wild rose bushes.

After fifteen minutes of tough slogging, they broke through into a small clearing where a narrow stream trickled over moss-covered boulders lining the banks. The soft ground was wet and spongy from the previous night's rain.

"Damn." Aiden's curse broke the silence.

She couldn't help giggling at the frown on his handsome face. His once-pristine white sneakers were covered in mud. "You really should buy a pair of hiking boots."

He grunted, and sloshed on, sinking up to his laces in muck.

They followed the stream along the narrow, winding deer trail and scrambled up a steep bank to a ridge.

Puffing from the rigorous climb, she paused and took in the surrounding view. Green forest stretched before her with no trace of civilization, no clear-cuts or buildings, nothing but a vast expanse of mature pine and fir forest and the winding ribbon of the river sparkling in the sunshine. They were in the backcountry where few park visitors ventured.

A haunting, echoing screech split the air, and high above, a bald eagle soared on the air currents in the azure sky.

"Man. This sure is pretty." Aiden pointed at the stunning view. "Have you been to this area of the park before?"

She shook her head. "I usually head east toward the river and Mercer Lake."

"I don't know about you, but I'm starving, and this looks like a great place for lunch." He shrugged out of the backpack and set it beside a large boulder. On the way to the park, they'd stopped at a deli, and he'd picked up a sandwich for himself, and a raw beef bone for Tracker.

They perched on top of the boulder, and he munched on his shaved beef and beet relish on dark rye.

She bit into the ham-and-cheese sandwich she'd made and grimaced. The bread was dry, and the cheese stale. It was all she could do to swallow it down.

He must've noticed her eyeing his yummy-looking feast because he held up his sandwich. "You want half?"

Her mouth filled with moisture, but she shook her head, and nibbled at her sandwich, fighting to hide her displeasure.

He swiped the back of his hand over his mouth. "Look, here's the deal—I'll eat half of your sandwich, and you can have half of mine. Okay?" Before she could refuse, he picked up the other half of her ham-and-cheese and took a big bite.

She grabbed the sandwich half he offered before he changed his mind. The first bite was heaven, the next even better, and she couldn't help the moan of appreciation that escaped her mouth.

He chuckled. "I know, right? Delicious." He chomped another bite of the ham-and-cheese sandwich, swallowed, frowned, and grabbed for the water bottle and slugged back a drink.

"Something wrong with your sandwich?" she asked, hiding a smile.

He drank more water. "It's—"

"I'm sorry." She laughed. "I haven't been to the store in a while, and that sandwich was the best I could do with what was in the fridge. Not my best effort." His rich, male laughter shot a frisson of heat to her core.

"Like I said, it's—" He coughed and gulped more water.

"Edible," she supplied. "I really am a decent cook. You should try my spaghetti carbonara." She put two fingers together and kissed the tips. "Delicious."

His laughter stilled, and his dark eyes smoldered. "Is that an invitation?"

The moisture in her mouth evaporated, and all she could think was, *yes, please, yes*. But enough common sense remained that she kept her mouth shut and didn't say a word, though her heart raced.

An awkward silence prevailed. The tweeting of birds was drowned out by the sound of Tracker gnawing on his bone.

Aiden finished his last bite, brushed crumbs from his pants, crumpled the packaging from the sandwiches, and stuffed it into the daypack. "What did you do to get on the wrong side of my partner?"

"Detective Breacher?"

He nodded.

Heat climbed her neck and flooded her face. "He didn't tell you?"

"Joe and I—" He shook his head. "—we don't talk much." His dislike of his partner was written across his handsome face.

That didn't surprise her. The two men couldn't be more different. Detective Breacher was prickly, to say the least, and Aiden was... Well, Aiden was pretty darn charming.

Focus on his question. The admonition blazed through her, and she sat up straighter and faced him. "After Charlene was abducted, my family never recovered." Even to her own ears, her voice sounded wooden, as if she were describing events that had happened to someone else, events that hadn't destroyed her family and left behind a lifetime of guilt.

His jaw hardened. "It must've been terrible."

"It was. It still is." She blinked back tears. "But Charlene's disappearance was worse for my parents. They passed away several years ago, but after Charlene was taken, they went through hell wondering if they'd ever see their daughter again.

"Our lives were never the same. We didn't stop searching, not for one minute. Over the years, my parents hired countless private investigators to look for her. They remortgaged the house so they could offer a reward. They even went to a psychic who promised to help." She picked up a pebble and tossed it over the bank. "As the months and years passed, they lost hope. They died without knowing where their daughter was or even if she were still alive." She hiccupped a sob. "You don't know what that's like. No one does, not really, not until something bad happens." She tossed another rock.

He rested his hand on her knee and gently squeezed, offering unspoken support.

She inhaled a deep, steadying breath. "After my parents died, I continued the search for Charlene. The police, with all their experts, couldn't find her, so I determined I'd do everything in my power to find my sister and the monster who took her.

"I went to the police station almost every day and pleaded with the authorities to keep searching." Her face heated. "I don't blame them for being annoyed. I was a pain in the ass, but I refused to stop. My sister is out there somewhere. I'm the only one left, the only one who cares. I have to find her." She bit her lip hard to stop the fresh tears. "I have to."

She swallowed past the lump in her throat. "The police are convinced Charlene's dead. They found traces of her blood in the farmhouse—lots of blood. But I know she's alive. I know it deep in here—" She patted her heart. "—and I refuse to give up looking."

She played with her hair, smoothing the tangled strands with her fingers, avoiding his gaze. "Detective Breacher was assigned to the case. He wasn't a detective then. He was a rookie, but I was angry the cops had given up on Charlene, and I blamed him. I organized a press conference, and I called Breacher out in front of the media for not doing his job." She swatted a mosquito that landed on her arm. "He didn't appreciate that."

Tracker grabbed his bone in his mouth and loped off into the surrounding forest.

"I get it. You want closure." Aiden picked up a twig and twirled the stick between his fingers. "You want to know the truth about what happened to your sister. You want the man who took her and the other girls, caught and punished. No one blames you for that."

"Breacher does." She inhaled a deep breath. "I may not have gone about the situation in the most diplomatic manner. He was the officer who came to our house the morning after Charlene was abducted." She chewed on her bottom lip, worrying the cut. "He assured my parents she'd run away and would be back home soon. He didn't believe them when they told him she didn't have a boyfriend, and she'd never leave home willingly. Not without saying goodbye."

"What did Breacher do?"

"It was more like, what he *didn't* do." She rubbed the back of her neck. "He didn't do *anything*. He wouldn't even open a file and told us we had to wait forty-eight hours before we could report her missing."

She waved away a buzzing insect. "If it hadn't been for my mom finding the blood on Charlene's pillowcase the next morning, two days would've passed before the cops returned to investigate. Two days! Can you believe that?"

She blew out a breath, fighting to calm the fury that exploded out of her when she thought of Joe Breacher and his incompetence. "Once the investigators found the blood spatter on her pillow, they started looking into the case. But by then, it was too late. Isaiah took my sister and drove sixteen hours across the state to that farmhouse where he held her and the other girls captive until the cops raided it three weeks later."

Aiden nodded. "You've blamed Breacher ever since."

Her cheeks flamed. "I may have overreacted. I mean, he was new on the job, and he was following protocol. I shouldn't have set up that news conference. I shouldn't have said what I did, but I was angry, and I blamed him for so many things...for not acting sooner, for not realizing the missing girls' cases were connected, for not finding my sister." She swiped at her damp eyes. "I even blamed him for my parents' deaths. I called him an incompetent fool."

"That explains why he has a chip on his shoulder where you're concerned."

She nodded. "In my defense, he messed up, and evidence that could've helped find Charlene was compromised or ignored until it was too late."

"I haven't worked with Joe long, but I think he means well. He's just a little rough around the edges."

She fished in the backpack, pulled out two granola bars, and handed him one. "I'm going to have to beg to disagree with you on that."

Sharp, frantic barking cracked the air, and Tracker

burst through the forest and galloped to Aiden, circling his feet, barking.

"What's wrong, boy? What is it?" Aiden asked.

The dog whined and tucked his tail between his back legs.

Aiden crouched and petted Tracker, but the dog refused to be comforted and ran toward the trees, stopped, and raced back to Aiden. "Something has him upset." He shot her a look. "You stay here. I'll see what this is about. He can't have gone far. He was just burying his bone."

She opened the flap on the holster on her hip, tugged out the can of bear spray, and slid back the plastic trigger guard. "I'm coming with you." He opened his mouth as if he were about to argue, but she stopped him. "I was a Girl Scout." She held up the canister. "Always prepared."

He nodded. "All right. Let's go."

Chapter 22

Aiden followed Tracker into the dense bush, shoving aside branches and clambering over gnarled roots and downed trees. Candace was so close behind that when he slowed to thrust a branch out of the way, she stumbled into him. Not that he minded. Not. At. All. The brush of her soft womanly curves against his back felt good. Damn good.

Tracker's barking grew more frantic.

Aiden frowned. What the hell was Tracker's problem? Had he spotted a bear? His heartbeat kicked up a notch, and he patted the revolver strapped to the holster under his light jacket. Bear spray was all well and good, but there was nothing like a bullet to the heart to stop a charging beast.

He wiped sweat from his brow and hurried his steps to keep up with the excited dog. Candace, no slouch in the fitness department, stuck to his heels. Damn dog. He should be tracking down clues to find the missing girl or questioning Candace like the captain had ordered him to do instead of chasing after a dog that was probably on the hunt after a squirrel. He opened his mouth to call Tracker back but stopped.

Tracker paced in tight circles, whining, his tail between his legs, his ears back. Casting an imploring look at Aiden, he darted behind a clump of wild rose bushes, disappearing into the thick vegetation.

"What's with him?" Candace mopped her gleaming face with a tissue she'd tugged from her pocket.

"I don't know. I've never seen him behave this way." He wiped the sweat off his brow and peered through the shrubbery. "Tracker! Come here, boy."

Tracker's excited barking echoed hollowly as if he were in a large, empty room.

Aiden shoved the prickly branches aside, wincing as tiny thorns pierced his skin. Fragrant pastel-pink rose petals floated to the ground. Hidden behind the thick tangle of vegetation was an opening in the rocks.

"Is that a cave?" Candace leaned over his shoulder, her warm body brushing his.

He sucked in a breath at the contact but forced his focus on the narrow fissure. "I'm not sure, but Tracker's in there." The hole was recessed beneath an overhanging rock ledge and was hidden by the prickly wild rose bushes and thick tangle of green leafy plants. "Here, boy."

The dog didn't appear.

Aiden glanced at his watch. He didn't have time for Tracker's antics. "Looks like I'm going to have to go in and get him."

"Take this." Candace pressed a small LED flashlight into his hand.

"You weren't kidding about being prepared, were you?" The desire to taste her lips again hit him like a blow to the solar plexus.

She grinned. "I told you I was a Girl Scout." Her smile widened. "I also have a GPS, a whistle, and a topo map of the park stuffed in my pack."

"You're quite the gal." With her flushed face,

tangle of long, shining dark hair, and brilliant blue eyes, she was achingly beautiful. Every cell in his body reacted, and he gawked like a schoolboy with his first crush, unable to look away.

The splashing river, chirping birds, buzzing insects, and Tracker's frantic barking faded into the background. Drawn by a powerful force, he leaned closer, his gaze fixed on her mouth.

Tracker's barking amped up and sliced through his daze. Aiden stiffened and dragged his gaze away from her moist lips. An odd mix of relief and regret washed over him. Saved by Tracker.

Man's best friend.

Maybe.

He shot Candace what he hoped was a stern look. "Wait here." Tightening his grip on the flashlight, he crouched, and twisting and turning, squeezed his head and shoulders through the tight opening. Razor-sharp rocks scraped his back like claws, and jagged pebbles gouged his knees and palms.

Once through, he stood and brushed dirt and rocks from his jeans. Streaks of light filtered through the matted vegetation, revealing a cavernous dark space. He switched on the flashlight and inched forward. The thin beam of light didn't pierce the inky darkness more than a few feet, and it was impossible to determine how big the cave was.

The air was heavy with the scents of damp earth, the sour tang of decay, animal feces, and creatures long dead and rotten. He shone the beam of light overhead. The rocky ceiling, stained with streaks of rust and yellow, arched high above. A dark furry mass shifted, and high-pitched squeaks resounded as a colony of bats protested the light intrusion.

Tracker burst out of the darkness and sprang toward Aiden, knocking him back a step, licking Aiden's face, slobbering over his shirt in his joy at seeing him.

Aiden ruffled the soft fur behind Tracker's ears. "What the heck are you doing in here, boy?"

Tracker barked, turned toward the rear of the cave, ran a few steps, looked back at Aiden, and barked again.

The streak of daylight streaming through the narrow entrance darkened, and Candace crawled into the cave. She stood and brushed dirt off the knees of her canvas hiking pants. "Wow. This cave is huge. I wonder how many people know it's here. It's not marked on the park map." Her eyes shone in the dim light cast by the flashlight. "The early indigenous people who lived in this area probably used this cave as a shelter or place of worship. There could be pictographs on the walls or projectile points buried in the dirt."

"I hate to burst your bubble, professor, but look over there." He directed the beam of light toward a blackened ring of rocks surrounding charred chunks of wood, burned and crushed tin cans, and half-melted plastic water bottles. "We're not the first modern people to find the cave."

She crossed to the fire ring and picked up a stick with a charred end and stirred the gray coals. A cloud of soot and ash floated in the air. She crouched and brushed ash aside. "What's this?" She picked up a small chunk of red plastic. "It looks like a hair clip."

"Put that down." Tension made his voice sharper

than he intended.

Her brow furrowed. "What?"

"Please put that back where you found it."

The lines scoring her brow deepened, but she did as he asked and set the clip in the gray ash of the firepit. She wiped her hands on her pants. "What's wrong?"

He tugged out his cell phone from his back pocket, powered it on, and nodded his chin at the red barrette. "I've seen a hair clip like that before."

She exhaled a gust of air. "Of course you have. They sell them in town at Bernadette's Bits & Bobs. Lots of girls wear them in their hair."

He stared at his phone screen. *Come on, come on.* The damn phone was taking forever. Finally, the small screen lit with a blue-white glow. No bars. He wasn't surprised. Even if the park had cell service, the thick stone walls of the cave would block reception.

Tapping the photo icon, he waited for his bank of crime scene photos to open. He flipped through the photos until he found the picture he wanted. Amanda Jacobs's youthful face grinned back at him. It was the photo from the missing person's poster, the picture her parents had given to the police. He enlarged the picture. At this high resolution, the image was blurry, but clear enough. His gut tightened. Holding Amanda's long black hair back from her face on one side was a red plastic hair clip with a raised flower design on one end.

Heart pounding, he crouched and picked up the barrette and held it in the palm of his hand. The clip was partially melted, its daisy-shaped design distorted by the heat of the fire, but there was no question—the piece of red plastic was a girl's hair clip, the same color and design as the one in the photo. He reached into his coat pocket and slipped out a small plastic evidence bag and tilted his palm and slid the clip into the bag. Sealing the bag, he stuffed it in his shirt pocket.

"What's going on, Aiden? Why is that barrette so important?"

"Amanda Jacobs has a similar red hair clip." He showed her his phone screen.

Her gasp was loud in the cavernous space. "Oh my God. *She* was here." She pressed her hand to her chest. "Amanda was in this cave, wasn't she?"

His heart raced as she vocalized his thoughts. "Let's not jump to conclusions. This hair clip could have belonged to anyone. Lots of girls use them. Like you said, you can buy them in town." He knew that for a fact. As part of his investigation into the case, he'd noticed the red barrette in Amanda's hair and checked the local stores. Bernadette's Bits & Bobs sold the same barrette in a variety of colors.

"It's hers. I know it is." Her eyes widened. "That means those footprints I saw last fall could have been Amanda's." Her face paled. "But how did her barrette end up in this cave? Did—"

He held up his hand to silence her.

"What is it?" She shuddered and wrapped her arms around her chest. "Is there something in here? A wild animal?"

He shook his head. "I can't imagine any beast would still be in here with the way Tracker was barking up a storm." Yet, his inner alarm bells were going off like a four-alarm blaze. He ran the beam of light over the cave floor. The hard-packed dirt was covered in dried leaves, twigs, and heaps of tree needles blown in by winds. It was impossible to make out tracks, certainly no human ones, but the floor was scuffed as if someone or something had moved about.

There could be any number of explanations for a girl's hair barrette to be in this hidden cave. The fire pit contained melted plastic water bottles and metal food tins. Maybe a family out for a hike had run into a rainstorm and sought shelter in the cave. But what if Candace was right? Amanda Jacobs's kidnapper could've used the cave to hold her. No one knew about the cave's existence. No one would think to look for Amanda there. He swallowed, but his mouth was bone dry. But if that were the case, where was she now?

Tracker barked and dashed into the back recesses of the dark cave.

High above, the bats squeaked and fluttered.

The hairs on the back of Aiden's neck prickled. Some scent had attracted the dog to the cave, an odor that made him nervous. Tracker had never run off before, but today he'd crawled through a hidden rock fissure into a cave. He shot Candace a glance. "Wait here."

Her pale face shone with a ghostly luminescence under the flashlight's glow. "Are you kidding? I'm not staying here by myself." She held up the can of bear spray. "Besides, you might need this."

He wasn't surprised she refused to do as he asked. She was strong-willed. She'd shown amazing fortitude in the face of adversity and survived the ordeal of her sister's kidnapping and gone on to achieve a successful career at the college. "Okay. But stay behind me."

Shining the thin beam of light into the stygian darkness, he clasped her hand and crept toward the sound of Tracker's excited barking. After a few steps, the cave narrowed, and the rock walls pressed in. The floor sloped downward, and piles of broken branches, dried leaves, and old animal feces littered the uneven ground.

Tracker stopped barking, and in the ensuing silence, the steady drip of water, and the furious pounding of Aiden's heart were deafening.

The scratch of nails on bare rock grew louder, and Tracker trotted toward them, his tail waving like a flag.

"What's that in his mouth?" Candace's whisper reverberated against the damp walls. "It doesn't look like a stick."

Aiden crouched and grasped Tracker's collar. "Drop it, boy."

The dog dropped the object and sat, tail swishing the dirt, panting, waiting for praise.

Aiden petted Tracker's big velvety head. "Good boy." But he wasn't looking at the dog. His attention zeroed in on the long, cream-colored object lying on the dirt.

Candace inched nearer. "Is that what I think it is?"

He focused the beam of light on the bone. The long shaft was about a foot long with rounded ends. His gut twisted. "I have a bad feeling about this."

She crouched beside him. "Can you shine the light closer?"

He angled the light, so the brightest stream spilled over the bone. "What do you think?" She was an anthropology professor, and from what little he knew of the discipline, physical anthropologists studied ancient human remains. Maybe she could tell if they were looking at a human bone or an animal one.

She picked up a twig and nudged the bone closer.

"This is a tibia."

"A tibia?"

"A shinbone. You know, the long bone that connects your knee to your ankle."

His heart lurched. "Are you saying it's human?"

She shrugged. "I'm not one hundred percent certain. Deer tibias are similar in size and shape to human shinbones. I'd need to do a microscopic study of the bone's interior to be sure. Animal bones are denser than humans."

"So, it's a deer bone?" Some of the tightness in his chest eased. A predator had dragged its kill into the cave. That explained everything.

She sat back on her heels and met his gaze. "Maybe. But if I had to guess, I'd say the bone is human." She wiped her cheek leaving a smudge of dirt on her pale skin. "If we had more pieces of the skeleton, I could be certain."

He pointed into the darkness ahead. "Tracker found the bone back there." His mind whirled with a dozen scenarios, none of them good.

Tracker was a cadaver dog, trained to search out human remains. The poor animal was still agitated.

That could only mean one thing—there were more bones. He heaved a breath and stood. "He's already contaminated the area, but we'll have to be careful. This cave could be a crime scene. Let's have a look."

They shuffled toward the rear of the cave, and he swept the beam of light over the scuffed dirt floor. His heart thumped as if he'd run a marathon, and his breath huffed in and out. He patted his gun, finding comfort in its familiar bulk, tempted to slide it free of its holster. The cave narrowed, and he crouched down and placed his hand on Candace's arm. "Careful. Ceiling's low here. You don't want to bump your head."

She nodded and sank to her knees.

A few more crawling steps, and the penlight's beam swept over a pile of freshly disturbed dirt and a ragged hole where Tracker had dug into the soft ground. The depression was the size of the bone Tracker had found.

"Look." Her voice was hushed as if she were afraid of disturbing the denizens of the cave. She pointed a few feet away where a cream-colored bone jutted out of the dark earth. Crawling closer, she brushed the loose dirt from the exposed bone with the back of her hand revealing a larger object. She fell back on her heels. "Oh my God!"

Moisture drained from his mouth, and the day took a serious turn for the worse. "Awww, shit."

Chapter 23

The skull was human. You didn't need her expertise as a physical anthropologist to determine that. The elongated shape, the presence of a chin, the size of the empty eye orbits, left no doubt. The flesh had rotted, but fine strands of long dark hair clung to a patch of desiccated scalp.

"Is that what I think it is?" Aiden's deep voice resonated in the cavern.

"It's a human skull." She licked her dry lips. Were these the remains of the person who'd left the bare footprints in the snow last November? Amanda Jacobs? Her heart skittered.

"Is the skull old?" He cleared his throat. "I mean, can you tell how long it's been in the cave?"

She sucked in a ragged breath. "There's very little weathering, so it's not prehistoric." Using light, feathery strokes, she brushed away more dirt and pointed at the skull's gaping mouth. "Shine the light here." She squinted under the bright beam, trying to bring the skull into focus. Damn it. She should have brought her glasses.

He angled the pinpoint of light. "What are you looking for?"

She eased the jaw open, exposing a set of even white teeth. Her heart sank. Picking up a twig and using it as a pointer, she tapped a dull silver discoloration in a back molar. She pointed at another similar marking in another molar. "These are modern dental fillings."

He sucked in a noisy breath. "How old was the vic—" The clearing of his throat was loud in the dark cave. "How old was the person when they died? Can you tell?"

She knew what he was thinking, and she shared his fear, praying she was wrong. "Teeth are one of the ways to determine the age of the person at the time of death. Throughout our childhood, teeth erupt and are lost according to a predictable time frame." She pointed at the incisors. "These front teeth are permanent adult teeth and would have erupted when this individual was between six and eight years of age."

She squinted in the thin, wavering light. "The permanent teeth are all present. That usually happens when a child is between ten and twelve years old." She gasped and fell back on her heels.

"What is it?"

"Our wisdom teeth usually erupt when we're around eighteen years old." She nodded at the jawbone. "This mandible doesn't have any wisdom teeth." She met his gaze. "The skull belonged to an adolescent." A sob hitched in her throat, and tears blurred her vision. "How did a child's bones end up here?"

Aiden's face was devoid of expression, but the pulse in his jaw ticked like a metronome. "Can you tell if the skull and tibia belonged to a male or a female?"

"There's no pronounced brow ridge." She pointed at the skull's smooth forehead. "Women tend to have a rounded frontal bone like this skull, and female eye sockets are often round with a sharp upper edge." She swiped her hand across her damp face, wiping the

207

streaming tears. "A young male wouldn't have developed a heavy brow ridge." Scooching closer, she feathered more dirt from the skull. "The features of the skull, combined with the length and width of the tibia bone, indicate this person was probably a young female. But I can't be positive."

He gaped at her. "You really know your stuff."

"I've identified human remains in the field before." She swallowed back bile. "But this is different. The bones I unearth in excavations are thousands of years old."

"So, it's possible that these could be Amanda Jacobs's remains."

She shook her head. "I don't think so. The skull and tibia are free of flesh. Amanda's only been missing a few months. Body decomposition begins less than five minutes after death, and there are four distinct stages. A lot of factors affect the rate of decomp—humidity, exposure to the elements, the mineral composition of the soil, animal predation, and even what season of the year it was when the person died. There are…" Her voice trailed off. She was lecturing and telling him more than he probably wanted to know, but stepping into the role of instructor gave her much-needed emotional distance from the horror of the bones.

He waved his hand for her to continue.

"Full skeletonization can take anywhere from a month to a year or more." She pointed at the ground. "The soil in this cave is sandy loam. There's a bit of humidity, but the temperature would be pretty constant. Given that, I'd guess a body wouldn't break down very fast. Three months isn't enough time for the flesh to be this decayed."

He nodded. "So, if these bones aren't Amanda's, whose are they, and how did they end up in this cave? You said it's not on the park map, and even the locals don't know of its existence."

Her gaze skittered over the skull and tibia, and she shivered. Someone knew the cave existed. They'd entered the hidden cavern, built a fire, and heated cans of food. Somehow, a young girl had died in the cold and dark, her body buried in the dirt until scavengers, and Tracker, had dug up her remains.

Aiden's warm breath washed over her. "I know this is hard, but we'll figure out what happened. Trust me."

She leaned into him, desperate for his strength and solidness.

He gently squeezed her arm before releasing her and turning toward the entrance. "Come on. Let's get out of here before we compromise the scene any more than we have."

She didn't budge. "We're not leaving the bones. We can't. It's not right."

He smoothed a strand of hair behind her ear. "This cave is most likely a crime scene. The forensic technicians will want everything left as we found it."

"But—"

"I'm sorry, Candace, but we have to leave them. It's the only way we can find what happened. Somewhere, someone is looking for her, grieving her loss, filled with questions, just like your family. They deserve to know." He crossed to the entrance and gestured for her to crawl through the narrow fissure. "Now come on. Let's go so I can call for back up."

With a last look at the haunting skull and its empty eye sockets staring up at the ceiling, she squeezed between the slabs of rock and emerged into blinding sunshine. It was still daylight. Impossible to believe less than an hour had passed since they'd entered the cave.

Tracker bounded through the opening, followed by Aiden.

"Come on. Let's find that cell service." He stuffed the flashlight into the backpack, hefted the nylon straps over his shoulders, and grasped her hand. "Are you okay?"

A lump welled in her throat at the compassion in his warm hazel eyes. She nodded, though she wasn't okay. Not by a long stretch. Finding the skull and tibia, and knowing someone, probably a young girl, had died in the cave hit her hard, and resurrected all her past grief and guilt.

Dark shadows filled his eyes turning them a deep-sea green. "Attagirl."

Their gazes connected, and for a heartbeat, she forgot the shock of finding the human bones and lost herself in his warm, approving gaze.

He coughed, cleared his throat, and looked away, but he kept his long warm fingers threaded with hers. "Let's go."

They didn't speak as they hurried back to the parking lot, not stopping for rest or water breaks.

As if he sensed their urgency, Tracker trotted at Aiden's heels, not pestering them with sticks to throw.

They didn't encounter any other hikers on the trail, and by the time they reached the parking lot, the sun was on its way down. Theirs was the only vehicle.

She peered into the lengthening shadows under the looming trees, afraid the man with the dark beard was watching from the shadows. But other than a crow cawing from atop a lofty fir tree, chickadees flitting amongst the aspen leaves, and a squirrel scurrying across the rough ground, the forest was deserted.

Aiden unlocked the car and opened the passenger door. Before she slid in, he touched her arm, stopping her. "We'll figure this out. I promise."

Inches separated them, and she sucked in a shaky breath. Her eyes were level with his chin, revealing the dark shadow of whiskers. "Aiden—" His name expelled in a gust of air. Her arm tingled where he'd touched her. She gulped and fought to focus on the day's shocking discovery. "Why didn't the K9 unit find the bones in the cave?"

"I don't know." His brow furrowed. "That area was beyond the search parameters. The cave's thick stone walls could've blocked the scent unless the dogs were close, like Tracker was." Opening the back door, he ushered Tracker onto the back seat and then slammed the door. Moving around to the driver's side, Aiden opened the door and settled behind the wheel. He tugged out his cell phone from his pants pocket and studied the screen. "Damn. No service."

"You should be able to pick up a few bars a couple of miles down the road."

"Good." He slid his phone back in his pocket. "I'll make the call, and after I drop you at your place, I'll double back and meet the crime-scene techs." He started the car and sped out of the parking lot.

She stared through the windshield, not really seeing the road, or the rich dark earth of the plowed fields prepared for planting, or the yellow-and-purple wildflowers dotting the ditches. An image of the cream-colored bones rose before her, and she swallowed back the acrid taste of bile.

They were almost in the city limits before he spoke. "You saw the strands of hair on the skull?"

"Yes." She rubbed the tightness at the back of her neck.

He slid her a look. "Does hair color change when a body decomposes?"

She frowned, struggling to recall everything she'd learned about body decomposition. "Oxidation can occur and alter the pigment in hair strands, but the hair on that skull was either a very dark brown or black when the person died. I'm certain of that."

"The same color as Amanda Jacobs's hair."

Her heart skipped a beat. "Yes, the same."

He skillfully navigated the rush hour traffic, but his face was bleak, and it was obvious his focus wasn't on the road. "A young woman's body was found in Lynn Canyon yesterday." He clicked on the blinker and pulled into her driveway. Switching off the car's engine, he faced her. His hazel eyes glittered with golden specks in the warm rays of the setting sun. "We haven't ID'd the body yet, but the victim was in her teens, and she had long black hair."

"Both Amanda Jacobs and the murdered girl from Lynn Canyon have long black hair?"

He nodded.

Her heart raced like a trip-hammer in her chest. "Why did you come to my house this morning?"

"I wanted to ask if you remembered any new details about the attack the other night."

She waved his words away with a dismissive flick of her hand. "But that's not really why you were there, was it?"

"No, it wasn't." His gaze strayed to her hair. "Your hair is long and black. Just like the other victims. I believe there may be a connection."

Chapter 24

His shocking words hung in the air like vultures.
She shuddered and touched her hair. "Are you saying
hair color is the connection?"

He stared at her, his gaze assessing. "You tell me."

"Come on. That's ridiculous. The victims are
young girls in their teens. Why would this man target
two different age groups? I'm not an expert, but I watch
crime shows on television, and even I know that's not
how these predators work. They pick a type and stick to
it." She squeezed her hands between her knees to stop
their trembling. A sob hitched in her throat, but she
swallowed it back and clenched her hands so tight the
pain of her nails digging into her palms edged out this
new terror.

Aiden stared out the window, a pulse in his rigid
jaw beating.

The suffocating silence thickened until she
couldn't breathe. "You think—" She swallowed.
"You're saying—" She struggled to swallow again. "—
you're saying I was attacked because of my *hair*
color?"

"No, I'm not saying that. Not at all." He scrubbed
his whiskered chin. "I'm just thinking out loud. Forget
what I said."

Forget what I said.

As if she could forget. Her heart thundered,

threatening to burst through her ribs.

Tracker sat up, leaned his head on the back of her seat, and whined.

Grasping her hands in his warm ones, Aiden eased her fingers open, loosening their death grip. His gaze met hers. "All I'm saying is that until we know more about what's going on, promise me you'll be careful."

A chill rippled along her spine, and she shuddered. "Do you think I'm in danger?"

He didn't respond, but the expression on his handsome face told the truth better than words.

"You don't have to worry about me." She picked up the can of bear spray she'd set on the dash. "If anyone suspicious comes within spitting distance, I'll blast him in the face."

Her feeble attempt at humor failed, and his face remained stony. "Just be careful."

She freed her hands from his, unclasped her seatbelt, and grasped the door handle. She didn't want to leave, dreaded stepping out of his car and entering her empty house. His strong, comforting presence was all that was holding her together. But he had to deal with the remains they'd found in the cave. He was a cop, and he had a job to do. "What happens next?"

"The forensics team is on their way to the park. They'll scour the cave and search for more bones and other evidence." He tapped his fingers on the steering wheel. "If we're lucky, we'll find some clue that will help identify the victim and explain what happened."

She rested her hand on his thigh. "Promise you'll keep me informed." The hard muscles tightened beneath her palm, and a dizzying heat flooded her nether regions. She jerked her hand away, her face on fire, heart pounding. "I know you can't tell me all the details, but please let me know about the remains."

His jaw pulsed, and he studied her with shadowed eyes. "Of course."

"Thank you." She opened the door and climbed out.

"Don't forget this." He reached into the back seat and held out her backpack.

She grasped the strap. "Thanks."

"Thank you for what you did today. If it weren't for your insistence that we head to the park to search for Amanda, we wouldn't have found those bones."

"Tracker did all the work. He's the one who found the cave."

Hearing his name, Tracker stuck his head out of the open back window and woofed.

She petted him. "You were a good boy today, Tracker."

The dog's mouth opened in a wide, toothy grin, and he licked her hand, leaving a trail of drool.

She gave him a final pat and stepped back from the vehicle. "See you later, buddy."

Aiden called from inside the car. "I'll make sure Detective Breacher knows how helpful you were."

She grimaced. "Good luck with that."

He started the engine, and with a quick wave, backed out of her driveway and sped down the street, sirens blaring, lights flashing.

Her body was heavy with exhaustion as she plodded to the front door. Finding the bones was upsetting. The fact the victim was probably a teenage girl was even harder to bear. The victim's family was waiting for their loved one's return, not knowing what happened. Now they'd find out their daughter was never coming home.

Not alive.

But at least they'd have closure. Fishing in her pocket for her house keys, she inserted the key in the lock, and stilled. The nerves on the back of her neck tingled with the primal awareness someone was watching. She spun around, scanning the neighborhood.

A red car passed slowly on the street. The driver tooted the horn, and her next-door neighbor waved and steered the car into his driveway. He opened his door and stepped out. "Hey, Candace. How's it going?"

"Hello, Ron. I'm fine." The lie slid off her lips. He was a good neighbor, always willing to help if he noticed her struggling with some minor house repair. His wife, Myrna, often brought a plate of fresh-baked cookies over for a treat. "How about you?"

"I'm still on the right side of the ground, so can't complain." He chuckled and strode across his lawn to the row of decorative bushes separating the two properties. A frown marred his ruddy face. "A shame about this hedge."

"Hedge?" She tried to gather her thoughts, to focus on what he was saying, but all she could think about were the bones in the cave. "What about the hedge?"

He pointed to a flattened section of evergreen shrubs. "I noticed the damage a few days ago, and I've been meaning to talk to you about it." He shook his head. "Looks to me like some big animal was trying to make a home here." Bending over, he picked up a broken branch. "We're going to have to replant this bush."

Now he had her attention. Her full attention.

"What—" She gulped. "—what sort of animal?"

He shrugged. "Dunno. But whatever it was, it was big. Sure did some damage."

Her hand fluttered to her pounding heart.

"If you're okay with going halves, I'll pick up another few plants on the weekend. Before long, I'll have this hedge looking as good as new."

She stared at the flattened and broken bush, her mind racing. Had someone hidden in the bushes and spied on her? Did that explain her unease these past few weeks?

"Candace? Are you okay?"

She jolted, realizing Ron was talking. Inhaling a shaky breath, she forced a smile to her stiff lips. "I'm fine."

His eyes narrowed. "Are you sure?"

She nodded.

"So, you're okay with me repairing this shrubbery? It shouldn't cost too much. I'll do all the work."

"Yes. Thank you, Ron. That's great."

The frown didn't leave his face. "Myrna and I are just next door if you need anything. You know that, right?"

"Thank you, Ron. You're a good neighbor. I don't know what I'd do without you."

"Well, let's hope you never have to find out." He chuckled. "See you around." He recrossed the lawn to his car and grabbed two bulging plastic bags from the back seat. With a friendly nod, he juggled the bags and his house keys. Managing to open his front door, he disappeared into his house.

She stood, frozen, studying her surroundings. A frisson of unease chilled her spine.

The neighborhood was quiet—no other traffic, the sidewalk and front lawns empty, no barking dogs, or children playing. At this time of day, most of her neighbors were inside their homes preparing supper, and the kids were doing homework.

The sun had gone down behind the distant snowcapped mountains, and streaks of mauve and crimson filled the sky. The streetlights hadn't flickered to life yet, and early evening shadows stretched across the lawn. The neighborhood looked peaceful and normal. So why was she unsettled? Her body was strung so tight she feared her muscles would snap.

The tall row of decorative shrubs separating her front lawn from her neighbor's was filled with shadows. From somewhere inside the tangled bush a branch snapped.

She pressed the palm of her hand over her mouth, cutting off a scream.

Nothing stirred...the leaves didn't tremble...the bushes didn't rustle...nothing.

She forced a shaky laugh. Aiden's warning had set her on edge. She was imagining all sorts of threats where none existed. Finding the bones had amped up her sense of impending doom, but at least she hadn't been alone. Aiden had been with her, and she'd leaned on his calm strength. An image of clinging to his chest, kissing him, caressing the soft hair at the back of his neck, rose before her, and her face flamed. Maybe she'd leaned on him a bit too much.

You think?

She fumbled as she twisted the house key in the lock, turned the door handle, opened the door, and stepped inside. Closing the door behind her, she followed her usual ritual and twisted the deadbolt, slid the security chain home, latched the door lock, and tugged on the door to ensure all the locks held. She set the security alarm, and a sense of relief washed over her when it responded with a familiar, reassuring beep.

Hurrying into the living room, she edged the curtain aside, and peered out. The street was quiet. No stranger watched from the bushes. But her heart still pounded, and she couldn't shake her unease.

She strode back to the front door and rechecked it was securely locked. The alarm showed a steady, reassuring red. Heading to the back door, she ensured all those locks were set. Next, she toured the house, stopping at each window, making certain it was sealed and locked.

Finally able to breathe, she returned to the kitchen and flicked on the overhead light. Turning on the tap, she filled the kettle and set it on the stove. A cup of tea was just what she needed to settle her nerves.

As she waited for the kettle to boil, she stared out the dark kitchen window, unable to ignore the feeling someone was out there watching. Her face, pale and haunted, stared back at her. She shuddered and tugged down the shade covering the window.

For months, she'd been on edge, hyper aware of her surroundings. When the nightly phone calls started, she'd had the locks installed on her doors and windows, and the security system put in. The past few weeks, the sensation she was being watched was so strong she'd started packing mace with her when she left the house.

She grimaced. The mace hadn't helped the other night. Her attacker still managed to drug her. If it hadn't been for those students passing by, who knew what would have happened? She rubbed the goose bumps on her arms.

Ever since Charlene had been abducted, Candace had lived on edge, each day filled with a thousand what ifs, weighed down by a dark burden of guilt. Overnight she'd changed from a happy, carefree twelve-year-old to a shadow, filled with the certain knowledge her sister's abduction was her fault, and her parents wished it was she who'd been taken, and not Charlene.

The man who kidnapped her sister and the other victims was never caught.

The rescued girls described their abductor as tall and broad shouldered, with thick muscles. He had a crescent-shaped scar on his right hand. His hair was long and dark, and he had dark-brown, penetrating eyes, a cruel mouth, and a thick, dark beard.

The police created a composite drawing, and his picture was shown all over the media. A nation-wide manhunt ensued, but somehow, Isaiah eluded capture. To this day, his whereabouts remained a mystery.

Two of the girls had been missing for almost two years; two others had been held captive for six months. Charlene was the most recent girl Isaiah abducted, and the three weeks she was missing felt like an eon to her worried family.

The girls ranged in ages from thirteen to sixteen, and like Charlene, they'd been taken from their bedrooms in the middle of the night. When Candace saw the photo of Amanda Jacobs on the missing person's poster on the bulletin board at the police station, something about the girl's appearance twigged, but she hadn't made the connection.

Not then.

But now that Aiden had pointed it out, the resemblance was impossible to ignore. Amanda Jacobs had long dark hair, *and* she had blue eyes. Just like Charlene. And Candace. She chewed on her bottom lip.

Five young girls were abducted and abused twenty-two years ago. The same nightmare scenario was playing out again, but the perpetrator couldn't be Isaiah. According to the Forgotten Five victims, Isaiah was in his early fifties. He'd be an old man now.

The man who'd attacked her the other night was young, and strong and fit with hard muscles. If the assault on her was connected to the current kidnappings and murders, the attacker wasn't Isaiah. The man who took her sister hadn't returned to unleash a new wave of terror on the community. He couldn't have.

The high-pitched whistle of the kettle pierced her dark thoughts, and she switched off the burner, hefted the steaming kettle, and poured boiling water into the teapot. Grabbing the small pill bottle from the shelf above the sink, she twisted open the cap and tapped out two triangular, green pills and popped them into her mouth.

Her heart rate slowed, and her breathing quieted as an instant wave of relief flooded her bloodstream. She'd been on a steady diet of antianxiety pills since she was twelve, but she'd stopped taking them when she started grad school. For the next ten years, she didn't touch a pill. But ever since she'd found the bloody footprints and encountered the bearded man in the forest, her anxiety had ramped up, and she was back on the pills. She jumped at every sound and constantly looked over her shoulder, fearing a lurking stranger was following her. The violent attack on campus and the nightly phone calls added to her tension.

She poured steaming tea into a mug, added a spoonful of honey, and stirred. The clinking of the spoon against the edge of the ceramic cup was loud in the silent kitchen, and the calming, earthy scent of chamomile filled the room. Holding the mug with both hands, she sipped.

Her cell phone rang, and she choked on a mouthful of hot tea. Her cup fell from her nerveless fingers and shattered on the tile floor. Hot tea and shards of ceramic sprayed across the room. She looked at the wall clock. Her heart jerked.

Her nightly caller! Once again, she'd forgotten to silence the ringer.

The plastic cell phone case vibrated across the countertop as if it were a venomous snake as the phone rang again and again.

The incessant ringing finally stopped, and she released the breath she was holding. Tottering on shaky legs to the counter, she ripped off several sheets of paper towel from the roll under the cupboard and knelt on the floor and mopped at the tea and bits of broken cup.

The phone rang again.

She sagged onto her bottom, uncaring that sticky, warm tea soaked into her pants, and sharp shards of the broken mug dug into her thighs. The anonymous caller phoned night after night, refusing to leave her alone.

Enough!

Tossing the sodden wad of paper towels on the floor, she surged to her feet. Before doubt weakened her resolve, she snatched up the phone and hit the answer button. "What the hell do you want?"

Heavy, labored breathing filled the line.

She closed her eyes and inhaled a shaky breath. "Stop calling me, you jerk. Do you hear me? Stop. Now. Call again, and I'll go to the police." She hit the end button and dropped the phone on the counter. A warm rush of affirmation filled her, and she pumped her fist in the air.

Look at that. She'd stood up to the bully and told him where he could get off. Damn straight she had. The counselors were right—being strong and fighting back felt good. Damn good. She sashayed a little dance across the kitchen.

The phone rang.

The screen read Unknown Caller.

Her elation evaporated like mist in the air, and the bluster vanished, leaving her wilted and teary.

So much for bravery.

Chapter 25

Aiden stared at the flickering computer screen. A lump the size of a block of concrete settled deep in his gut. He scrubbed his hands over his aching eyes and looked again. Nothing had changed. The same shocking report from the medical examiner's office flashed on his screen.

Joe strode over, a mug of coffee gripped in his hand. He sank with a groan onto a chair beside Aiden's desk and stretched out his legs. "What's got you looking so sour this morning?"

Aiden rubbed his two days' growth of whiskers and swiveled the monitor so Joe could see the screen. "This is the report from the ME on those bones Candace Cooper and I found in the cave in Creighton Springs State Park." He pointed at the color photographs of a tibia and a human skull. "The ME sent them to the State lab for examination by their forensic specialist. No question, the bones are human."

"And?" Joe slurped coffee. A few drops dripped onto his shirt, combining with several other stains.

"Candace was right. The skull is from an adolescent female between the ages of twelve and sixteen." He huffed out a breath. "A team of crime scene investigators went over the cave with a fine-toothed comb and found several other bones belonging to the same individual."

Joe grimaced. "Is it Amanda Jacobs?"

Aiden shook his head. "The mineral absorption in the bones indicates they've been in that cave for at least six months. Probably longer."

"Jesus. Another victim." Joe chewed on a fingernail and spat a chunk of nail on the worn linoleum floor. "How'd she die? Can the medical examiner tell cause of death from the bones?"

Aiden shook his head. "Teeth marks on the bones indicate predation by carnivores. After the victim's death, an animal, a bear, or coyote, probably, scavenged the body and scattered the bones about the cave. That's why some are missing."

"Poor kid." Joe plunked his empty cup on the desk with a loud clatter. "Any ID on the bones?"

"Nope." Aiden's gut knotted, and a sour taste filled his mouth. His stomach burned, and he opened his desk drawer and rifled through a tangle of paper clips, loose change, pens, and stacks of sticky notes searching for the bottle of antacids. Grasping the small, plastic container, he unscrewed the child-safety cap and poured out two pink tablets. Stuffing them into his mouth, he chewed, grimacing at the dry, chalky, over-sweet cherry flavor. This case was going to kill him. He'd been popping antacids like candy.

"No one's reported her missing. There's nothing in our data base of a missing teen that fits the time frame." He rubbed his burning gut. "It's like this girl vanished, and no one gave a damn." Anything involving missing kids punched his buttons, but this case was really getting to him. A bunch of missing girls, all with similar physical characteristics, and now these bones that belonged to a young female found in that isolated

226

cave in the state park.

Add in the possibility of a connection to a twenty-two-year-old kidnapping case, and you had a catastrophe of the highest order. How did Candace fit in? Was the attack on campus the other night related? Was it a failed abduction attempt? His brain swirled with all the unanswered questions.

"Earth to Loverboy. Hello? Are you with me, or are you dreaming about that hot Cooper babe? How did your interview go with her anyway?" Joe pursed his fleshy lips. "I can't figure out how you two ended up in that park. Interesting interrogation technique." Joe's voice dripped sarcasm.

Aiden frowned. Joe's disparaging remarks rankled more than usual, especially since they hit so close to the truth. Aiden was attracted to Candace, and he had crossed the line…not once, but twice. An image of holding Candace in his arms and kissing her sweet lips flashed before him. He cleared his throat. "Dr. Cooper's interview went fine." He kept his voice level, hiding his embarrassment.

Joe's smirk widened. "I bet it did." He winked lewdly.

Aiden reined in his annoyance and continued with his report. He tapped the keyboard, and a close-up photo of a human jawbone and teeth appeared on the screen. "The forensic experts compared the teeth of the victim in the cave to dental records of missing teenage girls across the country for the past five years."

"And?" Joe arched his shaggy, gray brows. "What did they find?"

"No match." Another sharp pain stabbed his gut, and Aiden winced. He grabbed the antacids and popped two more pills. "I don't know how her remains ended up in that cave, but I have a bad feeling." He popped another pink tablet. "A real bad feeling."

Joe narrowed his eyes. "So, you think the same perp did the victim in the cave, and the body found in Lynn Canyon, and snatched Amanda Jacobs?"

"Not only that—" Aiden sat forward and clicked buttons on the keyboard. Another image appeared on the screen. "Take a look at this." Earlier, he'd arranged the facial photos of Amanda Jacobs and the victim murdered in Lynn Canyon on a single screen. At the last moment, he'd added one final photo to the lineup.

Joe leaned closer and peered at the screen. He frowned and reached into his shirt pocket and tugged out a pair of reading glasses and slipped them on. "You're shittin' me, right?"

Aiden shook his head. "I wasn't sure at first, but when you look at the photos together, the similarities are impossible to miss." He tapped each photo on the screen with the eraser on the end of his pencil. "All the females are Caucasian, all have long dark-brown or black hair, and all have distinctive blue eyes. They even have similar builds—tall and slim." He sank back on his chair. Every time he looked at these photos, his gut spasmed.

Joe's brow furrowed, and a line carved deep between his bushy gray eyebrows. "I see the similarities between Amanda Jacobs and the murder victim from Lynn Canyon." He rubbed his stubbled chin. "It's a stretch to think they're connected, but it's a possibility." He tapped his finger on one of the photos. "What I don't get is why you included Candace Cooper. Sure, she looks a bit like the other victims, but she wasn't abducted." He sat back and crossed his arms over his barrel chest. "If you ask me, you're so desperate to find this perp, you're seeing patterns where none exist."

Was Joe right? Was Aiden reaching at straws? He studied the array of pictures, and his body tingled with the certainty he was on to something. "Look at her." He stabbed a finger at Candace's photo. "She fits the type…tall, slim, dark hair, blue eyes. Just like the others."

"As do hundreds of other women." Joe's mouth twisted. "She's at least fifteen years older than the other victims. These guys don't usually go for adults…too hard to control."

"I've got a bad feeling that the cases are all connected." Aiden ground down on his back molars. The more he studied the photos, the more certain he was of his theory.

Joe's lip curled. "You've done it again, haven't you?"

"Done what?" Aiden flinched under his partner's stare down.

"You've fallen for that woman." Joe shook his head. "Don't bother to hide it. I can see it in your eyes." He pushed to his feet. "Jesus, man. Why the hell are you going down that rabbit hole again? Didn't you learn your lesson in Seattle? You're already at the ass end of the universe. Do you want to end your career for good?"

Aiden opened his mouth to protest but thought better of it and clamped his lips tight. It killed him to admit it, but Joe was right. Aiden was attracted to Candace. Hell, if he were honest with himself, what he felt for the very pretty college professor was more than simple physical attraction. Something deep inside him sparked when they were together, something visceral and real, something he'd never felt with another woman.

He had to fight his feelings, no matter what it took. He'd been burned before. He couldn't—wouldn't—let the same mistake happen again.

But Candace wasn't anything like Marissa, and the situation was completely different. Candace had nothing to gain by befriending him, and she was a victim, not a suspect in a crime. But he'd thought Marissa was innocent of any wrongdoing too…until she wasn't. Until she proved to be a killer, and an innocent child was dead.

He swallowed back his guilt and misgivings and hit the Print button. Lurching to his feet, he grabbed his worn suede jacket from the back of his chair and shrugged into it.

"Where you goin'?" Joe clamped his hands on his hips, looking for all the world like a stern father demanding to know his teenage son's plans.

"To talk to the captain. She needs to know about this."

"What the hell? You're making a big mistake." Joe's frown deepened.

"Maybe. But it's my mistake to make." He strode to the printer and picked up the paper from the tray. His words sounded braver than he felt. He was putting his career on the line. If this hunch didn't pan out, he'd lose the captain's respect, and probably be demoted to riding a desk in the police station lobby directing people to where to pay their traffic fines.

Joe's glower followed him out of the crowded

detectives' room and down the hall to the captain's beveled-glass door.

He quelled his rumbling gut and tapped on the wood frame.

Captain Cerroli looked up and gestured for him to enter.

He shoved open the door and poked his head in. "Got a minute, Captain?"

She heaved a heavy sigh and nodded. "I suppose. Come in, Farrell." She pointed at the teetering stack of paper on her desk. "Those remains you found in that cave in Creighton Springs State Park have stirred up a hornet's nest. Every police department in the country is sending me photos of missing teens." She tugged off her glasses and rubbed the smudged lenses on the tail of her police-issue blouse. "You wouldn't believe how many missing girls there are in this country. It's a national disgrace."

He met her tired gaze. "I have a pretty good idea." When he worked in Seattle, his assignment was missing persons. It wasn't long before he noticed the majority of the missing were women, and most of those were under twenty-one. A staggering 31,000 girls and young women went missing in the States last year, almost three hundred of them in Colorado alone.

The captain slipped her glasses over her nose and sat back on her chair and crossed her arms over her chest. "Okay. What do you need?"

"Anything new on the bones we found in the cave?"

She flipped through the piles, scattering reports. Grasping one, she read the label and handed it to him. "This just came in. We got an ID, but no cause of death."

He opened the folder and studied the missing person's report. His gut iced with each typed word. The remains had been identified using dental records. They belonged to a fifteen-year-old girl from Bishop. She'd been missing for nine months. Her foster parents hadn't bothered to report her disappearance. They assumed she'd run away like she had twice before and had decided to let her go this time. Of course, they also hadn't notified child social services, and so the foster parents continued to receive the monthly subsidy checks. His lip curled. Nice people. Real nice.

He slid the first page behind the second and stared at a color photo of the victim.

And there it was.

His heart stuttered. The connection confirmed.

"I can tell by your face that you see what I see."

The captain's voice broke through his dismay. He met her red-streaked, tired eyes. "She looks like Amanda Jacobs."

She nodded. "They could be sisters."

He set the paper in his hand on her desk. "Take a look at this."

She studied the faces of the young women.

The drone of voices, footsteps clomping down the hall, ringing phones, and a burst of male laughter seeped through the closed door.

Aiden slid a glance at his watch and tapped his foot on the floor. His gut screamed he needed to get out of there. They were looking at a serial abductor, and he had no doubt Candace was a target. The attack on her the other night wasn't random. No damn way. For some reason, the perp who'd abducted, then killed those other girls, had targeted Candace. He'd failed in his first attempt. He'd try again.

Aiden had to warn her.

Finally, the captain looked up. The furrow between her eyebrows had deepened, and she seemed to have aged a dozen years in the space of a few minutes. "I'd better call the chief." She chewed on her bottom lip. "He's not going to be happy, but it's time we let the FBI know we're looking at a serial kidnapper."

His heart sank at hearing his worst fears spoken aloud. But then she spoke again, and he realized there was an even worse fear.

Chapter 26

The doorbell pealed.

Candace's hard-won serenity vanished, and she rolled up from the yoga mat and turned down the recording of the soothing sounds of ocean waves surging onto a sandy beach. Tucking stray hairs into her long braid, she crossed to the window and slid the edge of the curtain aside.

The late afternoon sun shone across the shaggy front lawn. A vehicle was parked at the curb—a familiar black SUV.

Her heart raced, but not from fear, definitely not fear. She hurried to the front door and unlocked all the locks and opened the door wide. "Aiden." She couldn't stop the smile breaking out on her face.

Instead of the light, teasing grin she expected, his face remained stony, and shards of flint shone in his hazel eyes. "I need to talk to you."

"Okay." She stepped aside. "Come in."

He brushed past her and waited in the foyer while she relocked the door and reset the alarm. Then he followed her down the short hall to the living room.

"Do you want something to drink? I can make coffee."

He held his body tight, his muscles taut, his shoulders stiff. "Sit down, please. We need to talk."

Okay, so this wasn't a social call. Heart lodged in

her throat, she perched on the couch.

He shrugged out of his suede jacket, laid it across the back of the couch, and sat on a chair facing her, staring at his hands.

The ensuing silence swelled and grew until she could hardly breathe. "Where's your dog? It's Sunday. I thought Tracker would be spending the day with you."

"I'm working. Tracker's stuck at home today." He continued to stare at his hands as he clenched and unclenched them on his lap.

Her heart rate sped up. "Is there a new development?"

He met her gaze for the first time since he'd sat down.

That was worse than him avoiding her gaze. His eyes were dark and hard, his jaw rigid, his mouth a thin line. Anger, and something else, something she couldn't put her finger on, radiated off him in almost-visible waves.

"What is it? What's happened?" Her hands flew to her chest, and she pressed hard to slow her racing heart. "You identified the bones in the cave. Are they Amanda Jacobs's remains?" The room swirled as her mind raced, fighting against the awful reality.

He shook his head. "They're the remains of a fifteen-year-old girl from Bishop. She went missing nine months ago."

"Bishop?" She blinked. "So, it's not—" She swallowed as his words sank in. A wave of relief washed over her, immediately followed by guilt. Some poor girl was dead, and she was happy it wasn't Amanda. "What happened to her? Bishop's a long way from here. How did she end up in that cave in

Creighton Springs Park?"

He shrugged. "We don't know. Not yet."

She digested his news. He'd promised he'd keep her informed, and he was a man of his word. "Thank you for telling me."

A pulse in his jaw ticked. "There's more."

"Did you find Amanda Jacobs?" She swallowed. "Is she okay?" Even as the questions spilled out, the dismal truth was revealed in the stark lines of his face. Amanda was still missing.

"No. Nothing on her yet." He swallowed, his Adam's apple bobbing in his tanned throat. "Remember I told you about the victim found in Lynn Canyon?"

She nodded.

He stood and reached in the back pocket of his faded jeans and pulled out a piece of paper, unfolded it, smoothed the creases and handed her the paper. "Tell me what you notice."

Her hands shook so much, the faces on the paper blurred. She grabbed her glasses from the coffee table and slipped them on and lay the paper on her lap. Her breath caught in her throat as she studied one face after another. She looked at him. "Are these the girls who went missing?"

He nodded again.

She expelled her breath in a rush. The room spun, and she closed her eyes and clutched the cushions and held tight. When she opened her eyes, nothing had changed. The world was still insane. "I don't understand. Why am I included in this array of pictures?"

The furious ticking in his jaw ramped up. "Look at the pictures again. Look at all the photos."

She didn't have to look. She knew what he was getting at. The second she'd seen the photo array the resemblance had struck her like a slap to the head. It was gut-wrenching to look at the youthful faces, filled with hopes and dreams for the future, knowing those dreams had been cut short.

"Candace?"

She blinked and met his gaze. Her mouth was dry, swallowing almost impossible. "All these young women have the same color hair and eyes. You mentioned this similarity yesterday, but then you told me to forget that you said that. Are you telling me now that you believe these crimes are connected because of a physical similarity between the victims?"

She handed him the paper and wiped her damp palms on her leggings. She refused to accept the terrifying possibility he presented. To do otherwise would be to slip into a yawning chasm of despair. She forced a lightness to her voice. "Sure, there's a resemblance, but it doesn't mean anything. Lots of women have the same combination of hair and eye color. It's not that unusual."

He nodded. "You're right. Lots of women have long dark hair. Not so many women with dark hair also have light-blue eyes. It's a unique difference."

"Those girls—" She pointed at the paper in his hand. "They're younger than me. I'm almost twice their age."

He folded the paper and stuffed it back in his pocket. "I think you might be in danger."

Her breath blasted out in a noisy gust. "Wha-what?"

His brow furrowed as he paced across the small

living room. "Think about this, Candace. You resemble those girls, and you were attacked the other night. If those frat boys hadn't interfered, you'd have been abducted. Don't you think there could be a connection?"

She swept a shaky hand across her forehead. "No. I don't. The man who attacked me was a mugger. He wanted my purse, that's all it was, a simple mugging." Even to her own ears her protestations sounded unbelievable, but to accept what he was telling her, to face the horrible reality, was too much to bear.

He stopped pacing and faced her. "So then why did he leave your purse behind when he fled? Most purse snatchers don't inject their targets with ketamine."

And still she persisted, hoping she'd convince herself. "I don't know. Maybe when those students called out, he was so desperate to get away, he forgot about my purse."

"You said he knew your name. That alone means the attack wasn't random." He strode toward her and crouched at her feet and grasped her hands.

The instant jolt of awareness caught her off guard, and she inhaled a quick breath. Her first reaction was to snatch her hand free, but the warmth of his palm against hers, the rasp of his callused fingers, was comforting, and she was too weak-willed to do anything more than sit there staring into his earnest gaze.

"Look, Candace. I don't want to frighten you, but the blood work from the victim in Lynn Canyon showed she had ketamine in her blood—the same chemical composition as the ketamine your attacker injected into you."

She yanked her hands free and jolted to her feet.

Lurching around him, her legs rubbery, she stumbled across the room. She had to move, had to escape the terrifying scenario he painted. "Are you saying you think the person who killed that poor girl, attacked me?"

He rose to his feet. "It's a definite possibility."

She clenched her hands into tight fists as the truth she'd been dodging these past days hit home like a bullet to the heart. "He was planning to *kidnap* me?"

"Maybe. I'm not sure, but like I said, it is a possibility. One we should consider." He advanced and set his palms on her shoulders, forcing her to meet his gaze. "I'm not telling you this to frighten you. That's the last thing I want to do, but we have to consider the evidence. You were attacked. The man who attacked you injected you with high-grade ketamine. The victim in Lynn Canyon was injected with the same ketamine. There's a pattern there. We'd be fools not to see it."

She blinked back tears. This couldn't be happening. She'd suffered heart-wrenching tragedy in her life. One Cooper sister kidnapped was enough. What sort of just God would inflict this on her? Was it because she should have been the one taken so many years ago, and not Charlene? Because Charlene's abduction was her fault?

Aiden's deep voice broke through her shock. "The medical examiner checked the hair samples found on the skull in the cave. Apparently traces of ketamine can be found through chemical hair analysis. The drug is present for months postmortem." He rubbed his chin, the rasp of whiskers loud in the small room. "The captain just told me the results." He expelled a long breath. "We found traces of the same ketamine used on you."

His pronouncement was like a bomb detonating in the room. She struggled to think through the maelstrom raging in her brain.

He studied her for several long seconds. "I believe we're looking at a serial kidnapper, and I think, for whatever reason, you've been targeted."

Chapter 27

He regretted his words the second they left his mouth. Knowing you were on some maniac's list to be abducted would shatter anyone. And she wasn't just anyone. She'd faced tragedy most of her life and lived in a nightmare few could imagine. Now he'd added another horror.

Her face was ashen, and her body quaked as if a strong wind would blow her over.

"Candace?"

She didn't say a word, didn't blink, didn't acknowledge he'd spoken.

"Candace, are you okay?" Dumb question. After what he'd told her, what the hell did he think?

"I'm not sure. It's a lot to take in."

"I hate to ask, especially now, but this is important." He sat close beside her, wanting to offer comfort, but afraid to take her in his arms. Afraid that wouldn't be enough, that he wouldn't be able to stop at just holding her, that he'd want so much more. "Is there anything new you remember about the attack the other night? Anything at all?"

Her brow furrowed. "I didn't see his face, but he was taller than me and muscular. I think he had a beard, but I can't be certain." She yanked a tissue from a box on the coffee table and clutched it in her hand. "Maybe I imagined that."

"The last time I was here, you received a phone call."

If possible, her face paled even more.

The urge to take her in his arms and comfort her was overwhelming, but he fisted his hands and shoved them deep in his pockets and shifted a few inches from her. "Does the caller speak? Does he threaten you? Do you recognize his voice?" *Whoa. Slow down. Don't rush her.* He'd been doing this job for years. He knew how to interview a victim of a violent crime. He had to tread lightly, speak softly, give her time to come to grips with the violence she'd experienced.

But that was the problem. She wasn't just another victim. Not anymore. Right or wrong, he had a personal stake in this. His worry for her safety was making him go too fast, and he was overwhelming her with his questions.

She shook her head. "He doesn't speak, but I know someone's on the other end of the line, listening. I hear his breathing." A shudder rippled through her slim body. "He called last night, and I told him if he called me again, I'd report him to the police."

"You said *him*. Why are you so certain the caller's a man?"

The furrow between her brows deepened. "I don't know. It's just a feeling I have, but I suppose it could be a woman." She leaned back against the couch, obviously exhausted.

He didn't want to further interrogate her, not now, not when she was so fragile. But a young girl was missing, and Candace's life could be in danger. The case was speeding up. He felt it in his bones. Every second counted. "You said you thought the man who

242

attacked you had a beard. What made you think that?"

"I think I felt the brush of a beard against my hands when I was fighting him off." She clutched the damp tissue in her hand and closed her eyes. After a moment, she opened them and met his gaze. Her vivid blue eyes glistened with fresh tears. "This is probably nothing, but a man was sitting in a gray truck several stalls over from where I was parked at the mall the other day."

She inhaled a shaky breath. "I'm certain he was watching me. He had a dark, bushy beard, and he wore a black cap pulled low over his forehead. He looked like the man from Creighton Springs State Park." Tears trembled on her long eyelashes. "Am I seeing boogeymen everywhere? Am I freaking out for no reason? Am I going crazy?"

He slid closer and pressed his hand on her warm, slim thigh to stop its shaking. "You have every reason to be spooked. You were attacked and assaulted, and you're receiving prank phone calls. Only a fool would be complacent." He forced a smile and attempted to lighten the tension that had her body strung tight as a bow. "You're no fool. I knew that the moment I met you. You're strong."

Her soft lips curved in an answering smile.

For a heartbeat, he felt ten feet tall, like a hero in one of those old western movies he'd loved to watch as a kid.

In the next breath, her smile faded, and worry darkened her eyes. "Do you really think all these events are connected?"

His heart bled at her vulnerability. She was holding on by a thread, but she was holding on, showing an inner strength he admired. "I don't know, but I promise you I'm going to find out."

"What if—" Her slender throat worked. "—what if the bearded man abducted Amanda Jacobs?" Hysteria coated her voice. "What if he killed that poor girl in Lynn Canyon and attacked me at the college? And that girl whose bones we found in the cave? Maybe he killed her too."

The panic in her blue eyes broke his restraint, and as if he were watching from a great distance, he saw himself gather her in his arms and hold her close. "I won't let anyone hurt you. You're safe with me." Even as he held her and whispered the soothing words, a feeling of impending doom filled him, along with the certainty the perp wasn't finished with his crime spree, and more young girls' lives were at stake.

Her narrow shoulders shook with sobs, and he tightened his arms. Only a stonehearted man would stand by and watch her anguish. He wasn't stepping over the line, he was helping a traumatized victim deal with a crisis. All part of his job.

Yeah, right.

He pushed aside the snide inner voice. Wrong or not, he couldn't ignore how good it felt to hold her. She fitted against his body like she was made for him. The sweet, floral scent of her dark hair, the silken wisps brushing his neck, the fullness of her breasts against his chest—

A loud ringing broke the moment of intimacy, and he dropped his arms and jolted to his feet. He sucked in several deep breaths and fished in his coat pocket for his cell phone. Glancing at the call display, he groaned. His partner had impeccable timing. "What's up, Joe?"

"You need to get here now!"

"What's going on? Where are you?" He shot her a glance.

She sat hunched on the cushions, her face buried in her hands, her quiet sobs filling the room.

"I'm at the precinct. Get your sorry ass over here. There's something you gotta see." Joe's tone was crankier than usual. "You have ten minutes." The line went dead.

What the hell?

He looked at Candace, and his heart lurched.

Her eyes were puffy and red from crying, and tears streamed down her cheeks.

Every cell in his body urged him not to leave her, not like this, not when she was so frightened. Not when she needed him.

But did he have a choice? Joe's tone made clear something big was going down. He ground his teeth until his jaw ached. He was a cop. He used to be a damn good one. He liked to think he still was. Heaving a breath, he stuffed the phone in his pocket, snatched his coat from the back of the couch, and shrugged into the suede jacket. "I'm sorry, but I have to go. Will you be okay?"

She sniffled and nodded.

His heart lurched. Her bravery nearly broke him, but duty called, and his career was important. "I'll be back as soon as I can. Don't leave the house, and don't let anyone else but me in." *Wait!* He was coming back? Tonight?

She rose and crossed to him, placing her hand on his arm. "Thank you."

He blinked, stunned by the jolt of electricity that zinged through his body at her simple touch. "I'm just doing my job."

Right. Keep believing that bullshit, and you'll be in the same pot of hot water as you were in Seattle.

Her mouth trembled as she attempted a smile. "Thanks for being here, for telling me what's going on. For understanding why I'm so upset…" She shrugged. "For taking me seriously. Not many cops—"

He cut her off. If she knew the effect holding her in his arms had on him, she wouldn't be thanking him, she'd be calling Internal Affairs and reporting him for unprofessional conduct. "I'll be back." He sucked in a breath. What the hell? Was he determined to dig his grave? "I promise." And there it was—the clincher. He might as well hand her the shovel and ask her to cover him with dirt.

Looking into her luminous blue eyes almost brought him to his knees, and more than anything in the world, he wanted to stay and protect her. Nothing else mattered. Not his career, not his self-respect. Nothing. Just her and her safety.

She smiled a tremulous smile. "I'll be waiting."

A wave of longing rushed through him, but he tore his gaze from hers, turned, and headed for the door. He fumbled with the series of locks, but finally had them all unlocked and wrenched open the door. "Make sure you lock up." His voice was a hoarse croak.

Before he could make even more of a fool of himself, he escaped out the door and almost ran down the walkway to his car.

Chapter 28

He was still thinking of her when he pushed through the doors to the station, waved at the lone security guard, and strode through the deserted lobby to the back stairs. Candace had looked so frightened and alone. He hated to leave her after dropping the bombshell that her attacker was possibly a serial abductor, and she was his next target.

But he didn't have a choice. Something big was up. The urgency in Joe's gravelly voice made that clear. And so, he'd done one of the hardest things he'd ever had to do in his life—he walked out her door and left her. Once in his car, he'd set the sirens blasting and the lights flashing and raced to the precinct.

As soon as he found out what Joe wanted, he'd head back to Candace's house. His gut pinged with the certainty she was in imminent danger. Like a typical serial perpetrator, her attacker would be upset Candace had escaped his clutches. The bastard wouldn't give up. He'd strike again.

And soon.

He rubbed the knot in his gut and almost turned the car around. How could he have left her? What was he thinking? She needed protection. But then he recalled the series of disastrous events that had severed his career in Seattle, and his promise to himself that it would never happen again.

247

Candace would be fine. She had good-quality locks on her doors and windows and a state-of-the-art security system. He ignored the tingle of unease in the deepest pit of his gut and bounded up the stairs two at a time and loped down the short hall to the detectives' bullpen. Shoving open the glass door, he wove through the maze of desks and empty rolling chairs.

Instead of the usual cacophony of ringing telephones and the buzz of loud conversations, the room was eerily quiet. Joe was the only person in the office. The other detectives were at home enjoying their Sunday evening with their families and nursing hangovers.

Joe hunched over his desk, studying a thick file. Four, large, dust-covered cardboard boxes were stacked on the floor beside his desk.

"What's up?" Aiden dragged a chair over to Joe's desk, turned the chair around, and straddled the seat, crossing his arms on the chair's back rail. "What's so urgent you had to call me away from a witness interview?"

Joe set down the sheaf of papers and smirked. "You were with that broad again, weren't you? If I didn't know better, I'd suspect something was going on with you and the good professor."

Joe's sarcasm rankled, but Aiden didn't bother defending himself. What would be the point? Joe wouldn't believe him no matter what he said. Besides, the sooner Aiden learned what his partner was up to, the sooner he could get back to Candace. "Why did you call me down here?"

Joe lifted the top file on his desk and handed it to Aiden.

Aiden studied the grimy, coffee-stained cover and frowned. "What is this?"

"Duh." Joe's lip curled. "A file folder."

Aiden ground down on his back molars so hard he wouldn't have been surprised if a tooth cracked. "Where did you get it?" As far as he knew the department had gone digital years ago. Paper copies of the files of solved and unsolved cases were stored somewhere off site.

"I ordered them a few months back. Took this long for the files to get here." Joe sat back and smoothed the palm of his hand over his short gray hair. "Gotta love modern technology. In the old days these files would have been in a filing cabinet in the basement. Now they're all the way over at the state capital in some warehouse." He frowned. "Makes no sense, if you ask me."

Aiden strove for calm. He didn't have time to sit around looking at old, solved cases and bitching about how things had changed. He waved the folder in the air. "What's in here that has you so fired up?"

Joe's chair squeaked in protest when he sat back and crossed his arms over his ample chest. "Open it and see for yourself."

Aiden flipped open the cover. The heading on the top document caught his attention, and his body stilled, every cell standing at attention. The file was an investigation into the Forgotten Five abductions. "What the hell? Why are you looking at these old files?"

Joe's smile was more a feral grin than an actual smile. He pointed to the boxes on the floor. "Took me hours to go through these dusty old files, but my hunch and solid, dogged police work paid off." He clasped his

249

hands over his chest and twirled his thumbs. "While you were out flirting with the pretty professor, I was doing the hard work."

Aiden wanted to punch the smug expression off Joe's face. Instead, he fisted his hands and dug deep for patience. "Are you going to tell me what you found? Or do I have to guess?"

The corners of Joe's mouth twitched. He nodded at the file in Aiden's hand. "Flip through to the second-to-last page."

Aiden heaved a weary sigh and rifled through the thick file. Page after page of reports of investigations, witness interviews, ME reports, black-and-white photographs of fingerprints, building exteriors and interiors, crime scenes... He stopped. Ice glazed his gut as he stared at the photographs of the five girls. His eyes burned, but he couldn't look away, couldn't blink.

"Well? What do you think?" Joe's smoker's-roughened voice broke through Aiden's stunned shock.

Aiden met his partner's gloating gaze. "Jesus! How did someone not catch this when Amanda Jacobs went missing?"

Joe rubbed his red-streaked eyes. "From the moment I saw her picture, something twigged, but I couldn't put my finger on what it was. I had a gut feeling, so I put in a request for those files. They arrived this morning, and I've been looking through them ever since." He nodded at the page filled with photos. I found that an hour ago. That's why I called you in."

Aiden studied the youthful faces of the Forgotten Five victims and shuddered. "You did good, partner." He fought to keep the surprise out of his voice. "This is damn good detective work."

Joe sat up straighter and beamed. "Then you see the same thing I do?"

Aiden nodded. "The Forgotten Five victims all have long dark hair and light-blue eyes. Just like Amanda Jacobs, the victim from Lynn Canyon, and the girl whose bones we found in that cave in Creighton Springs State Park." He'd known the cases were connected. Damn right he had. Now they had indisputable proof. He handed the file folder to Joe. "It can't be the same perp. The Forgotten Five case was over twenty years ago. The man who took those girls would be too old to be committing these crimes."

"Agreed." Joe opened another case file and handed it to Aiden. "This is a police artist's sketch of the man who held the Forgotten Five victims."

Aiden's hand shook as he opened the folder and studied the face of the monster who'd kidnapped five young girls and tortured them on a rustic farm deep in the woods. The man in the drawing was middle aged with strands of gray in his long, greasy dark hair and thick beard. Deep lines scored his weathered face. The investigators at the time had put his age as late fifties.

Joe shoved back his chair and stood. "Want some coffee?"

Aiden was too fixated on Isaiah's composite sketch to look up. His mind whirled as a thousand scenarios played through his brain in vivid technicolor. But the loudest inner voice screamed that Candace was in danger.

The earthy smell of dark roast filled the air, and Joe shoved a steaming cup of coffee into Aiden's hand. "Drink up. You look like you could use the caffeine."

"Thanks." He sipped and winced as the hot coffee burned the tip of his tongue and tapped the drawing. "This guy was in his fifties. He'd be in his late seventies now. If he's even alive. He'd be too old to be running around abducting young girls."

Joe slurped coffee. "Looks like we have a copycat."

Aiden's gut clenched. "They never found the perp, did they?"

Joe shook his head. "No. By the time the FBI raided the farm, Isaiah was long gone, along with one of his victims."

"Charlene Cooper."

Joe nodded. "It was never spoken of aloud, but we all figured someone on the force leaked intel about the raid, and the perp knew we were coming. He grabbed Charlene Cooper and took off just hours before our guys could take him down." His mouth tightened. "You should've seen that place. The poor girls were chained to metal pipes in the shed, terrified he'd come back and punish them if they tried to escape. Worse crime scene I've ever attended. Bar none.

"I don't know how any of those girls survived. That son of a bitch messed with their minds and bodies big time. He made them call him Isaiah, as if he were some sort of Biblical prophet." Disgust laced his gruff voice. "By the time they were freed, they needed counseling. One of the victims killed herself a year later. Another ended up on the streets strung out on drugs." He shook his head. "It was a fricken' nightmare."

Aiden gripped the chair back, his nails digging into the hard plastic. Candace's sister was one of those girls.

She'd been snatched from her bedroom and held hostage for twenty days, enduring unthinkable abuse at the hands of the monster who'd taken her.

When the police raided the farm, Charlene wasn't one of the emaciated and battered girls found chained in the shed. She was never seen again. The theory was that Isaiah killed her, but even though investigators scoured the farm and nearby woods, using high-tech sonar to check beneath the ground and K9 search teams, her remains were never found.

He slammed the file closed, unable to look at the sick bastard who'd ruined five young girls' lives. But Isaiah's bearded face was branded on his eyeballs. Aiden slurped another gulp of the high-octane coffee. "The man Candace Cooper saw in Creighton Springs Park the day she found those bloody footprints in the snow had a dark beard. You knew that, right?"

Joe grimaced, his cheeks flushing red. "Yeah."

"And yet, you dismissed her report."

Joe shrugged. "What was I supposed to do? She's a pain in the ass. Her sister was one of the Forgotten Five. She's been hounding us for years, making all sorts of baseless accusations. I couldn't trust what she said."

"She reported suspicious activity to the police." Raging fire burned through him. "It was your job to investigate."

"I did." Joe huffed a breath, but his gaze shifted sideways. "I took her statement, and I went out there with a couple of uniformed cops and searched the forest."

"How well did you search? Did you sit in your car with the heater running and look at the snow outside? Was that the extent of your so-called search?"

Moisture beaded on Joe's forehead. "What did you expect me to do? The temperature had dropped, and it had snowed a good foot the night before. I nearly froze my ass off." He grabbed a crumpled paper napkin from the desk and blotted his face. "Searching was a waste of time. The chances of finding anything were slim to none."

Aiden lurched to his feet and tossed the file folder on Joe's desk, disgust at his partner's laziness like a beast raging inside him. He stormed across the room.

"Where are you going?"

Joe's voice followed him out of the bullpen and down the short hall to the captain's office. When he'd arrived, he'd noticed her office light was on. The pressure from her superiors was intense, and she was putting in the overtime hours just like him and Joe.

Not bothering to knock, he slammed open the door so hard it bounced back against the wall.

Captain Cerroli looked up and frowned. "Farrell! What the hell?"

He strode to her desk and towered over her, no longer able to rein in his fury. "These abductions are all connected. Breacher found photos of the Forgotten Five victims." He pounded the desk, uncaring that his actions would likely end in his being fired or demoted to traffic detail. "The girls all have similar appearances. We're looking at a serial." His other fist hit the desk.

She sat back and crossed her arms over her chest. "So, what are you planning to do about it?"

He blinked. "Me?"

"Look, Farrell, I know you got yourself in hot water in Seattle, but you're a good cop and an even better detective. I saw that from the first day you started here. No one works harder than you or puts in longer hours."

He blinked again. She was saying all the words he'd wanted to hear, words that exonerated him, words he thought he'd never hear again. A week ago, he'd have been jubilant, but now her praise didn't matter. Not when Candace was in danger, and Amanda Jacobs still missing. "We need to protect Candace Cooper. She's in imminent danger. She saw the guy who tried to abduct her." He wanted to pound his fist on the desk again, but a spark of restraint remained in his brain, and instead, he clenched his hands so tight his fingers ached. "Let me take her into protective custody."

She nodded. "Okay."

"Okay?" He'd expected a fight.

"I trust you, Farrell. Do what you think is best."

A warm flush washed over him. "What about Amanda Jacobs? What's the department doing about finding her?"

"I don't have a choice." She grimaced. "This thing is bigger than we can handle. I don't have the manpower." Her gaze slid from his. "That's why I'm here on a Sunday. I've called in the FBI. They'll be here tomorrow afternoon."

The FBI? His gut lurched. Once the Feds arrived, he'd have to turn over all his evidence. They'd take control of the investigation. *His* investigation. He'd be cast aside, a spectator to his own case.

"I know how you feel, but believe me, I don't have a choice." Her eyes narrowed. "Twenty-four hours. You have until then to work the case. Let's see what you can do. I don't care about the overtime."

Twenty-four hours.

Twenty-four hours to find Amanda and catch the scumbag who took her. Twenty-four hours to keep Candace safe. The task was daunting, but he'd do his damnedest. Damn right, he would. Twenty-four hours was a good solid day. There'd be no sleeping, no resting. He'd make every second count. He jerked around and strode to the door.

"Oh, and Farrell, make sure you follow the book. This case is exploding. Lots of eyes are on this. I don't want the Feds coming back at us. My butt's on the line here." She narrowed her eyes, pinning him with a hard gaze. "Yours too."

He nodded. Her meaning was clear. If he messed up this case, his police career was over. Refusing to think of the consequences, he grasped the door handle and charged out of her office.

He tore out of the precinct and ran down the back stairway, taking the stairs two at a time. Flinging open the door, he raced across the parking lot to his car. His hand was on the door handle when a voice stopped him.

"Where the hell do you think you're going?"

He sighed. He didn't have time for Joe. Not now. Not when he had to reach Candace. "Leave it alone, Joe." He flung open the car door and jumped behind the wheel and inserted the key in the ignition. A shadow fell over him.

Joe leaned into the car, his face inches from Aiden, his coffee-laced, sour breath blasting. "I thought we were partners."

Aiden bit back his impatience. Joe was right. They were a team, and his partner deserved to know what Aiden was up to. He heaved a sigh. "I'm going to Candace Cooper's house. If your theory's right, we have a copycat kidnapper out there, and she's the only one who can identify him. That makes her a target."

Joe pulled back a few inches. "Good idea. You do that while I continue scouring those old files. I can't help but think there's something else in them we've missed." He stepped back. "Keep me posted."

Aiden started the car and shifted into gear, jammed his foot on the gas, and roared out of the lot.

Chapter 29

Aiden sat in his car and stared at Candace's house as he fought to slow his heart rate. The FBI was taking over the case the following day. *His* case. He punched the steering wheel. The second the Feds rolled into town, they'd swan into the precinct in their fancy suits and ties and take charge. The next thing he knew, he'd be standing on the sidelines twiddling his thumbs, picking the hay seeds out of his hair. He bit hard on the inside of his cheek. Well, the Feds weren't there yet. This was still his case, and he had a witness to protect.

He shoved open the door and jumped out of the car, slamming the door so hard the SUV shook. The loud bang provided some satisfaction. *His case.* The affirming words rang through him. Damn right it was. He straightened his jacket and threaded his fingers through his hair and strode up her walk and jammed his finger on the doorbell.

The familiar peal echoed from behind the solid wood door.

He waited, tapping his shoe on the concrete porch.

No answer.

He rang the bell again.

Nothing.

The hairs on the back of his neck stiffened. Her car was in the driveway, so she had to be home. Besides, he'd told her not to leave the house. Maybe she was sleeping, or in the shower, or…

Knowing full well she'd have the door locked and bolted, he twisted the door handle anyway, but reeled back on his heels when the door opened. What the hell? The ping in his gut morphed into a giant punch.

He reached under his jacket and slipped out his service revolver. Heart pounding, he pushed the door open wider and stepped inside. All three locks were undone, and the alarm was off. Sweat popped out on his forehead. He stilled his rapid breathing and listened. The refrigerator hummed, a clock ticked somewhere in the house, but the loudest sound was the echoing silence of an empty house.

A dozen scenarios ran through his brain. Maybe she'd run to the store. No. She would have had to drive, and her car was still parked in the driveway. Or, she'd run out of coffee and stepped out to borrow some from a neighbor. Possible, but he'd told her to stay home and keep her doors locked. She was a smart woman. She knew there was a chance she was being watched, that the man who'd attacked her could strike again. She wouldn't have left the house, and she certainly wouldn't have left her door unlocked.

No way.

Not willingly.

He tightened his grip on the gun and edged down the hall and into the living room. The television was on, the sound muted. A stack of student papers was on the table by the couch, a mug of what looked like coffee, with a greasy film of cream congealed on its surface, beside it. A red marking pen lay on the carpet in front of the couch.

Heart racing, adrenaline pumping, he moved

through the small townhouse, clearing one room after the other, ending with the kitchen.

And that's when the full horror of the nightmare hit.

Shards of broken glass littered the floor. A chair was overturned, and a picture of Candace and her sister that had hung on the wall beside the stove, lay on the floor, the glass cracked. The matching long black hair, light-blue eyes, and smiling faces of the two girls stabbed like a knife to his chest.

Something bad had happened in this room, something violent, something he should have been there to stop. He'd let her down. He wasn't there when she needed him. Candace trusted him, and he'd failed her.

He surveyed the room, and his shoes crunched glass, but he was careful to not contaminate the kitchen. She was the most cautious person he knew. She'd never let a stranger into her house. Never. But there were no signs of a break in, and the alarm wasn't set. So, what happened? More importantly, where was she?

He fished out his phone and called for backup. What the hell? His hand was shaking. It was his job to protect her, but if he were honest with himself, her safety was more than a job. So much more. He didn't know if he could live with himself if something happened to her. No matter what the fallout, he'd do whatever it took to find her. He just prayed the perp had left something behind, some piece of evidence that would indicate where he'd taken her.

****

Aiden winced and rubbed his burning gut as he slurped bitter coffee. How many cups had he drunk tonight? Six? Seven? The astringent taste of acid filled his mouth. Probably more. Probably a lot more. But still he downed the hot coffee, even the dregs. If he was going to get through this nightmare, he had to stay alert and on top of his game.

Somehow, someone had entered Candace's house and abducted her. The fact she hadn't gone willingly was reinforced by a bloodied steak knife, a smear of blood the crime scene techs had found on a kitchen drawer, and the broken glass, fallen picture, and overturned chair.

They weren't certain the blood was Candace's. They'd have to wait for analysis back at the lab to know that. Maybe she'd fought back against her attacker, and the blood drops were from the perp. That'd be one way to track the bastard down. If he'd ever been incarcerated, arrested, served in the armed forces, or worked for a police department, they'd have him. He rubbed the burn in his gut. This wasn't the movies, and cases were never solved that easily.

The cops had been there for hours. They'd questioned the neighbors and scoured the neighborhood for evidence, but no one had seen anything unusual.

One neighbor, an older lady who lived across the street, thought she saw a young woman knocking on Candace's front door, but she was watching her favorite game show and hadn't noticed if Candace opened the door to the woman or not. She didn't notice anything unusual about the young woman.

There'd hadn't been any cries for help, no suspicious activity, nothing...just a normal, quiet Sunday night.

The alarm company's records indicated the alarm had been turned on when Aiden left the house hours earlier, but an hour later, someone had turned off the alarm, using the appropriate code. It hadn't been reset.

She'd disarmed the alarm. Had she been forced to? It was the only scenario that made sense. The back door was locked up tight, all the security in place, but the front door was unlocked. The perp must've entered and left by the front door. He'd risked a neighbor or someone passing by on the street seeing him. But no one had, so his gamble paid off.

Aiden scrubbed the back of his neck. Somehow the perp had taken Candace out of the house without anyone seeing him. She wouldn't have gone willingly, and she would have fought, unless... His heart stuttered. Had the attacker used ketamine on her again? The questions, one after the other, raged through his aching brain. What the hell happened? Where was she?

His phone rang, the loud peal breaking through his turmoil. He fumbled the phone out of his jacket pocket, glanced at the screen, and frowned. "What the hell do you want?" He spit out the words through clenched teeth.

"Hey, don't bite my head off."

"Sorry." This disaster wasn't Joe's fault. No, this fiasco rested squarely on Aiden's shoulders. He'd messed up. He'd left a key witness alone and vulnerable. He just prayed to whatever gods were listening that Candace wouldn't pay the ultimate price for his mistake.

"You still at the house?" Joe asked.

"Yeah." He didn't know why he was still there. The crime-scene techs had left long ago, and other than a uniformed officer stationed at the front of the house to protect the scene, he was alone. He should be doing something, anything but standing there beating himself up. But what the hell could he do? There weren't any clues, no suspects to track down, no leads, nothing. That feeling of helplessness filled him with a fury so strong it was all he could do not to smash his fist into the wall.

"Well, hold on to your hat, because I got some big news."

Joe's gruff voice dragged Aiden out of his dark thoughts. "News? Like what?"

"The captain put a rush on this case, and the crime-scene geeks came through."

Aiden's heart started thumping. "And?" Joe wouldn't be Joe if he didn't drag this out. "What did they find?"

"The blood found at the scene is B positive. Dr. Cooper's blood is A negative, so the blood must be the perp's. The DNA results won't come back for at least a week, but it looks like he was wounded." He paused, and the line hissed. "They found blood trace in the front hall as well."

Aiden sucked in a ragged breath. Candace had fought back, but the kidnapper still managed to drag her out of the house. Fury, mixed with a hefty dose of fear, raged through him. He'd kill the bastard. Damn right, he would, and then he'd stuff his sorry ass in jail.

"But wait, there's more."

Aiden stiffened, his senses on high alert. "What?"

"They found animal hairs in the kitchen. A lot of hairs. No idea yet if it's dog or cat hairs, but I'm pretty sure the good professor doesn't own a pet."

The air hissed out of his lungs. "Pet hairs?"

"Yep. Just like those found at the Forgotten Five

263

crime scenes."

Aiden's mind spun. Were the hairs the result of transfer from his clothing? He owned a pet, and he'd been in Candace's kitchen. "Where—" He swallowed. "—where were the pet hairs found?"

Papers rustled as Joe searched for the information. "Says here they were located by the fridge and in front of the cupboard where we found the blood smear."

Relief surged through Aiden. He hadn't contaminated the scene. As soon as he'd noted the signs of struggle, he'd been careful to stay out of the kitchen. When he'd been there the other day, he hadn't gone near the fridge or the cupboard. The pet hairs couldn't be from his clothing.

"You still there, partner?"

"Yeah."

"Well, that's not all I discovered. I told you I was looking through the old Forgotten Five case files. Guess what I found?"

Aiden bit back his irritation. He didn't want to play this game with Joe. Not tonight. Not when his brain was ready to explode. "Tell. Me." Each word was bitten off like a separate chunk of ice.

"Funny thing with good police work—it ain't sexy. It involves lots of drudgery. Most of the time it's a waste of effort. But…"

Aiden wanted to scream at his partner to spit it out, but there was no rushing Joe Breacher when he was in this mood. He bit back the expletives burning the tip of his tongue.

"But—" Joe huffed out a wheezing breath that indicated he was smoking in the office, which wasn't allowed, but something Joe did when no one was around. "—I came across an interesting character in my research. Twenty-two years ago, during the initial investigation into the Forgotten Five case, the task force interviewed hundreds of people, but didn't come up with a single viable suspect."

Joe inhaled and exhaled loudly as he smoked his cigarette, punctuated by a raspy cough. When he'd finished hacking up a lung, he cleared his throat. "When I reviewed the files, I discovered that one of the individuals questioned at the time was a veterinarian. Apparently, a witness thought she saw this guy acting suspicious near the scene of one of the abductions."

Aiden's breath whooshed out. "A vet!"

"Yeah." Another phlegmy cough. "The cops checked him out, but he had a solid alibi, so they crossed his name off the list of possible suspects."

Every hair on Aiden's body stood at attention. This was it. He knew it. This was the break they were waiting for. "You were looking into veterinary clinics. Do you have a name?"

"Martin Strawski." Another, prolonged, wet cough. "And you won't believe this—he's still at the same address."

"Thanks, Joe. This is great." Aiden ended the connection and stuffed his phone into his pocket. Heart racing, he tore out of the empty house, waved at the duty cop, and jogged to his car.

I'm coming, Candace. Hang on. I'll be there soon.

Chapter 30

"Time to wake up, Candy Girl."

The singsong voice came from far away. She fought to open her eyes, but her eyelids were too heavy. Her head pounded like a drill was spiking through her brain. She tried to swallow, but her tongue was too thick, her mouth dry, as if stuffed with cotton.

A blast of icy water drenched her face and body, knocking her head back. Her skull struck something hard and unforgiving. She screamed, her eyes flew open, and she blinked at the blaze of blinding light. Water filled her mouth, gagging her...impossible to breathe...drowning...

As suddenly as the deluge began, the glacial spray stopped.

"Do I have your attention now, Candy Girl?"

She spit out a mouthful of water and sucked air into her burning lungs. Water streamed off her hair and dripped down her cheeks, puddling on the cement floor. She struggled to focus, but a nimbus surrounded the single blazing light, and everything was a colorful blur. The pounding in her head intensified, and she feared her skull would split open.

Another blast of freezing water slammed her, cold water flooding her mouth and nose. She spluttered and strained to block the torrent, but she couldn't move her arms. They were locked behind her back.

Again, the punishing rush of water ceased, and she struggled to her knees. Shivers wracked her body, and her teeth chattered. She squinted into the blinding halo of light. Blurred shapes turned into objects, and she gasped.

A tall, muscular man, with coarse, shoulder-length dark hair and a thick black beard stood over her, grinning, exposing startling white teeth.

Her heart threatened to burst out of her chest, and she mewed in terror as she struggled to escape, but she couldn't move her leg. She blinked away dripping water. What the hell? She blinked again. A metal band encased her right ankle above her sodden cotton sock. A chain led from the restraint to a rivet embedded in a cement wall. She tugged and jerked, but the shackle held firm.

She was chained to a wall, and the man who'd attacked her on campus, the same man she'd seen in the forest all those months ago, the man who'd watched her from his truck in the mall parking lot, was standing over her.

This was a nightmare, another of the frightening dreams that plagued her almost every night. She was at home, asleep in her bed, safe and sound. If she woke up and opened her eyes, she'd see that none of what was happening was real.

Cruel male laughter filled the small room, echoing off the rough, cement walls. "Good. You're finally awake, Candy Girl." His terrifying grin widened, and he rubbed his hands together. "I've been waiting."

Her throat closed tight, and she had to force out the words. "How do you know my name? What do you want with me?"

"All in good time, Candy Girl. All in good time." He twisted a tap on the wall, and the water pouring from a short, green plastic garden hose stopped. "First, we need to establish a few house rules so we can be friends."

"Who are you?"

He chuckled. "I thought a smart girl like you would've figured that out. I mean, you're a college professor, aren't you, *Doctor* Cooper?" He dragged a rusted metal chair across the floor and settled onto the dented seat, his knees spread wide, his broad hands resting on his muscular thighs. A deep cut puckered the skin on his left arm. The cut was red and puffy and inflamed.

A vague memory of grabbing a knife from the drawer and stabbing him rose before her. Was that real? Had she wounded him? She couldn't remember. Her hands were bound behind her back, and when she fought to free her arms, the strapping dug into the skin on her wrists. The heavy chain attached to her ankle rattled as she kicked and flailed, hoping to break free, but her efforts were futile. She sank onto the floor, chest heaving. "You kidnapped me. You drugged me, didn't you? You injected me with ketamine just like you did before."

"Sorry about that, but—" He shrugged. "—how else did you expect me to get you out of your house? You're a real spitfire." He pressed his hand over the wound on his arm and winced. "I had to do what I had to do." His smirk grew. "That ketamine's great stuff. One little prick and you're out cold. I saw it used once on a black bear." He chuckled. "The zookeepers wanted his knackers cut off." He made a sad, pouty face. "Poor beast didn't know what hit him."

"You're a veterinarian?" Fear turned her body to ice. The police had theorized that Isaiah was a vet, but they'd also suspected the abductor was a long-haul trucker, or a travelling salesman. But this man couldn't be the same monster who took Charlene and the other girls. He was too young to be Isaiah. "Who are you?" She bit back a moan. The pounding in her head was so fierce her thoughts were foggy.

"I'm not a vet. Just an animal lover." He smoothed his hands over his thighs, raising a small cloud of what looked like dog hairs. "You can call me Abraham."

"What do you want with me?"

"I'll leave you to figure that out, Candy Girl. It'll give you something to do." He grinned and rose to his feet. "We'll chat later once the ketamine has worn off."

"Where's Mary? She was there, wasn't she? She was at my house with you." Her heart skipped a beat. Her memories of what happened were vague and disjointed, but Mary Jorgenson, one of her first-year students, was somehow involved in this nightmare. She was certain of that.

He rubbed his hands on his camouflage-patterned pants and smirked like he had a big secret. "Our little Mary served her purpose."

"What have you done with her?" Horror seeped through her confusion, and it was all she could do to breathe. "Did you hurt her?"

"Let's just say, Mary outlived her usefulness." His thick lips curled in a smile.

He'd killed Mary! An icy chill settled over her. He was a murderer, a cold-blooded killer.

"Let's get back to business. If you do exactly what

I say, we'll get along just fine. If not?" He shrugged, making it clear she wouldn't like the consequences of disobeying him.

His arrogance pierced her brain fog and lit a fire inside of her. She opened her mouth to tell him to go to hell.

He held up his hand stopping her. "That's another rule. Don't speak unless I give you permission. Don't even bat an eyelash." His brow furrowed and he scowled. Deep lines carved on either side of his wide mouth.

"If you're a good girl, I'll release your hands, and you can feed yourself...*if* I decide to give you food, that is. I might even let you use the bathroom...if you're really good." He crossed his arms over his massive chest. "You see, Candy Girl, you're mine. All mine. No one knows you're here. No one will ever find you. The sooner you accept your fate, the better."

His words pelted her like a deadly hail of bullets, striking her dumb, but she wasn't defeated. Not yet, not by a long shot. She gathered a pool of saliva in her mouth and spit. The gob landed on the scuffed toe of his black, leather combat boot.

He reeled back, his dark eyes glaring. "What the hell?"

"I won't—" Her tongue didn't work right. "I won't do what... you... say." Each word was an affirmation. She refused to be a victim. No. Damn. Way. And she sure as hell wouldn't follow his *rules*.

He smoothed his fingers over his bushy, dark beard. When he removed his hand, he was grinning. "I followed you for months, you know, watched you when you were in your house, at work, out running on the trails and shopping. At first, I wasn't sure you were worth the effort. Not until the other night when you told me off on the phone."

"Wha-what are you talking about?" But then she got it. "You're the one who's been calling me!"

"Guilty." He smiled like a proud father whose child had arrived at the correct answer. "I hoped you'd be feisty." He cackled, the cruel sound filling the small, dank room. Striding toward a dented metal door, he wrenched it open. "You be good now. Don't go anywhere." He laughed louder at his joke and stepped through the opening. The door slammed shut behind him with a bang, followed by the metallic thunk of a bolt sliding into place.

She huddled on the floor, knees drawn to her chest, sobs clogging her throat, tears flooding her eyes. The ketamine lingering in her blood took over, and she closed her eyes and gave in to the pressing darkness.

****

She jolted awake, and a moan of agony ripped from her mouth as a muscle in her right thigh spasmed in an agonizing knot. Stretching her leg, fighting to ease the unrelenting pain, she bit back another groan. As the cramp eased, she lay on the cold, wet floor panting. For the first time, she took in her surroundings.

A single light bulb, lit by what looked to be a hundred watts of power, hung from a twisted, colored wire attached to the water-stained ceiling, illuminating the small, windowless room. The cement walls were patterned with mold stains and long zigzagging cracks. Warped wooden shelves lined the walls. A thin stream of dirty water trickled from the nozzle of an old plastic hose into a rusted drain in the center of the cement floor. A foul stench of decay permeated the tiny room. The only way in or out was a battered metal door

She rubbed her throbbing thigh muscle and stilled. Her hands were free! Raw, red lines crusted with dried blood encircled both wrists, but she could move her arms. Sometime while she'd slept, her captor had entered the room and undone the ties binding her hands behind her back. She shuddered at the thought of him touching her while she slept.

Her head throbbed, and her mouth was desert dry, her tongue swollen and furred, her lips cracked and bleeding. A small, plastic water bottle was set on the floor beside where she lay. She grabbed the bottle. Her hands shook as she fought with the twist-off cap. The water slid down her throat like silk, easing the tightness and clearing the cobwebs from her head. She wanted to drain the bottle dry, but she didn't know when he'd bring more water, and so, after another sip, she replaced the cap and set the water bottle back on the floor.

A three-foot long chain attached to a metal band encased her ankle like a manacle and tethered her to the wall. The chain rattled when she jerked her leg, but the band around her ankle held tight. A large, rust-colored blotch stained the floor.

Blood? She shuddered. Had he kept someone else prisoner here? Amanda Jacobs?

The stark horror of her situation hit like a bomb, and she collapsed onto the unforgiving floor. Her stomach spasmed, and she heaved. She managed to roll onto her side before hot, acrid bile spewed out of her mouth and splashed the floor. The sour stench of vomit added to the room's revolting miasma. Spent, she lay back and wiped her mouth with the back of her hand.

Tears thickened her throat, and she gave in to despair.

Once again, bone-deep exhaustion took over, and she slept.

Chapter 31

When she awoke, the throbbing ache in her head had eased from a full-on nuclear explosion to a cluster bomb blast. Gingerly, she pushed to a sitting position and leaned her back against the cold cement wall. A new water bottle and a granola bar lay on the floor beside her. She shuddered. He'd been in the room again while she slept.

She rubbed at a small ache on her neck where a scab had formed over a tiny puncture wound in her skin, and a low moan escaped her cracked lips. The familiar effects of ketamine washed over her—confusion, disorientation, exhaustion. She wrapped her arms across her chest and focused on the elusive fragments of memory of how she'd ended up in this cell-like room, chained to the wall, held captive by a monster.

She'd been at home, sitting on the couch marking term papers, waiting for Aiden. The television was on, but she'd muted the sound, wanting to concentrate on the essay before her...

Rain spattered the living room window, sounding like the sharp claws of a beast scratching to get in. By the date on the calendar, it was officially spring, but this was the Rockies, and a chill was in the air. She'd turned on the gas fireplace, cranking the setting to high. The room was cozy with the warmth from the flickering flames.

The doorbell pealed, and she startled, dropping the papers on the couch. Her marking pen slipped from her fingers and rolled under the coffee table. She checked her watch. Six o'clock. A trill of excitement fluttered in her stomach. Aiden had returned earlier than she'd expected.

With his tall, muscular build, broad shoulders, dark, wavy hair and hazel eyes, he was one handsome man. But her attraction to him was about more than his good looks. For the first time since Charlene had vanished, she felt a true connection with another person, a bond that struck deep into her soul.

He'd told her about the tragic events in Seattle, and in turn, she'd revealed the truth about what happened the night Charlene was abducted. Their shared burdens of guilt drew them together, and she'd opened her heart to him, feeling as if she'd known him forever, rather than a few weeks.

The doorbell pealed again.

What was she doing standing around fantasizing when her dream man was at her door? With a skip in her step, she headed to the front door, but halted, her fingers poised on the top lock. Aiden had warned her to be careful. He'd made her promise she wouldn't open the door to anyone but him.

She peered through the door's security peephole. Her breath gusted out, and she stumbled back a step. A young woman stood on her front porch. She recognized the student from her Social Anthropology 101 class. What was her name? Mary. Mary Jorgenson. Why would Mary be at her front door?

She peeked again.

Mary looked agitated as she paced across the small stoop, wringing her hands. Her face was pale, her eyes wild, her auburn cloud of curls in riotous disarray.

A sense of unease settled over Candace.

Mary gave up on the doorbell and pounded on the door. "Dr. Cooper, are you there? Please, let me in. I need to talk to you. It's important." Her voice was edged with panic.

Candace's first instinct was to undo the locks and fling open the door to the troubled young woman, but she hesitated. The situation didn't feel right. Maybe she was overreacting because of Aiden's warning, but she couldn't shake the certainty that something was off.

Mary pounded the door again and pressed her finger to the doorbell and held it there. "Please, Dr. Cooper. You said we could come to you for help."

Candace chewed on her bottom lip. Mary was right. Candace always told her students she was there for them, and they shouldn't hesitate to come to her if they needed help, either academic or personal. But she couldn't shake her disquiet. "How did you know where I lived?" she called through the closed door. At the start of term, she provided her students with her office hours and her cell phone number, but she never gave out her home address.

There was a moment's silence. "I looked you up in the faculty directory. Your address was in there. Please, Dr. Cooper. This is important."

Of course. Her home address was in the faculty directory, but that booklet was only available to faculty members, not the students. But there was the Internet, and all information was accessible to anyone with a computer and the World Wide Web. Anyone with the

276

barest of computer skills could track down her home address, her mother's maiden name, or the name of the primary school she'd attended. It was that easy.

Silencing the voice in her head warning her she was making a mistake, she undid the locks and opened the door.

The second she saw the fear in Mary's blue eyes, she knew she'd made a fatal error. A trickle of ice ran up her spine. "Mary, what's going on?"

Mary's face crumpled. "I'm so sorry, Dr. Cooper. He-he made me do it."

"What?" But she knew, oh she knew. Even before the tall, bearded man stepped out from behind the shrubbery, she knew she'd made a mistake. Her heart stuttered, and she stumbled back and slammed the door.

A large, boot-clad foot blocked the door from closing. He shouldered the door open, shoving her back against the entryway wall and surged inside, dragging the terrified Mary with him.

The door slammed closed.

A voice inside her head screamed at her to run, but her knees were locked, her feet planted. She whimpered and gaped at her worst nightmare. This was the man who'd attacked her on campus, the man who'd watched her at the mall, the man from the state forest.

She reached for Mary, pleading silently for help, but the young coed just stood there watching, chewing her fingernails, regret lining her youthful face as sobs wracked her slight body.

"Well, hello, Candy Girl." He grinned, exposing vividly white teeth. "Remember me?"

A scream built in Candace's throat, and adrenaline coursed through her, breaking her paralysis. She spun and ran, racing for the back door and escape.

He caught her in the kitchen and grabbed her arm and slammed her against the wall, knocking a picture to the floor.

Elbowing him in his side, she broke free and scrambled behind the counter, tearing open a drawer, searching for a weapon.

He roared and swiped his hand over the countertop. A teapot, cups, and a sugar bowl hit the floor and smashed. Shards of ceramic sprayed across the room.

Grasping a steak knife, she turned, muscles tensed, ready to fight.

He lunged toward her and lifted his hand, revealing a plastic syringe.

She screamed, but he jammed his hand over her mouth, cutting off her cry for help. A familiar sharp pin prick, a burning sting, and an unsettling warmth flooded her as the drug he'd injected flowed through her veins.

No! *The scream was silent.* No! *Her knees wobbled, weakened. With her last ounce of strength, she lifted the knife and stabbed him in the arm. Blackness filled her vision, and the knife clattered to the floor. A heartbeat later, her legs collapsed, and she slid into the abyss.*

Candace shook her head and blinked back tears. Her worst nightmare had happened. She'd been abducted by the man she'd seen in the forest all those months ago, and again at the mall. He'd been following her for months, and he admitted to making the frightening phone calls. He'd even confessed to murdering Mary.

She sank onto the cold floor, drew her knees to her chest, and curled into a fetal position. A fresh wave of tears filled her eyes, and her shoulders shook as she sobbed. She was being held in this cell-like room, chained to the wall like an animal.

Had Charlene felt this same fear and helplessness? Her sister left behind a loving family who missed her and spent years searching, prodding the police to action, never giving up. Who would look for Candace? She didn't have any family, not a boyfriend, or even any close friends.

She'd devoted her life to finding her sister and building her career. There hadn't been time for love or friendship. Her students would wonder what happened to her when she didn't show up on Monday for the last classes of the semester, but they'd be more relieved to be set free than concerned about her absence.

Eventually, someone from the college would report her missing, and the police would be called to investigate. Maybe Aiden would be placed in charge of the missing person's case. He was a dedicated cop. He'd search, but would he find her? Thousands of missing women and girls were never found. She'd become another sad statistic. Misery overwhelmed her, and once again, she gave in to tears.

She lost track of how long she lay on the dank floor, but her hips ached from the cold seeping into her bones, and her body was stiff, her muscles throbbing. She bit down on her bottom lip until she tasted blood. The fresh pain drew her out of her self-pity fest. She wiped her damp face with the back of her hand.

Pushing up on her bottom, she sat up, blinked away her tears, and surveyed her prison. Rescue was unlikely.

No one knew where she was. No one would find her. Not until it was too late. Happy endings only happened in the movies. People disappeared all the time and were never found. They were forgotten and given up for dead. Just like Charlene. If she was going to get out of there alive, she had to use her brains. Escape was her only option.

A loud squeal of metal rent the air, and the door swung open.

She scrambled back against the unforgiving cement wall and drew her knees to her chest. Her heart pounded so loud, she feared it would burst free.

The bearded man stepped into the room and studied her for a long, agonizing minute, his fierce dark gaze assessing. He nodded and rubbed his hands together. "So, shall we begin our lessons?" A wide grin split his bearded face, but his eyes were cold and flat.

Chapter 32

Aiden tightened his grip on the steering wheel until his knuckles stood out stark white, and his hands ached. A trip that should've taken twenty minutes was taking twice as long because Joe demanded to come along. He slid a glance at his partner.

Joe lounged on the front passenger seat picking at a ragged cuticle.

Aiden hadn't wanted to wait for his partner. Hell no. Candace was missing. Abducted, for Christ's sake. Every second counted. Every. Damn. Second. But Joe insisted. He'd even gone so far as to threaten to go to the captain if Aiden didn't swing by the precinct and pick him up.

Aiden blew out a breath, striving for calm, and swerved around the corner. The rear of the car fishtailed on the pavement, leaving rubber skid marks on the asphalt.

Joe, who refused to wear a seat belt despite regulations, let out a surprised whump as his right shoulder slammed against the passenger-side door.

As childish as his actions were, Aiden smirked. *Served the jerk right.* He jammed his foot on the gas, and the powerful SUV shot down a straight stretch. They passed through a heavy industrial area on the outskirts of Briggston. The street was lined with garages, their service bays open and cluttered with heavy-duty rigs and stacks of discarded tires and rusty mufflers.

A factory, with boarded-up windows and plastic bags, broken glass bottles, and old newspapers flattened against its dingy brick walls, looked like it had been closed for years.

Without slowing, he wrenched the wheel and skidded into the parking lot of a rundown strip mall and bumped over the cracked and buckled pavement.

The SUV bucked over rain-filled potholes, bouncing Joe out of his seat. The top of his head smashed against the padded roof. Cursing, he rubbed his head and resettled on the seat, clutching the sides of the seat cushion. "Jesus, man. Who taught you to drive?"

Aiden ignored his partner and focused on steering the heavy vehicle around the deep potholes. He sped past a nail salon, a massage parlor, a liquor store with heavy metal bars covering its front window and glass door, and a thrift shop.

He jammed on the brakes. The vehicle squealed to a stop, raising a spray of gravel. "We're here." Ripping the keys from the ignition, he thrust open the door and leaped out of the car and charged toward the row of small, rundown businesses.

A hand grasped his arm and drew him to a halt.

He shot Joe a glare. "What the hell, man?"

Joe didn't release his hold. "Whoa, partner. You can't go in there hot and heavy demanding answers. We need a plan."

Aiden thrust off Joe's hand. "Oh, yeah? Watch me." But he didn't move. As much as he hated to admit it, Joe was right. The son of a bitch who took Candace could be in there holding her captive, prepared to kill her if the cops burst through the door. He sucked in a steadying breath, fighting the rush of adrenaline that had spiked through him the second he discovered Candace was missing, "How do you think we should do this?"

"You own a dog, so you know the drill. Walk in there like you want to make an appointment…you know, for shots or something." Joe shrugged. "Get a feel for the place. Find out if the doctor's in. See if you can talk to him."

Aiden nodded. Joe's plan made sense. Maybe if he saw the guy, he'd get a read on him, be able to tell if he was involved. "Okay." He shot Joe a look. "What are you going to be doing?" He half-expected Joe to say he'd wait in the car in case backup was needed, but for the third time that day, his partner surprised him.

"I'm gonna walk around back and make sure no one takes a flyer out the back door."

"Sounds good."

Joe headed off, and Aiden sucked in three long, steadying breaths, pasted what he hoped was a pleasant smile on his face, and strolled toward the vet clinic. A neon sign, with several burned-out letters, hung above the door and read "Briggston Animal Care Hospital." Beside it was a smaller, flashing sign indicating the clinic was open for business.

The place had seen better days. A long, jagged crack spidered across the large, dusty front window as if someone had kicked it. The white trim had yellowed, and a small pile of last fall's leaves clustered against the crumbling foundation.

As he approached the door, it opened, and an

elderly woman stepped out, cradling a small, whimpering dog in her arms.

He grabbed the door and held it open.

She smiled and squeezed by him. "Thank you so much. My poor little Bitsy is upset." Her arms tightened around the scruffy pup. A white gauze bandage was wrapped around the dog's quivering middle. She petted its head. "Poor Bitsy. Did that mean vet hurt you?"

Unable to resist, Joe smoothed a light hand over the tiny dog's velvety head.

Bitsy raised her head and looked at him with sad, sorrowful eyes and whimpered again.

"What happened to this poor little pooch?"

The woman made a kissy face at the dog. "My little girl had to get spayed." She planted a kiss on the dog's head. "I know, sweetie," she cooed in baby talk. "Mama's sorry, but you know it had to be done, and Dr. Tammy says you'll be fine in a few days." She looked up at Aiden, and the tiny lines around her mouth deepened. "The neighbor's male cane corso has been sniffing around my poor sweet Bitsy." She shuddered, and her gray bob bounced. "No way was I going to allow that to happen. My poor girl—"

Aiden had stopped listening. Dr. Tammy? He frowned. That wasn't the name of the vet they were looking for. He cut off the woman's tirade against the unneutered cane corso in mid rant. "I thought the vet here was Dr. Strawski."

She tutted. "Oh, no. Dr. Strawski hasn't worked here for years. Dr. Tammy took over the practice—" She paused and wrinkled her forehead. "—maybe fifteen, twenty years ago? Maybe more?"

Aiden opened his mouth to pepper her with questions, but Bitsy took that moment to squirm in her owner's arms and let out a piteous whimper.

"Oh, dear. I have to get this poor baby home." The woman hurried past Aiden and headed to a small compact car parked in the lot.

Some of Aiden's adrenaline faded. From what the old lady said, the perp they were looking for hadn't worked there in years. Was this another dead end? He opened the door wider and stepped inside and wrinkled his nose at the heavy stench of antiseptic, urine, and bleach common to all veterinary clinics. A chorus of frantic barking echoed from the back of the office. Tracker hated going to the vet, and it was all Aiden could do to drag him there for his annual shots.

He approached a desk with a young, attractive blonde-haired woman sitting behind it talking on the phone. She smiled warmly at Aiden and held up a finger, indicating she wouldn't be long.

He used the time to check out the waiting room.

A wooden bench was set against one wall and three plastic chairs against the other.

A man sat on one of the chairs holding a struggling and meowing black cat on his lap.

A black rubber mat covered the cracked linoleum floor. Posters of pet rescue societies and advertisements for high-end pet food covered the grungy white walls.

"How can I help you?"

He swung back to the receptionist and reached into his pocket and tugged out his wallet. Flipping it open, he showed her his badge and ID. "I'd like to ask you a few questions." No point pretending to be a customer if Strawski was long gone.

Her smile faded. "Is something wrong?"

"I'm looking for Dr. Strawski. Is he in today?"

Her eyes widened. "Dr. Strawski? The only vet we have is Dr. Tammy."

He studied her, searching for signs of subterfuge, but her confusion seemed real. "Let me talk to Dr. Tammy."

She jumped up from her desk. "Of course." She hurried across the room and opened a closed door. The barking increased in volume and eased when the door closed behind her.

He glanced at his watch and frowned. Time was ticking. Every passing second was one second longer Candace was in danger, one second closer to when the Feds took over. He was about to follow the woman, when the door opened, and the receptionist and another, much-larger, gray-haired woman in navy-blue scrubs stepped into the waiting room.

The receptionist followed and returned to her desk.

The older woman's gray hair was skinned back from her weathered face in a tight ponytail. She was tall and broad shouldered and looked like she wouldn't have a problem wrestling a pregnant cow to the ground. "I understand you're looking for someone." Her voice was brisk and no-nonsense, making it clear he was interrupting a busy day.

The bells above the door chimed, and a man walked in, restraining an excited golden retriever on a leash.

As soon as the dog spotted the cat, it lunged and started barking.

The cat yowled and attempted to claw its way up the owner's neck.

Dr. Tammy stepped to the interior door and motioned for Aiden to follow.

The door closed behind him, cutting off the excited barking. He was in a small exam room.

The vet leaned against a padded counter and crossed her arms over her ample chest. "How can I help you, Detective?"

"I'm looking for Dr. Strawski. Our records show this is his place of business."

She was shaking her head before he finished speaking. "This is my clinic now. I've leased it from Dr. Strawski ever since he retired fifteen or so years ago. That probably explains why his name is still on the business license." Her eyes narrowed. "Why are looking for him? Is he in some kind of trouble?"

Aiden cursed under his breath. Another dead end. "You wouldn't happen to know where he went, would you?"

"I'm afraid he's dead."

"Dead?" Aiden's heart sank. "Are you sure?" Damn. Their one lead was dead in the water. Literally.

She nodded. "I used to pay him directly, but for the past ten years, my rent checks go to a real-estate company."

Damn and double damn. Aiden gritted his teeth. This trip was a waste of time. He stared at the institutional clock on the wall ticking away the seconds. Every cell in his body demanded he get the hell out of there and dig up another lead, but Candace's life was at stake, and so he asked one more question. "Do you mind if I have a look around?"

The furrow between Dr. Tammy's brows deepened. "What're you looking for, Detective?"

He ignored her question. The vet clinic was a dead end, but he wouldn't be doing his job if he didn't at least search the place.

She blew out an aggrieved breath. "Okay. Go ahead, but all you're going to find are sick dogs and cats."

She followed on his heels as he looked into each room of the small clinic. She was right. There were lots of miserable-looking pets lying in metal cages whining. The sight broke his heart, but the vet was helping them, and when they recovered, their owners would come and pick them up and take them home. He turned back to the vet. "Thanks for your cooperation. I'll get out of your hair." He opened the door that led into the waiting room.

"Detective Farrell?"

He paused and looked back at her and arched his brows.

"I don't know if this'll help, but Dr. Strawski's son is still around. Maybe you could talk to him."

Aiden's heart jerked. "His son?" This was the first he'd heard of a son.

"He comes and helps out every week or so. He's a bit—" She grimaced. "—different, but he loves animals, and so I let him help." A frown creased her brow. "Come to think of it, I haven't seen him in months. I hope he's all right."

Aiden's gut pinged with the certainty this was the man they were looking for.

"Can you tell me what he looks like?" And there was the clincher. "Does he have a beard?"

"Why, yes, he does." She smiled. "His father had a beard as well. They looked a lot alike. No question they were father and son."

His heart rate sped up to the quadruple digits, but he had to be certain. He pulled out the composite sketch Candace had helped create and showed it to the vet. "Is this him?"

She nodded.

Bullseye! "What's his name?"

"Abraham. Abraham Strawski."

Got the bastard. "Do you have an address?"

"I'm sorry, I don't." She threaded her fingers through her short hair. "I pay him under the counter. You know, in cash. I know it's not right, but this place doesn't make a lot of money." She gestured at the crated animals. "People around here don't have much, some are homeless, others are seniors living on a fixed income. They can't afford veterinary fees, so they come here. I help them."

"You're not a qualified vet."

"No, but I know what I'm doing. I help these animals." Her eyes watered. "Are you going to shut me down?"

A small, mixed-breed dog lay in the crate in front of Aiden, a bandage wrapped around the emaciated creature's back leg.

A cat paced inside another cage, pawing at the metal bars, meowing.

Aiden knew the law. He should report the woman for operating an illegal animal clinic. But that would close her down, and then what would happen to the animals? He blew out a breath. "No, I won't report you."

"Thank you, Detective." She smiled for the first time. "You must be an animal lover."

Maybe so, but he'd just agreed to look the other way and ignore a criminal offense. Would he ever learn?

Chapter 33

She had to find a way out of the cell. But how? She rubbed her aching hands, bruised and swollen from fighting to free her leg from the metal ankle band. The sharp edges of the cuff dug into her skin, and blood seeped from her wound. Every time she moved, the chain clunked on the cement floor, reminding her of the hopelessness of her situation.

She'd lost track of time and had no idea how long she'd been in the cold cell. The tiny room didn't have a window, and the light bulb hanging from the ceiling was always on, glaring in her eyes, making it impossible to tell if it was day or night.

Every inch of her body ached from straining at the metal tether as she searched for escape. Her throat was raw from screaming and calling for help, even though she knew it was hopeless and no one heard her pleas.

She sank onto the floor and once again gave in to tears. There was no escape. Not from this room. Not unless she dug through solid cement with her fingernails. Her bruised hands, with their dirty, broken nails throbbed, a testament to her frantic efforts.

The only way out of the room was if by some miracle, she overpowered her captor. She tugged the chain tethering her to the wall like a dog. But then what? She still had to break free of the damn shackle. She didn't have a weapon, unless she could wrap the plastic hose around his neck and beat him over the head with the metal chair. Picking up an empty plastic water bottle, she tossed it across the room. It hit the wall and bounced on the floor.

The clang of the bolt sliding free jolted her out of her misery. She jerked up, her back pressed against the wall, fear icing her heart.

The door swung open, and the bearded man stepped into her cell. "Wakey, wakey, Candy Girl."

His cruel gaze met hers, and she swallowed back another sob. She'd be damned if she'd let him see her cry.

He tsked. "You've been a naughty girl. I've heard you yelling for help." He grabbed her sore hands and squeezed. "You don't really think you can escape, do you? These walls are thick. Whoever dug this old root cellar knew what they were doing."

A bolt of agony shot through her as his fingers dug into her raw wounds. She bit her lip to stop a scream, refusing to give him the satisfaction.

He tutted again and released her.

Before she recovered her breath, he drew his foot back and kicked her. Hard. The pain in her hip took her breath away. She cowered on the floor, covering her head with her hands, tears burning her eyes.

He slammed his boot-clad foot into her thigh again.

She couldn't hold back the scream as agony ripped through her. Another blow and another, until she was sobbing, pleading for him to stop, begging for the pain to ease.

The blows ended as suddenly as they began.

Pain roared through her like a freight train. She sucked in a shaky breath and bit back a moan. Her chest was on fire. Every breath was like a knife stabbing. Had he broken her rib?

"That's what happens when you're a bad girl." Beads of sweat glistened on his brow as he towered over her, his arms crossed over his massive chest, a look of smug satisfaction on his brutish face.

She wiped the snot and saliva from her face. "What do you want with me? Are you going to kill me? Is that it? Is that why you kidnapped me?"

He stared at her for a long time. "I think you know, Candy Girl. Oh, yes. I think you do."

She shook her head and instantly regretted the movement, as a tsunami of pain radiated from her rib through her body. The room dimmed, and blinding shards of light flashed. She sagged against the cold wall, her body limp. She was done fighting, done struggling, done trying to escape. She couldn't take any more pain. All she wanted was blessed oblivion.

Her captor's cruel laughter filled the small room and followed her into the darkness.

****

"Rise and shine."

The rough, taunting voice pierced her brain, and she groaned and burrowed deeper into sleep.

A hand grabbed her shoulder, nails digging into her bruised muscles, and someone shook her.

Consciousness returned, and she lurched up, a wave of pain flooding her. Her chest was on fire, every breath an agony. "Wha…"

"Come on, sleepyhead, wake up." He shook her again.

And just like that, the nightmare returned. "Please don't hurt me." The whine in her voice disgusted her, but she didn't want him to hit her again, wasn't sure she could handle any more torture.

"Hurt you?" He crouched before her. "I don't want to hurt you, Candy Girl."

His dark eyes glinted with a manic madness that terrified her.

He shrugged off a black canvas bag strapped across his chest and removed two plastic water bottles and a granola bar. "Can't have my Candy Girl going hungry, can I?" He dropped the bottle and granola bar at her feet. "Eat up. You're going to need your strength."

She didn't move, couldn't budge an inch. Her body was too sore, her spirit shattered.

He nudged her leg with his booted foot. "Aren't you going to thank me?"

She tensed, preparing for more blows, but a spark of dignity remained in her soul, and she glared, putting all her loathing into her scowl. "Go screw yourself."

He shook his head and tutted. "Now, that's not smart. Not smart at all." Jumping to his feet, he booted her in the thigh.

She screamed at the white flash of searing pain.

He loomed over her, his eyes piercing. "Now, say thank you like a good girl."

She shook her head, refusing to play his sick games.

"Woo hoo." He slapped his hands on his thighs and grinned. "I knew you'd be a challenge. That's why Father chose you."

"Wha-what?"

"You didn't know?" He chuckled. "You were the Chosen One. Your sister wasn't supposed to be taken that night. You were." His smile broadened, exposing his too-white teeth.

The air in her lungs exploded out of her mouth in a loud gasp. "Me? What are you talking about?"

"Father watched you for months. He went to your house that night to collect you, but your sister woke up and ruined his plans. He had to take her instead."

A prickle of sweat broke out under her arms. "You're *Isaiah's* son?"

He hooked his thumbs into his pants pockets and puffed out his chest. "The lightbulb finally goes on."

"Is… Charlene…is she alive?"

"Come on. You can't be that stupid."

Her fight drained, and she collapsed on the floor. A sob tore at her throat. Charlene was dead. Gone. Had been for years. And now Isaiah's son had Candace. Would this nightmare ever end? "What do you want with me?"

"You don't know?" He arched his dark brows.

She shook her head. "No."

His smirk widened, and he laughed again.

"What's so funny?"

"You." He spit the word out between giggles. "You have all those fancy degrees, but you don't know shit." He huffed out a breath. "Let me ask *you* a question— why do *you* think you were chosen?"

Fear rippled beneath her skin like a serpent. "I—" She struggled to swallow over the stone clogging her throat. "—I don't know."

"Because you look just like her."

"Like whom?"

"Mother." His eyes took on a faraway look, and he smiled. "You all look like her." He leaned closer and smoothed his large hand over her braid, toying with the dark hair. "She had pretty hair, just like yours. And her eyes were the same shade of blue."

He turned and strode toward the door, wrenched it open, and left without another word.

The door slammed closed, and the lock slid into place.

Chapter 34

Aiden pounded his fist on his desk. Damn it! Why was this so difficult? When Dr. Tammy told him Strawski had a son, Aiden was elated, figuring it'd be a snap to locate the guy. He rubbed his burning eyes. *Yeah, right.* Nothing about this case was easy. He'd been sitting at his desk all night, searching police and state databases, looking for Abraham Strawski, but there weren't any hits.

It was as if the guy didn't exist. Other than Dr. Tammy's memories, there weren't any records to prove Strawski had ever had a son. The kid hadn't been registered for a birth certificate, had never attended school, never sought medical attention, and never owned a vehicle. At least, he hadn't done any of those things under the name Abraham Strawski.

And where did that leave them?

Another dead end.

He stared at the clock on the office wall as it ticked away the seconds. He was wasting time. Candace had been taken eighteen hours ago. Every minute she remained missing, the odds of finding her alive decreased exponentially.

Not good. Not good at all.

He should be doing something to find her. But what? Every lead led to a dead end. They had nothing. Zip. Nada. Not a damn thing except a few pet hairs. The

DNA results on the blood found in Candace's kitchen weren't in yet, even though the captain had put a rush on them. But he didn't expect them to help. Abraham Strawski was a ghost. His DNA wouldn't be on file.

He threaded his fingers through his hair, fighting off the despair threatening to destroy him. Where was she? Was she still alive? His heart lurched. Candace was a strong, resourceful woman. She'd survive this. He refused to think otherwise.

His cell phone rang, the piercing tone cutting through his dark thoughts. He grabbed the phone off his desk and scanned the screen. Joe. He frowned. Why was his partner calling him at five in the morning? "What's up?"

"Meet me out front."

"What—"

"There's no time for questions. Get your ass out here now."

The urgency in Joe's rough voice had Aiden grabbing his jacket off the back of his chair and running through the deserted bullpen and leaping the stairs two at a time. His breathing was heavy by the time he burst through the front doors and onto the sidewalk.

Joe's official sedan was idling at the curb.

Aiden opened the door and slid onto the passenger seat. "What's up? What's so urgent you're out at this time in the morning—" Before he finished speaking, the car took off with a jolt that threw him back against the seat.

Joe accelerated down the street, far exceeding the speed limit. He leaned over to the console and flicked on the flashing lights and wailing siren. Taking the next corner with screeching tires, he sped down the empty street.

Aiden strapped on his seat belt. "Are you going to tell me what's going on?"

Without taking his eyes off the road, Joe grunted. "You're not gonna believe this." He skidded around another corner.

"Believe what?" Aiden clenched his hands into fists. "Look, Joe, I don't have time for your games. I have to find Candace before it's too late."

"Amanda Jacobs."

"What about her?" Damn. They'd found her body. He braced for the news.

"A runner was out jogging on the trails in Creighton Springs State Park early this morning." Joe slid him a look. "What's with those athletic types? Who in their right mind goes running through a forest in the dark? I mean, haven't they heard about bears?"

Aiden bit his lip, but he knew better than to say anything. Joe was enjoying stringing Aiden along. He'd get to the point, in his own good time. "People like to keep fit."

Joe grunted. "Stupid people, you mean." He swept down the street, the buildings a blur.

Bright lights loomed ahead. Aiden sat up. "What are we doing at the hospital?"

"Didn't I tell you? That fool of a runner found Amanda Jacobs. She's alive."

Aiden's breath whooshed out. "Amanda's alive?"

Joe nodded as he screeched to a halt in front of the Emergency entrance. The siren died, and the police lights turned dark. He faced Aiden. "She's alive, but poor kid's in critical condition."

Aiden only heard his partner's first words. Amanda

was alive! She'd beaten the odds and survived more than three months' captivity. A ray of hope surged. If Amanda had escaped her captor after all this time, Candace could as well.

Joe's jaw worked as he chewed on a wad of gum. "First reports are that she's emaciated, severely dehydrated, and suffering from hypothermia. From what the cops on the scene told me, she was naked and delirious." He tutted. "Poor kid. She's been through a rough time. It's touch and go if she makes it."

"We can't talk to her?" Aiden drummed his fingers on his thighs and slid a glance at the digital clock on the console. Time was ticking. "Then why are we here?"

"Don't get your panties in a twist." Joe grabbed the car keys and shoved open his door. "The runner who found her is here. He has one of those fancy satellite phones, and he called from the park for help. The poor guy was so shocked to see a naked girl in the woods, he tripped over a root and sprained his ankle. The EMTs transported him to the hospital for treatment." He climbed out of the car. "I thought you might want to chat with him."

Aiden sucked in a steadying breath and followed. His mind whirled with a thousand possibilities. This could be it. This could be the break they'd been praying for. If the same perp who took Amanda was the one who'd abducted Candace, they were in the money. *If* Amanda recovered. And *if* she could identify her kidnapper.

A lot of ifs, but he had a new spring in his step as they pushed through the sliding glass doors and rushed into the bustling Emergency ward.

Chapter 35

The waiting room was crowded, and every seat was filled with people holding bloody rags to their heads or wrapped around their injured hands, looking pale and haggard. Others paced back and forth across the large room, hands pressed to their stomachs or chests, moaning in obvious discomfort. Red-faced babies wailed in their parent's arms, and toddlers whined. Hunched under a tattered blanket on the floor in a corner, a blond-haired man shouted obscenities.

The glass entry doors slid open with a whoosh, and two EMTs rushed in, wheeling a stretcher bearing a woman writhing in pain, her mouth and nose covered with an oxygen mask.

Two nurses and a doctor joined the ambulance techs, and the woman was hustled through a swinging door into the Emergency ward.

Joe and Aiden threaded their way through the throng to a desk manned by a nurse in dark-pink scrubs. Her pale-blonde hair was tugged back into a ponytail that bounced with her every movement.

"Excuse me," Aiden said. "We'd like to see one of your patients."

She barely glanced up. "Take a number—" She pointed to a machine that dispensed numbered tickets. "—and someone will see you as soon as possible." She returned to her paperwork.

Joe and Aiden exchanged looks.

Joe slipped his ID wallet out of his coat pocket and slapped it down on the desk. "We don't need a number."

She stared at the police badge and photo ID, and then looked up. Her gaze shifted from Joe to Aiden.

Aiden flashed his ID.

"How can I help you, officers?"

"Detectives." Aiden slipped his wallet back in his coat.

She nodded.

"We'd like to talk to one of your patients."

She nodded again. "It's a full house this morning. You're going to have to do better than that. Do you have a name?"

"Tom Wakefield," Joe said.

She consulted a chart and pointed down a corridor to her left. "He's in room 435, cubicle number three."

"Thanks," Aiden said, but the harried nurse had already returned to her reports.

"Come on." Joe tugged on Aiden's arm.

They found room 435 easily enough. Cubicle three consisted of a narrow hospital bed with a curtain around the bed providing the illusion of privacy. One side of the curtain was open, and a lean, fit-looking, middle-aged man lay on his back on the bed. His right ankle was wrapped in a tensor bandage and was supported by a pillow.

"Mr. Wakefield?" Aiden stepped forward and flashed his ID.

"You're the police? I've been waiting for you." He shifted on the bed and winced as he adjusted his injured ankle.

Aiden nodded at the man's bandaged ankle. "How's your ankle doing, Mr. Wakefield?"

"Call me Tom." He stuck out his hand and winced again as the movement shifted his ankle. "This sprain will keep me off my feet for a few weeks, but the ankle's not broken at least." He grimaced. "It's nothing compared to that poor girl's injuries." He rubbed his hands over his face as if trying to erase his memory of Amanda's wounds. "Is she going to be all right?" He sagged back on the pillow. "No, of course she won't. How could she?" He looked at Aiden with a pleading gaze. "How is she doing?"

"Still unconscious at last report," Joe said. "We'd like to talk to you about how you found her."

"Of course." Tom's Adam's apple bobbed in his thin throat. "I was out for my early-morning run." He grimaced. "I'm training for the state cross-country marathon race in August. I like to run the trails at Creighton Springs State Park. They're challenging and—"

"Can you get to the point?" Joe asked.

"I'm sorry. Of course." Tom twisted his hands together on his lap. "It was still dark, but I had my headlamp, and the trail's pretty wide, so I was fine. I run there three times a week before work. I'm a foreman at the mill, and—"

"You pack any bear spray with you?" Joe interrupted again, his opinion of night runs more than clear.

"Of course, but I've never had any problems. Not until today." Tom swallowed again, and his face paled.

"Tell us what happened," Aiden asked. Maybe Tom would be able to tell them something that would help find the man who took Candace. It was looking more and more certain the same man took both women. The connection to Creighton Springs State Park was impossible to ignore. His gaze strayed to the clock on the wall.

Tom settled back against a pillow. "Like I said, I was running on the trail—"

"What trail?" Impatience wafted off Joe in almost-visible waves.

"The Turnkey Trail. It's the one that starts at the parking lot and swings past Mercer Lake and along the Eggleston River and up to the ridge and back."

Aiden nodded. He and Candace had walked part of that trail the day they'd found the cave with the human remains buried in the dirt. "And then what happened?"

"It was still dark out, but I had on my headlamp. I saw something on the trail ahead. It wasn't moving, but I heard moaning, as if an animal were in pain." He inhaled a shaky breath. "At first, I thought it was an injured deer or bear, but as I got closer, I realized it was a person…a young girl." His eyes reddened.

"Go on. You're doing great," Aiden encouraged. The poor man was struggling with the horror of what he'd seen. Who could blame him? Finding a severely injured girl on a remote trail in the woods would have been terrifying.

Tom sniffled and swiped his hand over his damp eyes. "When—" He swallowed. "—when I saw it was a girl, I didn't know what to do. She was lying on the ground, naked, covered in dirt and blood. There were gashes on her thighs and her stomach…as if someone had beaten her." He grabbed the blanket covering him and squeezed his hands until his knuckles turned white.

"She was hurt real bad.

"There's no cell reception in the park, and my wife makes me carry my satellite phone." He met Aiden's gaze. "You know, just in case." He hiccupped a shaky breath. "I called 911 right away. When the girl saw me, she screamed. She wouldn't let me touch her, and she tried to crawl away, but her leg—" He shook his head. "I was just trying to help her."

"Did she say anything? Anything at all?" Aiden leaned closer, his muscles tense.

Tom's forehead furrowed, and he was quiet for so long Aiden wanted to grab him by the shoulders and shake the words out of him.

Finally, Tom nodded. "I'm not sure she knew I was there to help her. I think she thought I was someone else." He looked at them with pleading eyes. "Maybe the man who hurt her?"

"Why do you say that?" Aiden prodded.

"She was moaning and crying, and she covered her head with her hands as if she was afraid I was going to hit her. It was hard to understand what she was saying, but I think she spoke a name."

"What name, Tom?" Aiden's gaze zeroed in on the man.

"I'm not sure." He looked at Aiden and then Joe. "Something biblical." He scrunched up his forehead. "Maybe Adam?" He shook his head. "No. That's not right. Abraham? Yes. That's it! I'm sure of it."

Joe and Aiden stared at each other as the man's words sank in.

Aiden moved a step closer to the bed. "Think very carefully, Tom. Are you sure she said Abraham?"

"I think so. She said the name a few times. She was

so scared. I think she thought I was him."

"Did she say anything else?" Joe asked.

Tom shook his head. "She passed out after that. I covered her with my coat and sat with her while I waited for the paramedics." He blew out a ragged breath. "Poor girl. She's only a kid. What the hell happened to her?" His eyes opened wide. "She's not that girl who's been missing for months, is she?" He pressed his hand over his mouth. "Oh my God. Did I find Amanda Jacobs?"

Not wanting to give away any information, Aiden ignored his questions, thanked the man, and he and Joe left the room and headed down the brightly lit corridor for the exit.

"Are you thinking the same thing I'm thinking?" Joe asked.

Aiden nodded. "Strawski's son's name is Abraham. That can't be a coincidence."

"You bet your life it ain't." Joe popped a gum bubble with a loud crack. "Strawski must be Isaiah. We never caught that monster. You don't suppose he's back at his old tricks, do you?"

Aiden shook his head. "Isaiah would be in his late seventies now; too old to be attacking and abducting women. Besides, the vet at the clinic said he was dead."

"So, what's the deal then? A copycat?"

"I think Junior's following in Daddy's footsteps." Aiden's gut lurched at the nightmare possibility, but he was onto something. Damn right he was. Every cell in his body vibrated.

They stopped at the front desk.

The same nurse manned it. She looked up when Joe tapped his fingers on the desk and sighed. "What do you want now?"

Aiden eased Joe aside and took over. Sometimes Joe's abrasive personality rubbed people the wrong way. Sometimes? He smiled at the nurse and read her name on the badge pinned to the front of her scrub top. "Diana, I wonder if you could check and give us a status report on another patient brought in this morning."

She returned his smile. "Sure. No problem, Detective…?"

"Farrell, but you can call me Aiden." He ignored Joe's snort. "We'd like to know Amanda Jacobs's current condition."

Her face altered. "That poor girl. I heard all about her. It's terrible what happened."

"How's she doing? Can we see her?"

She shook her head. "I'm sorry, but she's in surgery. She has a fractured arm and dislocated shoulder, to say nothing of all her other injuries."

Aiden's gut knotted. What sort of man would do that to a young girl? But she'd survive. He'd bet a year's salary on that. She was strong. She'd somehow managed to escape her captor. She was going to make it. He refused to consider any other outcome. He'd make damn sure he caught the monster that hurt her and toss him into a cell. "When will we be able to talk to her?"

"Not for several hours." She batted her eyelashes and smiled coquettishly. "Why don't you give me your card, and I'll call you when she's out of surgery?"

"Thanks, Diana." He ignored her blatant flirting and smiled. "That would be great." He slipped a card out of his wallet and laid it on the desk.

She picked the card up and slipped it into her breast pocket, smiling at Aiden. "I'll talk to you soon, Detective."

He flashed her another smile and turned and headed into the Emergency waiting room, through the waiting throng, and to the hospital front doors.

Joe followed, and once they were seated in the sedan, he turned to Aiden and smirked. "Still using the same tactics that got you in trouble in Seattle, Loverboy. Guess you haven't learned your lesson."

Aiden brushed off Joe's snarky comment. Too much was at stake to waste energy arguing with his partner. "Come on. Let's go. We need to get to the state park and check out the scene. Maybe we can find something that will tell us where Amanda was held, something that might lead us to Candace."

"You're pretty sure the same guy who's been holding Amanda all these months is the one who took the Cooper woman." Joe started the car.

"I am. It's too much of a coincidence that Candace saw those footprints in the park in November, and Amanda turns up there this morning. There has to be a connection."

"And you think he's holding her somewhere in the park." The bright-yellow fluorescent lights of the hospital shone on Joe's rugged face. "Then what are we sitting here for? Let's go find her." He shifted the car into gear, and they roared out of the parking lot, sirens blaring, lights flashing.

Chapter 36

She lay curled on the cold, damp, hard floor nursing her wounds. Each inhalation was like a shard of glass stabbing her chest. Every inch of her body ached, and her thighs were black and blue from where Abraham had kicked her. A lump the size of a golf ball throbbed on the back of her skull.

A shudder wracked her, and she moaned at the electric jolt of pain the tiny movement caused.

Isaiah murdered Charlene. She and her parents had searched for years, praying that someday they'd find Charlene.

Finally, Candace knew the horrible reality, but she wished she didn't. Far better to believe her sister was alive and well somewhere, living with amnesia, unaware of her past or the family who missed her. There was comfort in ignorance. The light of hope had kept her going year after year.

She bit hard on her bottom lip to stop another sob escaping. Charlene was dead, and the son of the man who'd killed her now held Candace hostage. If she didn't want to meet the same fate as her sister, she had to act, and act now. Before it was too late.

Pushing up against the wall, she struggled to find a comfortable position. The chain attached to her ankle clanked, and shooting stabs of fire flared in her bruised ribs. Her head throbbed, and she squeezed her eyes shut and swallowed back bile. The acrid taste filled her mouth, and she grabbed the water bottle lying on the floor and twisted off the cap. Her hand shook as she lifted the bottle to her mouth and gulped a mouthful.

A loud clank of metal sounded as the bolt slid back. The door opened, and Abraham stepped into the room, carrying a small plastic tray with a bowl on top. He set the tray on the floor beside her and backed away. "I brought you some soup and crackers."

The savory smell of warm, meaty broth filled the small room. Her mouth watered, and her stomach rumbled. The bowl was filled to the brim, chunks of meat and vegetables floating in the steaming broth. There was also a small, plastic-wrapped package of soda crackers on the tray.

Abraham crossed his bulging arms over his muscular chest. "Aren't you going to thank me?"

She bit down hard on her ragged bottom lip, the pain giving her strength. "Thank you." The words galled her, but she'd learned her lesson. The slightest sign of disrespect earned her a hard kick and more pain. If she had any hope of escape, she needed to be healthy.

He nodded approvingly. "Eat your soup. You need to keep up your strength. I have plans for you."

She wanted to tell him what he could do with his soup, but all she'd had to eat was a granola bar, and she was starving. There wasn't a spoon, so she lifted the plastic bowl with both hands. The soup smelled like heaven. Her stomach rumbled again, and she slurped. The meaty broth slid down her throat and into her belly, sending tendrils of warmth throughout her body. She ate the rest of the soup and set down the empty bowl.

Ripping open the package of crackers, she stuffed

them into her mouth, all the while aware he watched her every move. When she'd finished her meal, she leaned back against the wall, wincing at the stab of pain in her ribs. "What have you done with Amanda Jacobs?" He'd hinted there were other women. Maybe Amanda was one of his victims.

His dark eyes turned icy. "Amanda was a bad girl."

She shivered. *Was*? Was Amanda dead? Had he killed her like he'd killed Mary and those other girls? "Where is she?"

"Gone."

Fresh tears burned her eyes. "Did you kill her?"

He exhaled a hard-done-by sigh. "She didn't follow the rules." He shook his head as if he were discussing a recalcitrant child who refused to tidy her bedroom. "I thought that after the first time she tried to escape, she'd learned her lesson, but…" He shrugged.

"Those footprints I saw in the snow last November in the park were hers, weren't they? She was escaping you." The truth blurted out, along with a bucketful of guilt. If only she'd done something more that afternoon, maybe she could have saved Amanda.

"It was supposed to be you that day, you know. I'd been keeping track of you for months, and I followed you to the park. You were all alone, and the park was deserted." He spread his big hands wide. "It was almost as if you were asking for it, but when that little bitch escaped, I had to go after her." His narrowed gaze pinned her. "You called the cops, and I had to grab Amanda and clear out of the area." He jammed his hands on his hips and glowered. "It was all your fault. And Amanda's, of course. She broke the rules. That was naughty of her, but I punished her. No one disobeys me."

A chill rippled through her at the menace in his brown-eyed gaze. *Stop talking. Now. Stop asking questions.* The warning blazed through her. But she couldn't stop. She had to know the full scope of the nightmare. "What—" She gulped and gathered strength, prepared for the full brunt of his rage. "—what about the other girls? What happened to them?"

"The others?" He smiled sadly. "They weren't very smart either." He shrugged. "I tried to train them, just like Father taught me, but they wouldn't learn." He fixed her with a hard gaze. "Not like you, Candy Girl. You're smart. Real smart. You'll learn. I know you will." He rubbed his hands together. "We're going to get along great."

Insanity gleamed in his eyes, and her stomach roiled. He'd never release her. Never. She'd be his prisoner until the day he decided she wasn't following his rules. And then he'd kill her. No one would find her body. No one would know what happened. An ache, deep in her heart, throbbed. Would Aiden keep searching? Or would other cases of missing women take over, and he'd move on?

Stop feeling sorry for yourself. You're not dead. Not yet. You're smart, just like he said. You can get out of this. Just figure it out. The words, blasting like bullets, firmed her resolve. She squared her shoulders. "What happened to your father? Is Isaiah still alive?"

He picked up the tray and strode to the door but paused with his hand on the door handle. "Father passed several years ago." His eyes shone with unshed tears. "He was sick for a long time…cancer, I think. He wouldn't go to a hospital. He didn't trust doctors or the system." His gaze pierced her, the light of insanity blinding. "Before he left me, he made me promise to carry on his legacy. And so, I have." His chest swelled as if he were proud of his actions.

"Sleep well, Candy Girl. I have big plans for you tomorrow." He opened the metal door and slammed it shut behind him.

The lock slid into place.

Chapter 37

Aiden shivered and rubbed his arms. He'd lived in Colorado for months. You'd think he'd know better by now. He should've worn a warmer coat.

Springtime in the Rockies wasn't balmy. Fresh snow capped the nearby mountains, and there was a definite chill in the early morning air. The sun had just risen over the mountains, and the pinks and yellows of dawn's early morning light softened the looming shapes of the trees.

The second he'd learned Amanda had been found on a park trail, his gut pinged. If the same perp who abducted Amanda also took Candace, Candace was being held somewhere in the vast park. He just had to find her. The sooner the better. On the drive to the park, he and Joe had contacted the Parks Branch, and their contact mentioned Sam Wheeler, a retired park ranger.

Sam had agreed to come right away, and ten minutes ago, he'd pulled up in his rusted, four-wheel drive, super-cab truck, spewing dark clouds of diesel into the cold mountain air. In his seventies, the former chief park ranger at Creighton Springs State Park had been retired for the past five years.

From what Aiden had been told, the man knew every inch of the vast park.

Sam leaned against his truck, his arms crossed over his narrow chest. He wore a heavy down jacket, faded jeans, worn-and-scuffed work boots, and a faded black-felt cowboy hat pulled low over his lined forehead. Thin strands of snow-white hair curled at his neck. He sported an old fashioned, white, handlebar mustache. His leathery skin and deep tan were a testament to the many years he'd spent outdoors. In spite of his wrinkles and white hair, his body was lean and tough, his stomach flat, and he looked younger than his years.

"Yep." He nodded. "I know pretty well every inch of this park. After more'n thirty years keepin' an eye on the place, I sure as hell should." He turned his earnest gaze on Aiden. "Hope I can help y'all find this missing woman." He shook his head. "It's a damn shame what goes on in the park these days. In my day, the biggest issues we worried about were poachers and folks leaving their campfires unattended."

A cold wind kicked up, and fingers of icy air slid down the back of Aiden's neck. He shivered again. "Do you have any idea where someone could lay low for a few months, somewhere no one would notice them?"

Sam pushed back his hat and scratched his freckled forehead. "This here's a mighty big park, one of the largest in the state." His breath formed a cloud in the cold air. "I heard about that cave y'all found a week or so back." He grimaced. "Could've knocked me over with a feather. In all my years workin' here, I never heard a whisper about a cave in that section of the park."

A snowflake floated past Aiden's face. What the hell? It was March. He refocused on the retired park ranger. "Do any other places like that cave come to mind? We're pretty sure this guy kept a girl imprisoned here in the park for months."

More snowflakes swirled in the wind.

"Brrr!" Joe tightened his coat around his neck. "It's as cold as a witch's tit out here."

Sam nodded. "That's springtime in the Rockies…sunny and hot one minute, freezing your ass off the next."

Joe reached into his coat pocket and pulled out a crumpled cigarette package. Sliding a cigarette out, he fished in his other pocket and grabbed a lighter. Holding up the cigarette, he pointed toward the police cruiser. "I'm just gonna grab a quick smoke. Be right back." He hurried to the car, opened the driver's side door, climbed inside, and slammed the door closed. The car rumbled to life, and a plume of exhaust filled the air.

"We really need your help, Sam," Aiden urged. The clock was ticking. They had to find Candace. And soon. "You know this park better than anyone. A woman's life is at stake. Give us something, a bear den, another cave, an old cabin, something."

"I hear ya, Detective. Ever since I got your call, I've been givin' this some thought." He slipped off his Stetson and scratched his scalp and rocked back on his heels. "There is one place that comes to mind. It's a stretch, mind you, but it's the only structure I can think of."

Aiden's heart raced. "Tell me."

"Years ago, when I first started work here in the park, a bunch of fellas used to ride their snow machines on the park trails. There quite a group of 'em. Mind, that was before the regulations changed. Now there's no snowmobiling permitted within the park boundaries. The whole darn park is a protected area. No motorized vehicles of any kind allowed off the main road."

Patience wasn't Aiden's strong suit, but some informants just couldn't be rushed.

Sam coughed, a deep raspy sound. "Those snowmobile fellas wanted to build a warmin' hut." He chuckled. "Can you imagine?" He shook his head. "Anyhoo, they applied for permission, but were denied. The Parks Board didn't want any buildings erected in the park, leastwise, not without the proper permits." He grimaced. "You know how the government works…reams and reams of paperwork even if you just want to revarnish a picnic table or change the brand of toilet paper in the outhouses."

He set his hat on his head and reached into his coat pocket and drew out a red-checked cloth handkerchief and blew his nose. "Damn cold today. Weatherman says it's supposed to snow a good six inches. My hip's been acting up. It don't take kindly to the cold and damp." He eyed Aiden. "Don't let anyone tell you that gettin' old is the golden years." He blew his nose again, inspected the contents of his handkerchief, and stuffed it back in his pocket. "Where was I?"

"The snowmobile warming hut." Aiden gritted his teeth, wanting to wring the information out of the old man. Only a miracle stopped him.

"Ah yeah." Sam nodded. "When they got turned down, those boys came direct to me and pled their case." He huffed out a raspy breath. "Call me a soft touch, but I couldn't see where there was a problem with them buildin' a small hut, especially when they were plannin' on doin' all the work."

"Where was that? What area of the park?"

"If I recollect, it was back behind Mount Redson, over by Sisters Creek." He shifted, winced, and rubbed his hip. "I been there a few times, but that was years ago." His mouth curled in a smile. "Those boys sure knew what they were doin'. That hut was somethin', all right. It even had a root cellar, for Gawd's sakes. Can you imagine? I mean, what were they thinkin'?"

Adrenaline surged through Aiden, and his heartbeat sped up a dozen beats. "Is the hut still there?"

Sam shrugged. "Don't rightly know. When the Parks Board shut down all snowmobilin' in the park, those boys stopped comin' 'round, and the hut fell into disuse. The trail to the hut washed out a few years ago. Far as I know, no one goes there anymore." He shook his head. "Funny, I almost forgot about that shack."

"Can you show me where it is on a map?" Every cell in Aiden's body tingled, his muscles strung tight. This was it. He knew it.

Sam opened the front door of his truck and leaned inside. He tugged out a stained, folded map from the glove compartment, opened it, and spread it on the hood of his truck.

Aiden moved closer. The wind whipped at the map, and he struggled to hold it flat.

Snowflakes spotted the paper.

Sam pointed at a spot on the map. "Hut was here. Not sure if it's still standin', but this is where it was."

Yes! Aiden wanted to fist pump the air. He'd found the bastard's lair. "Can I take this?" He folded the map and held it up.

"Sure, but it won't do you much good."

He frowned. "Why not?"

"You can't drive there, and like I said, the trail's

washed out."

Aiden clenched his hands in frustration. "So how are we supposed to get in there?"

"I just called for a chopper and a SWAT team."

Joe's smokey breath blasted Aiden. He hadn't heard his partner approach.

"They'll be here in twenty minutes."

Sam nodded. "That's one way to get there."

Joe looked smug. "That's what I thought."

Chapter 38

Candace stared at the light bulb until her eyes burned, but she didn't blink and didn't look away. She needed to get the hell out of that locked room before Abraham returned. Hours earlier, she'd heard a muffled sound of a distant door slamming. Since then, silence. He'd left. Maybe he'd gone for supplies. But she was alone. Of that she was certain.

A horrible thought entered her mind...what if he never came back? What if he'd left her there to starve? No one knew where she was. No one would find her. She'd never see Aiden again. Despair weighted her heart, and she lay on the cold cement floor, her knees drawn to her chest, hot tears washing her face.

With no outside light penetrating the tiny cell, she had no way of knowing if it was night or day. The hours blended one into another. Thirst raged through her, and her stomach growled with hunger. The last food she'd eaten was the soup and crackers. How long ago was that?

She had no idea where she was being held or what Abraham's plans for her were, but judging by the string of dead and injured women he'd left in his wake, unless she escaped, no one would see her alive again. She'd disappear. Just like Charlene, and that poor girl the police had found dead in Lynn Canyon. Like Amanda Jacobs.

Maybe he was also responsible for the death of the anonymous girl whose bones she and Aiden had discovered in the park cave. A sob clogged her throat.

Tears streamed from her eyes, blinding her, seeping down her cheeks, dripping onto her dirt-crusted shirt. Somehow, she had to escape. She scrubbed her hands over her face. Think. Study the room. Examine every inch. There had to be a way out.

The walls were made of solid-looking concrete. There weren't any crumbling patches through which she could dig a hole and escape. Besides, she was chained to the wall. She jerked her leg and rattled the chain like she had a thousand times before, but the metal ring embedded in the cement didn't budge. She'd spent countless hours fighting to break the clamp around her ankle, but other than broken nails and blisters on her hands, she hadn't made any progress.

Think! There had to be something she could use to escape.

She took inventory—a plastic water hose, a metal chair, six empty plastic water bottles, and a heavy-duty plastic bucket filled with her waste. She grimaced. Not even a Special Forces expert could finagle a weapon with those simple supplies.

She curled back on the floor, too exhausted, too filled with hopelessness, to do anything other than cry. The tiny, windowless room would be her crypt. She'd die there. Not now, maybe not tomorrow, but Abraham would kill her. Of that she was certain.

She'd almost accepted the inevitable. The oblivion of death was preferable to lying on the cold, hard floor, in that brightly lit room that smelled of rot, despair, and her own waste. Her only regret was she'd never see

Aiden again, never again feel the comfort of being held in his arms, his lips on hers… She squeezed her eyes closed.

****

The twenty-minute wait for the helicopter felt like twenty years. Aiden passed the time pressing Sam for more details on the snowmobile warming hut and the surrounding terrain.

Joe waited in the car, the motor idling, steam from the car's exhaust clouding the air. He'd asked Aiden if he wanted to join him, but Aiden was too fired up to sit twiddling his thumbs in a warm vehicle.

Adrenaline pumped through him, and his body vibrated with the need for action. He couldn't stand still, and so he paced. From one side of the empty parking lot to the other, again and again, listening for the rumble of a helicopter over the roar of the wind. The temperature had dropped a dozen degrees, and the snow swirling in the air was thicker and starting to stick to the ground.

He raised his coat collar, huddled into his light suede jacket, and shoved his cold-numbed hands deeper into his pants pockets. Questions swirled like the snow through his brain. Was his gut instinct right? Had Abraham Strawski taken her? Was Candace being held in the snowmobile warming hut? Would they find her? Would she be alive when they did?

And what about the perp? Would they take him down? He sure as hell hoped so. If Abraham Strawski somehow managed to escape, Aiden vowed he'd track the bastard through the very gates of Hell and make damn sure he paid for what he'd done. Not just to Candace, but to all his other victims.

"Aiden."

Joe's voice broke through his inner storm, and Aiden turned to the car.

Joe had the window rolled down and gestured for Aiden to come closer.

Aiden strode over. "What's up?"

"Get your ass in here, and I'll tell you." Joe punched a button, and the window rolled up.

Aiden heaved a sigh and walked around to the passenger door, yanked it open and climbed in. A blast of warmth hit him. Joe had the heater cranked up, and the air inside the car was tropical. The windows were fogged and beaded with condensation. He unzipped his jacket. "What's going on?"

Joe wiped a bead of sweat from his brow. "The captain radioed. Looks like they caught the guy who raped Laurie Ann Carson. He broke into a girl's dorm room and attacked her. Lucky thing her roommate walked in and called the cops."

Aiden's breath whooshed out. "So, he's not our guy."

Joe shook his head. "Doesn't look like it." He reached over and turned the heater down a notch. "The chopper pilot just radioed. He's delayed. This weather isn't helping. The visibility is crap."

Aiden's heart sank. "How much longer will they be?"

Joe shrugged. "Another couple of hours at least. They can't take off until the storm eases."

"What?" Aiden pounded his fist on the dash. "No way. We have to get in there now. We can't wait two hours. Candace's life is at stake. Every second could mean the difference between life and death."

C. B. Clark

Joe's eyes narrowed. "You really like this girl, don't you? She means more to you than just a pretty face."

Aiden chewed on his bottom lip, and then decided to hell with it. "You're right. I like her. I like her a lot." He smoothed the palm of his hand over his damp hair. "I don't know what it is, but she's special to me, and we have to find her."

There was a beat of silence, filled by the smooth rumble of the motor and the blast of hot air from the vents.

Joe cleared his throat. "Well, then you should go and get her."

Aiden furrowed his brow. "What are you saying?"

"You can't let your past control you. You made one mistake. So what? Everyone screws up. It may surprise you, but even I've messed up a few times." The corners of his mouth twitched. "Candace Cooper isn't a mistake. And she's in danger."

Joe was right. He needed to find her. And fast, before he was too late. But how? That was the million-dollar question, the one that tore at his heart.

"Look, man." Joe gripped Aiden's arm. "I made a mistake a long time ago." He licked his lips. "I didn't act when I should have. I thought I knew better than anyone. I regret that. I've regretted it every single day since and…" His voice broke, and he released his hold on Aiden's arm and sat, staring straight ahead at the fogged windshield, blinking.

Another long beat of silence.

Were those tears glimmering in Joe's eyes? Aiden had never seen his partner express any emotion other than sarcasm. And what was he talking about? What case did he regret?

"Aiden?" Joe's rough voice was loud in the thick silence. "Why the hell are you sitting here on your ass when your girl needs you?" He arched his shaggy brows. "Go get her, Loverboy. Be a hero."

Aiden sagged against the seat. "But you just said the helicopter's delayed."

"I'm willing to bet my pension there's more than one way to get in there."

Aiden stared at the falling snow melting on the hood from the heat of the engine. Was Joe right? Was there another way to access that old warming hut? The bigger question was—did he have a choice? Candace was in deep trouble. He knew where she probably was being held. He had to save her. It was as simple and as complicated as that.

An idea popped into his brain, and he wrenched open the door and jumped out of the car. "You're a genius, Joe." He slammed the door behind him and rushed over to Sam's truck.

The retired ranger was sitting inside the rumbling vehicle, keeping warm.

Aiden tapped on the driver's-side window.

Sam rolled the window down. "What's up, Detective?"

"The helicopter's delayed due to the weather. Is there any other way to reach that hut?"

Sam pursed his lips. "I'm not surprised about the chopper. This snow's pretty heavy, and with the wind, there's no way anyone would fly. You'll be lucky if the storm ends before tomorrow."

Aiden fought against despair. "Could I walk to the cabin? Is that a possibility? Or ride an ATV?"

Sam shook his head. "It's too far to walk, and like I told you, the trail's washed out. You'd never make it. Not even on a quad."

The energy seeped out of Aiden's body like air leaking out of a balloon, and it was all he could do to remain standing. "So that's it then? We have to wait for the chopper." A dozen scenarios flashed before him, each more terrifying that the next. The longer Candace remained with her abductor, the greater the risk. It was simple statistics that every cop knew.

Sam shoved his hat back from his forehead. "There is another way."

"There is?"

"Yep. It won't be easy though, especially with this storm." The old ranger studied Aiden. "You look tough enough. Maybe you could handle it."

"Tell me. What do I have to do?"

"How good are you on a horse?"

Chapter 39

She awoke with a start and lay still, listening. Something—a noise, a change in the air—had awakened her. A distant thud of a door slamming echoed from behind the locked metal door of her cell.

He was back!

Her heart thudded so hard she feared it would burst out of her chest.

A metallic screech rent the air as the bolt was drawn back.

She flinched, and inhaled a breath, digging deep for strength, preparing. This was it. Her last chance. D-Day.

Another scrape of metal, and the door swung open. "Well, hey there, hi there, ho there, Candy Girl." Abraham grinned. "Did you miss me?"

"What do you want?" She refused to play his games. Even if he beat her, she wouldn't bow down before him. Not anymore. She was stronger than that. She gulped. At least she hoped she was.

"You haven't figured that out yet?" He stuffed his hands into the front pockets of his cargo pants and smirked. "And I thought you were smart."

She gripped her hands so tight her fingernails dug into her skin.

"This —" He pointed at first her and then himself. "—you, me, we're a circle." He chuckled. "You can call it the circle of life, if you like. Father started the circle when he recruited those girls all those years ago, but the police raided the farm where he was keeping them and ruined his plans." He scowled, and the furrow between his dark brows deepened. "Father didn't like loose ends. I don't much either."

Her breath whooshed out at the menace shadowing his dark eyes. This was the end, the moment he killed her. Unless she stopped him.

Keep him talking. Distract him. Do something. Anything.

"You must be proud of your father." She nearly gagged at her words, but she needed to convince him she was going along with his insane plans. "Isaiah and his exploits were all over the news. He's famous. The media still runs specials on the anniversary of the Forgotten Five's rescue."

He puffed his chest out with obvious pride. "His name really wasn't Isaiah. His real name was Martin Strawski. The name Isaiah was given to him by the Prophet one night in a dream." His eyes gleamed. "Before Father passed, he made me promise I'd finish his life's work. Close the circle, like I told you. Once I've done that, everyone will know my name too. I'll be famous. I bet they even make one of those true-crime documentaries about me."

She shuddered at the light of insanity glowing in his dark eyes. His father had kidnapped young girls and kept them in horrendous circumstances, abused and beat them. Now, in his quest to fulfill his father's insane plans, Abraham had followed the same evil path. "How many others have there been?" She had to know every vile act he'd committed.

"A few." His gloating smirk transformed to a glower. "You and that cop boyfriend of yours ruined everything. I had it all planned. I chose the girls I wanted, and I organized everything. I found the perfect disposal places in case—" He smiled, revealing sharp canines. "—you know, in case the girls didn't follow the rules."

"It was you!" A rush of blinding shock swept over her, threatening to drag her down into oblivion. "You did it. You killed that girl and left her body in the cave in Creighton Springs State Park." Why was she so shocked? He was crazy. Life meant nothing to him in his insane quest to complete some sort of senseless circle of life his father had started. She squeezed her eyes closed. She couldn't look at him a second longer, not without throwing up.

His rank body odor thickened the air, and she opened her eyes. He loomed over her, so close the scuffed toes of his boots brushed her thigh. "You should be honored, Candy Girl. You're one of the chosen."

She spotted the festering stab wound on his arm, and a small glimmer of hope flared. He wasn't invincible. She'd hurt him once; she could do it again. Without giving herself time to realize the stupidity of what she was about to do, she fisted her hand and punched as hard as she could upwards into his crotch.

He grunted and hunched over, cupping his hands between his legs, and fell to his knees, landing with a thud on the hard floor.

She swung her fists, punching his kidneys, his stomach, his face, wherever she could reach, as hard as she could, again and again.

He collapsed onto the floor.

In a blur of motion, she scissored his body between her legs and squeezed. Her ribs screamed, but she fought through the blinding pain and tightened her hold. All those years of running had hardened her thigh muscles, and she pressed.

He fought back, and in seconds was free, springing to his feet, snarling. "You bitch."

She scrambled to her feet and slammed her fist into his rock-hard stomach, his chest, his back...landed another blow between his legs, one to his nose. Blood spurted. Another punch glanced off his bearded chin. Her hands throbbed, her chest heaved, but she fought on, knowing that if she stopped, he'd kill her. He landed a blow to the side of her head, and she screamed at the flash of pain. Tears burned her eyes.

He shoved her hard, and she tripped over the chain and fell with a hard thud that knocked the wind out of her. Before she caught her breath, he landed on top of her, suffocating her with the weight of his big body. Pain shot through her, and spots filled her vision. She blinked away the darkness and fought on, twisting, kicking, spitting...

He laughed, a deep-throated belly laugh, so unexpected she stopped struggling. The expression on his face staggered her. He was toying with her. He wanted her to fight him. The rage drained out of her, and she sagged beneath him.

He'd won. She couldn't win this fight, not against the man's insanity. It was over. All over.

His hot, stale breath blasted her. "Well, that was fun." He grinned. "Stupid, but fun." His eyes turned cold. "You have to be punished for your disobedience.

You know that, don't you?"

She shuddered, struggling to mask her fear, refusing to give him the pleasure. Gathering saliva in her mouth, she spat. The gob of spittle landed on his bushy beard. "You bastard!"

He reeled back and wiped his beard with the back of his hand. His eyes narrowed, and if looks could kill, she'd be dead. "You're gonna regret that, Candy Girl. Oh, yes you are."

She braced for his attack, but then froze. Somehow during their struggle, the chain attached to her ankle had wrapped around his legs. A plan formed in her panicked brain, a crazy plan, one with no chance of success, but a plan all the same. The timing had to be perfect. Heart pounding, she waited for him to move, to shift his weight.

He planted his hands on the floor on either side of her head and pushed to his knees.

She tensed. Any second now.

Just as he realized the chain was wrapped around his ankles, she jerked her legs hard and yanked him over.

He fell, landing with a thud on the hard cement floor. His head struck the ground with a hollow thunk. His eyes widened, and his mouth opened. Fury raged in his eyes. He jammed his hand on her neck, cutting off her air.

Her lungs, starved of oxygen, burned. Dark spots blurred her vision. She flailed, desperate, her fingers prying at his cruel grip. Darkness loomed. She needed air. Now! Her hand brushed something hard and metal. In the dim recess of her mind, she knew it was the metal chair. She grabbed it by a leg and dragged it closer.

He was so intent on killing her, he seemed oblivious to her efforts.

She stopped trying to pry his fingers from her throat and, with the last of her strength, lifted the chair with both hands and slammed the heavy metal on his head with a sickening clunk.

He grunted, released a gust of fetid air, groaned, and his eyes fluttered closed.

The pressure on her throat eased, his hand fell away, and he collapsed, sprawling atop her like a suffocating blanket.

Gasping, sucking air into her lungs, she shoved against his unresisting bulk. Inch by inch, she pushed off his heavy body. Panting, exhausted, her injured ribs screaming, she climbed to her feet, the desperate need to escape driving her.

His eyes were closed, but his chest was moving up and down. He wouldn't stay unconscious for long.

She crouched over him and fished in the front pockets of his pants, searching for keys. She touched cold metal. Yes! Dragging out the key ring, she inserted a key into the lock on the metal band encasing her ankle and twisted. The lock didn't open. She tried another key. That one didn't work either.

His legs twitched, and he groaned.

Her hands shook as she slid another key into the lock. With a quiet click, the manacle sprang open. Scrambling to her feet, she stumbled to the door and wrenched open the heavy door.

He groaned again, a low feral growl, and crawled to his knees, staggering to his feet. Blood dripped from his nose into his beard. "You goddamned bitch! You'll pay for this. Mark my words. You'll pay."

She whimpered and slipped through the opening and slammed the door behind her.

Heavy footsteps sounded on the other side of the closed door.

No time to slide the bolt in place. Heart in her throat, she fled up a short set of wooden stairs and down a narrow, dark hall and burst into a small room. Light seeped through the warped slats of a single boarded-up window and filtered across the dirty, planked floor. A bedroll, with a sleeping bag on top, lay against one wall. The crackle of flames came from a rusted iron wood stove set in the center of the room.

A loud wrenching screech echoed as the metal door opened.

He was coming!

She raced across the room, stumbling over the uneven floorboards, toward a wooden door. Grasping the handle, she flung the door open, and plunged through the opening. A blast of cold air struck first, and then a blinding swirl of snowflakes blowing in the frigid air.

She was outside! She'd done it. She'd escaped. But now what?

"You can run, but you can't hide from me, Candy Girl. Your sister tried to escape too, but she learned her lesson. She didn't get very far. No siree. Father saw to that."

Heart racing, a scream building in her chest, she ran into the blizzard.

Chapter 40

Aiden tightened his grip on the reins as the sure-footed horse clambered up the steep, narrow trail.

Somehow, even with the snowy gusts, the gray gelding managed to follow the faint indentation of the old, overgrown path.

They'd been riding for over an hour, climbing through dense stands of coniferous forest as they ascended the mountain.

With each plodding step, Aiden bounced up and slammed down on the hard, leather saddle.

They'd left the trees behind and travelled through the alpine on a trail that snaked around stunted scrub pines and snow-covered mossy tufts. The horse waded in the tall grass and splashed through shallow, snow-covered marshes. The temperature had dropped, and the heavy snowflakes swirling in the bitter wind were blinding.

They'd left Joe at the park parking lot, waiting in his warm car for the helicopter with the SWAT team members. He wasn't happy with Aiden's decision not to wait for backup. Aiden grimaced. Unhappy was putting it mildly. Joe had been livid. Even now, two hours later, memories of their argument stung.

"I'm telling you, Aiden. You're making a rookie mistake." Joe huffed out his chest and stuffed his hands in his coat pockets. *"You don't wanna screw with your*

career. Not now. Not when you're just getting your feet back on the ground."

"But you're the one who told me not to wait for the chopper. You told me to go and get Candace."

"You caught me in a weak moment." He scrubbed his hand over his whiskered chin. "Now I've had time to think about it, I'm having second thoughts." He huffed out a breath that fogged in the cold air. "Look, I know I've been a mean bastard, but it was for your own damn good. You needed hardening.

"I never shoulda said anything. I shoulda kept my damn mouth shut. You're new here. You haven't proven yourself. If you go all maverick, you'll get canned." His gaze met Aiden's. "You're good at your job. Don't do anything to screw with that. The chopper will be here soon, and then you can save your girl. A few more hours won't matter. You know that. This is your career we're talking about."

Those were the most words Joe had ever spoken at one time.

Aiden forked his fingers through his snow-dampened hair. Part of him—the career-driven, sane part—knew Joe was right. What Aiden was about to do would guarantee his dismissal from the force. Breaking protocol was a career killer.

But he didn't have a choice. Candace was in trouble. He had a chance to save her. For the first time in years, he didn't give a shit about his damn career. All he cared about was saving the woman he loved, consequences be damned.

Climbing into Sam's rusted four-by-four, he settled on the torn-and-stained upholstery of the passenger seat. He looked at Joe. "I'm doing it."

Joe shook his head. "Jesus, man. Wait for backup. You know the rules. You can't ride in there like some cowboy out of a goddamned spaghetti western and save the girl." He spat on the frozen ground. "Things don't happen that way in real life. You know that, right? Wait here for the chopper."

Aiden shook his head. "Not a chance."

Sam, seated in the driver's seat, cleared his throat. "If we're doin' this, Detective Farrell, we best get goin' before the storm gets much worse."

Aiden nodded. "Let's go."

Sam fired up the truck, and black diesel smoke billowed in the air.

Aiden waved at Joe. "I'll see you on the flip side, partner."

Joe grimaced. "Shit, man. I'd better not wear any flak from this. It's all on you. You—"

Aiden slammed the heavy door with a resounding thunk, cutting off Joe's tirade. He nodded at Sam. "Let's do this."

Sam pressed his foot to the gas, and the truck roared out of the parking lot, leaving a plume of black smoke billowing in the air with the snowflakes.

Joe raised his hand and gestured.

Aiden stared. Was that a thumbs-up? Nah. No way.

In the next minute, they'd left Joe and the parking lot behind, and Aiden focused on the upcoming rescue operation.

Sam Wheeler drove on rough back roads to a corral a few miles from the park boundary, where the rangers kept saddle horses for when they had to access the backcountry to check on the park's wildlife or search for lost hikers.

After Aiden confessed that he hadn't ridden a horse since he was a kid, Sam chose a tall, gray-speckled mare named Sally for him. He saddled the animal and helped Aiden climb onto the saddle.

Sam mounted his own horse, a beautiful black gelding, and expertly guided his horse out of the corral and into the dense forest.

Aiden's horse seemed to know the backcountry, and all Aiden had to do was hang on and pray he didn't fall off. His thighs were chafed raw from gripping the sides of the horse, and his butt...well, his butt was damn sore from slamming down onto the hard saddle. But none of that mattered, not the pain and discomfort, nor the cold. He was on his way to find Candace.

Sally stumbled over a snow-crusted rock.

Aiden clung to the saddle horn and dug his feet into the stirrups, barely managing to hang on.

Ahead, Sam looked over his shoulder and peered through the blowing snow. "How ya doin', son?"

Aiden grimaced. "Okay, I guess."

Sam chuckled. "You're not much of a rider, are ya?"

"Does it show?"

Sam laughed again. "Well, if you can hang on a bit longer, we're almost there. We just have to angle down this mountain and into the valley." He pointed. "If it weren't for this snowstorm, we'd probably be able to see the hut or what's left of it."

Aiden's heart sped up. They were almost there. Finally. For the first time since he'd agreed with Sam's wild suggestion to ride horses over the mountains to the old snowmobile warming hut, doubt assailed him. What if Candace wasn't there? What if he'd read the situation

C. B. Clark

wrong, and the kidnapper had taken her somewhere else? If so, he was wasting valuable time.

But if he wasn't wrong, he had to be prepared. He didn't know what the situation was down there. He could be riding into a disaster. If his theory was right, and the man holding Candace was the same person she'd encountered in this very forest months ago and the one who'd attacked her the other night, the perp had at least one long rifle and a knife.

He squinted into the sleet. Joe was right. Aiden should've waited for backup, but time was running out. He was certain this was Abraham, the man who'd kidnapped Amanda Jacobs and held her captive for months. The monster had killed the victim whose bones he and Candace had found in the cave. He'd probably murdered the girl in Lynn Canyon too.

And now he had Candace.

Aiden would take down the bastard. He wasn't waiting for backup that could take hours to arrive. He patted his police-issue revolver strapped in its holster on his hip. He hadn't ridden all this way over rough terrain to sit back on his ass and wait for the cavalry.

The horse slipped and dropped down a foot, bouncing Aiden in the air. His butt landed on the saddle with a painful thump. He shook off his dark thoughts and focused on staying on top of the beast. He just hoped he could walk once they reached the hut and he climbed off the horse.

They descended the steep, treed slopes of Morrisey Mountain into a narrow, forested valley where a small creek was visible through the heavy snowfall. Under other conditions, the valley, with its views of the surrounding snowcapped mountains and untouched, verdant forests would be beautiful.

But not today, not when a blizzard raged, and his heart pounded so fast he feared it would beat out of his chest. Adrenaline surged through his veins, tightening every muscle, focusing his mind, preparing him for the upcoming battle.

Sam reined in his horse and waited until Aiden's horse sidled beside him. He pointed across the valley. "Do you see it? The snowmobile hut's over there, against that big boulder, by the creek." He exhaled, his breath a plume of white in the cold air. "You might be onto something, Detective. Looks like someone's fixed it up a bit."

Aiden peered through the squall. The falling snow had transformed from hard, icy pellets to large fluffy flakes. Was it wishful thinking or was the storm easing? He spotted rocks, the creek wending through the narrow valley, and lots and lots of trees. "I can't see a hut. Are you sure this is the place?"

Sam snorted. "I worked this park for over thirty years. I know every damn inch of it. I'm sure."

"You didn't know about the cave." Aiden couldn't help pointing that out. If Sam was wrong about the cave, he could be wrong about the hut. He wasn't a young man. Maybe he was losing his faculties.

"I should've known about that damned cave." His shoulders drooped. "Guess I don't know this park as well as I thought."

Guilt flooded Aiden. Way to go, buddy. Take your frustration and worry out on an old man. "Look, Sam. I'm sorry, I—"

Sam cut off his apology. "Do you smell that?"

A whiff of woodsmoke drifted on the frigid air.

They were close. "Show me again where that hut is."

Sam squinted into the wind and snow and pointed. "It's hard to see because the wood's weathered, and the walls blend in with the rocks." He reached into his saddle bag and pulled out a pair of binoculars. "Here. These'll help."

Aiden held the binoculars to his eyes and studied the valley floor again. He blinked to clear his vision.

A person in a red shirt burst through the trees, staggering across the snow-covered ground.

His heart skittered. Candace! Fear was all too visible on her pale face. He shifted the binoculars and peered to the right. His heart almost stopped.

A bearded man, wearing camouflage-patterned clothing that blended into the forest cover, chased after Candace. A rifle was gripped in his hands.

Aiden wiped the moisture from his eyes and handed Sam the binoculars.

"Do you see them?" Sam called over the gusting wind. "Looks like there're two of 'em, and one's chasing the other. This doesn't look good, they—"

Aiden didn't wait for Sam to finish. "Stay here!" He kicked his horse in the sides and clung to the saddle horn and hung on for dear life when Sally responded and cantered down the mountain, slipping and sliding through the loose rock scrabble.

The clatter of Sam's horse racing after him rose above the wind. He should've known Sam wouldn't listen. He hoped the old man knew enough to stay under cover if bullets started flying.

Aiden's teeth rattled, his butt screamed in agony with every hard bounce, and his arms ached from gripping the pommel, but he leaned back on the saddle and allowed the horse her way. His gaze never left the two running figures.

The distance between them had shortened.

Candace stumbled and slowed, and his breath caught in his throat.

The man chasing her was catching up.

He prodded the horse, urging the poor beast to go faster. *Hang on, Candace. Hang on. I'm coming.* The fervent prayer ran through his brain in an endless refrain.

I'm coming.

Chapter 41

Breath gusting in and out of her burning lungs, she sprinted through the trees, dodging boulders, leaping over half-buried roots, slipping on the wet, snowy ground. Her feet, clad only in thin cotton socks, were frozen, but she yelped as the sharp edge of a rock sliced her heel. A flashback of the footprints in the snow she'd seen so many months ago, blood smears marking the heel imprints, rose before her. A sob choked her throat.

She risked a glance over her shoulder and shuddered.

He was gaining on her.

Digging deep for strength, she ignored the burn in her muscles and raced across the snowy ground. She had to get away. But where to go? She was in a dense forest, miles from anywhere.

Snow-covered mountain peaks loomed overhead, and fresh snow swirled in the bitter wind and settled on the ground, concealing roots and rocks.

She stumbled and cried out. Her injured rib screamed in protest, the pain almost driving her to her knees.

"I'm coming for you, Candy Girl."

His taunting voice chilled her to the bone, but she tamped down the paralyzing fear. She wouldn't give up. Never. Pushing harder, pumping her legs, flying over the snowy ground, scrambling over downed trees, and tumbling down gullies.

A loud curse rent the air.

She glanced over her shoulder, and a spurt of elation flared.

Abraham lay sprawled on the snow. In the next second, he let out a roar and clambered to his feet. "Run all you want, Candy Girl." His maniacal laughter filled the cold air. "You can't get away. There's nowhere to go." He started after her again.

She couldn't outrun him. She had to find somewhere to hide. Until what? Help wasn't on the way. No one knew where she was. How long could she stay hidden in the frigid backwoods before hypothermia set in?

Fear eating at her insides, she ducked under a branch and raced into the forest, hoping to lose him in the trees. She swerved around a fallen tree and crawled over a deadfall, ignoring the sharp branches ripping at her clothes, gouging her skin.

His tortuous breathing, pounding feet, and angry curses grew louder.

A sob tore at her throat. She wasn't going to make it. She'd tried her best, but her best wasn't good enough. This was how she'd meet her end—hunted like an animal, chased to the ground. Once he caught her, he'd kill her. Not right away. He'd want her to suffer. But he would kill her. Of that she had no doubt.

A sob burst free, and tears blinded her. Her foot caught on a root, and she went down hard, landing on the icy ground with a thump. Pain spiked through her knee, and she moaned. She struggled to rise, to run, but her knee collapsed beneath her. She buried her face in her hands, not wanting to see his gloating smirk when he caught her.

This was it. The end.

"Police! Stop where you are. Now." The sharp command rang out.

She lowered her hands and blinked. And blinked again.

Aiden stepped out of the trees and stood, his legs braced wide, a large revolver clenched in his hands and pointed at Abraham.

Abraham skidded to a stop, his wide-eyed expression of shocked surprise almost comical.

Aiden! He'd found her. A miracle had happened. Somehow, he'd tracked her down to this remote valley. The lump clogging her throat thickened, and her eyes burned.

His hold on the menacing-looking gun was steady, his steely-eyed gaze fixed on Abraham. "Hands up, asshole!"

Abraham glared, dropped the rifle, and turned. Roaring like a ferocious beast, he charged.

She screamed, and struggled to rise, but he covered the ten feet between them in seconds, grabbed her shirt collar, and yanked hard, hauling her to her feet, slamming her against his body.

His sour sweat gagged her, and she shoved against the hard wall of his chest, fighting to break free of his iron grip. His arm jammed her throat, cutting off her air.

"Let her go," Aiden's quiet command rent the air. He didn't move, didn't flinch, the gun in his hand steady.

Abraham laughed and tightened his arm. "Make me, Loverboy. That's what they call you, isn't it? I read all about your *little* mistake in Seattle."

The pressure on her throat was agonizing. Stars burst behind her closed lids. She flailed, twisting, kicking, fighting for breath. The iron band on her throat tightened, and darkness beckoned, but she fought on, refusing to give in. The monster wouldn't win. Not this time. She drew her right leg up and drove her heel back into his groin.

He emitted an oomph.

The second the unrelenting pressure across her throat eased, she sucked in a breath, and with a twist of her body, threw herself onto the ground, landing with a jolting thud.

A flash lit the air, followed by a deafening bang.

Abraham staggered a step, and then sagged onto the snowy ground, landing on his knees beside her. A pool of blood stained the snow beneath his thigh. He turned his head and met her gaze. "What have you done, Candy Girl? You've ruined everything. We haven't closed the circle. I thought you understood."

She swallowed bile and scrambled back from his insanity.

"I said, 'hands up,' asshole." Aiden moved closer, the barrel of his gun pointed at the wounded man.

Abraham cursed, and his eyes burned hatred, but he slowly raised his arms over his head.

Aiden shot her a quick glance, and the corners of his mouth lifted in a brief, reassuring smile. Yanking Abraham's arms behind his back, he cuffed the man's wrists and read him his rights. He nodded at her. "Are you okay? Did he hurt you?"

"I'm fine." Her throat burned, her body ached in a hundred different places, her knee was swollen, and the slightest movement set her ribs on fire. But she was free. She'd made it out of that cellar, and just like in the movies, the handsome hero had saved her. You bet she was all right.

A whinny sounded along with the thudding of a horse's hooves on hard ground. A man wearing a battered cowboy hat rode into the clearing on a beautiful black horse. "I see you didn't need my help, Detective." His gaze switched to her, and he smiled and tipped the brim of his hat. "I gather you're Candace."

She nodded, trying to wrap her brain around the sight of a cowboy riding in on a horse.

The man on the horse grinned. "You must be somethin' pretty special." He nodded at Aiden. "This guy went through a hell of a lot of trouble to get here." He jerked his thumb over his shoulder to a small stand of trees where a gray horse was tethered to a branch. "Sally gave him quite a ride. Your man won't be walkin' straight for a week."

She turned to Aiden. "*You* rode here on a horse?"

He rubbed his butt and winced. "I had to get here somehow."

She opened her mouth to tell him how glad she was that he was there, but her voice was drowned out by the thundering roar of a helicopter.

The whup, whup, whup of the rotors filled the valley, resounding off the mountains.

The noise increased in intensity, and she covered her ears.

A blizzard of wet snow, pine needles, and dirt swirled as the large black helicopter settled onto the ground, rotors whirling, motor roaring.

The door opened, and six men, dressed in black

346

combat gear and heavily armed, jumped out and swarmed Aiden and his prisoner.

Aiden stepped out of the crowd of armed men and crossed to her, a frown marring his handsome face. "You must be freezing." Shrugging out of his suede jacket, he draped it over her shoulders. "This coat isn't much, but it's the best I can do right now. As soon as we get you on the helicopter, I'll get you some blankets."

She huddled into the jacket's warmth and inhaled, savoring the comforting scents of leather, fresh air, and Aiden. "Thank you." Tears stung her eyes. "Thank you for saving me."

"You don't have to thank me." His eyes glistened, and his Adam's apple bobbed in his throat. "I'm just glad we found you." He swallowed again. "I don't know what I—"

"Detective Farrell," called one of the SWAT members. "We need you over here for a minute."

Aiden leaned close and tugged the lapels of his jacket over her chest. "Don't go anywhere. I'll be right back." He turned and strode to the helicopter.

Detective Joe Breacher climbed out of the chopper. He hunched in his heavy coat, the thin strands of his gray hair whipping in the tumult of air. A smile wreathed his rugged face, and he strolled over. "Glad to see you, Professor." He jerked his thumb at Aiden. "Loverboy was pretty worried about you. He took a risk not waiting for backup. I told him that riding a horse over that mountain in the middle of a blizzard to rescue the girl like John Wayne could end his career, but he wouldn't listen to reason. He had to be the hero." His smile widened. "Damn good thing he didn't listen to me."

She nodded, unsure how to take this new and softer version of Detective Joe Breacher.

His hooded gaze drilled into hers.

The roar of the helicopter's throbbing engine and Abraham's virulent protests faded into the distance, and a heavy silence settled like a blanket of snow in the air between them.

He stared off into the distance, fiddling with the buttons on his coat.

She'd hated this man for so many years, blamed him for not finding her sister, for not doing his job. But standing there in that remote mountain valley, with snow dampening his coat, his hair tangled, there was something vulnerable about him, something she'd never seen before.

He coughed and cleared his throat. "I'm real sorry about your sister. I've wanted to tell you that for a long time." He shuffled his feet, digging furrows in the snow and blew out a breath. "I messed up. I should've called for backup that first day." For the first time, he met her gaze. "I hope someday you'll forgive me." Sincerity shone from his faded-blue eyes.

"Thank you." She swallowed over the lump clogging her throat. "I appreciate that."

He nodded, coughed again, and turned to Aiden and thumped him on the back. "Well, well, well, partner. I see you pulled it off. Who would—" A frown creased his forehead. "What the hell?" He moved closer to the cuffed prisoner. "Abe? Is that you?"

Candace stood frozen, a spectator to the unfolding scene, her injuries forgotten in the rising tension.

Abraham, fighting his restraints and mouthing

obscenities, ignored the detective.

"I asked you a question." Joe's voice rang with authority.

"What's going on, Joe? Aiden asked. "Do you know this guy?"

Detective Breacher smoothed the palm of his hand over his windblown hair. "I sure as hell do." He shook his head. "I can't believe this." He turned to Aiden. "*He's* our perp? You're sure?"

Aiden nodded.

"So that's how Isaiah knew about the raid on the farmhouse." Joe lunged at the prisoner and grabbed his collar. "You jerk! You told him, didn't you? You told Isaiah we were coming for him."

Abraham cackled. "You never were the sharpest knife in the drawer, were you, Joe? All these years, and you're just figuring it out." His laugh was cut off when the burly detective plowed his fist into his smirking face.

Candace bit back a gasp.

Breacher's face turned purple as he let loose more blows.

Blood spurted from Abraham's nose and mouth, dripping red onto the snow.

"What the hell?" Aiden grabbed Breacher's arm and hauled him back. "Joe, stop! Don't do this. He's not worth it."

Chest heaving, sweat glistening on his brow, Breacher shoved off Aiden's grip. He adjusted his coat but stayed where he was.

The SWAT members dragged a bruised and bloodied Abraham into the helicopter.

"What was that all about, Joe?" Aiden asked, his

eyes flashing fire.

Candace limped closer. "What's going on, Detective Breacher?"

The detective wiped his brow. "I know that guy. He used to work at the Precinct in the mailroom. He was a kid then, eighteen years old at the most, but I remember him. He had a smart-ass comment for everything." His breath gusted out in a white plume.

"He was the one who warned Isaiah about the raid." Another wheezing breath. "I always suspected someone in the precinct told him, and that's why Isaiah was able to skip out with your sister mere hours before the cops raided that farmhouse."

She reeled back, wincing at the pain in her sore knee. "Abraham worked at the police station?"

Detective Breacher nodded. "He did until he got fired for leaking confidential information to the press."

"So, he knew about the planned raid to rescue the Forgotten Five?" she asked.

He nodded again.

She struggled to wrap her mind around his astounding revelation. Abraham was the reason her sister wasn't rescued with the other victims. His father was the one who killed Charlene, but Abraham was just as responsible, just as guilty. A primal rage filled her, searing her body, flaming out of control. Hot tears scalded her eyes. Her legs wobbled and she stumbled.

"Hey." Aiden grabbed her and enfolded her in his arms, holding her close, pressing her head against his chest. "It's over. We got him, Candace. We got him."

And just like that, the wave of hatred abated, and she breathed deep, inhaling the cold mountain air and Aiden's familiar masculine scent, listening to the steady thumping of his heart. She pulled back, sniffled, and met his gaze. Her heart flip-flopped, and comforting warmth spread throughout her body. "We did, didn't we? We got the monster."

Chapter 42

She opened the front door and smiled as a rush of warmth flooded her. "Aiden. Hello. Come in." Stepping aside, she motioned for him to enter the house. "I was just going to put on a pot of tea. Join me."

He followed her through to the kitchen and leaned against the counter. "How've you been?"

"Fine." She smiled a brittle smile. "Just fine. How are you?" She set the kettle on the stove to heat, and bit down on her bottom lip. *How are you*? Could she be any lamer? Next, they'd be discussing the weather. "How's Amanda Jacobs? Did her surgery go well?"

He nodded. "She's still in the hospital, but I spoke to her doctor this morning. She's expected to make a full recovery."

"That's good. Real good."

Amanda had survived months with Abraham, showing enough fortitude to escape twice. She'd recover physically, but her emotional wounds would take years of therapy to heal.

A fragment of guilt raised its head. If only Candace had done more to find the girl on that long-ago afternoon when she'd spotted Amanda's tracks in the snow.

As if reading her mind, Aiden said, "It's not your fault. You know that, right?" His gaze delved into hers. "You wouldn't have found Amanda that day, no matter what you did. She told us that Abraham caught her and moved her out of the park to an old travel trailer parked in an empty, wooded lot just outside of town. He didn't move her back to the park until a few weeks ago." He shifted closer and trailed a warm finger along her bare arm. "There was nothing you could've done to help her."

She knew he was right, but she'd never really forgive herself. The what-ifs of her life would haunt her all her days. She just had to learn to live with them.

"I missed you."

"You missed me?" For the first time, she took in his unshaven cheeks and the dark circles under his eyes. She hadn't seen or heard from him since he'd rescued her from the mountains. At least, she hadn't seen him in person. He and his partner were the heroes of the hour, and it seemed every time she turned on the television, they were on one news show or another.

Joe Breacher loved the limelight, and he grinned like a Cheshire cat at the cameras as he described his part in the daring rescue.

Aiden—not so much, especially when the media uncovered the unfortunate events that had transpired in Seattle. He held his body stiff and still, his expression blank, and only gave the briefest of answers to the reporters' questions, letting Joe speak for both of them and take the glory.

"I saw you on TV." She grimaced. "Sounds like Detective Breacher was a real hero."

"Yeah. Good old Joe. He's quite the guy." He pushed away from the counter, his golden gaze drilling into hers. "I—" His throat worked. "—I wanted to see you." He shook his head. "No, that's not right. I *had* to see you."

Butterflies fluttered in her stomach. "You did?"

He moved another step closer, his expression serious. "Do you have any idea how terrible it was for me when I went to your house and found you'd been abducted?"

She shook her head. "No, I—"

"It was the worst day of my life." He threaded his fingers through his hair. "I thought I'd never see you again. And then when I finally found you, that man was chasing you…" Moisture shone in his eyes. "I saw the bruises and the pain on your face and knew he'd hurt you." He swiped his upper lip. "I was terrified I wouldn't reach you in time."

"But you did." She grasped his hand and squeezed. "You saved me. If it hadn't been for you riding that horse over the mountain, I'd be dead."

"I don't ever want to feel that way again." He inhaled a noisy breath. "I love you. Do you know that? I couldn't bear if something happened to you." He tugged her closer. "Candace Cooper, I love you."

"Really?" Inches separated them. She breathed in his unique scent…freshly laundered cotton, citrus, and him.

He nodded.

He loved her! Joy filled her heart. This wonderful, decent, strong man loved *her*. She smiled her first real smile in days. "I love you too, Aiden. I've loved you for weeks." She moistened her lips. "Kiss me. Please."

A slow smile spread across his handsome face, and he slipped his arms around her. "I never thought you'd ask." He pressed his lips to hers.

Finally.

She buried her hands in his hair and hung on as he deepened the kiss. Her body melted against his as if it were a chocolate bar under a searing sun. She opened her mouth, drinking him in. The kettle whistled, but she blanked out the high-pitched squeal and focused on him and the sensations rioting through her.

He pulled his lips away, his chest heaving. "You'd better get that."

She groaned and slipped out of his arms and stumbled over to the stove and shut off the burner.

The whistling stopped.

"There's something I have to tell you."

And just like that, her euphoria vanished. She turned and faced him. "What is it?"

He stuffed his hands into the front pockets of his faded jeans. "We found Mary Jorgenson. Looks like Abraham killed her and hid her body under some tarps in your neighbor's shed. The neighbor was away and didn't discover her body until this morning. I'm sorry."

Her throat worked, but no sounds emerged. Poor Mary. Another of Abraham's victims.

"I'm afraid there's more." He rubbed his hand over his chin, the rasp of beard loud in the silent kitchen. "The crime-scene techs found human bones in the forest behind the snowmobile warming hut. DNA tests showed they're your sister's remains."

She swallowed, and her knees wobbled. Grabbing onto the counter, she held on tight. Abraham had hinted that Charlene was dead, that his father had killed her shortly after the police raid, but to learn her sister had been held in the same root cellar in the forest floored her. "Do—" She swallowed. "—do you know how she died?"

"According to the medical examiner's report, she had a broken arm and two broken ribs, but death was probably caused by a blow to her head." His jaw worked. "Her remains were discovered at the bottom of a ravine under a log. We think she was running away, but Isaiah caught her and killed her."

Tears filmed her eyes. Charlene died fighting, determined to escape. That was just like her big sister. She never gave up. Candace wiped away her tears. After all these years searching for answers, she finally knew what happened.

"I'm so sorry. I know this news is a shock, and not what you wanted to ever hear, but you deserve to know the truth."

"Thank you for telling me." She wiped her damp eyes with the back of her hand. So now she knew. Charlene was gone, had been dead for years. A lump clogged her throat, and she bit back a sob. Her sister would never walk in the door and call her Candy Girl again. All those years searching, hoping, praying for a miracle were over.

Inhaling a shaky breath, she grabbed a tissue from the counter and wiped her eyes. "I'm glad the police finally found her. Maybe now she can be at rest." At long last, the burden of guilt she'd worn like a shield, slipped from her shoulders. For the first time since Charlene vanished, she felt light and free. She'd found her sister. Just like she'd promised her parents. Now was her chance to start healing, to look toward the future rather than dwell in the painful past.

He enveloped her in his strong arms and drew her close until her head rested against his chest.

His heartbeat thumped in her ear, and she pressed

closer, burrowing into his embrace, seeking his very essence. A sense of being protected and loved washed over her. She'd seen the worst mankind had to offer. Now was her chance to experience the best—together with this man. She stood on tiptoes and pressed her lips to his, instilling all her deep feelings into the kiss.

Hours—or was it minutes later?—the kiss ended, and his gaze fixed on her. "You're quite a woman. You know that?"

"I do." She smiled, but then she remembered something Joe had said after she was rescued, and her happiness faded. "Was your captain angry?"

"About what?" His brow furrowed.

"Joe told me you didn't wait for backup when you rode that horse over the mountain. He said you could lose your job."

"I could have, I guess." He shrugged. "But I didn't care. I needed to do whatever it took to find you."

"But you're okay? You still have your job?" She knew how important being a detective was to him, and she couldn't bear the thought of being responsible for him losing his career.

He smiled. "We caught a murderer who kidnapped and murdered young girls across the state. The mayor's ecstatic with all the positive press. I'm the golden boy." His grin widened. "You can't punish a hero."

"You certainly can't." She pulled him close for another deep kiss. When she drew away, she was short of breath. "Do you want to bring that handsome dog of yours and go hiking tomorrow?"

"Hiking? Are you up to that? You had some pretty serious injuries."

She threaded her fingers through the soft dark curls

C. B. Clark

at the nape of his neck. "I'm still sore, but I think I can handle a walk in the woods. The weatherman says it's supposed to be a beautiful day."

The corners of his mouth twitched. "Really?"

She nodded.

He heaved a heavy sigh. "I guess I'll have to buy a pair of hiking boots if I'm going to hang around with you."

"Don't forget the bug spray." She chuckled. It felt good to laugh. Damn good. Her laughter was cut off when he claimed her mouth with his in another deep, soul-penetrating kiss that took her breath away.

Oh man. She loved him. Her hero. Her rock. Her future.

A word about the author…

C.B. Clark has always loved reading, especially romances, but it wasn't until she lost her voice for a year that she considered writing her own romantic suspense stories. She grew up in Canada's Northwest Territories and Yukon. Graduating with a degree in Anthropology and Archaeology, she has worked as an archaeologist and an educator, teaching students from the primary grades through the first year of college. She enjoys hiking, canoeing, and snowshoeing with her husband and dog near her home in the wilderness of central British Columbia.

Thank you for purchasing
this publication of The Wild Rose Press, Inc.

For questions or more information
contact us at
info@thewildrosepress.com.

The Wild Rose Press, Inc.
www.thewildrosepress.com

www.ingramcontent.com/pod-product-compliance
Lightning Source LLC
Chambersburg PA
CBHW051130030726
47504CB00004B/788